JUNKYARD DOGS

For Lynn Evans (who will always be Miss
Consigny to me) and teachers like her,
who create space for young writers.

—K. H.-C.

Published by Peachtree Teen
An imprint of PEACHTREE PUBLISHING COMPANY INC.
1700 Chattahoochee Avenue
Atlanta, Georgia 30318-2112
PeachtreeBooks.com

Text © 2023 by Katherine Higgs-Coulthard
Cover illustration © 2023 by Lisa Marie Pompilio

Jacket design by Adela Pons and Lily Steele
Composition by Amnet Contentsource Private Limited
Edited by Jonah Heller

Printed and bound in January 2023 at Maple Press,
York, PA, USA.
10 9 8 7 6 5 4 3 2 1
First Edition
ISBN: 978-1-68263-540-7

Library of Congress Cataloging-in-Publication Data
Names: Higgs-Coulthard, Katherine, author.
Title: Junkyard dogs / Katherine Higgs-Coulthard.
Description: First edition. | Atlanta, Georgia : Peachtree Teen, 2023. |
Audience: Ages 14 and up. | Audience: Grades 10-12. | Summary:
"Some people dream of happily ever after, but all 17-year-old Josh
Roberts wants is a roof over his head and for his little brother to be
safe"-- Provided by publisher.
Identifiers: LCCN 2022040802 | ISBN 9781682635407 (hardcover) |
ISBN 9781682635414 (ebook)
Subjects: CYAC: Brothers--Fiction. | Family life--Fiction. | Missing
persons--Fiction. | Fathers--Fiction. | LCGFT: Novels. Classification:
LCC PZ7.1.H5455 Ju 2023 | DDC [Fic]--dc23
LC record available at https://lccn.loc.gov/2022040802

JUNKYARD DOGS

KATHERINE HIGGS-COULTHARD

PEACHTREE
Teen

CHAPTER

01

"TIME-OUT, WOLVES!" THE ANNOUNCER SHOUTS.

Matt slaps my back and the guys sprint over. Coach leans in, jaw rigid, breath reeking of Twizzlers. "You got this, Josh. That's your bucket."

The buzzer sounds and we jog back out onto the court. The ref straight-arms me the ball. I bounce it once. *Whomp.* Look at the scoreboard.

75–74.

Whomp, whomp. I let the ball become the slow, lazy pulse of the gym, let it drown out the yelling and jangling keys of Warsaw's fans, who outnumber ours ten to one, even though we're only an hour from home. *Whomp. Whomp, whomp.* Drown out the cheerleaders with their "Thir-TEE-two! Thir-TEE-two," and Matt saying, "Come on, man, let it fly." Just me and the beat of the ball.

Whomp.

Whomp, whomp.

"Come on, Joshie!" a kid yells, and my eyes go right to where Twig would be—second row from the top. I almost convince myself I see him there, Dad right behind him, long arms draped over Twig like the shoulder harness of a roller coaster. I blink against the picture, but my mind puts Mom up there too, next to Dad, her hand over her eyes; she never could bear to watch me at the line, even back in the when, where this image belongs—back in middle school. Uncle Stan would be up there too, laughing at Mom and urging her to look, but she wouldn't. Twig would blow a raspberry, try to crack me up. My lips curl at the almost memory.

"Come on, Joshie! Nothing but net!" the kid shouts, and I see him—not Twig—just some random kid in the stands waving a poster board cutout of a Wolf wearing a Woodson High jersey. The ref snaps his fingers in my face, ripping a hole in the nostalgia just big enough for the ball in my hands and the net fifteen feet away.

I set the ball, overlay the rim with the ball's top curve, let my breath whistle, and pull the trigger.

Up, up, and—

"Yessssss!" the announcer yells. "Josh Roberts brings the score even with two seconds to go!"

The ref tosses me the ball, harder this time, his eyes all *Let's get this over with.* I lock my elbows, let the force reverberate along the tendons and bone, keep my heartbeat inside my chest.

Whomp. Don't look at the boy who is not Twig.

Whomp, whomp. Don't look at Coach, although his voice pierces my concentration. "You better nail that shot, Roberts!" he yells. "Nail it!"

I stare at the net, dripping from the rim like saliva. *You still hungry?* It opens its mouth for me and I stuff the ball down its throat.

The announcer's voice is drowned out by the fans, but none of that matters right now. Warsaw's forward is already in motion, lobbing the ball downcourt where it careens off the corner of the backboard. The buzzer sounds.

Now I look at the boy who is not Twig. The dad who is not mine is lifting him into the air, the mom who is not mine is smiling so huge, she might be crying, but the kid's eyes meet mine and he's yelling, "Yay, Joshie! Yay!" just like Twig would be. I blink hard and when I look back, they're gone. Lost in the churning mass of teammates and cheerleaders and Coach, hands clapping my shoulder, my back, my arm.

Most of the guys rush through their showers, but I stand in the steam, let it soak through my skin to the muscle beneath. By the time I come out, toweling my hair, everyone else is already packed up and waiting with Coach.

"Nice shot," he says, his voice implying ownership, like he coached it into me over the last two and a half years.

Coach doesn't own that shot any more than Matt or Nick or the rest of the team. I own it. Me and Stan and the hours we spent in the junkyard, him feeding me the ball, me feeding it to the basket we pieced together from an old milk crate and some chicken wire. "That basket's starving, Josh. Hungrier than your worst day. It's a bear, Josh, towering over you—blinded with rage and ready to rip out your guts and eat them steaming in spring's shitty snow. That basket's a bear and you gotta stuff that ball down its mother. Fucking. Throat."

But Coach is in my face, the guys all watching, and so I grin and say, "Yeah, it'll do," and then Coach herds the guys toward the door, toward the bus, and I toss my towel in the heap on the floor and follow.

Matt's saving my seat in the back. The playlist on his phone's fired up and everyone's talking so loud, I can't tell what song's playing, just that there's a backbeat to the conversation. We bounce along, replaying the game, analyzing each shot, each foul, until the bus glides into Mickey D's and everyone flows off, comes back with shakes and fries and burgers, filling the bus with the stench of grease on grease. The acid in my stomach roils and revolts.

"You eat?" Matt asks, tipping his bag at me. I look away from the fries, nod, dig in my pocket for the roll of Tums I pinched from Gas n'Go. Thumb a few into my mouth. Chew. It helps. Matt downs two Quarter Pounders and enough fries to feed a village of trailer park kids.

Nick hangs over the back of his seat, breathing onions and pickles in my face. "You get pickles?" he asks. He reaches for Matt's bag. "I ordered no pickles, this thing's covered in them."

Matt yanks his bag back, grins. "No pickles, but, dude, I ate it already."

"Shee-at." Nick balls up his sandwich and launches it at Matt.

It rebounds off his forehead and lands in my lap. I jump up, knock it to the floor. "Man, that's nasty! Don't be throwing that crap at me."

"Chill, man," Nick says. "You been pissed all night."

"Yeah?" I shoot back at him. "So what?"

"So nothing. I just don't get why you got a stick up your ass."

"I don't get why you're worrying about my ass. Mind your own fucking business." I sit down and hunch my shoulders toward the window.

I can see Matt's reflection in the rain-splattered glass, watching me. When he turns back to Nick, I toe the crumpled sandwich into the corner and reach down. Slip it into my jacket pocket.

Back at Woodson, the bus belches us into a lot packed with parents, classmates, cheerleaders. I let the crowd swallow me, suck me into its self-congratulatory swarm, but my mind has drifted to the burger in my pocket. Everyone ignores the rain and the maintenance guy's not so subtle hints until he loses his patience and kills the lights for good. The bus driver hangs out after the lot clears, fiddling with something in his trunk, waiting, I know, for my ride to appear. Finally he calls across the lot to ask if I need to use his cell.

I hold up my wallet like it's a phone. "Dad's on the way," I tell him. "Be here any minute." That's good enough for the bus driver, who climbs into his car and is outta there without so much as a glance back.

For a second I believe my own lie. I look up the road like any second Dad'll screech into the lot in Gran's pissyellow Datsun. *A day late and a dollar short*, as Gran would say. Except even Gran would have to admit that while Tye Roberts is always broke, he is never late.

I pull Nick's discarded burger out of my pocket and wolf it down in two bites, tossing the wrapper into a puddle. Then I stuff my hands into my empty pockets, duck my head, and start to walk.

CHAPTER

02

I'M BARELY OUT OF THE PARKING LOT BEFORE MY JACKET IS soaked through and my shirt sticks to my flesh like a thin layer of ice. No amount of blowing on my hands can keep the cold from needling my fingertips. I dart from blacktop to mud puddle to avoid being pancaked by cars doing at least twenty over the speed limit, their headlights blinding me.

Gran lives about two miles east of town. While the idea of a warm towel and a dry bed sounds great, as soon as I see the split-rail fence at the front of Gran's trailer park, I want to turn around. Looks like Santa did a flyby and tossed his cookies all over it. Huge red and green bulbs, half of them burnt out, drip from fake garland. Couple of glittery bells lie forgotten in the dead grass, like Mac got the garland up, realized how pathetic it looked, and said, "Screw it."

Less than a week from Thanksgiving and "Jingle Bells" already blares between bursts of static from the speakers outside the office. People used to ask me what I wanted to be when I grew up. I said the usual stuff—firefighter, policeman, creepy sewer-dwelling circus clown. Now if somebody asks me, I'm gonna say homeowner, that way nobody can put speakers right outside my house and pipe that crap into my ears 24/7.

The seasonal vomit-fest has hit about half the trailers in the park and I know by Sunday, it'll consume every lot except Gran's. That's when Mac awards the prize for the best decorations. The way everybody gets all jazzed, you'd think he was giving away free Hamburger Helper for a year, instead of the ten bucks off January's lot fee. Gran never decorates. Says the prize isn't worth the migraine she gets from all those flashing lights. But really, why would she bother jumping through hoops when she gets a discount from Mac every month?

Gran's trailer is around the third bend. Her Datsun's parked exactly how it was when I left for school that morning. Gran leans against the rail of the little jetty of wood she calls a porch. She's bundled up in a blanket, smoking. Smoking outside is the one thing she listens to me about—Twig can't be showing up at school reeking of weed. Without so much as a hi, Gran holds the blunt out to me. I wave it off. I've told her a hundred times I don't do that junk, but she says there's always hope.

She sizes me up and makes a sad puppy face at my wet clothes and chattering teeth, but doesn't move out of my way so I can go in to get dry. She doesn't ask about the game or why I walked home in the freezing rain. Instead she says, "Where's your dad?"

"Beats me. Supposed to pick me up."

"Supposed to pay the rent, too, but I don't see that happening, now do I?" She inhales quick and deep, holds it, tapping that foot of hers, and I know it's coming.

"Look, Gran, I just got home—"

"Home? I told your dad a hunnert times this ain't nobody's home but mine. My name on the leash. My name on the utilities."

I hate the way she says that word, "leash," but it's exactly right. That four hundred bucks a month is a tether around all of our throats and she doesn't let any of us forget it.

She rips right on past the rent and lays into me about the grocery bill, even though me and Dad know better than to touch anything she buys except the Sunday dinners she serves. We stash our own food in the back bedroom—ramen noodles and peanut butter straight out of the jar. All Gran has to feed is herself and Twig. Well, and Mac on the nights he ditches his wife and kids. Maybe if she didn't smoke up half her Social Security she'd have enough to cover that.

Gran snuffs out her blunt and tucks it under the fake geraniums she calls her potflower. Then she fixes me with those black eyes of hers. "You know what he gone and done? That *father* of yours?"

Spittle flies as she says the word "father," and it's all I can do not to step back to avoid the spray. I know what she's gonna say, same thing she always says when she doesn't know where Dad is.

"Took off again, I know it. Long gone, if you ask me." She links her thumbs and flutters finger-wings toward the sky. "Bye-bye, birdie. Shoulda named him that—Birdie! He took off and left you two here. Took the damn dog, though. I told him I ain't raising no more kids and I ain't. I'd rather kept that dog. At least it's good for scaring off the raccoons."

Any energy I had left after the walk drains out of me. I've been so distracted by her tirade, I haven't noticed the absence of Axl whining in the back pen. Dad never takes Axl with him on a job. Never really pays any attention to that poor old dog. It's me who feeds him and cleans out his pen. Twig who puts him on a chain and reads to him out back of the trailer. Twig. That kid is gonna be just devastated.

"Gran, I'm getting hypothermia out here."

She huffs and heads into the house, not bothering to hold the door for me. "Don't drip on the linoleum," she snaps. Her voice rebounds in the emptiness of the trailer.

I want to tell her that I wouldn't drip on the linoleum if she had a doormat like everyone else in the world, but I bite the words back. You'd think after living here so long I'd get used to the echo, but I just can't. I've been in plenty of other trailers—kids in the park are always running in and out of each other's like it's one big happy family—but nobody ever comes in Gran's because it's just plain spooky. "Where's all your stuff?" a kid asked me the one time I had dragged a friend in, shortly after me, Dad, Twig, and Axl had first arrived on Gran's doorstep five years ago. "It's invisible," I told him. He'd rolled his eyes at me, but Gran heard us by then and hollered at me to get "that white trash" out of her kitchen.

It's going on eleven thirty, but Twig's still up. I find him cross-legged on the floor in front of the TV, my beat-up basketball in his lap. "Horse?"

"Go to bed, little dude. It's almost midnight." I start to walk away, but his shoulders slump. "It's raining ice shards. I'm not going back out there."

"How about *2K*?" Twig scrambles for the Xbox controller and holds it out to me. "I'll let you be the Bulls."

He blinks up at me. Now there's a kid who has mastered puppy dog eyes. "*Let me*, huh? Little man, I'm always the Bulls. I gotta get changed first."

He calls after me, "Just one game, I promise."

Yeah, right. But I nod like I believe him and go to retrieve some dry clothes from the room we share with Dad. Gran's trailer might be as barren as the United Center on a Tuesday morning, but our room could take up a whole episode on *Hoarders*. One wall is nothing but boxes stacked floor to ceiling—mine and Twig's are open, spewing clothes like Mount St. Helens. Dad's are closed, the flaps tucked under each other haphazardly, like a kid's do-it-yourself pinwheel. His pile leans against Mom's. Only her boxes are sealed, a pyramid small and fragile, two on the bottom, one on top. Her name is printed neatly on each in black Sharpie and below that a date so long ago, it's irrelevant, like the expiration date on a box of Twinkies.

I snag a shirt and a pair of torn sweats from the heap and head down the hall. The bathroom's my favorite part of Gran's trailer. It's small as a closet, but there're no boxes and no empty echo. I wrestle out of my wet clothes and throw them in the tub. I'm tempted to climb in after them, turn the water on as hot as it can go, but soon as Gran hears the water rattling the pipes, she'd be banging on the door, yelling that water "ain't free." Besides, Twig's waiting. My towel's bunched up in a corner like someone used it to mop up the floor. I pick it up, give it a sniff, then use it to dry off before spreading it over the shower rod where it can air out.

When I come out of the bathroom, Twig's already got the game fired up. He hands me a controller and hits start. For a few minutes I don't think about Dad or anything else that might disappear in the night. Twig's all speed. He jams on the sprint button and sure, he scores some quick points, but me? I'm more about the strategy. Twig's never been good at spotting a pick. You'd think after about a bazillion losses Twig would give up, but each time I win, he leans in further, holds his controller tighter, and goes straight for the basket.

We're in the third quarter when Twig says, "Gran thinks he's gone again."

The cramping in my hands tells me we've been playing at least an hour. I nod, pretending to concentrate on the game. After a few minutes, Twig says so quiet, I almost don't hear him, "Is he?"

Ignoring him would be easy. *If he really wants an answer, he'll speak up*, I tell myself. But I know better. I was about his age when we lost Mom. Wanting an answer isn't the same as needing one. "What do you think?" I say at last.

"Axl went with him."

"Yeah."

Another minute passes before Twig says, "He's stayed put real good, 'cept for that one time."

I nod again. No reason to point out that the one time he's talking about was half Twig's childhood. And that the times before that were so frequent, we'd need an abacus to tally them up. No reason to tell him any of that or what Gran says about not raising any more kids. But her words bounce around inside my head. If she's right and Dad is gone, where does that leave me and Twig?

Before long, Twig's players start lagging and I know he's fading. Each time I look over, he shifts positions and rallies. When he sprawls out on his stomach, holding the controller with straight arms stretched like Superman playing *2K* in midair, I know he's toast. Couple plays later the controller clunks to the floor. A streamer of drool hangs from his mouth. I switch off the game and scoop Twig up. He mumbles something that sounds suspiciously like "I ate all the ice cream" as I tote him down the hall to our room. Door's shut again, but I manage to scooch Twig up to my shoulder so I can free a hand for the knob. Ozzy hisses and races out between my feet. I settle Twig on the bed and go after the mangy furball, taking a few scratches for my troubles.

"Should just let Gran cook you," I tell Ozzy. I pin him against my body so he can't shred my arms. When I bring him back into the room, he scrambles straight for Twig, curling up next to him like the world's ugliest teddy bear.

I kick the door shut and climb into the bed, flopping around trying to get comfortable on the lumpy pile of rocks we use for a mattress. My hands slide under the pillow and recoil at the feel of something under there. For half a second I think Twig brought home another cat. But there's no fur and it doesn't move. Just some crumpled paper. Or a note. My eyes fly open and I swat at the light switch, blinking partly from the sudden glare and partly from shock. Wads of cash litter the top of the bed like bills from a generous but overworked Tooth Fairy. Ones, tens, more than a few twenties. And right in the middle is a note from Dad scrawled on the back of a receipt:

Have to see a man about a horse. Take care of your little bro.

CHAPTER

03

IT'S NOT MY ALARM OR THE EARLY MORNING LIGHT streaming through the filmy window above the bed that snaps my eyes wide open; it's the weight of someone staring at me. I bolt upright, hyperaware of the fact that there's more money in this room than most of our neighbors make in a week.

"Dad left a note?" Twig asks.

He's sitting cross-legged on one of Dad's sturdier boxes, holding the receipt in both of his hands like it's a map he's trying to read, the money in a small stack next to him. I scoot to the foot of the bed so there're only inches between our knees, and gently take the note from him.

"Yeah. The money, too."

"What's it say?"

"Says he went to see a man about a horse. That we should take care of each other until he gets back." It doesn't exactly say that he's coming back, but the fact that Dad's cursive is practically illegible gives me the leeway to embellish a bit.

"Why do we need a horse?"

"Not a real horse. That's just something Dad says sometimes when he's following up on a lead for a job."

Twig nods, but his eyebrows knit with worry. "Is the money from him? Why does he need a job if we have all that money?"

I lean over and retrieve the bills, fanning them out in my hand. "I know it looks like a lot of money, but it costs a lot more to pay rent, buy food."

This news only deepens the creases in his forehead.

"Wanna help me count it?"

The invitation propels Twig off the box and onto the bed. He takes the money from me, smoothing the bills and sorting them into piles with a gleam in his eye that reminds me of when he played the banker in Monopoly the one time Dad took us to a game night at the library. Once the bills are stacked, he counts them. Seven ones. Two tens. Five twenties. One Benjamin.

$227. I can't help but wonder where the hell Dad got that kinda dough. On the daily, he's likely to have more bruises than bucks. The most I have ever seen him with is $250 and that's after spending every waking moment on the thirtieth scraping it together in time to pay Gran rent on the first.

$227. I say the number aloud and Twig's eyes light up like we've won the lottery, but that amount of money isn't going to last us long. Especially if Gran gets a whiff of it.

As if summoned by thought, Gran's voice screeches through the trailer like nails against prefabricated metal. "Woodrow!"

If Gran's up, that must mean it's at least—my eyes go to the clock—nine. I grab my gym bag. "Hey, stash that somewhere safe, will ya?"

Twig nods earnestly. I know he wants to come to the gym, but he doesn't ask. Instead he hops up to hide the cash. "Good luck!" he calls after me.

The rain from last night has stopped, but moisture hangs in the air and chills me right through my jacket. I hop the bus to the Center. The first time Stan woke me up early on a Saturday so we could go shoot hoops at the Center, I spent the whole bus ride dreaming about what it was gonna be like to step up to the same free throw line toed by Jordan, Wade, Walker. My heart sank like a brick when the bus dropped us in front of a two-story building labeled "Center for the Homeless." But Stan didn't notice. He ushered me down the back alley to a side door. Pride shone on his face as he introduced me to a man roughly the size of a refrigerator. "Dwayne," he said, clasping a hand on my shoulder, "this here's my boy. Gonna play for the Bulls one day." A big ring of keys jangled in Dwayne's hand as he unlocked a door and led us into the gym. "Better show me that free throw then, kid." It may not have been the United Center's court, but it was still a real court. The sheen of polyurethane beneath my feet, the white-hot glow of the nylon net and massive plexiglass backboard made me feel real too. I've come here every Saturday since—with or without Stan. The last five years, it's been without.

Dwayne's chatting up some dudes on the corner, but he spots me getting off the bus and throws up his hands. I swing my hip around and fire a behind-the-back pass, which he pretends to catch and layup. The guys nod at me and I nod back, heading down the alley to the side door, which Dwayne left propped open with a rock. The gym's empty this time of day, which is how I like it. I shed my jacket and my old shoes. Wedge my feet into my hoop shoes and try not to notice that they're starting to pinch a bit. Dwayne already wheeled the ball cart out for me. The first two balls are flat, but the third one is perfect. I lose myself in the bounce and rebound of free throws and three-pointers, casting glances at the clock every so often. The game's not until one and it's just a scrimmage, but being late means being benched, so at eleven thirty I swap out my shoes and throw on a dry shirt.

I start for the door, but the scent of sweet peppers and onions draws me back toward the cafeteria in the hopes of seeing a friendly face. Despite Dwayne's VIP treatment, the Center's policy is clear: no unaccompanied minors.

A woman with hair the color of pond scum waves at me. She looks vaguely familiar, so I make a beeline for her table. She pats the bench next to her. "Come sit, baby boy. How's your dad?"

She smiles, showing teeth so gappy that you could park a Buick between them, and it clicks: she works at the Gas n'Go. She's the one Dad always hits up for cigarettes. Trina, Tina, Tracey—something with a *T*. "Ah, you know. He's the same as always."

"Well"—she reaches over and pinches my cheek like I'm five—"you look like a half-starved puppy. Let me go grab you one of those burritos?"

"I sure would like that."

Trina, Tina, Tracey returns moments later carrying a bloated burrito draped in cheese, nestled between piles of rice and beans. Instantly my mouth floods with so much saliva, I literally have to run my sleeve across my face to keep from slobbering all over myself. She holds out a fork and watches with wide eyes while I wolf the whole thing down.

I got five minutes to make the bus to Woodson, so before she can grill me about my dad or drag me into small talk,

I thank her for the food and head through the gym toward the back door.

Dwayne greets me at the end of the alley, eyeing my thin jacket. "Need to get you a real coat. Winter's on its way."

Nothing I can say to that, so I shrug.

"Hey, you seen your dad lately?" he asks.

"He took a gig someplace."

"Since when?"

I flip pages in a mental calendar, trying to pinpoint when I last saw Dad. Definitely saw him Wednesday; that's when we talked about him picking me up from the game. Could he have left that long ago? Seems like I would have found the cash under the pillow sooner if he had, but I really don't know. "I dunno. Yesterday, I think."

His lips pinch together, biting back something he doesn't want to say.

"What?"

He looks at me, hard. "Nothing. I just worry about you kids."

It's cold as hell, and I gotta catch the bus so I ask him straight out, "What's going on?"

His shoulders slump. "Stan's back in town."

"Stan?" For just a second I see Uncle Stan bringing me here for my first time on a real court, Stan standing beside me at the free throw line telling me to feed the basket, Stan up in the bleachers cheering me on. Except there's no way he could be talking about that Stan. That Stan's been gone for years.

"Yeah, he showed up here looking for your dad and—"

"Stan who?"

"You know, *Stan*. Your dad's old pal."

I feel like Dwayne pressed the pause button on my brain. I just stand there trying to get my head wrapped around the possibility that we're talking about the same Stan. When I finally do manage to speak, I say, "My dad's friend Stan?"

"Josh—"

"Is he here now?" I start toward the door. If Stan is here, maybe he's working with my dad. He and Dad used to be inseparable, disappearing all the time up to Holland or over to New Carlisle to score a load of junk to pick through at our old farmhouse. Maybe Dad's doing junk runs with Stan again. Maybe he's back already. Except why leave us that cash, then? And where's Axl? None of this is making any sense.

Dwayne shakes his head, grabs my arm. "Josh, I don't think your dad—"

"Did Stan say where—"

"Josh." Dwayne pulls harder on my arm, turning me back so we're face-to-face and putting both hands on my shoulders to keep me from pulling away. Behind him, the twelve-o'clock bus blows by. "That's what I'm trying to tell you. I think your dad took off *because* Stan is back."

"What? That can't be right."

Dwayne shrugs. "I'm just saying, your dad was sitting there playing cards with the guys. In walked Stan and everybody was all around him talking to him about where he'd been and what he'd done and when the crowd cleared, your dad wasn't there. He just took off."

Dwayne's words clank around in my brain like rocks in a dryer while I cut through side streets trying to get to the Transpo station in time to catch any bus headed toward Woodson. I'm too worried about being late to the game to think clearly, and I keep getting tangled trying to make sense of everything.

Dad wasn't himself after the fire all those years ago. None of us were. And Stan just disappeared. Dad should have been happy to see Stan walk back through the door. Why would he just take off? Dwayne's gotta be wrong about that.

Four buses idle at the station when I round the corner on Lafayette. I scan the signs and spot the one headed east. Of course it's the one at the farthest end of the platform.

"Wait!" I shout at the guy stepping aboard. "Hold the bus!" I yell again as the doors close after him. The bus heaves itself away from the curb. I smack the back panel as hard as I can. The brake lights flash and the bus stops. The driver eyes me as I fumble with the fare. "Thanks for stopping," I say.

"You're welcome," he says, and without missing a beat he adds, "Next time you hit my bus, I'm backing over you."

CHAPTER

04

COACH SHOOTS ME A LOOK AS I TROT OUT ONTO THE court, but the guys are already doing their layups and I jump in line. Mason makes his shot and comes in behind me.

"You missed pregame," he says, loud enough for a few of the guys to turn in our direction, but I stay face forward, watching Nick get the next rebound. Matt flashes me a *You good?* look. I lift my chin in a quick *Yep.*

Mason bumps me from behind and I turn to give him a good-natured smile that melts when I see the leer on his face. "I said, you missed pregame," he repeats, like he's talking to someone so deaf, they need one of those old-fashioned ear horns.

Matt glances back at me again just as Nick releases the ball in a pass to him. The ball smacks Matt hard on the arm. "Fuck!"

Mason sneers and jerks his thumb at Matt and Nick. "Got your girlfriends all distracted."

"Man, mind your own fucking business," I tell him.

"This team is my fucking business and if you—" He punctuates the word with a finger in my chest.

My hands are in motion before my brain can think this through. I shove him hard, both hands flat on his chest, and step forward as he staggers back. "What's your problem?" Our faces are so close, I can see the spittle from my question on his cheek.

Matt's between us now, whispering at me to let it go before Coach—but Coach is already coming across the court, his face a dark storm. I step out of the way so Coach can get to Mason, put him in his place for messing with a teammate, but Coach grabs me by the jersey and hauls me off the court. He tosses me at the bench and I sit, hard.

The game buzzer sounds. The team comes over, ready for the lineup. Coach doesn't even look at his clipboard—the starting lineup's been the same every game since freshman year. Instead Coach uses the clipboard as an extension of his pointer finger, jabbing it at us as he barks out names and positions. I'm on the bench the first two quarters, but that's nothing new. Coach usually reserves me for when we're down.

The team plays hard, but we go into the third quarter down by five. I peel off my warm-ups, ready to go in. Matt's at my side, whispering to watch for Fifteen's elbow on the rebound.

Coach barks the sub. "Mason in for Matt."

Matt laughs, but the look on Coach's face makes it clear he's not joking. Everyone's eyes go to me, on the bench like a little kid in time-out.

"What?" Coach shouts. "You gonna stand here holding hands or go play some ball?"

His words jolt the team into action and they huddle up for Wolves on three, but since me and Matt are both on the bench, there's no one to lead it. Mason thrusts his hand out. "Wolves on three!" he shouts, and the guys all put their hands in too, but when Mason gives the count, it's only him yelling "Wolves!"

"This is bullshit," Matt mumbles as he slides closer to me on the bench.

"Just a scrimmage," I tell him with a shrug.

What I want to say, but don't, is bullshit from Coach is nothing new. Subbing Mason instead of me is a mistake, even Coach knows that, and if he didn't, it becomes painfully obvious when Mason loses the ball right after a hard pass from Nick because the guy never learned to keep his guard up. I lean forward, elbows on knees, like I'm just as into the game as I would be if I had set foot on the court. I clap when Nick makes a jump shot and smack my hand on my knee when Pokagon's defender denies a three-pointer. The guys keep passing to Mason, and he keeps losing the ball, and before long we're down by ten. I refuse to look at Coach when he comes to the bench for subs, and keep my eyes on the court when he subs out Nick but leaves Mason in.

Nick plops down between me and Matt. By now Matt's so angry that the red blotches on his cheeks have red blotches. He looks like he got in a smackdown with an orangutan. But as pissed as he is, Matt doesn't say anything and that's what I appreciate about him. Nick, on the other hand, is cussing a blue streak. Most of the guys are nodding along. Except, soon as Coach paces in our direction, Nick's voice trails off and the guys' heads go still and it's really just me and Matt staring daggers at Coach as he eyes us.

"You're in," Coach says. Matt and Nick are looking at me, but Coach isn't. He snaps his fingers right in Ramón's face. "You hear me, kid? You're up."

Ramón hasn't seen one second of game time since he joined the team as a transfer last year. Matt claps him on the back and gives Ramón a push to get him off the bench and on the court. I can feel the guys watching me as Ramón stumbles over to the scorer's table. "Go for Number Seven," I call after him. "Do that peel and squeeze we practiced last week."

Soon as the ref subs him in, Ramón calls for a switch with Sadiq. At six foot five, Sadiq literally is head and shoulders above Ramón, but he leaves Pokagon's center for Ramón to guard and lines up against the shortest kid on their team (who still has six inches on Ramón). Ball's in and Pokagon passes to their center, but Ramón quick-steps around him and snatches the ball. He bounce-passes it between the dude's legs to Sadiq and then streaks up the court. Mason's wide open, but Sadiq baseballs it past him. Ramón catches it, bounces it once, and then goes up for the shot, just as Pokagon's Fifteen throws an elbow. Blood flies, Ramón goes down, but the ball is already in the air and damn if it doesn't go straight into the basket. Blood's dripping from his nose like a freaking faucet, but even the largest ice pack we've got isn't big enough to hide that grin on his face.

After the scrimmage (which we lost by a landslide), Coach finds me in the locker room. "You like the way that game went? Watching another man lead your team? Watching them get their butts handed to them on a platter?"

I shake my head.

"I'm sorry, I didn't hear you."

I look him in the eye. "No, I do not."

"We need you on the court, but you don't warm up, you don't play. Simple as that."

I don't bother going home after the scrimmage. I never do. On the weekends, kids roam Gran's trailer park like packs of wild dogs. They flow in and out of trailers, grabbing snacks between rounds of sledding, pickup games on the busted-up concrete of a basketball court, and Capture the Flag or

Zombie Apocalypse. Twig doesn't exactly have friends, but he's little and often overlooked, which makes it easy for him to just follow along with whatever group notices him the least. Gets him plenty of free meals and the protection of the pack.

Mac's wife takes their kids over to her mom's on Saturdays, so he'll be at Gran's, helping her fix whatever she broke on purpose this week to get him there. When he's done, Gran'll offer him a beer that she buys with the money that Dad gives her for groceries and Mac'll stay all day, sitting on the couch and belching while Gran bats her eyes at him.

Instead I pile into Matt's pickup with the rest of the team. Matt, Nick, and Ramón sit in the front—Matt because it's his ride, Nick because he's Matt's next-best friend after me, and Ramón because he says he doesn't mind riding with the gear shift between his legs. Most of the guys enjoy riding in the back because it's like a party—everyone laughing and yelling, waving at pretty girls or talking trash to guys in other cars. I sit back there because it's the only place in the world I feel truly at peace. When I perch on the wheel well, the air hits my face like an ocean of ozone and I have to work to catch gulps of air from the tidal wave churning and crashing into me. The guys are part of that torrent, their voices breaking through like seagulls fighting over French fries on the beach. In those moments, sailing at seventy down the highway, I feel myself break apart at the subatomic level—my molecules mingling with the oxygen and hydrogen to flow away on that current of air and water. In those moments, I know what it'd be like to get out of here. Leave Gran and her shitty trailer, Dad and this on-again, off-again thing he considers parenting, Coach and all his "Simple as that." I'd ride that tsunami until it dashed itself against the shore and then I'd break into a million pieces.

Except . . . Twig.

The mall is pretty packed when we roll into the lot. Matt angles his truck into a spot too small for even a normal-sized car, and the three of them wriggle out through the slider between the cab and the bed. Ramón wonders out loud how the other driver will get in his car, but Matt dismisses the question with a shrug. As soon as the mall's automatic doors swoosh open, Mason and a few guys head for the pizza place. My stomach tries to claw its way out of my belly to follow them. Instead I follow Nick to the Philly cheesesteak line. Easier to watch raw beef being fried up than to see slices of pizza piled high with pepperoni and sausage and knowing none of it is for me. Nick orders shakes, fries, and a nine-incher with onions and jalapeños.

Soon as he walks away, I ask the cashier for a cup of water.

She gives me a look like I asked her for the keys to the store and says, "Seven cents for the cup." I flip a dime at her and tell her to keep the change. She takes her time getting my cup.

By the time I get to the table, most of the guys are slurping the dregs of their shakes. Matt scooches over to make room for me. "Jeez," I say, looking at his tray. An eggroll and fried rice, some kind of chicken. Pepper steak. He has more food than me and Twig eat all weekend.

"They messed up my order," he says, holding out a fork to me. "I'm allergic to sesame."

Grateful for the mix-up, I scoop up a forkful of sesame-seed-ladened chicken. It's halfway to my mouth when I notice the man sitting a few tables over. It's not the man who draws my attention; he bears little resemblance to the snapshots framed in faded memories. But the way his hands move—worry and wring, tumble and turn, the continuous hand over hand over hand—drags me instantly back to the lot with its makeshift hoop, Stan rocking back and forth, his hands wringing as he barks at me to feed the bear.

"What is it?" Nick asks, twisting in his seat to follow my gaze. "Hottie?"

I force myself to stop staring, and focus on moving the fork to my mouth, chewing, swallowing. There's no way that's him. The hair's all wrong, for one thing. Then there's that jacket. Stan used to make fun of guys who wore leather. Said they looked like walking cows.

Nick smacks my fork-lifting arm and rice sprays across the table. "Dude! Quit holding out! Where is she?"

I scan frantically for any half-cute girl, but Nick zeroes in on a short skirt in the Philly Express line and calls out to the guys, "Babe at three o'clock."

The resulting hot-or-not debate gives me a chance to study the man in the tattered bomber jacket off to our left. His fingertips have settled around the opening of a brown paper bag and he's staring down into it like if he looks hard enough, whatever's inside will tell him some incredible secret. People change over time, but if this is Stan, time has not been his friend. The military haircut is gone, replaced by an orange fisherman beanie and thick hair, more gray than black, jutting out in all directions. He still has his funky James Franco mustache (also more gray than black), but his chin and neck look like a thirteen-year-old's attempt at sheering a goat. The more I study him, the less sure I am this is Stan. Maybe if I could see his face straight on . . .

As if on cue he turns and looks at me. It's Stan, it's definitely Stan.

My hand lifts in a wave, hesitates, and then transforms itself into a visor shielding my eyes. I lean over and pick the sesames off a larger-than-normal piece of chicken with meticulous attention to detail. As much as I want to get up right now and ask Stan where my dad is, that idea falls solidly in the dumbass category. There's no telling if Stan recognizes me and now is not the time to find out. There would be no end to the shit tossed my way if the guys got wind that this crazy-looking homeless man is my pseudo-uncle.

I shovel in two more bites of chicken, then scoop up the tray and head for the trash. "Let's hit the arcade," I call over my shoulder.

"Hells to the yeah," Nick shouts.

As the team races past me, I hazard a glance back. Stan's turned in his seat and his eyes widen as they meet mine. His chin lifts in a quick nod and he pushes up from his chair. My head twitches an involuntary *No*. I hold up a finger and glance into the arcade, thinking maybe if the guys are distracted, they won't notice me slip away to talk to Stan. Everyone's gathered around the change machine. Someone must've put in a five, because they're grabbing up quarters like kids fighting over a bag of Skittles. Perfect timing, but when I turn back, Stan is already gone.

CHAPTER

05

NO SIGN OF STAN OR DWAYNE AT THE CENTER, BUT THE guys smoking out front tell me Stan isn't there. "Might be over to the laundry," one says, flicking a cigarette butt in the general direction of Our Lady of the Highway Laundromat. I know where he means. Dad used to get vouchers from the Center to wash our clothes there for free, and I liked to tag along when I was younger because it was fun to push around the big metal laundry carts. I wonder if they still have that old-fashioned vending machine and if it still sells Bit-O-Honey and Chiclets.

Before I cross the street, I can see the guy is right about Stan being in the laundry. He's pacing in front of Our Lady's plate-glass window, bare-chested, wearing nothing but a baggy pair of long johns. The pacing is something I remember too, like the hand-wringing. Mom used to call those his Stan-erisms. "Some people got so much nervous pent up inside them, they just gotta let it out," she explained. "When Stan gets to pacing, you let him be until he settles down a bit." I never listened to that advice when I was a kid and I'm not about to start now.

"So," Stan says before the bell over the door stops its jangle. "I ain't good enough to meet your friends?"

He hasn't turned, hasn't even looked at me, and to be honest, that really pisses me off. This man disappears from my life for what—five years?—and now he's on my back for not jumping right up to introduce him to my teammates? He'd know them all if he'd stuck around. Hell, he'd probably be our coach instead of Nelson. All those words jam up in my throat and I'm about to spit them at Stan until he turns around to face me and says, "I sure missed you, boy."

"I—uh—" I force a cough to cover the way my voice cracks, and plop down in a chair backed up against the window, the plastic cold as concrete. "You always do the laundry in your underwear?"

Stan frowns at the dryer, then laughs. "Be done any minute. You need a wash?"

"I'm good." I wait, listen to the slow breath of the dryer, let the heat coming off it warm me. Pretty soon Stan sits too. Doesn't look at me. There's so much between us, so much I know, but even more that I don't, and I don't know how to ask. He clears his throat a time or two like he wants to tell me something, but never does. After a minute, his hands get to rolling. I wait. When he starts that body rocking, I reach out and touch his arm, tell him I missed him too. He stills but doesn't look at me.

"You seen my dad?"

"You ain't?"

"Not in a few days."

Stan glances at me then past me out the window. "He'll turn up. Always does, am I right or am I wrong?"

"This time feels different. He left a note and he took Axl and . . ." For some reason I stop short of telling Stan about the money Dad left under the pillow. I don't tell him what Dwayne said either because that's gotta be wrong. "He'd want to know you're here. We should find him."

Stan's rocking again, real slow. "A note, huh? What'd it say?"

"Just that he had to see somebody and I should watch over Twig."

Stan stops rocking and leans back in his chair. "Little man always cracked me up. Gotta be about ten now, huh? He play ball too?"

"Twig's nine. We really need Dad to . . ." I stop short of saying *be a dad*, because I don't want to sound like a little kid.

"You got someone taking care of you, though, right? Your dad didn't leave you all alone."

"Well, yeah, we're staying with our grandma, but—"

"Sheeeeeet. That woman never cared much for me, but guess that made us even."

"So, I just wondered if you had any ideas where he might be?"

"Man don't want to be found, ain't no finding him."

It had not for one second occurred to me that Dad might not want to be found. Dwayne's words start tumbling again—*I think your dad took off* because *Stan is back.*

No, that's just crazy. I shake my head to clear the thought, and fish a couple of quarters from my pocket and cross over to scan the offerings in the candy machine. It's the same one I remember, with the pull knobs, but the candy's all been replaced by single-serve packets of laundry soaps, shave kits, deodorants. I drop the coins back into my pocket. When the time runs out on the dryer, Stan yanks a faded black T-shirt over his head and pulls his jeans on over the long johns, hopping to get them up over his jutting hip bones. He grabs more shirts and some tighty-whities from the dryer and stuffs them into his pack. Stan pulls on his coat and slings the pack over his shoulder. "You coming?" he asks.

You'd think after not seeing each other for so many years, we'd have a lot to say, that Stan would ask me all kinds of questions about school and Twig, but Stan just isn't that person. He tells me he's been hanging at this place they call the Castle and that the guys there used to do some jobs with Dad. That maybe they'll know where he went. We walk in silence, me in front, him three steps behind and half a step to the right. Everybody's got quirks, but Stan's got more than most.

It's only about five blocks from Our Lady to the Castle, but it takes us forever to walk it because Stan keeps stopping at all the intersections to wait for the green even though the road's deserted. Once the light changes, I have to wait for Stan to perform his little OCD rituals—on north-south roads he spins twice before he steps off the curb; east-west, he spins four times. And he always waits for the light to change before he does it. When I was a kid, I thought it was fun to watch Stan walk through the city. Well, more fun to watch other people watch him walk through the city. All that spinning and rocking makes stroller-pushers cross the street and minivan mommas lock their doors at stoplights. But I'm not in the mood to be entertained right now. The November wind cuts through my jacket like it's nothing more than a T-shirt. I just want to find Dad and get home. Stan's cold too. I can tell by the way he just keeps walking, chin to the wind, not stopping to talk with any of the guys on the street along the way.

The Castle turns out to be the old Chemco factory. I must have passed by this place a million times, but it was always just one more block in downtown's Lego landscape. It never occurred to me this boarded-up, busted-out building might be one of my dad's hangouts.

Stan eyes the building. "You wait here."

"Here?" The word catches in my throat, making me sound like I'm smack in the middle of puberty. Stan heads around the side of the building without a response. The nearest streetlight's in pieces on the ground. The whole place stinks from the carcass of a burnt-out car. Shadows lurch and loom along the ground from wind-whipped tree branches. My brain does a quick inventory of every scary movie I've ever seen. "Screw that," I say, and trot to catch up with Stan.

The back door's got the daddy of all locks on it, a big padlock. I'm thinking, *How's he gonna pick that?* and next thing I know the door swings wide without Stan so much as touching the lock.

Stan snorts at the look on my face. "Nice trick, huh?"

He shows me how the padlock just looks like it's attached. All that really holds the door closed is a rusted wire hanger someone rigged inside to keep the door from swinging in the wind. We step inside and Stan pulls the door shut. Darkness blots out the first floor; the boards over the windows repel even a hint of the outside world. Stan navigates the maze of abandoned cubicles on autopilot and I scurry to keep up. A mix of mold and God knows what—dead raccoon?—stings my nose.

"Where would he be?" Even my whisper echoes in the complete silence.

"Who ya looking for?" A deep voice rumbles right next to my ear and I almost pee my damn pants. My shin bangs against something sharp and I stumble backward. Invisible hands grab my elbows and thrust me after Stan, who just keeps moving, oblivious to it all. I stare toward a pool of blackness that seems darker than the rest.

"Looking for Tye Roberts," I say, but whoever grabbed me has faded away and doesn't answer. I can't see a frickin' thing.

The stairwell is quiet. Stan's hand shoots out and presses me square in the chest, all stop. We stand there, frozen. I squint trying to see Stan, imagine him head cocked, listening. I listen too, the tiny hairs on my arms prickling.

"What?" I whisper, my voice too big for the small space. Stan ignores me. He's doing something. Shuffling papers on the ground. Something metallic clunks then rolls across the cement floor of the stairwell. A low growl reverberates in the darkness. Hard to tell if it's human or animal. Stan shoves his pack at me and shuffles on the floor again. A moment later, metal raps against the stair railing. One long, two quick. *Cluuunk, clunk-clunk.* The response—*tap, tap, tap*—comes quick and the growling stops, replaced by wet, throaty breathing. Stan takes back his pack but holds on to the pipe. He clicks his tongue and I'm not sure if he's calling me or whatever is making that awful noise. I inch up the stairs with my back flat against the wall so if the breathing thing decides to attack, I'll have a chance in hell of fending it off. God, I wish I had a flashlight.

No one's on the stairs. We wind around one landing, up more stairs. I only realize it's getting lighter when I make out the shape of a body propped in the corner of the next landing.

"Watchman," Stan says, no longer whispering. "What's up?"

The body on the floor shifts. "Blue sky. Starlight. The good Lord." The man rattles off the list like groceries he'll never be able to afford. He knocks the white tip of his cane on the rail again. *Tap, tap, tap.* Stan taps back, his knuckles muted on the cold metal.

"Sail on, wayward friends," Watchman says.

"Sail on," I tell him.

Two more flights and we're apparently at our destination. The city didn't waste wood on boarding up the windows here—they blackened them with thick paint that smells like tar and lets in pinpricks of light, like tiny stars sucked into a black hole. Stan marches straight off across the universe and I scurry to keep up, caught between dueling fears—losing Stan in the darkness versus tripping over a dead raccoon and falling through the wood-rot floor.

A soft blue glow blooms at the edge of my vision and relief floods through me as Stan heads in that direction. We round a corner and push through a gauzy curtain stapled across the opening in the wall. I expect to duck through into a cubicle like the ones downstairs, but this is a real room, dimly lit by a pair of glowing fish—Nemo and his blue side-kick—plugged into a multisocket extension cord, draped over an old coatrack in the corner. The end of the cord fish-tails across the floor, hitches up with another cord, and slithers out a crack in the window.

A guy's sitting cross-legged, his back to the far wall, flipping cards onto the floor. He is clean, freshly shaven. Not like the rest of the guys who hang out at the Center or in places like this. His white shirt almost glows in the dimly lit room. If it weren't for the raggedy purple scarf draped over his shoulders, he could be fresh from a photo shoot. He looks up. His eyes hold the glint of a feral cat's, adding an air of danger, like Johnny Depp as Captain Jack—you just aren't sure if he's a good guy or a bad one. The girl next to him doesn't seem to notice us. Her face is half hidden under a ripple of black hair. She kneels next to the guy, flicking a card from her own stack atop each of his, scooping up the pairs, tossing them into his pile or hers. Mostly hers.

"Who's he?" the guy asks Stan. His tone is neutral, curious, but his eyes hold suspicion.

Stan bounces on the balls of his feet. "This is Joshie. Josh Roberts. Tye's boy."

The girl's head jerks up and I see her eyes for the first time. Sad, round, impossibly black. Two small stones in an arctic landscape. "Sorry," she says, so softly I'm not sure I hear her right. I want to ask what she's sorry for, but more than that I want to ask why she's so sad.

The guy is standing by now. The two of them could be brother and sister—willowy, stick thin, like a good breeze would bend them in half. But his hand on her shoulder and the way he's squared off against me tells me I was right to be wary. He might just be the kind of branch that snaps back when pushed.

"S'kay," I say, accepting an apology I don't understand because of those black, black eyes.

Her face softens just a bit, but that only makes the guy's free hand tense into a fist by his side. He takes a step toward me, pointing a finger at my chest. "Okay, you're Joshie. She's sorry. Now that that's settled, you happen to bring back the money?"

"What money?"

The guy looks at me like I'm a moron, and the memory of those crumpled bills tickles against the tips of my fingers. Oh, *that* money. Before he can say anything else, the girl's whispering to him. He leans down to hear her and I think it might be a good time to get the heck out of Dodge, but then he's looking at me again and so is the girl and I realize they're waiting for an answer to a question I didn't hear.

Stan touches me on the arm and nods back toward the way we came, but for some reason it matters to me that they think they have some claim to that money under my pillow, so I ignore the question they asked and repeat my own. "What money?"

The guy snorts, but the girl steps closer to me, so close I can smell her breath, sugar-sweet like white-iced cookies. She stares up at my face like the truth might be written across the arc of my eyeball. But there's something written in her look too. More than suspicion. That sadness I saw dance across her features when she first saw me pools in her eyes. I expect her boyfriend to step between us, but he doesn't. Stan doesn't either, but his fingers are on my arm, *tap, tap, TAPPING*, a kind of Morse code I can't translate any better than I can make out the reason behind all that sadness.

"He doesn't have it," she says casually, then plops back down to her spot on the floor like the money matters less than the next card in her stack. Her eyes flit up to me once more. "Ruthie," she says.

Instantly the tension drains from the room. Stan's hand drops from my arm and he squats near Ruthie, his face relaxing.

"Chick," the guy says, and without warning, his hand's in mine, pumping it twice in the same handshake Coach teaches the freshmen before the first recruiter surfaces at the edge of the court each fall: up, down, up, down, hold, and release. The handshake feels less practiced when this guy, Chick, uses it. His scarf bounces comically with each pump, but I don't crack a smile. He motions to a spot on the floor for me to sit and I do. The whole situation is just so surreal.

One second ago this guy was acting like he'd rather punch me than say hello and now we're all friendly? Just because this Ruthie girl says I don't have the money?

"You like cards?" Ruthie asks. I don't actually, but she's dealing me a hand already. Answers seem to be optional here.

She puts the pile on the floor between us and flips four cards faceup, aligning the edge of each with one side of the pile to make a cross. Ruthie scoops up her cards and holds them close, under the veil of her hair. Chick lays down the ten of hearts on top of the jack of spades and turns to me expectantly.

I'm still trying to catch up. "What game is this?"

My question is met with a *tsk* from Stan and ignored by Ruthie and Chick. I stare at the cards on the floor: ace of diamonds, nine of clubs, seven of diamonds, and Chick's ten of hearts. The seven cards in my hand hold no clues. Judging by the game of War we walked in on, I figure it can't be too complicated. I lift out a red eight and put it on the black nine. Stan immediately covers it with a seven. I smile, proud to have cracked the code, but everyone's staring at their cards like there was never any doubt. Ruthie's all concentration as the game goes on, but Chick and Stan trade info on a few of the new guys holing up downstairs and make predictions about the weather.

As fun as it is sitting in an abandoned building playing cards with two people who think I stole their money, I'm impatient. Stan seems to have forgotten why we came in the first place, because as far as I can tell, we're not getting any closer to my dad here than we were at the laundry. Now they're talking about sports and I know Stan's gonna do what Stan always does and brag about teaching me to nail that free throw, but instead he says, "Josh's going to help us. Just till Tye turns back up."

"No." Chick answers so fast, he overlaps Stan.

"Help with what?"

Stan shoots me a *Shut up, I'm handling this* look and tells Chick, "I'm not asking. He's in, temporary-wise. Just till Tye—"

"And I'm saying no. I don't know this kid from Jesus Christ. And if you brought him here expecting—what? What did you expect?"

Stan looks at me, right in the face, and says, "He's a good kid. He'll work off what his dad took."

Suddenly it all makes sense—why this dude is acting like I stole his Hershey bar, where that money under my pillow came from. I force my eyes to stay locked on Stan's and make my voice go low. "Fuck you talking about? My dad isn't a thief."

Stan says something, but Chick's voice drowns him out. "Nah, man. You right. Stealing other people's hard-earned cash don't make him a thief, it makes him a fucking—"

The two of us are on our feet quicker than Rodman on a loose ball. There's a *click* and something silver flashes in Chick's hand. But Stan's quick too. I'm not afraid of a fight. Living in the park, I've been in my fair share, but Chick's hands aren't up like they should be for a fight. They're out to the sides. The second it takes for Stan to step between us is all the time my brain needs to pair the flash and *click* with the flick of a switchblade.

"Aw, now, we're all friends here," Stan says, his hands stretching palms out to each of us.

"Ain't friends with no fucking crook."

"Well, now that's just what I was saying. Josh is a good kid. He ain't a crook."

"My dad isn't a crook!" I shout at them both. My brain is screaming, *Shut the fuck up, you're making things worse,* but at this point it's either double down or admit they might be right about my dad taking their money. I jab my finger at Chick. "This is bullshit. I didn't come in here to get accused of stealing your shit."

Ruthie sidles up from behind Chick like a cat, putting one hand on his shoulder and running the other hand down the length of his arm until they're holding the knife together. She leans in and whispers something to him, and then she's the one holding the knife. It disappears somewhere. Ruthie's hands smooth Chick's stupid purple scarf.

"Not really fair to accuse a man who's not here to defend himself," she says, then to me and Stan, "Why don't you two go see about finding Tye? Let him clear the whole thing up."

Stan puts his hand over my forearm and eases me toward the stairs.

As soon as we step outside, the wind whips the door right out of Stan's hands, slamming it against the side of the Castle with a *boom* that echoes through the city streets like a gunshot. In Gran's trailer park a noise like that would've caused lights to blink on, one after another, illuminating a ripple of paranoia through the community. But here, where abandoned buildings loom over abandoned streets, the only response is the distant bark of a dog.

"Stan," I call, my breath short, steamy puffs as I race to keep up with him as he takes off chin down into the swirling snow. "What was all that about? Stan!"

But he keeps moving, quick, despite the drag-ass cross-country-skiing kind of trail his tennis shoes make along the sidewalk. When he pauses to spin before crossing Main and Sample, I grab his arm and stop him.

His eyes snap to my hand on his elbow. "Boy." For a second neither of us move. Then I release him and he's off again, but still half turned back to me. "Said it 'cause it's true. He took it, you'll pay it off."

I stay back a few feet, even when he stops at the next corner, figuring what to say to that. I could tell him he is full of it, that Dad wouldn't have taken their money, but seeing as how wads of cash turned up under my pillow with Dad out of work and I need Stan to help me find Dad, that might not be the best response. I consider telling Stan that I have the money, but again something holds me back. As far as trust goes, I probably have more holes in my socks than people I can trust. But Stan is one of them, so that's not it. It's just the gut feeling that Dad wouldn't steal money from friends. And if he did, it was for a good reason. So instead of arguing, I yell another question after Stan. "What were you guys talking about? That you want my help with?"

Now Stan stops of his own volition. He studies my face. "Your dad had a surefire job. Brought them two into town to work it with me and your dad's crew. We coulda really raked in some dough, but then one of your dad's guys took off. Then Tye up and disappears. Could use some more muscle on the job. Figured you could help. Not that you got much. Muscle, that is."

My biceps flex defensively under layers of shirt, hoodie, coat. Coach keeps us lean and mean, he likes to say, quick and hungry. Lots of sprints, jump rope, ladders mixed with ball handling and shots. But we hit the weights, too, twenty minutes twice a week, jockeying with football and track for time in the gym. Whenever one of the guys complains (usually a freshie), he gets an earful of "If you don't have stamina, you don't have squat." Then to drive home the point, Coach gives all of us a couple sets of parallel squats before we get back on the bench.

"Muscle enough," I tell Stan.

He nods. "Muscle enough for some things. Enough for this job, anyways."

"What job?"

He takes off walking again.

"Stan. Stan! I don't want any frickin' job! I just need to find my dad."

Stan stops again. His shoulders slump and he turns back to me, slow, patient. "I know, Joshie. But life is hard on the streets. Eventually you'll need the money. Job is yours when that time comes."

Gran's snoring on the couch when I ease open the door. Twig's still up though. He's twisted up in the blankets on the bed with a book propped against Ozzy, like that cat is his own personal bookstand. Next to them on the bed is Axl's metal bowl, full of the cheap kibble from the feed barrel.

"You know Ozzy isn't gonna eat that, right?"

Twig frowns. "He might. I poured some milk on it."

I make a mental note to dump that out before the milk sours and stinks up the room. It's weird that Twig didn't jump up and start begging to play *2K* the second I walked in the door. I sit on the edge of the bed carefully so I don't tip the bowl.

"Hey, little dude. You know Axl's safe with Dad, right?"

He nods, but doesn't look up from the book.

"Gran give you any trouble today?"

"The usual. Dad's a no-good piece of junk, you're following in his footsteps, and I'm not far behind because all men are worthless."

"Sounds about right." I lean over and gently tap the book. There's a weird lizard eye on the cover. "Can you put that away for a minute? We need to figure some things out."

Twig snaps the book shut, which causes Ozzy to hiss and leap from the bed.

"You know that's Dad's money, right? Not money for us to spend except on necessities. We gotta make it last until Dad comes back." I'd been thinking all day about how stupid it was to leave that money with Twig. He knows the value of a nickel way better than I did at nine on account of living on nothing but scraps from Dad and Gran his whole life. That doesn't mean he wouldn't be tempted, though. When I was his age, if someone had handed me a pile of cash, I would have been off to the mall. Would have bought two Big Mac meals and a huge bag of Reese's Cups and passed out sugar-drunk playing Mario Kart in the arcade.

Twig huffs at me. "I know, I know. I'm not an idiot, Josh. Gran's the one to worry about. I put it somewhere safe."

That little dude might not understand everything about our situation, but he gets more than I give him credit for. Dad usually pays Gran the rent on the first of the month and you can bet Gran will be asking for it as soon as she wakes up December first.

"Yeah? Where'd you stash it? In your box?"

Twig huffs again. "No. Gran might find it there." He scoots out from under the blankets and gestures at our pyramid of boxes. He's wearing one of Dad's old flannel shirts that's so big, it hangs on him like a nightgown. "I put it in one of Mom's."

I get to my feet so fast, the blood can't keep up and black spots dance before my eyes. Mom's boxes are still stacked—two on the bottom, one on top. The tape still lies flat and smooth across the seam of the flaps. For all appearances, none of the boxes have been opened in years.

"I didn't open them."

"Then how'd you get the money in there?" My voice is harsher than I intend and Twig cringes.

I sit on the edge of the bed, eyeing the stack of boxes that are Mom's. I don't really know what's in them, besides the money Twig stashed in there. They've been sealed since before we moved in with Gran. Since . . . Mom didn't need those things anymore.

"It's in this one," Twig says, gently pivoting the smallest of Mom's boxes to expose a hole in the side for carrying the box.

It's a great hiding spot. Probably the best spot in the whole house because Gran knows better than to touch Mom's boxes. She'd tried once, told Dad he shouldn't keep perfectly good clothes lying around when others could make use of them. But Dad had told her he'd deal with Mom's things when he was good and ready and meanwhile, she better keep her fucking hands off his shit. Only time I ever heard him cuss at Gran. Only time he ever stood up to her.

But the thought of that money in with Mom's things twists my stomach. Whether Dad stole it from Chick and Ruthie or not, Dad didn't come by it honestly. Not without a job. Not that much money. The need to move it is as intense as it is irrational.

There's no getting the money out the same way it went in, though. My jacket is draped over the bedpost and I reach into its pocket for my key so we can cut the tape with its sharp edge. I take the key and lean over the box, hesitating. It feels wrong to open Mom's boxes. Like we're snooping, violating her privacy. I know she wouldn't mind; Mom had never closed doors, never kept secrets. Even when I was little, she'd let me play in her dresser drawers with her socks and silky pajamas; in her drawer of curlers, the pins of which I'd pretend were hungry alligators and use to bite her toes under the kitchen table when she had her coffee; her special drawer with beaded necklaces and rings that look like treasures retrieved from gumball machines.

It isn't silk or jewelry, socks or curler pins that greet me as I lift the flap of Mom's box. It isn't anything at all but everything at once. I think I am ready, that I have steeled myself, but a thin tendril of memory slips in on the smell of stale smoke. It's not Dad's Pall Malls from before Mom badgered him into quitting or the sweet aroma of Gran's weed that clung to her clothes when she came to visit us in the old farmhouse. It's not the hickory or oak that I'd help chop when I was too small to do more than break off branches to burn in the pit so we could roast marshmallows and make s'mores and pretend we were camping. It is metal, black and twisted beyond recognition, upholstery melted into formless lumps, sizzling linoleum, and crackling wires. Flaming curtains jumping and twirling from the steaming spray of fire hoses and the fluffy white clouds Mom and I had painted on the ceiling over Twig's bed flaking like charred snow.

I gag and rub at my eyelids, but the memories claw their way through, creep into my ears, and cram into my nose and throat, suffocating me. I curl into myself, trying to scream, but I choke on the black smoke that presses in around me and I am dying but I have to find my mom. I have to get to her and Twig. The room spins and I know that all of us are dying.

I wake up on the bed. Twig starts when my eyes flutter open. He dips a cloth into a bowl of water, wrings it, and presses the coolness against my forehead. He watches me with concern but doesn't say anything. As Mac's voice drifts in from the hall, I realize why: Twig's eavesdropping.

Mac's asking if I've ever done that before, freaked out, lost my shit like that. Gran tells him I had night terrors after my mom died, but grew out of them. Like I'd outgrown losing my mom the way I would a pair of shoes or gym shorts. That's easiest for Gran to believe, so I learned long ago to let her think that. Twig knows the truth, though, because me and him share this bed. I calm his fears of shadows and monsters under the bed; he holds my hand and brings me cool cloths on the nights I wake up burning and drenched in sweat.

Mac says something else, which I don't catch.

"Well, you won't have to put up with it much longer," Gran tells him. Her words and the eagerness in her voice make my temperature drop so fast, the rag feels warm against my skin.

I think about what she said to me the night Dad didn't come home—about not raising any more kids—and I wonder what she and Mac are cooking up. She can't ship us off to any relatives; we don't have any.

Maybe she's heard from Dad. Except we'd know if Dad were on his way. Someone would have spotted him and word would have trickled down. When Dad comes home from rambling, he arrives like the Bulls on a parade float after the championships: full of stories about this adventure or that town. And when Twig begs to go, Dad always tells him he'll take us along when we're grown enough, although if seventeen isn't grown enough, I don't know what is. Not that I'd want to go anyway. I just don't see what Dad gets out of roaming town to town. Maybe when he had Stan to roam with. They were like Magic and Kareem. I used to dream of having a friend like that to explore the world with. But after

Stan disappeared, rambling seemed like such a lonely way to live.

And then there is the shit Dad has to take from Gran when he gets back. Yelling and cussing. Telling him she isn't no *orphan-inch* for him to dump his children at. Gran can never stay mad at him long. He flips her cash from some trash he picked up in one town and sold as treasure in another and soon they're back to their uneasy truce. As much as I want to believe that is how it will be this time, I feel in my gut something is different. The money under the pillow, the way Dad didn't bother to pick me up from the game. The note. Axl. It just doesn't feel the same.

"Don't worry," Twig whispers. "I hid the money again. It's between Mom's boxes." When I don't respond, he asks if I'm okay.

"Long as I got you," I tell him.

"Where am I gonna go?" he says with a laugh. And it's easier to let him think it's that simple, so I do.

CHAPTER

06

SUNDAYS ARE FAMILY DAYS. OR AT LEAST THEY WOULD BE if Twig and me had a family. We do our best, though. I could use about two more days of sleep, but I roll out of bed and shake Twig awake at 9:45 because I know he'll be devastated if we miss the Hot Light at Krispy Kreme. The lady behind the counter gives us the evil eye, but we're just asking for our free doughnut, just like every other customer in the store, so she can't kick us out. Twig's doughnut is gone in two seconds flat, but he eats mine slowly, making it last. We walk the short distance from breakfast to the mall, Twig so consumed with licking every bit of sticky icing from his fingers that I have to bodycheck him to keep him from stepping into a pothole the size of the Grand Canyon. A group of girls is in our usual food court booth, so we sit farther from the arcade than I would like. Makes it hard for me to do my calc homework and still keep an eye on Twig as he obsessively checks the floor and machines for runaway quarters. After a bit, the girls move into the arcade. Twig gloms onto them right away, leaning in to vicariously play whatever games they pick. *BurgerTime* and *Dig Dug*. Two games Twig doesn't particularly like, but they're better than watching the opening animation on *NBA Jam* over and over.

Twig had been quick to re-stash the money while Gran and Mac woke me up; he's a smart kid. He knows what that money has to do. But it still must have been hard for him to walk out the door this morning empty-handed knowing that one bill from that pile of cash could have bought him a turn or two on the joystick.

The restaurants in the food court have started prepping for the lunch crowd. Smoky mozzarella from Wood-fire Pizza mingles with curry and saffron from Taste of India, and my stomach growls so loud, the girl in the next booth glances up. I pay seven cents for a cup of water to tide off the hunger until the sample trays are put out. By the time I come back, my usual booth is empty. I'm gathering up my stuff to slide over when I catch movement out of the corner of my eye.

"This seat taken?" Ruthie asks, but she's already planted herself across from me.

I start to say hi, but my mouth twists at the sight of swollen flesh around her eye. It's so purple, it looks like Twig colored it with a marker. I manage to ask if she's okay.

She shrugs. "I've had worse."

"He hit you before?" My hands clench into fists and I picture myself wiping that smug look off Chick's face.

But Ruthie's shaking her head. "Wasn't Chick. He protects me. Before I met him, there were lots of lowlifes. None of them too good at taking no for an answer. Always somebody wanting to be my pimp, my sugar daddy, or my baby daddy."

"So which is Chick?" I ask.

"Less of a dick than you."

"Sorry. I just don't think that Chick—"

Ruthie leans forward across the table like she's going to whisper something to me, and I stop mid-sentence. She doesn't whisper, but her voice is low and shakes with anger.

"Listen, *Joshie*. I'm trying to like you. But the truth is, you're the asshole here. You don't know shit about me or Chick, so don't come in thinking you know what's best for me. I've been on the streets since I was fourteen. Chick is the only man who's ever given a shit about me. He's got my back and I'd have him in my corner in a heartbeat over some little boy who doesn't have the guts to admit his father's a thief."

"He's not—"

"Yeah, he's not a thief. Keep telling yourself that."

The word *bitch* itches at the tip of my tongue, except I know better. It's not just that calling her that would probably get me dick-punched, it's that that word doesn't fit her. She's tough, that's as plain as the black eye, but she's not a bitch.

"Then why'd you stand up for me with Chick?"

"I didn't stand up for you. I just said you don't have our money. That doesn't mean Tye didn't take it." She picks up my cup without asking and takes a long drink.

Her lips leave a slight smear of pink on the rim of the cup. To keep myself from staring at her mouth, I ask, "So what happened?"

"Cops. They hardly bothered us in the last town, but here, they're all over us. Ever since that thing with Wade. His family's been pressuring them."

"Wade?"

"One of your dad's guys. Part of our crew. He took off our first night in town. Big fight with Stan and he was all 'I don't need this shit.' Just fed up, you know? But his family reported him missing and they're after the police to pin the disappearance on someone from the Center. Same old shit: all homeless are whack-jobs and tweakers, you know?"

I'm trying to wrap my head around the fact that the cops gave Ruthie her black eye when Twig pops up out of nowhere. "Who's your girlfriend?" he asks, wriggling his eyebrows so ferociously, it looks like a couple of fat caterpillars are belly dancing on his forehead.

Ruthie laughs and tousles Twig's hair, which he normally hates, but for some reason finds totally tolerable in this situation. Before I can even introduce them, Twig has already invited Ruthie to join us for lunch and is leading her toward Chow Chang's, his absolute favorite. He marches right up to the sample lady and takes two skewers with a "Don't mind if I do." The lady smiles at him and Ruthie, but scowls as I reach for a sample. Tastewise, I can take or leave bourbon chicken, but my stomach's about to jump out of my torso and grab that chicken if I don't.

Ruthie hesitates at the counter like she's trying to figure out what to order, but Twig links his elbow through hers and drags her toward Zito's. Just the thought of their marinara meatballs already has my stomach growling. We make the rounds—munching on samples from each restaurant and joking about a seven-course meal until we come to Dairy Queen.

Ruthie steps right up to the counter, but Twig tugs on her sleeve. "They don't give samples."

She *yeah-yeah*s him and orders three Dilly Bars. She pays for them and holds one out to Twig. He glances at me.

"I—uh—lost my wallet," I tell her.

"Dessert's on me," she says. "You bought lunch."

Twig gobbles his Dilly Bar and races back to the arcade. Ruthie and I sit on the edge of a planter and eat our ice cream. I had never considered the way someone eats their ice cream to be a window into their soul, but I am fascinated by Ruthie's technique. I just bite off chunks. Ruthie, though. *Man.* She takes a tiny nibble at the edge of the chocolate coating and creates an opening to suck the ice cream out. I have to look away to keep from embarrassing myself.

To get my head straight, I ask her, "So, Chick? He's really an okay guy?"

She ducks her head while she swallows a mouthful of ice cream. "Yeah. We been together awhile, you know?"

"He sure dresses nice. Like something out of *GQ* or whatever."

"Yeah, he says you gotta project on the outside what you are on the inside. Something his grandad used to say."

I laugh. "Oh yeah? What's with the scarf, then? Is that to project his inner crazy cat woman?"

Ruthie's smile vanishes and her eyes drop to the floor. "Yo, dude. I *made* him that scarf."

"Oh shit, I'm sorry." I feel like smacking myself upside the head. "It's nice, you know?" *You know?* Great, now I'm talking like her too. She's gonna think I'm mocking her.

Ruthie throws her head back and laughs. "Ha! Fooled you! I hate that fucking scarf—but his nonna gave it to him and no matter what I say, he won't take it off, you know?"

Just like that, she's not just pretty, she's stunning. It's like the sun had been hiding behind a cloud—a beautiful silver-lined cloud—and now it's sparkling in her eyes and singing in her laughter and I am blinded.

Eventually Ruthie says she better take off, and Twig and I head back to the trailer park. We pass the kiddie playground. That's the one area of the park that Mac stays on top of. He's out there constantly picking up trash and sanding the wooden teeter-totter. I think his wife makes him do it so she won't have to spend her whole day pulling splinters out of the butts of their five—yes, *five*—little kids. Up ahead, there's the court. The rims have been empty since before we moved in with Gran and one of the backboards is missing a chunk near the top like Godzilla took a bite out of it. Fat chance Mac'll ever fix that. His kids'll probably be more into NASCAR.

It's warm for November and kids are out on the court waiting for us. Well, waiting for me. As soon as they spot us, they're vying for who gets to play on my team. I stand back and let them fight it out. I don't really feel like playing. The whole thing with Ruthie at the mall has me off-center and now I feel bad for letting her pay for the ice cream. But these kids aren't gonna take no for an answer. When the teams are divided up, I hold out my hands and someone feeds me the ball. Playing with the kids at Oak Creek Court is completely different from real ball. Real ball, I know what my teammates are gonna do. Real ball, there're rules. With these guys, anything goes—no one to call foul if someone throws an elbow or an insult. Most of the kids are little, like Twig's age, so you wouldn't think it'd get too bad, but last fall one kid straight-armed another off the ball and the kid who took the hit got pissed. He grabbed the other player by both ears and head-butted him.

But usually it's pretty chill.

The other team has the ball to start. Twig's on my team. That's an unspoken rule. If I weren't there, they probably wouldn't even let him on the court. For somebody who sucks as bad as Twig does, it's pretty impressive that he even wants to play. Nobody but me ever passes to him because as soon as he gets it, Twig practically hands the ball to the other team, high dribbling it out in front instead of tight and low. "You gotta teach him some skills, dude," Matt told me once. I've tried, but Twig's so, well, twiggy, that the ball rebounding off the pavement sends shock waves up his arms. Only thing I can do is pass it to him and then snatch it back when the other team takes it. Most guys would realize they suck and give up, but not him. The thing with Twig is, he still likes to play. He's out there smiling and joking with the guys and doesn't notice that they don't joke back, that they pretty much ignore him.

Today is different, though. Something's got TreyAnn in a mood. "What the crap?" she yells at Twig the first time he loses the ball. But I get the ball back, so she moves up the court and goes up for an easy layup when I send it her way. We let Twig take the throw-in because it's something not even he could mess up, except today he does. The ball hits the tip of his shoe and skitters across the blacktop to the other team, who takes it right down and scores. TreyAnn says something I don't quite hear and Jason laughs and says, "Cuz he a spaz."

"Really?" I shout across the court. "We're on the same team—cut the shit and play or get off the court."

They give me a look, but I'm older and got about fifty pounds on them, so they shut their mouths and move up the court. Twig comes up alongside me and says real quiet, "It's okay, Josh. They don't bother me."

"It ain't about whether they bother you. You gotta stand up for yourself or you'll be sitting down your whole life."

He rolls his eyes at me, like that's the dumbest thing he's ever heard. I know it's just a line of BS—if he tries standing up for himself with this group, he'll no doubt get knocked on his ass. And unlike in the movies, this crew doesn't give respect to someone for *trying* to stand up for himself. The only way to get their respect is to stand up and stay up, and it can take a whole lotta bloody lips and black eyes to build up that kind of tough when you're as small as Twig.

It seems like we're gonna get a real game going for a bit, but then I send a bounce pass toward Twig and TreyAnn steps in front of him to steal it. She sends it to Jason and they head up the court and after a second so does Twig, but it's the look on his face during that one second when he doesn't move that kills me. He's not pissed or angry. Not hurt or sad. He just purses his lips and gives a small nod, like *Well, why not?* and then trots after TreyAnn and Jason. My legs kick in and I sprint down the court like I'm on a racetrack and whip that ball outta Jason's hand. I don't bother dribbling, just come full stop. "You want the ball? We're on the same god-damn team. If I want you to have the fucking ball, I'll give it to you." And just like that I straight-arm it to TreyAnn so fast, it hits her right in the gut and folds her in half. Jason goes to help her and one of the other little dudes whose name I can never remember yells at me, all indignant, "What the heck, man? We're just playing ball."

But they're not just playing ball, and I'm done with their games. I grab Twig by the arm and drag him off the court.

"Josh!" he yells, trying to pull away, shouting about not wanting to leave and how he's not going back to Gran's, but I don't listen to anything he says until he plants both feet and yells, "I want to play with my friends!"

That makes me stop cold. I can't stand how freaking gullible he is. It's so obvious nobody likes him, but he tags along behind those kids like a lost puppy and wags his tail when they toss him their used-up bones. I just want to smack some sense into Twig, but I don't hit him. Instead I hold Twig tight by his upper arms. "They're not your friends. You're just some kid they let hang around so they can get me to play."

And then Twig's whole face crumples like a wadded-up test with a big red F at the top. I'm about to tell him I'm sorry. That I didn't mean it and he's a great kid and those other kids are shit, but before I can say anything, he kicks me as hard as he can and my grip slips long enough for him to wrench away and take off running. Of course I go after him, but my shin feels like it's shattered and I don't know how, when he's such a little kid, so I hobble as fast as I can. He rounds a corner headed God knows where, but it ain't Gran's. Fuck.

I look for Twig back at the playground. Not sure why, but my gut tells me that's where he'd go. He's there—curled up in the little yellow room at the top of the swirly slide. He pretends not to hear my "Come on down," and I grimace with each step up the ladder, wondering if it's possible for a sixty-pound kid to shatter a tibia with one kick. When I get to the top, he's got his arms across his knees, head down, and the hood of his Notre Dame sweatshirt pulled up. "Twig?" He pivots away from me. "Twig? I'm sorry. I didn't mean it. I'm just tired of you letting those guys treat you like that."

He mutters something into the corner.

"Hey, dude. My leg is killing me. Can I sit?"

He scoots over a bit and I ease my rear onto the edge of the platform, my legs hanging down. "Twig? You hear me? You gotta stop taking their crap."

Twig's shoulders shake and I think maybe he's crying, but when I try to turn him around to hug him, he shakes me off and looks at me full in the face and I'm shocked to see he's laughing. Like borderline-crazy laughing. I say his name again, but that makes him laugh harder. The only thing I can do is wait. "You know what's so funny?" he asks.

I'm afraid to ask, but there's nothing else to do, so I say, "What?"

"I get that they think I'm nothing. Why wouldn't they? My name's Twig for Pete's sake!"

"We can start calling you by your real name. You wanna be Woodrow? Woody?" I offer, but neither one of those is gonna go over any better. Only two ways to go with that— *Toy Story* or penis jokes.

But Twig's laughing again. "It doesn't bother me that they think I'm a loser. I don't care what they think. But you think I'm a loser too."

"No, I don't." I mean it when I say it, but as soon as I hear the words, I know they're a lie. I love him, but he doesn't do anything to stand up for himself. Basketball's not the only thing in the world, but he's not good at soccer or track and God forbid he step on the football field, one tackle and he'd snap like a— "Twig?" I say, trying to come up with some way to make him think I think he's not a loser.

"You think I *let* them treat me like that. You think I don't know that they hate me. I'd have to be an idiot not to know it, Josh. They tell me every day what a waste I am. I don't let them do that. They just do. If I avoid them, they find me, so I might as well just get it over with. Let them say their crap then play some ball. It's not like I have anyone else to hang out with."

That last statement probably isn't meant as a jab, but my stomach clenches like one landed anyway. He doesn't have anyone else to hang around with because I'm always at practice or school. And now, with Dad gone again, most of the time Twig's alone with Gran. I wouldn't wish that on my worst enemy. Speaking of Dad, he should be the one here right now. That's what dads are supposed to do. They're supposed to be there when their kid gets beat up or picked on. They're the ones that teach you how to throw a punch, how to stand up for yourself. Except our dad apparently didn't read the playbook. I wish I knew where he was right now. I wouldn't bother asking him about the money or how we're supposed to take care of ourselves without a mother, without a father. I'd just walk right up to him and punch him in the face for not being here when Twig needs him.

But I don't know where Dad is, so it's up to me to get Twig off the slide and help him cope in the real world of trailer park bullies. I tell Twig I'll fix things, but instead of that helping, it just makes him start laughing again. "You don't get it, Josh. My big brother can't fight them for me. That won't help."

"Okay, so what do we do?"

Twig sighs. "We wait it out. I won't be nine forever. Bullies grow up and think about more important things."

"Like what? Jobs?"

"No, girls." Twig smiles and I smile with him, but I think about kids like Mason who never stop talking trash and the guys Ruthie has to face on the streets who never stop treating others like trash and my heart aches for Twig.

Sunday is the one day we can count on Gran for a real dinner. She must have seen some show back in her formative years when she was deciding what it meant to be a family, some sitcom where the whole family gathered on Sunday for dinner. Whatever the reason, Gran considers Sunday dinner mandatory family time. She cooks a big meal—usually chicken-fried steak or Hamburger Helper lasagna, or if she manages to not smoke up all her Social Security, ham slices and fried potatoes with canned green beans. Salty, but better than ramen noodles any day.

Today she's banging around in the cabinets, pissed off because she was gonna make her favorite tuna casserole but she apparently forgot to buy the tuna. Not that she'd ever admit that. Instead she's cussing a blue streak about us kids eating her out of house and home. Finally she ditches the casserole idea and calls me into the kitchen to get down her meat loaf pan from above the stove. My stomach rejoices.

I know a lot of kids hate meat loaf and Gran would never take a prize for hers, but after a week of the leftover crap my friends don't eat and the Center's noodle-roni, punctuated by snack crackers and an occasional pudding pack, Gran's hamburger-stuffing-egg-ketchup loaf tastes like heaven. Twig wrinkles his nose at the mushy broccoli and watery melted cheese Gran spoons onto his plate, but when she's not looking, I scrape it onto mine and wolf that down too. The best part is the potatoes, though. Gran uses those box-of-spuds, but she adds steamed milk and melted butter and even though it's the consistency of soup, that stuff is good. I eat two bowls of that, dipping the meat loaf in it like bread. I think about going back for a third bowl, but Gran scowls at me and gets up to clear the plates, so I know I better lay off or she's gonna start yapping at me about wasting food.

I swear, she's the only person I've ever heard say you were wasting food by eating it. Most parents make their kids clean their plates and for them, wasting food would be not eating it. Gran, though. She stashes the leftovers away in little plastic bowls, which she labels and dates and then throws away the next day without anyone eating because she can't stand them cluttering up the fridge. I watch her box up those potatoes and a horrible thought comes to me. Tuesday, those potatoes will be in the trash behind the trailer. Maybe even some of the meat loaf if Mac doesn't use it for his lunches. I think of the guys who stand by the trash at McDonald's waiting for spoiled kids to throw away half their meals, and my stomach turns. But is it really dumpster diving if it's your own food you're digging out? And it's not like the food would be all nasty—it'll still be in those little plastic bowls.

Twig's in a better mood, so we play some *2K* until it gets so late, his eyes keep dipping shut. "Time for bed," I tell him. Too tired to protest, he drops his controller and half sleep-walks down the hall. I follow along to make sure he stops off at the bathroom and doesn't pee in the utility closet like that one time he actually did sleepwalk. While I've got him in the bathroom, I remind him to brush his teeth. That wakes him up enough for him to ask me to tuck him in. I guide him down the hall to our room, but as soon as I open the door, I know why we had meat loaf for dinner.

"Aw shit, dude! Our whole room smells like fish!"

Ozzy licks his whiskers and full-body-stretches across the bed like an old man who ate too much. Two tuna cans sit empty near my pillow. I pry open the window and toss them out into the bushes, leaving the window open a crack to banish the oceanic aroma.

"For real, man. If you want to keep that cat, you can't be feeding it Gran's food."

"But he was hungry," Twig says with a yawn.

"Ain't we all?" I say back. "Now climb on up there and go to sleep. You got school in the morning."

I tuck him in next to Ozzy, who hisses at me for trespassing in his bed.

I kick off my shoes, then consider putting them back on. Maybe I should go look for Dad. Even if he does plan to come back, last time he took off, he was gone for weeks. Chick's accusation and Dwayne's insinuation that Dad might have taken off because of Stan swirl in my brain. I wonder if Dad's in over his head or if he really is away on a job. If he'll come home in a week or a month, ambling up the drive in his raggedy denim jacket and busted-up white tennis shoes. I hold on to the image of him coming home, as if I can will it to happen. But daydreaming isn't gonna bring him home and I can't just sit on my hands and wait. What if he's in real trouble?

I reach for my shoes, but Gran yells my name down the hall.

She's in the kitchen, rummaging in the junk drawer, and doesn't hear my "Yeah, Gran?" until I touch her lightly on the arm.

She slams the drawer and shakes her head, tight-lipped and pissed about something. I don't want to ask what's wrong, but what else am I supposed to do, so I ask.

"Same thing that's always wrong. Your dad ain't here and I gotta pick up his shit." She grabs the meat loaf pan from the dish drainer and holds it out to me. "Stick this back up there. And while you're at it, grab that box down, will ya?"

I put the pan up there and feel around the shelf. There's nothing there I can feel, but Gran tells me to give it a good stretch, that the box might have gotten shoved toward the back. I don't know what I'm reaching for and even after I find the box, it takes my brain a full second to process that my grandma just had me fetch a box of Trojans from her kitchen cabinet. I hold them out to her, but she bats them away.

"Them ain't for me! What am I gonna do with comdons?"

I resist the urge to correct her pronunciation and there's no way I'm gonna hazard a guess as to what she would do with them, so I toss the box onto the counter and put both hands in my pockets.

"I'm assuming you know what them are for?" she asks.

"Jesus, Gran, I—"

"Don't you 'Jesus, Gran' me! I did not ask your dad to run off and leave me a horny teenage boy. Do you or do you not know what to do with them?"

My face is so red, I'm sure flames will start licking at my collar any second, but I manage to nod.

"Mac says he saw you at the mall today with some floozy. I do not care who you screw. I do not care how many worthless little sluts you mess with. But I swear to God, if one of them little whores comes sniffing around here saying she's pregnant, you will be out on that fucking sidewalk faster than you can get your dick back in your pants. You hear me?"

"Gran—"

"Do you hear me?"

"Yes, ma'am."

"Now get your ass to bed."

I manage to take three steps toward the hall before the box of condoms smacks me on the back of my head.

CHAPTER

07

THE BUS IS LOUD—LOUDER THAN USUAL, ANYWAY. YOU'D think a bunch of high school kids would be impervious to a little snow, but it'd been coming down all day and the district canceled evening activities, including tonight's practice. Definitely good news.

I'm not usually one to use the words "beauty" and "trailer park" in the same sentence, but when I step off the bus, the snow covers all the ugliness like a coat of fresh paint. The manager's trailer, with its Christmas lights twinkling under a blanket of snow, looks a little like a Swiss chalet. If you look at it out of the corner of your eye and squint a little to block out the hulk of a trash bin. Twig's probably all suited up, just waiting for me to get home so we can attack the sledding hill he's been eyeing ever since the first flake fluttered down after Halloween. I'm rounding the bend to Gran's, mentally rummaging through our food stash, wondering if it's possible to make hot cocoa out of hot water and Nutella when a couple of guys from the park ambush me, pelting me with snowballs so powdery, they poof on impact. Same guys who shoved me in a mud puddle when we moved in with Gran. But they've long since realized I'm not a contender for their King of the Dump crown and the sudden storm's got them romping in the snow like little kids. I scoop up a handful and launch it back, but it doesn't pack well and disintegrates in midair.

A horn gives a polite *toot* and the guys move out of the road to let a bubble of a car slip through. "Slug bug, red," I say under my breath, but Twig isn't here for me to punch. Too bad, because he's up by two and without him around I can't count this one in our race to ten. Plus, he'd have gotten a kick out of the eyelashes stuck on its headlights.

As the car eases past, a snowball splats across its windshield. The driver, a young blonde, turns on her wipers and gives a small wave, but the guys are in full attack mode now, and she's caught in a firestorm of snow. The car lurches forward and disappears around the corner.

"Bish better not come back," one of the kids says. The venom in his words is more than territorial testosterone aimed at some trespassing college chick who, in all fairness, probably turned in here by mistake. Nobody in the park could afford a car like that and friends who have cars like that are even harder to come by. In fact, the last time I saw a nice car in here, it belonged to—

Oh.

The road is slick with wet snow and I nearly fall on my face twice, but I keep running. I take the stairs in front of Gran's trailer in one leap, but stop cold when I see a flattened circle in the snow on the rail where Gran usually sets her roach can.

I burst through the door. "Twig!"

My voice echoes in the emptiness of the kitchen.

"Gran?"

I start toward the doorway to the living room, but skid to a stop in front of the fridge. Our refrigerator—the surface of which is normally as shiny and free from clutter as the NBA's O'Brien Trophy—has been buried under a normal family's fridge. Report cards, school lunch menus, kids' artwork. I almost wonder if I'm in the wrong house. There are a few pictures poking out from between all the papers. I step closer to examine them. My fifth-grade face cheeses from between Twig's preschool photo and a picture of a family I barely recognize. They're at the beach. The man in the picture is laughing, his arm draped casually around a woman who is also laughing, her head tilting in a way that makes her ponytail cascade over her shoulder. The baby in her arms is laughing too, holding tight to that ponytail and looking at a boy in a shark swimsuit who's got his tongue sticking out and his fingers ringed around his eyes. I don't remember the shark swimsuit or that beach, but I do remember the smell of my mom's ponytail after a day in the sun and the girlish peal of Twig's giggles when I used to make that face.

My stomach lurches with a weird mix of homesickness and fear. That picture taped on this fridge is like finding an ice-cold can of Coke being carried across the Sahara by a scorpion. Gran doesn't put anything on the fridge. Gran doesn't have a single photo of anyone anywhere in her trailer. The only reason for her to put all this stuff on the fridge is to create a testament of her grandmotherliness for the woman in the red Volkswagen. She doesn't get to use my mom as a prop. I grab the photo and fold it so it will fit in my pocket.

"Gran!" I yell again.

And then I see the folder. Not on the counter or the table, but atop the microwave stand. A montage of happy kids' faces ring the words *Indiana Department of Child Services*.

"Twig!" I'm out the door and down the steps and after that red Volkswagen, even though I know it's long gone. I race all the way to the split-rail fence at the park's entrance before the pinch in my side cramps so bad, I double over, hands on knees, breathing like a bull on steroids. All I can think about is Twig in the back seat of that car on his way to God knows where.

"Dude? Man, you okay?" One of the kids who'd snow-balled the car tries to take hold of my arm, but I shake him off. He doesn't go away, though. "Come on, man, you're scaring your brother."

His words slip through the pain and fear and I look up to see Twig over at the McGlochens' trailer, clutching a sled to his chest like a shield.

I wait for Twig to go to bed before I smack the folder down on the couch next to Gran. Her eyes are closed, but she doesn't even jump at the sound of it hitting the plastic, just stares at me from under one half-open lid.

"What's this?" I know even as the words leave my mouth that this is not the way to handle Gran on this and, in fact, is absolutely the opposite of the way to handle Gran on this, but all the time Twig was doing his homework and eating his mac and cheese, the anger'd been roiling under my skin like a pot left to boil too long.

Her just lying there like that is making my fists clench and I wonder for half a second if that's part of her plan. Provoke me so I try to choke the living shit out of her and then have the police cart me off. Then no one can stand in her way when she dumps Twig in the system like an unwanted dog. I force my fingers open, drop my shoulders down and back, release the tension slowly through pursed lips.

"What is this?" I ask again.

Gran sits up, picks up the folder, and sets it on the coffee table. Then she says in a voice as even as the surface of a frozen pond, "I never wanted kids. Not your dad, not his whore of a sister. Work my ass off to get them two out of here. Finally getting back to living my own life. Got a job, got a man. Then your mom up and dies and I'm right back to raising kids again. 'Only till I get on my feet,' your dad said. Well, he ain't on his feet and he ain't gonna be on his feet now or never. He's content just laying on his back while the world picks up after him. I told him, me and Mac, we're gonna retire in Florida together and when that happens, ain't none of his *shit* coming with us."

She makes damn sure I know that's what she thinks we are—me and Twig. Dad too. My fists are balls again, pressing into my sides. She didn't ask for this. Fine, I get that. Neither did I, neither did Twig. But what I don't understand, what makes me want to punch her right in those dead eyes of hers, is why she hates us.

She stares back at me, daring me to say something. I swallow down the anger, my mouth twisting with the effort, swallow down the hate that wants to spew everywhere. Hating her might be what I want, but it isn't gonna help Twig any if I let her goad me. So I swallow and wait, forcing my breath into a slow, easy rhythm that matches the *tick* (in) and *tock* (out) of the clock in the kitchen. It takes some time before I feel calm enough to speak. Even more time until I trust the words I've assembled. I drop my eyes so she doesn't take what I am about to say as a challenge.

"Gran."

My voice cracks.

I clear my throat and try again. "Gran, Twig's just a little kid. Can't he stay? I'll leave tomorrow, you won't have to take care of me, but Twig—" There goes that crack again, and I stop long enough to swallow then plunge ahead. "Twig deserves a real home. None of this is his fault."

The instant I say the word "fault," Gran's eyes widen. My hands come up to brush away the word, but she's on her feet, screaming in my face. "Fault? Ain't my fault neither! Whole world expects women to pick up after lying, cheating husbands, good-for-nothing sons. Twig deserves? Twig *deserves*? What about what I deserve? What if I want a life, huh? What if I got plans? Can't do shit with you all clinging on my back. Far as you and Twig—you're just a couple of worthless boys on your way to being worthless men."

I press my lips together and wait for her to come up for air. When she does, I say the only thing that might get through to her. "I can pay you."

Her eyes narrow. "How you gonna do that?"

"I got a job." The lie comes easily.

"How much you got so far?"

Someone eavesdropping might think we were a couple of Wall Street wolves instead of a grandparent and a grandson. I convince Gran that I just started as a busboy at Denny's and barter down from the two-fifty Dad was giving her for all three of us to stay there to two hundred a month as long as I fork over the fifty Dad shorted her for November and move out first thing in the morning. She says I can come on Sundays to spend time with Twig. I want to remind Gran that me living here doesn't cost her anything—except for Sunday dinners, Dad and I had stopped eating her food months ago—but the kids on the folder stare up at me, their faces frozen in fake smiles, and I know they'd tell me to take the deal. Any deal.

It buys me some time, but not much. That fifty dips Dad's money to below what I need for December rent. And what if Dad doesn't come back? What if Gran decides two hundred a month isn't enough?

Packing my stuff is easier than thinking about all the what-ifs, so I focus on that. I leave the door open so the hall light casts enough light to find my shit, but not enough to wake Twig. I shove my underwear, socks, and the few shirts I own into my backpack, put my books on top. Zip it shut. The last thing I grab is some money. Dad's note is folded in with the bills. I peel off two twenties and a ten for Gran, pocketing the other ten and a few singles for bus fares and emergencies. The rest I put back where Twig stashed it. No sense tempting fate by walking around with that much cash. If we need it, *when* we need it, it'll be safer right here. I smooth the note against my jeans, running my fingers over the words.

Have to see a man about a horse. Take care of your little bro.

Yeah, Dad? How am I supposed to do that on $177?

I grab a pen from my backpack, intending to add a note of my own for Twig, but there's nothing I can say that is any less full of shit than Dad's *Have to see a man about a horse.* Anything that needs to be said, I should say to Twig's face. I crumple the note and toss it at the trash can in the corner, not even caring enough to see if it makes it in.

But telling Twig is impossible. I try the next morning over breakfast, when Gran is in the bathroom. Twig's snarfing down enough no-name oatie-o's to feed a kindergarten class while I nibble one of the few granola bars left in the closet. When he goes to pour himself thirds, I grab the box. "You gotta eat less," I tell him.

"I'm hungry."

"I know, but Gran'll get mad if you eat too much." What I'm really thinking is *Gran will have you hauled off*, but I don't want to scare him. Instead I tell him there's always a stash of snacks in the closet if he needs more food than Gran'll give him. He nods and lets me close up the oatie-o's. Gran flushes in the other room and I know I only have a second or two to tell Twig why he won't be seeing much of me. "Remember my friend Matt?"

Twig nods. "Matt's mom made you that birthday cake and you brought home some for me. Did I tell you my teacher is having us write letters to Santa? I think I'm gonna ask for a skateboard—"

"Twig."

"—but I really want to ask for a bike. Do you think Santa would bring me a bike?"

"Twig, I need to—"

"Like, I know that's a big thing, but if I'm really good?"

He sits there, waiting. And I wish that I could say of course Santa will bring him a bike. I swallow and try to start again, but all I get out is his name and then the bathroom door opens, and Gran comes back into the kitchen muttering that Twig'll miss the bus and she ain't driving him to school. Twig hesitates, not wanting to leave without an answer, so I pinch my lips shut and nod. "Mm-hmm. A bike."

Joy radiates across his face. He grabs his backpack and is out the door and I never told him.

CHAPTER

08

I'D PLANNED TO ASK MATT DURING PRACTICE IF I COULD stay on his couch just for a night, but Coach works us so hard, I don't get a chance. Then, in the last few minutes, I miss an easy shot.

"Take the line, Roberts."

I had hoped Coach didn't see the ball dip just below the rim and rebound back out. No such luck.

"Got eyes in the back of his head," Nick says.

"Got ears, too," Coach snaps. "You wanna join him, Levine?"

"Nope! I'm good."

Coach tosses me the ball. I step up to the line and ready my shot.

He hits the ball, trying to knock it loose from my grasp, but all my anger is in my fingertips and I'm squeezing that ball so tight now, it doesn't go anywhere.

"That how you hold the ball? Like a third grader?" Coach motions for Mason to pass him a ball. Coach swirls it in his hand until the grooves line up the way he likes. He raises the ball to the net like an offering. "Gentle. Light touch. That's what makes the ball want to fly. And put your toes right at the line."

My toes *are* right at the line. My toes have been at the line since before I learned to tie my shoes. I'm the best fucking free throw guy on the team and here Coach is taking me to school in front of all the guys like I'm seven.

"At the line, Roberts!"

My eyes snap up. I bite back the urge to tell him to shove this ball up his ass. I need this team. It's the only thing that keeps me real.

Coach points down at his feet. The green tips of his Michigan State Adidas aren't at the line. They're on it. If I do that in a game, I'll get called. Is that what he wants? Me to get called for line-stepping? He moves back and I take up his position. Toes on the line. No way I'm doing that shit in a game, though. I give the ball a bounce, hold it with the tips of my fingers.

Just before I release, Coach says, "Oh, and, Josh? You stand at that line until you hit one hundred in a row." The ball clanks off the rim.

Matt whistles through his teeth. "Sheesh, Larry Bird only hit eighty-nine percent."

The side of Coach's mouth twitches and he adds, "Each time you miss, give me stairs. Already owe me one. The rest of you, nice practice. Hit the showers."

Coach picks up his tattered Michigan State duffle bag and climbs the bleachers. As I pass him on my way back down, he doesn't even glance up from his stack of newspapers. He doesn't watch me shoot, just keeps gnawing licorice and reading like it's Sunday afternoon at Starbucks while my muscles seethe and my heart throbs with hate. When I hit eighty-nine, I look up. He's gone.

Matt's waiting in the parking lot, the windows of his truck down. A blues track plays nice and low. "Pride and Joy," Matt's absolute favorite. He's got his eyes shut, playing right along with Stevie Ray. I don't interrupt him, just open the door and climb on in. When the song ends, I clap and Matt says, "I wanna thank you so very much," in his perfect Stevie Ray voice.

"Still taking guitar lessons from that dude that lives behind the Gas n'Go?"

"I wish. He moved to Texas or somewhere. Speaking of Texas, wanna join the guys at Bruno's? They ordered enough for us."

We were not, in fact, speaking of Texas, but I let that go with a shrug. "Nah, man."

Matt shakes his head and starts the truck. "Can't let Coach get you down."

That's easy for him to say. Matt and the rest of the guys are always hitting the showers by seven. Most of the time Coach keeps me another half hour.

"He just wants you to be the best you can."

I side-eye Matt. He's serious. "If he wanted me to be the best I could be, he'd let me start. He knows I got the goods—I bring the game home every single time, man. The team gets down, I get in there and *bam!* put a few in the bucket. Coach hates me, plain and simple. He's a washed-up never-been and he resents me cuz he knows I got skill he ain't never had and he hates me."

Matt twists his body in the seat. "You got that all wrong. Coach doesn't start you because he's *saving* you. Like late-career Joakim Noah. Teams be saving him for when they need him. Keeping him fresh so he can get in there and put that other team down. Joakim, he the man for his team. That's you for us, you the man. You're complaining that Coach works you hard. I wish he worked me that hard. That shit's gonna get you noticed, get you out of here. The rest of us"—he pops the truck into drive—"we're just playing ball."

Forget asking Matt if I can sleep over; he'd probably take that as an invitation to tell me Gran's only kicking me out to help me be my best self. "Yo, man, drop me here."

"Here? Right here on the street? Man, don't be like that."

"Right here's good."

Matt pulls over and lets me out. There's a CVS on the corner. I walk into that drugstore like I got a whole list I'm shopping for and need to get to it. Soon as he drives off, I'm back on the street. Nick's house isn't too far from here, but the likelihood I can crash there is nil to no. Nick can't even drink a soda without asking his dad for permission.

Stan would probably let me bunk at the Castle, but the thought of sleeping in the same room as Ruthie and Chick is . . . problematic. I'm not sure which bothers me more, the thought that I might have to listen to the two of them making out all night or that Chick could try to kill me in my sleep. A small part of me thinks about what could happen if Chick falls asleep first. Maybe Ruthie and I could sit up and talk. I'm so deep in fantasizing about a fricking conversation that I don't notice Stan leaning against a lamppost until he says, "I gotta lead on your dad."

Stan walks toward downtown. He knows I will follow, and I do. Where else am I gonna go? He's calmer than usual, less spinning and counting, but still not normal enough to avoid attention. People give us a wide berth on the sidewalk. Downtown is not usually busy, especially in the middle of the week, but it's right before Thanksgiving and no one wants to cook, I guess. I glance in the big window as we pass Bruno's. The team's still in there, but Matt's truck isn't parked on the street. Couples spill out onto the sidewalk in front of Chicory Café. Puffs of e-cig vapor and strains of music drift in and among the bodies, and for a second I wonder what it'd be like to live in a studio apartment downtown instead of a trailer out at the edge.

Coach says we got a chance to change our lives if we keep our grades up and smile at the recruiters. He's not promising the NBA or anything—no one at Woodson dreams that big—but maybe a DII school somewhere in Indy or Detroit. Matt already plans to go to Bethel, and he's been talking to the recruiter there every chance he gets. Nick's wanted to play for IU since he could hold a ball. His dad's an alum, so he's got a shot. A few weeks ago Coach pulls me aside and introduces me to a guy from San Bernardino. I have to ask him where that is, because I never heard of it, but when he says California State, I nod. That I've heard of. "We hold a special spot in our program for Woodson," the recruiter tells me, his smile so sparkly, he looks like he stepped out of a toothpaste commercial. He tells me they've had a few players come through from Woodson—Lionel Wilcox and Quinn Kelley, to name a few—and he grips my shoulder and tells me I seem like their kind of guy. But all I can think of is Twig. If I go that far away, what'll happen to Twig?

"Recognize this place?" Stan stands in front of a closed-up shop, both hands on his hips, rocking back on his toes with the air of someone who's about to start crowing.

I shake my head. "Nope."

"Dad ever bring you by here?"

"Nope."

"Really?"

"Really. Why? This where he's staying?" I swipe at the greasy smudges on the front glass and use my hand like a visor to shield the glare from the downtown lights. It's completely dark in there. Nothing moves. Looks like it might've been an old saloon or something—a huge mirror lines one wall, a long counter in front of it. There's a hulking something across the room, maybe a piano, but it's too dark to really tell.

"Naw, he ain't in there. But he was gonna be."

"Yeah?" I wonder if the crew was planning to break in, rip out the fixtures, and sell them as scrap, but Stan is looking at the place more like a lovestruck teen than a treasure hunter. "What is this place?"

Stan points to the right of the door where wooden letters spell out *Sal's*. "I grew up here," he tells me.

"In a saloon?"

"Ayuh."

"You grew up in a saloon?"

"Ayuh," he says again. "Parents used to own it."

Maybe in the Roaring Twenties, I think, but instead I ask him what happened to it.

"Long story," he says like he'll fill me in later, but the truth is Stan never tells long stories. It was always Dad who filled me in when Stan threw out such teasers, which in this case means the details of Stan's saloon-inhabiting childhood may remain a mystery. I give him a few more minutes to stare at the building with that strange look of infatuation on his face and then I ask how this building will lead us to my dad.

"We were gonna buy it with the money, make it a diner," Stan says. "The three of us. Your mom, dad, and me."

Just like that I can hear Mom laughing, tugging at her apron as it hangs around Dad's thin hips, teasing that he and Stan are gonna burn the kitchen down with the bacon grease they're splattering all over the stove. She shushes, though, when Dad puts a cup of coffee in front of her, drops a Hershey's Kiss in it, and bends to kiss her forehead. I used to love watching the three of them on Saturday mornings, filling the kitchen with their laughter and love. So many ways our lives would be different if Mom were still here.

Stan walks off down the sidewalk at a brisk pace, although not as brisk as it would be if he weren't trying to avoid stepping on any cracks in the sidewalk. This crack-avoidance is new and annoying. Like trying to walk down the street with a four-year-old. But right now I am too preoccupied with thoughts of what it'd be like to live in a cramped apartment above a saloon-turned-diner to be irritated by Stan's irrationalities. We're headed toward the Castle, so I walk in silence behind him, not daring to hope my dad turned up there.

The Castle is less scary now that I've been inside and can anticipate Watchman's banging and the gaping holes in the floor. Stan and I make it up to the fifth floor. The Nemo and Dory night-lights cascade orange and blue across the floor, but it's so dim that the room seems empty until Stan clears his throat and a subtle shift of blue in the corner draws my attention. Dory's soft glow catches Ruthie's hair as Chick's hand moves through it. Stan *harrumphs* louder.

Chick makes a noise that might be "What?" but it is hard to tell with his mouth still full of Ruthie's tongue.

"Y'all need to get a fucking room," Stan says, his voice flat.

"Had one, until you showed up," Chick grumbles, but Ruthie hops up and gives Stan a hug, which he does not return. She tosses me a quick smile, but other than that doesn't acknowledge my existence. Probably a good thing, because Chick already hates me enough without knowing his girlfriend hung out at the mall with me over the weekend.

Stan leans down and snatches the bag of chips on the floor where Chick and Ruthie had been sitting. He eyes the label and scrunches up his nose. "I asked for nacho cheese."

"Get 'em yourself," Chick shoots back.

Ruthie takes the bag from Stan and pops a chip into her mouth. "I don't see why you won't eat these," she says, her words punctuated by crunching. "They're pretty good. We did try to get your nacho cheese ones, but all the good ones got moved up front, like they knew someone had been lifting them." She gives Stan a reproachful look that makes my heart pang with a memory of that same look on my mom's face when I refused to let Twig toddle along to the park with me and my friends. Stan doesn't seem to notice, though; he's leaning against the wall sulking about his nacho cheese chips. Ruthie grabs another chip and adds, "Oh, and no luck with Tye, either. Chick got a punch in the face for our trouble, though."

"You found my dad?"

"No . . . ," Ruthie says, like she is talking to a toddler, "I just said we *didn't* find him. We went to look at one of the spots he likes—down by the river under that bridge—and asked around. Usually something's going down, the guys there know. But we're asking around and Jimmy Dean spots us. Comes over, getting in Chick's face—"

"Goddamn Jimmy Dean," Chick says.

Stan pulls away from the wall. "Jimmy was down there?"

Ruthie nods. "That's what I'm saying. Can't nobody listen? Asking us who we think we are moving in on his turf. Like he owns this town or something."

"I told you guys, keep your head down. He finds out what we've been doing, he's gonna want in on it."

"Like we have anything to show for all our work." Chick shoots me an accusatory glare.

"Chick told him to bug off and *kapow!* Jimmy Dean socks him right in the eye and walks away without so much as looking at him."

"I'd a kicked his ass if it wasn't for my vision going all FUBAR. Gonna go back tonight and—"

Stan had started pacing but stops in his tracks and points a finger at Chick. "Stay the fuck away from him. You're lucky all you got was a punch in the face. You go back down there, Jimmy'll gut you like a fish."

"Pffff. Like to see him try." Chick turns to me. "Jimmy thinks he's king of the world. All bark."

"Wade might have something to say about that," Stan shoots back.

"Wade?" Ruthie repeats.

"What's Jimmy Dean got to do with Wade? You told us he left after that fight with you." Chick's eyes narrow at Stan.

"Ayuh, that's what I said and that's sure enough true. I didn't tell you what we was fighting about. Jimmy Dean tried to recruit him out from under us. Promising quick money. You know that boy was always about taking the easy way. I told him, you don't crawl in bed with a rattlesnake and expect to walk away with its rattle."

"You're saying Wade didn't leave? That he's working with Jimmy Dean?"

"No, I ain't saying nothing. But he didn't stay with us and he didn't go back home, now did he?"

I know it's not the best time to ask, but I have to know. "So you didn't find my dad?"

"No," Ruthie and Chick both shout at me.

"But you didn't really ask those guys under the bridge, right? I mean, Jimmy Whoever showed up and ran you off before you had a chance, right? So they might know something?"

"Don't get any bright ideas," Stan tells me. "Chick and me ain't the only ones Jimmy hates. You go spouting your mouth off about being Tye Roberts's boy, might find yourself in the intensive care ward over at St. Joe's."

Ruthie rolls up the bag of chips and tosses it down on her blankets. "Josh? I don't want to be harsh, but if your dad's this hard to find, maybe it means he doesn't want to be found. Have you thought about that? Maybe you should respect that. Maybe he disappeared for a reason and us chasing all over hell looking for him . . . Well, maybe that's not what's best for any of us."

Ruthie's voice is soft, like the tone can make the words sting less.

"You know what?" I snap at her. "You were right the other day. I don't know you. But that goes both ways. You don't have a clue what me and my dad are like, what we been through. You don't wanna help me find him? That's just fine. You can all go screw yourselves. I don't need your help."

I'm out the door and out in the cold before I realize I don't have anywhere to go.

Despite their warnings, I wind up down by the river. There are two bridges Ruthie could have meant. I head toward the one by Howard Park and—*bingo!*—a cluster of men are warming themselves around a burn barrel. I approach with caution. It's dark and I'm so focused on trying to see if I recognize anyone, maybe someone from the Center, that I don't notice an old guy leaning against the bridge's cement wall until he barks a "We know you?"

"Uh, no. Looking for Tye Roberts? You seen him?"

"Tye Roberts, huh?" the old guy echoes loudly, and a few of the men turn from their conversation to eavesdrop on ours. "Everybody knows Tye, right, fellas?" His question is met with a few affirmations. "Problem is, lately he's been pissing off the wrong folks. What he do to you?"

Now everyone is interested. The men circle around. Instinctively, my shoulders want to fold in, shrink, but I inhale a full breath of the night air and force my shoulders up and back. Not threatening, not aggressive. Just holding my space. Projecting a *We're cool* attitude. Like I usually talk to strangers. In the dark. Under bridges.

I'm not sure whether to admit our relationship or buddy up to the group like I'm just another guy Tye ticked off. I'm leaning toward the second option when the old guy swats my chest with the back of his hand. "Boy, don't piss yourself. We're just messing with you. True though, your pops been messing in some shit lately. Got himself poked last night."

"Poked?"

A small dude with a man bun translates. "Knifed. Surface wound, but bet it hurt like a mother."

"What? Last night?" Stan's words replay in my head— *Crawl in bed with a rattlesnake*—but instead of a rattle, I see the heat in Chick's eyes punctuated by the flick of a switchblade. "Who stabbed him? Do you know?"

The old guy puts a calming hand on my arm. "He's gonna be fine. Alek walked him over to the hospital to get stitched up. Right, Alek?"

"Yep," a voice from nearer the barrel responds. "Be good as new."

"Which hospital?" I ask.

"He ain't gonna be there—"

"Which hospital?" I repeat, near panic. I can't even think with words like "knifed" and "hospital" stuck in my brain.

Small dude points up the river. "Memorial."

I don't know where to go. Main entrance? Locked. Staff entrance? Locked. Then I realize I'm being an idiot and head to the emergency entrance. There's an ambulance in the bay and the whole room is packed with people. Some are crying; others are sleeping. The smell of antiseptic hangs in the room so thick that I taste it in the back of my mouth. It's better than tasting the smells that linger just under the antiseptic, though, vomit and BO. A sign orders me to check in with the receptionist, but the line there rivals the corner Dairy Queen when the temp tops ninety.

I'm considering trying to cut to the front of the line when a door slides open in the wall next to where I'm standing. A harried nurse steps out and calls someone's name.

"Excuse me? I'm looking for—" I try, but she cuts me off with a wave of her hand toward the receptionist. I swallow and try again, but she's already escorting the patient whose name she called through the invisible sliding door. She shuts it in my face. But another door slides open next to it and I manage to step in front of that nurse, and before he can say anything, I blurt out that I'm looking for my father, who might have been brought in last night.

He looks at me like he wishes he had a flyswatter. "You'll have to check with the visitors desk."

"Okay, where is that?"

"Main entrance." He brushes past me and calls a name. Across the room a woman stands and helps a boy with a large bandage on his head get up.

"But that's closed."

"Not during visiting hours," he informs me in what Twig would have called a Captain Obvious voice.

"Okay, but I'm not trying to visit. I just want to know—" I begin, but the nurse is already sliding another door shut in my face.

Across the room, there's a glass door under a sign that says "Admitted Patients Only." I'm thinking about making a break for it when I notice a familiar security guard watching me. He catches my eye and nods toward the way I came in. I nod and head for the parking lot. It takes him a few minutes, but Dwayne comes out, lighting up a cigarette.

He holds up his hand as he approaches and says, "Before you ask, he isn't here."

"My dad? Has he been here? Do you know where he is?"

He holds up his hand again, like I'm a puppy that he's trying to keep from jumping up. "Not here now, but he was. Came in last night holding his side and bleeding like a stuck pig. I don't know what happened to him, because they don't tell me stuff, but they patched him up and he left, so it couldn't have been too bad. You try the Castle?"

I blink, trying to transition from the idea of my dad bleeding like a stuck pig to the rest of what Dwayne is saying.

"Did you look at the Castle?" he repeats. "He hangs out there sometimes. With some kids about your age."

"Yeah, but he's not there. He was okay when he left? You sure?"

Dwayne nods. "The policy might be catch and release, but that doesn't mean we don't measure them first."

He's lost me again, but before I can ask him what the hell he's talking about, he changes the subject. "What's your good friend Stan have to say about your dad?"

"Not much. Hasn't seen him."

"Stan doesn't always tell everything he knows. And what he does tell is not always what he knows. You know what's good for you, you stay away from him."

I want to ask Dwayne when he turned into a fricking oracle, but there's squawking over his radio and he takes off at a jog toward the emergency room. I stand there in the parking lot watching him disappear inside the doors.

In the time that I've been at Memorial, the temperature has dipped. It's not even ten o'clock, but November in Indiana means it's already been full-on dark for four hours and anyone with any sense is bundled up somewhere warm. I just stand there, my breath hanging frozen in the air like empty cartoon speech bubbles. I don't know whether to be relieved that Dad is alive and still in town, or worried that he might be holed up somewhere, still bleeding. And if he's in town, why did he leave Gran's? That triggers a whole avalanche of questions—about whether he ever even left town, where he'd be if he wasn't at Gran's, wasn't at the Center, wasn't at the Castle. No motel would let him keep Axl, and he couldn't afford one anyway. None of his friends have places of their own. In fact, a few had come knocking at Gran's the first month we lived there, the same guys who used to camp in the junkyard or who Dad would sweet-talk Mom into letting sleep on the couch on the coldest days. If Dad were anyone else, the junkyard might be an attractive place to hole up. Except the city confiscated that after the fire and even if Dad could get in . . . he wouldn't.

Still, the thought keeps nagging at me that I should check it out. But not tonight. And not alone.

I don't relish the idea of going back to the Castle, but I don't have anywhere else to go. Maybe I can talk Stan into going out to the junkyard with me between school and practice tomorrow.

As I pass Watchman on the stairs, he tells me he's gonna start charging admission with all the traffic passing through. I don't know what to say to that, so I chuckle and say, "Yeah, okay."

As I come up the last few stairs, Stan's voice floats across the space. "So that's it?" he says. "You just gonna ditch our plan?"

I hesitate at the stairwell, not wanting to interrupt the conversation, curious about whatever plan they're discussing. Chick's voice is lower, muffled by the curtain. The only word I can make out is Ruthie's name. I creep halfway across the room, listening.

"So you already asked her?" Stan shouts. "No? Well, then you don't know shit, do you?"

"More than you. She deserves a real place. Running water! Real heat. You said we'd have that here. Come with me to South Bend, you said. Okay, we're here and it's no better than the last two towns. Except now we don't even have Wade and our money's gone. I'm starting to think you're just stringing us along. Ruthie and me, we—"

"Me and you, what?" Ruthie calls as she bounds up the stairs and nearly runs into me in the dark. "Hey, Josh." No anger, no *Guess you decided you do need us after all*. It's like the whole conversation where I said they could all screw themselves never happened.

Stan sweeps aside the curtain. "Chick here was just saying—"

Chick steps forward. "That me and you, we got history. That's all. Stan needs to respect that."

Ruthie tilts her head and eyes them, like she knows there's more to that conversation than they're letting on, but is willing to let it go. For now. "They were outta regular, so I got white chocolate." She tosses candy bars to Stan and Chick then shrugs at me. "Didn't know you were gonna be here. Want mine?" She tosses one to me and I fumble to catch it. My stomach reminds me that it's been a minute since the taco salad they served at lunch. My brain says, *Dude, you can't eat her candy*.

"I'm good," I say, holding it out to her.

Ruthie rips the corner of the wrapper with her teeth and peels it back to reveal two white Reese's cups. She takes one and pops the entire thing into her mouth, then reaches for my hand and folds it around the package containing the other one. Stomach for the win.

Ruthie and Chick settle down on the blankets, but Stan's keyed up. He paces in the small space between the boarded-up window and the curtain, eating the candy. His hands crinkle the empty wrapper like a fidget toy.

"Hey." I tap his arm as he passes and he turns to me. The look in his eye says he doesn't share Ruthie's *all is forgotten* approach to disagreements, but he doesn't tell me to leave. I contemplate apologizing, but since I didn't do anything wrong, I can't quite bring myself to do it. Instead I tell him I found out my dad is still in town. That he was treated in the hospital for a knife wound and released.

Stan throws up both hands. "See? I told you guys. Fucking Jimmy Dean!"

"Shit," Chick says quietly.

Ruthie smiles. "So you found him, then? Your dad? He okay?"

"Yes, well, no. I mean, the hospital patched him up and sent him out. But I didn't see him and I don't know for sure where he is. I think maybe he might have gone to the junkyard where we used to—"

"No."

We all turn to look at Stan, who's shaking his head like I suggested my dad had jaunted over to Jupiter. "That was the first place I looked when you came to me, son. I went there and checked it out 'cause I thought the same thing. But he wasn't there. Nope. No sign of him."

"Maybe you missed him? We could go tomorrow and look again."

Stan rubs the back of his neck. "You know as well as I do, that is one place he don't want to be. You neither. I only went to check to put it to rest. Save you the pain of going there yourself. He ain't there."

I nod. "Yeah. It's just that—"

"That place is nothing but pain. I'm telling you, your dad wouldn't step foot in there again if his life depended on it." Stan chucks the crumpled candy wrapper into a pile of trash in the corner.

He's right. I know he's right. Damn, I can't even open a box of Mom's things without freaking out. Why would Dad go back there?

"Need a place to crash?" Stan asks. "We got a few sleeping bags."

Ruthie's face is buried in Chick's neck and it's hard to tell if her "Mm-hmm" is in agreement with Stan's invitation or just a reaction to whatever's happening under that blanket. It's hard to believe that just this morning I woke up in a warm bed at Gran's. The whole day has been one thing after another and I guess I've been too much in denial about being tossed out of Gran's to make a plan. Maybe I could go back there. Sneak in the back bedroom window. Get out early before Gran notices. Or there's Matt's place. I'm still pissed at him for defending Coach like that, but I'd rather swallow my pride than stay here, like a fourth wheel tacked onto some busted-up tricycle.

"Nah, I got a place," I tell Stan.

I leave not sure if I'll wind up at Gran's or Matt's, but in the end the risk of getting Twig thrown out is just too high. Matt's truck isn't in the driveway. I sit on the front porch, intending to wait for him to get home, but Sammi, his Goldendoodle, spots me and whimpers at the window. Shushing her doesn't work. I try to slink off into the shadows, but Matt's mom opens the door and calls out, "Matt, is that you?"

"No, Mrs. Higle. It's just me, Josh." I lean forward into the light so she can see me. "I'm sorry if I scared you. I was just looking for Matt."

"He's not home yet, but you can come in and wait."

"That's okay, I—"

"Joshua. It is seventeen degrees out here. Get your rear end in this house."

God, I love that woman.

Mrs. Higle leads me into the kitchen and tells me to sit. "Hmmm, got some leftover pizza in here," she says, rummaging through the fridge. "You like olives?"

"Yes, please," I say. The only other thing I hate worse than olives is pistachio pudding—reminds me too much of Twig's baby vomit—but right now I'm so hungry, I'd eat olives floating in pistachio pudding.

Mrs. Higle nukes four slices of pizza and plops them down in front of me with a can of Barq's. "I'll go make up the couch for you," she says, like it's a given that I am spending the night.

No questions about why I showed up on their doorstep at midnight or whether I should text home to let them know I'm okay. Just *Here's some pizza. Here's the couch.* Matt has no idea how lucky he is.

CHAPTER

09

FIRST HOUR IS BRUTAL. DAVIS IS ON SOME RANT ABOUT the lack of textual support in our essays and if it wasn't for Ramón kicking the back of my chair every time my head dipped, I'd have fallen asleep for sure. Thank goodness it's a half day, so we're up and moving class to class every twenty-five minutes. Somehow I make it through the morning and I'm at my locker, stuffing books into my backpack when a sharp punch to the shoulder causes me to drop shit everywhere. I spin around ready to deck whoever had the nerve to come up on me like that, but it's just Nick and Matt.

Nick throws his hands up in mock surrender. "Dude! What the hell? We're yelling down the hall and you just walk by like we're nothing, then I come to entice you with burgers and shakes and you act like someone might be trying to stick a shiv in your back. Mason doesn't want you off the team that bad."

Matt laughs. "He's not worried about Mason." I wait for him to tell Nick I spent the night on his couch, to tell Nick the same story I told him about fighting with my gran, but instead Matt says, "He's been spacing out all week. It's a girl. Can't you tell when a guy's got it bad?"

Even though I know he's just yanking my chain, moonlight on ebony hair and the smell of strawberry shampoo send heat up my neck. I turn away and squat to scoop papers back into my math book. "I just got a lot on my mind."

"That shit with Coach? Crazy, huh?"

I look up at Nick and he raises his eyebrows. "What, you don't know? Some homeless piece of shit is stalking him."

I heft my backpack and slam my locker. "I gotta go."

"Wait—Josh—come on! Team's doing Five Guys."

I swallow hard and force my face to remain neutral. "Nah, man. I got this pre-calc test on Monday . . ."

"Like you're gonna study? Nobody studies the day before Thanksgiving, dude. A half day! Come grab some food with us. Get your head off that chick." Matt hooks an arm around my neck and hauls me down the hall a few steps. When I stop struggling, he releases me.

A few guys, including Mason, are waiting by Matt's truck. Ramón throws up his hands in exasperation. "What took you guys so long? The line's gonna be out the door by the time we get there."

"Then you better get in the fucking truck." Matt pops the locks.

Ramón was right about the line at Five Guys, so we head over to Wood-fire Pizza in the food court. The guys order the family special—two pies and some breadsticks.

"Twenty-two fifty," the cashier tells us, then scrambles to count the singles everyone tosses onto the counter. I flip my hand with everyone else, except there's no money in it.

"Another buck fifty," the cashier says.

Matt hands him another dollar. I sift through the change in my pocket for a couple of quarters and plop them down.

We eat the pizza while we cruise the mall, killing time until practice. The guys wolf it down like it's air that they're breathing, but I savor each bite, tasting the layers of pepperoni, peppers, cheese, even licking the runnel of grease from my wrist. Mason is uncharacteristically quiet. Nick is pissed that there's practice on a half day right before Thanksgiving. He won't stop bitching about how his family is gonna have to drive half the night to get to his aunt's in Tennessee. He threatens to skip practice, but we all know Coach would have his head on a stick.

Matt and Nick both have crushes on this girl, Ashley, who works at Claire's. Nick drags us all in there, pretending he wants a piercing so she'll talk to him. Nick already has a girlfriend—one of the cheerleaders—she's super smart and super busy. But she's a senior and will probably score a scholarship out of state. I think he's looking to trade her in. Ashley's pretty, but not in a cheerleader kind of way. She's friendly without being flirty and I can see why they like her. She brushes Nick's hair back so she can look at the prospective piercing site. Nick looks like he might pass out if she doesn't stop touching him. I drift further into the store, not really noticing much of anything.

Someone taps me on the arm. I look up into the face of a girl wearing so much blue eyeshadow, she could be a peacock. "Shopping for someone in particular?" she asks.

I tell her no and move away, but she follows me. "No girlfriend to buy something for? That's a shame. If I were your girlfriend . . ."

She's still talking, but I stop listening and move away again, feigning interest in some Disney jewelry. Snowflakes and glass slippers, honey pots and roses. A tiny blue fish that reminds me of Ruthie. I pick up the fish and almost drop it when the chatty salesgirl leans over my shoulder so close, I can feel her breath on my ear.

"That's cute," she tells me. "If you're three years old. Plastic charms are so toddler. If you want a real charm, you should—"

Her critique is interrupted by an ear-piercing shriek.

Matt walks Nick up to his door, holding his elbow like that'll keep him from passing out, and then practically runs back to the truck the second Nick is safely inside his own house.

"His dad is gonna kill him," Matt says.

"Maybe he won't notice," I say, although Nick has so much blood on his shirt, he looks like the girl tried to Van Gogh him instead of just piercing his ear.

On the way back to school the guys toss around what they're gonna tell Coach when Nick doesn't show up to practice. So far, the front-runner is that his dad accidentally backed over his foot. "Look at the bright side," Matt says. "Now Coach will have somebody else to be ticked off at."

The thought of Coach riding someone else's case instead of mine should be appealing, but Nick's hoping for a ride to college just like the rest of us. If he's smart, Nick'll take the stud out and let it grow closed. The guys'll cover for him if he tells Coach he got bit by a rabid bat or something.

Matt says we should say Nick got sick on mall food.

"Nick has the squirts!" Mason yells, his own joke making him bray like a donkey.

I want to punch him. Not really, but it's enough of a thought that I stick my hand in my pocket to keep it from flinching. My fingertips brush a small, cold something. It's the Dory charm. In all the turmoil of Nick's screaming, I must have shoved it into my pocket. That's just great. I think about the college applications my advisor waves at me every time I walk by her office. "It takes more than basketball to get into Division I. You need some other extracurricular—community service, chess club—just pick something!" I doubt she had shoplifting in mind.

Coach is in a crap mood. We're not even on the court before he yells at us to hustle up and asks if we need to do some stairs to wake up. He doesn't seem to notice Nick's not there. My head's everywhere but on the ball. I'm thinking about how the charm got in my pocket, wondering if my dad's okay or if the ER doc might've shipped him out quick because he couldn't pay, thinking about what Ruthie would say if I gave her the charm, how Chick would deck me if I did.

We're in the middle of running cones when Coach's "Get on out of here!" jerks me from my thoughts and nearly causes a twenty-guy pileup. Matt's in front of me and stops so quick, he trips over his own sneakers. Coach isn't yelling at us this time, though. Stan is leaning against the doorframe of the gym, totally chill, and Coach is all red-faced and crazy.

"Coach?" Mason calls. He trots over to them and stands with both hands on his hips. I'm hoping he tries to escort Stan out. That would be fun to watch.

Coach waves Mason off. "It's okay, he was just leaving. Weren't you?"

"Yep." Stan straightens and gives that slow grin of his that used to infuriate Mom. "Guess we'll find time to catch up later."

Coach puts a hand on Mason's shoulder and the two of them start back toward us, but Stan calls out, "Hey, Mitch."

Coach stops and turns back.

"Team looks great, by the way."

"Line up for three-man weave!" Coach barks at us.

Stan flashes us a quick two-fingered salute and slips out the door. When practice is finally over, I spot him waiting at the bus stop out in front of the school. I duck back into the building until everyone else is gone and then trot over to him.

"What the hell was that?" I snap at Stan before he has a chance to open his mouth.

"Just dropping in to see an old friend. Sometimes a man gets to missing his glory days."

"Yeah, well, Coach sure didn't seem to reciprocate the feels."

The smirk on his face tells me he already knew that.

"You know he takes that shit out on us, right? He was so pissed, he made us do stairs. Why you gotta poke him like that?"

"He misses me, he just don't know it yet. Some folk need reminding of where they come from. Four of us went to school together—me and him, your mom and dad. Since there ain't never gonna be a reunion, I figured I'd see how he turned out. Too damn big for his britches, that's how. Forgot everything he learned about ball, he learned from my dad. Now he's too good to talk to me."

I think about all those Saturday mornings with Stan laughing in the kitchen with my parents. Try to meld Coach into that mix. Can't see it. I can almost envision Coach, Dad, and Stan playing on the same team, grabbing burgers after a scrimmage, but when I try to squeeze Mom into a booth with them, the image disintegrates. She would have hated Coach.

The number two bus lurches to a stop in front of us. The smirk lingers on Stan's face as he gets to his feet and waits for the doors to open. "Actually stopped by to watch you a bit. You ever get that layup down?"

"Yeah."

We've missed the after-work rush, so the bus is nearly empty. Stan slides into the seat behind the driver. I pull a single from my pocket, smoothing it against my jeans before feeding it to the fare box. Before I can pass, the driver jerks a thumb over his shoulder. "What about him?"

Stan shoots me a *Pay the man* gesture. I dip into my pocket for another bill, mentally starting a tab that I plan to collect on.

I plop down across the aisle from Stan.

"Your dad help you?"

I rewind the conversation, trying to figure out what he's talking about. "What? With the layup?" He nods. "Nope. Had to figure that one out myself."

He turns to the window, watching the trees pass by. After a bit he says, "You know that wasn't my choice."

Just like that, I'm twelve again. Tension tightens my shoulders and I press my lips together, trapping the tangled knot of need. Losing my mom . . . no kid should have to deal with that. When all that happened, I needed Stan more than ever. When he just disappeared, I told myself it didn't matter, I didn't need him. And I didn't. Me and Twig got along just fine without him. We survived without Mom, without Stan. Dad moved us all in with Gran, gave us a roof and food. And those other things kids need? I made sure that Twig had them even if I didn't. Now Stan waltzes back in here and asks about my layup? Fuck him.

When I don't respond, he pivots in his seat to face me, but he doesn't meet my eye. His hands aren't wringing yet, but his fingertips trace small, quick circles on the frayed pleather of the seat back. "I woulda stuck around if I could. Woulda done anything for you boys. You gotta know that."

My filter finally fails. "How would I know that? My mom *died*, Stan. We lost her. Lost the house. Everything went to shit and you just kicked dirt over us and walked away. How could you leave us like that?"

Stan's head drops, chin to chest, defeated. It reminds me so much of the hangdog way Dad gets when Gran goes after him that I feel a little bit sorry for him. But it's not enough to dislodge the crusted-over hurt and anger in my throat, and it sure doesn't match the sorry I feel for two little boys and their dad, left behind to pick up all the pieces of their shattered lives. I smack the back of the seat and a woman two rows behind us looks over, startled, but I don't care. "Goddamn it, Stan! You owe me an answer. Where the fuck did you go?"

Head still down, Stan's lips press together so hard, they twist into a frown, and his chin moves like he's working out the words, getting them lined up. "I fucked up, kid. Plan went wheels up in a ditch. I did all I could to steer it back on the road, but it wasn't enough. Had to make a tough call. Stick around and drag your dad down or take off and let the blame follow me. I put you boys first. Always have. Always will."

I don't know what I expected to hear, but it isn't this. His words, his whole demeanor, are so radically different from what I get from everyone else—Coach's degradation, Dad's disregard, Gran's disgust—that I don't know what to do with it. We ride in silence for a while before I tell Stan what Dwayne said about my dad taking off because of him.

"Naw. Me and the crew came in couple weeks ago. Hooked up with Tye. We were working a job, had a run-in with Jimmy Dean. Soon after that Wade took off, then your dad. At first I thought maybe Jimmy got to him, but the money missing and that note he left for you makes it pretty clear he skipped town."

"But he didn't skip town."

Stan pinches the bridge of his nose. "I'm talking about us here—you and me—and you're back defending your dad. You don't have to convince me he's a good guy. He took the money for the same reason I left, okay? To protect you boys. Jimmy Dean was gunning for him. Only a matter of time before he showed up at the trailer and your dad didn't want nothing to happen to you boys."

"But he didn't leave, Stan. Maybe if he had, he wouldn't have been stabbed. Dwayne said—"

"Dwayne said? Dwayne said? *I'm* saying. Me. Known you your whole life. How long Dwayne known you? Think he loves you boys? I'm telling you, your dad is smart enough to know when to get out of Dodge. You keep asking around about him, you're gonna cause the one thing he was trying to avoid. Gonna get one or the both of you killed." As the bus rolls to a stop in front of the Center, Stan meets my eyes. "I know you can't forgive me for leaving, even if it was the only option. And I can't make it up to you, but I'm just asking for the chance to get to know you again. Maybe help you boys out a little."

I don't respond. Don't really know how to, so I follow him off the bus.

A few guys cluster near the entrance. One calls out, "Hey, Joshie." Stan ignores them and heads straight to the gym.

More guys are in there, practicing free throws. They wave at me and the heavier one calls out, "How about a game, Josh?"

He looks familiar. Might be a friend of Dad's—sometimes I think there isn't a guy over thirty who hasn't met my dad—but I don't feel like shooting hoops, so I give him an apologetic shrug.

Stan gives me playful shove. "Come on, kid. Let's show these old men how to play." Stan tosses his coat on the bench and bends at the waist, hands planted on his knees. Gradually he rolls up and then twists to the left, his back popping. He rolls his head around with cringeworthy cracks.

I can't help but laugh at all the racket. "Dude, that can't be good. You sound like a bowl of Rice Krispies."

Stan straightens. "Keeps me spry. Like Peter Pan."

Can't argue with that. I don't know if it's all that snap-crackle-and-popping, but Stan has always moved like a man half his age. Rhythm and grace, especially on the court. "Coulda been a Globetrotter," Dad used to say. When I was a kid, Stan tried to teach me his Moonwalk Dribble, but I just couldn't do it.

The chubby dude tucks the ball under one arm and holds out his hand. "Name's Ken."

Stan eyes him. "Tell ya what, you score a bucket on us, we'll learn your names. Till then shut up and gimme that ball."

The dude shoots me a *Is he for real?* look. I peel off my jacket and step onto the court.

Stan is ruthless. Every time he gets his hands on the ball, he drives straight for the basket and makes every shot. When the other guys get the ball, Stan snatches it out of their hands as easily as stealing candy from a baby. A sleeping baby. After the guys get pissed and walk off the court, Stan challenges me to a shoot-out. "Come on, Joshie. It'll be like old times. You and me. Mano a mano."

Standing here with Stan, just the two of us, takes me back to the days in the junkyard learning to play ball. We'd shoot it out and whoever won got to pick our pre-dinner snack—crustless PB&J (my fave) or a hot dog rolled up on a piece of bread with a pickle spear and some ketchup (his). Hanging with Stan was better than any day at the park with kids my own age. I spent the last five years missing him as much as I missed my own mom. But part of me holds back. Not just because of what Dwayne said. But because something in Stan is different than it was back then. It could be because I'm older now, but I don't think that's it.

"Nah. Been a long day."

"Gonna be a longer night. Chick's expecting me about nine. Let's get some grub."

I follow Stan through the Center to the kitchen. The dinner crew is long gone. He opens the fridge like he owns the place and pulls out a tray of some mooshy, shapeless Italian-smelling food. He slops heaps of it onto two plates. Puts one in the microwave. When the microwave dings a minute later, he holds the hot plate out to me. "You eat?"

The mall pizza is a distant memory. I shrug and take the food from Stan. We eat standing in the kitchen, leaning against the sink. I half expect the front desk lady or one of the security guards to come in and yell at us, but no one does. I wash our plates with warm water and dry them with paper towels while Stan scrapes some of the pasta into a plastic bread bag and ties it shut. "Ruthie likes noodles," he tells me.

I nod like bagging up noodles is something anyone would do.

Stan shoves the bag of noodles into his jacket pocket and heads for the door. "You coming? Could use your help."

I weigh the options. Could head to Matt's for a working shower and a full breakfast versus helping Stan and his knife-wielding homicidal friend with some potentially illegal job in twenty-degree weather. Clearly the latter. To be fair, heading back to Matt's also has risks. One night, no worries. Two nights . . . his mom starts to question my life choices. Plus, I need to bring in some cash. Gran is gonna be asking for that rent money, and if I don't have it . . . not to mention, that bag of noodles guarantees seeing that smile of Ruthie's again and what sane man would pass that up?

"Is Chick gonna be okay with me coming?"

"That matter?" Stan asks.

I shrug and stick my hands into my pockets.

Stan shoots me a long look. "Two things you need to know here, Joshie. I'm in charge. Me, not Chick. If I say you're in, you're in."

I nod. "What's the other thing?"

"That I don't answer to you, neither. What we do is dangerous and you can't be questioning me all the time. Don't matter if you agree, don't matter if it makes sense to you. I tell you to dance a fucking jig, you put on your tappity shoes and start sashaying your way acrossed the floor. You got that? Chick can't get that through that knucklehead of his, gonna come against trouble soon."

CHAPTER
10

IT'S WICKED DARK BEHIND THE CASTLE. THE MOON doesn't reach here and neither do the streetlights, just the dim glow from a light high up on the corner of another building filtered through the branches of a tree. Stan walks over to a low building that might have been a garage if it weren't so small. Storage shed, I guess. He doesn't go in there, just squeezes between the wall and a hedge. I wonder if I should follow him, but before I can, he's backing out, dragging something after him.

"You gonna help me with this or what?" Stan snaps.

"I got it," Chick says from right behind me, and I nearly jump out of my skin.

Ruthie materializes like a Cheshire, first a toothy grin then the full moon of her face as she steps away from the shadows. "Hey." It's more breath than word and sends goose bumps tickling up my arms.

"Hey," I say back. "We got you some—"

"Josh! Get your ass over here and help."

My eyes want to study the way the dim light turns Ruthie's hair into an onyx waterfall, but I force myself to go help Stan and Chick. Together we lift the awkward bundle.

As soon as we've got it out from between the shed and hedge, Stan lets go and drops back to talk to Ruthie. Chick and I heft what seems to be some kind of tarp, rolled up like a carpet, and my stomach drops for just a second as I realize it's a whole lot like the kind people in movies use to roll up dead bodies. But it's not heavy enough to be a body. (I hope.)

They don't tell me where we're going, and I bite the question back. I don't want to start shit with Chick again and it feels good to be near Ruthie. I hear her laugh when Stan hands her the bag o' noodles and it's almost good enough to imagine the accompanying smile.

We head away from the street, deeper into the complex. There're a few more buildings back here, storage sheds mostly, a few low garages, and then we're trudging across an open field toward a high chain-link fence. Barbed wire glimmers in the moonlight. Ruthie walks right up to it like she can just pass through and I half expect her to, but then she stops and bends down. I didn't realize how quiet it was back here until Chick drops his end of the bundle and metal things inside clang loud enough to make a dog bark a few streets away. Chick and Ruthie peel aside a portion of the fence, holding it wide enough for me and Stan to maneuver the tarp through.

Back here's an expanse of cement that was probably a parking lot or the footprint of a demolished building, but now it's a cracked desert, potholed and busted up and I have to watch my feet in the darkness to keep from tripping over the ridges and ripples of concrete. We leave the parking lot and head across a field of snow, the top layer crisp under our feet. Ruthie and Chick hold hands, and every once in a while Ruthie's laughter interrupts the crunching of our feet in the snow. I expect Stan to grouse at them, tell Chick to come help carry the tarp, but he doesn't. He watches them, though.

Ruthie pulls away from Chick and jogs up a steep hill. At the top she crumples to the ground and I think she's hurt, but then Chick is laughing and trying to get out of her way as she rolls down the hill at him. With her thin jacket and those leggings, she has to be cold, but she pops up and brushes the snow off like it's sand, then jogs back up to do it again. Stan and I go up the hill at an angle to avoid getting bowled over by her. There's no snow on top of the hill and the crunch of snow is replaced by the crunch of flagstone, gleaming just as white in the moonlight. Railroad tracks extend in both directions, west across cornfields and cow pastures, east through downtown South Bend. We head east. Stan's OCDing again and I stumble and trip with my end of the tarp before I realize his pattern of planting both feet flat on one tie before lurching to the next. We pass between two buildings and cross the bridge over Lafayette. Up ahead Chick and Ruthie are off the track, looking at something on the ground.

"Right about here," Chick calls.

We put the tarp down. Stan walks the rest of the way to Chick. "Ayuh," he says. He yells at me to bring the shovel. A shovel's not the only thing I find in the tarp: there's a crowbar, a couple pairs of gloves, an assortment of tools, a saw, and some kind of scissor-y thing that's big enough to give King Kong a haircut. Stan takes the shovel and scrapes the flagstone away, taps the tip of the shovel against dark metal, tells Chick to bring the crow.

While Stan and Chick are working on the manhole, Ruthie comes over and puts her arm through mine, leans her head against me like she's known me all my life. I try to focus on what Chick and Stan are doing—pulling tools from the tarp and lining them up beside the hole—instead of the tickle of her hair on my chin and the sweet smell of strawberries.

"Josh!" Stan yells.

"Yeah?" I have to clear my throat and try again to get the "yeah" to sound like it's coming from me and not some twelve-year-old girl.

"Get your ass down there."

Metal rungs disappear into the dark hole. "What's down there?"

"Ghosts," Chick says.

Ruthie laughs and holds the head of a flashlight under her chin and clicks it on so that her face glows ghastly. When I don't move, she bends down and traces the circumference of the hole with the beam of light. "S'not that bad," Ruthie tells me. "No rats or nothing. Just big-ass spiders."

"Why do I have to go down there?"

"Your job," Ruthie says. "Everyone else's been doing it since Tye bailed, but it was his job. Now it's yours."

"What's down there, though? Why does anybody have to go down there?"

Stan takes the flashlight from Ruthie and angles it so it illuminates some wires and pipes and other electronic-looking stuff. "Copper. You go down there, cut that piping out, *cha-ching*! Big money in copper."

"He's afraid of ghosts," Chick says.

No such thing as ghosts. Rats don't scare me. Spiders are fast little freaks, but a shoe will take care of them. What I don't like is the idea of going down in that dark hole. There's not much room in there. My brain flashes a happy little video of me down there and Chick kicking the lid shut. I glance around at their faces then up the track, half wondering if my dad might be in the last manhole they plundered.

Stan holds out a pair of gloves and the saw. "We'll talk you through it."

The gloves are squishy rubber and I feel like I'm wearing Gran's pink dishwashing gloves, which always make me think of the field trip my third-grade class took to River Farm. We got to milk a cow. There is an uncanny resemblance between the texture of a teat stretched full of milk and the cool smoothness of latex.

Chick leans in and says in a low, conspiratorial voice, "I hate those gloves, but it's better than the alternative."

"What's the alternative?"

"Electrocution." His face is dead serious.

Ruthie bumps her shoulder against mine and tells me Chick is just messing with me. He raises his eyebrows as if to ask if I want to test that theory.

Once I'm in the hole, the three of them lean over the opening, handing me tools and barking orders at me. The copper wire isn't easy to spot. It's coated in a gray material and bundled with about a thousand other wires, but I find it eventually and follow Stan's directions on how to clip the wire without risking certain death. It's not easy to concentrate with Chick making jokes about bomb diffusion. My fingers are stiff from the cold and they tremble as I separate the wires, clip the copper one, and coil it around my fist, leaving the rest of the wire hanging like spaghetti. Chick reaches down. I hand up the tools one by one.

"That everything?" Chick asks.

It's dark down here, but Ruthie flashes the light around so I can check if I missed anything. I tuck the coiled wire under my arm and start up the ladder.

"Hey, hand that up too," Chick says. His voice is light, friendly, but something in it makes me stop climbing and look up at him. He's leaning far into the hole, reaching down.

"What?" I ask.

"Gimme the wire." His mouth is smiling, but his eyes are hard.

"I got it." The wire is slick and I have to pause on the ladder to readjust it under my arm.

"You're gonna drop it," he tells me.

"I got it."

Chick moves out of my way as I reach the top. He starts tossing the tools onto the tarp. I drop the wire at Stan's feet. He says something, but I walk away. Ruthie's sitting on the rail, leaning over her knees, eating the mushy noodles out of the bag with her fingers. I'm cold and pissed and can't feel my hands. This isn't getting me any closer to finding my dad. I don't even know if Stan can help me find him. Maybe Ruthie is right and he doesn't want to be found. Or, and this possibility is feeling more real in light of the way Chick looked at me when I was in the hole, maybe Chick found him and tried to settle up that debt. Dwayne said he came into the ER bleeding—what if Chick got to him after Jimmy Dean stabbed him? He could be alone somewhere, in need of help.

Stan grunts as he bends to scoop up the wire and add it to the tarp. The three of them start walking along the track, not toward the Castle, but away from it. I'm tempted not to follow. I could go to the Center, start asking around for leads on Dad. Maybe Watchman knows something. If this were a folktale, that guy would be the sage in disguise. The old woman who needs help carrying a basket. The person who you're likely to ignore but who holds the answers to the whole story or at least your survival at the end of it.

"Josh!" Stan shouts. They've stopped. The tarp is on the ground. Chick and Ruthie are scraping away stones while Stan motions for me to join them. If I ditch them now, I could lose the one chance I have to find Dad. Except, Ruthie and Chick never actually said they would help me. Maybe they're just stringing me along to help them earn money with no intention at all to help me back.

"Josh!" Stan shouts again.

I chew my lip and then jog down the track to them. Ruthie, Chick, and I heft the lid off the manhole. Ruthie holds the light; I don the gloves and head down the ladder without a word. I've barely gotten to the bottom when I hear frantic whispers from up above. I start back up the ladder, but Ruthie waves me back down and tosses that flashlight at me. It ricochets off the metal ladder with a ping and winks out when it hits the ground. "What's wrong?" I ask.

"Take these," Chick whispers.

He and Stan start dropping tools down, one right after the other. I can't see them in the dark and something—a wrench, maybe—catches me across the bridge of the nose. Stars dance from the instant pain. Blood trickles into my mouth and I throw my hands up to ward off the other tools thudding to the ground around me like storm debris.

"What the fuck?" I shout at them.

"Shush! Someone's coming!" Ruthie tells me. "We'll be back."

And before I can respond, Stan and Chick slide the cover of the manhole closed.

I've only been in darkness that deep one other time.

I was supposed to be at school that day. Dad was away on one of his jaunts—up the tracks in Dowagiac or Decatur at some auction, so Stan and I had been out in the junkyard the night before, practicing shots on goal. He was trying to calm my nerves about tryouts for soccer. "Why you wanna play soccer anyway?" he'd asked. "You're a natural b-baller." He frowned at my answer that Matt and Nick and all the other guys played soccer and spat a big phlegmy wad in the dirt. "Okay then, it's just like basketball, line up your shot the same way." But it wasn't like basketball and no matter how many shots I could make on the court, I couldn't get one on the soccer field. "Why you so worked up?" Stan asked. "Put all that junk outta your mind and just focus on the post." I wasn't sure if he meant put tryouts and the fear of being the only boy in sixth grade to not make the soccer team out of my mind or the actual junk piled along the wall that held our makeshift goal, but either one was easier said than done.

We stayed out there until midnight, when Mom had finally had enough and shouted that I better get in bed. In the morning, my stomach cramped and squirted anxiety out both ends. Mom heard me in the bathroom, retching, and knocked on the door. "Josh? You okay, Bear?"

"Go away!" I shouted at her.

"We need to get going or I'll be late," she called back. I could picture her outside the door, Twig clinging to the white ruffle at the bottom of her waitress uniform, all ready for preschool in his Buzz Lightyear shoes and backpack.

"I can't go," I said.

"What?" Her voice had that hint of wanting to be patient but knowing that the bus would leave on schedule whether we were on it or not. "Joshie?" she called again.

I thought of Matt and Nick and all the other guys who'd make the team easily because their parents sent them to soccer camps and weekend travel leagues. Of their dads, who bought them actual goals to practice with instead of telling them to build their own goal by clearing a gap in the junk. Of their moms, who didn't have to drop them an hour early at school so they could get to crappy jobs at greasy diners and who would feel sorry for them and make them toast if their stomachs were upset instead of rushing them to quit barfing and get on the bus.

"Josh?" she called again, this time knocking like I might have forgotten she was out there. "I can't be late."

I flung open the door and shouted right in her face, hoping she could smell the puke on my breath. "I'm sick, okay?"

"I know, honey, but you're gonna have to power through it. I missed all that time last month when Twig was sick. I can't stay home with you. Just get to school. Then you can go to the nurse and lie down in her office. I'll come get you as soon as my shift ends at two."

"I'm not going."

"Josh—" But I was already shouldering past her and heading down the hall to the room I shared with Twig. "Josh!" she shouted. I slammed the door and wedged a chair under the handle.

Twig was crying now, yelling at Mom that he wanted to go to school. That it was Tod's birthday and he was bringing in Hostess cupcakes for his treat. Hostess cupcakes were a big deal. Add them to the list of things my family couldn't afford from Mom's waitressing and Dad's junkyarding. Now Mom was banging on the door, telling me we had to go.

"Go without me," I yelled. But I knew she wouldn't. I was twelve fricking years old and my mom wouldn't even let me ride the city bus by myself. If she lost her job for missing work, it was her fault for being so overprotective. Matt's mom would have let him stay home alone, but even as I thought that, I knew it wasn't true. It would have never been an issue for Matt because his mom didn't have to work. If he was sick, she'd bring him a cool washcloth for his head and some toast to settle his stomach and probably let him watch SpongeBob all day on the living room couch until he felt good enough to eat Hostess cupcakes.

"Josh!" she yelled again, then: "God bless it." A few minutes later I could hear her on the phone with her manager, saying she couldn't get to work because the boys were sick.

"I'm not sick!" Twig wailed indignantly.

Mom shushed him then said in a panicky voice, "No! Yes, they're really—No, I wouldn't call in if—Alice, wait!" She slammed down the phone. "God bless it, Joshua!" she yelled.

The last thing my mom would ever say to me.

I don't know how long I'm in that hole before metal grates against metal. Squinting up into the beam of a flashlight, I can't tell if it's cops up there or Stan until Chick calls down to ask if I'm still alive. Then I'm up the ladder and in his face so fast, he doesn't have time to react.

"You fucking asshole!" I shove him and he trips, landing flat on his ass.

"Josh!" Stan steps between us. "We had to go. The cops have been cracking down."

"You didn't have to lock me in there!"

Chick's brushing snow off his pants and mutters, "Not our fault you're a little bitch baby."

I step around Stan and go for Chick, but Ruthie catches my arm, yelling at me to let him be. I shake free and give Chick another shove, but this time he stays on his feet and comes right back at me. Ruthie steps between us and takes the full force of his blow right on the cheek. It knocks her clean off her feet. She lands, crumpled, and doesn't move. Chick and me race over to her, but Stan beats us there and growls at us to leave her alone. He turns her on her back and props up her head.

"Ruthie?" he says in a soft voice. "Ruthie, honey, you with us?" For a second it's my mom lying there, Stan bent over her smoke-smudged face, patting her cheek and saying, "Rosie, Rosie, honey. Stay with us." My stomach lurches and then it's just Ruthie again, saying she's okay and struggling to sit up.

"Let's just get you back to the Castle," Stan says. "Chick, Josh, grab our shit."

Chick and I eye each other. "There's no way I'm going back down in that hole," I tell them.

"Well, I'm not going down there," Chick shoots back.

"Fuck's sake, you're both useless," Stan says. He climbs down the ladder and hands the tools up one by one. After Chick helps him slide the cover on, Stan goes over to Ruthie and helps her to her feet. "You guys get the tarp," he says.

I'd rather toss Chick onto the tarp, and from the look on his face the feeling's mutual. Without taking his eyes off me, he stoops and gathers his end of the tarp. When I don't move, Stan snaps at me to get my head on straight. "This about you right now? Let's get her back to the Castle, eh? Sort this shit out there."

Except there's no sorting it out. By the time we get Ruthie back to the Castle, up the stairs, and settled on the blankets, the pain has really hit her. She's just lying there, her head on Chick's lap, silent tears trickling from the corners of her eyes. Chick's voice trembles as he asks if Stan thinks Ruthie might have a concussion.

Stan runs both hands through his hair. "Need to get her some Tylenol or some shit for that pain. Ice would be good too."

Chick nods. "Except how we gonna pinch that? They keep that shit by the register."

Stan looks at me.

Gran's medicine cabinet is full of Pepto-Bismol, Tums, and Rolaids. Her remedy for a headache is green, rolled in paper, and smoked. But the green in my pocket is another thing.

It's a short hike to CVS, but that's closed when I get there. Walmart is too far to walk. That leaves Gas n'Go and its convenience store pricing. I stand in front of the pain relievers, waffling between the generic acetaminophen and the real deal. I don't want to waste money just for the sake of a name brand, but what if there's actually a difference in how good the name brand works? The fact that I only have a ten-dollar bill and some change makes that decision for me. With taxes and a cup of ice, the money I stuffed into my pocket this morning is now down to seventy-four cents.

I make the trek back and Chick takes the acetaminophen from me without a thanks, but Ruthie's eyes meet mine and even though she doesn't say anything, I know she appreciates it. She dry-swallows a few of the caplets and lies back, asleep as soon as her head hits the pile of rags she uses for a pillow.

Stan is leaned back in the corner, rubbing at his boot with a wadded-up piece of newspaper. He looks up when I come over. "You damn kids bleeding all over me."

My fingertips tap the bridge of my nose gingerly. Pretty swollen, but the pain is nothing more than a low thrum. Definitely not worth wasting any of Ruthie's acetaminophen on. "Yeah, speaking of that, any chance I can recoup the money for the pain pills? Maybe add it to my share of the take tonight?"

Stan snorts. "That blow knock the sense outta your head? You owe us. Your share—which is pennies to the dime, by the way—goes toward payback."

"Come on, Stan. You remember my gran, right? She got me paying her rent just to keep Twig. I gotta get some cash coming in."

Stan spits on the toe of his boot and goes back to scrubbing it. "That old biddy never gave nothing for free. But Twig . . . you two boys used to sit on my feet and he would just giggle and giggle when I tramped around the house like a giant, yelling 'Fee, Fi, Fo' and pretending I didn't know you two was clinging to my legs. Remember that?"

I brush away Stan's attempt to drag me down memory lane. "Twig is hungry, Stan. Gran doesn't feed him much and I'm not sure how long she's going to be willing to keep him if my dad doesn't turn back up. I need to get some money—"

"Ayuh. That's what we're doing and we woulda had more of it coming to us if you and Chick spent more time working and less time pissing on each other."

"You guys locked me in a manhole, Stan! *He*"—I gesture at Chick—"hurled a fucking wrench at my head! I'm not supposed to fight back?"

"Oh, you wanna fight back?" Chick jumps to his feet and throws out his hands, beckoning me over. "Let's go, asswipe. Let's finish this shit."

Stan waves him off. "Go back to tending Ruthie and let me handle this."

But Chick isn't stepping down. "Yeah, gonna handle this like you handle everything else? You keep saying you got it, but I don't see anything getting any easier for us. And now I'm supposed to just let this little punk-ass kid—"

I laugh and turn back to Stan. "I thought you were in charge here. Isn't that what you said?"

Stan drops his boot and stands up slowly, deliberately. He points a crooked finger at Chick. "This is my house and you better sit the fuck down."

Chick shoos a hand at him. "Whatever, dude. You wanna play favorites, that's all good. When Ruthie heals up, we'll move on."

"You ain't going nowhere," Stan says in a low voice that rumbles just short of rage. "And you"—he turns on me—"I told you once, do not question me." He's shorter than me by about six inches, but he meets my eyes like we're level. Stares me down like he's Goliath and I'm just something clinging to his boot.

Fuck this.

I storm out of the Castle for the second night in a row.

CHAPTER

11

CINNAMON.

Ooey-gooey cinnamon.

Mom's brioche French toast and her cinnamon syrup.

A huge glass of milk. Dad and Stan joking in the kitchen. Laughter.

"Josh?" My mom's voice, soft. Her hand on my shoulder, calling me to breakfast. "Josh?"

I roll over and mumble that I'll get up in a second.

"Dude, did you just call me 'Mom'?" Matt smacks me on the shoulder. "Aw, little Joshie dreaming about his mo—" His laughter stops suddenly. "Oh man. I'm sorry."

"S'kay," I tell him. "Nobody wants your hairy ass for a momma. And just for the record, I was dreaming about cinnamon. What is that smell? Did your mom make French toast?"

He smiles, relief all over his face. "Nah, that's her cinny-buns. She makes them every Thanksgiving. You ain't tasted cinnamon until you've had one of these."

I fold up the blanket and lay it over the arm of the couch, lean the pillow up against it so the family room looks more like a family room and less like a homeless kid's been camping out there. "Aw, man, I forgot. It's a holiday. I should probably get going."

"Nope. Mom made you a cinny-bun. You gotta eat it or I will and last time I ate two of those, my stomach was so full that I threw up in my mouth a little bit."

The rest of Matt's family is already in the kitchen. His dad lifts his glasses and eyes me with a long, slow whistle. "Gonna have a helluva shiner, there. Hope the other guy got suspended."

My hand goes instinctively to my nose. Matt jumps in before I can say anything. "Nah, just a junk ball. Stupid Mason thinks he's clever with his side-pass."

"Gotta wait to see the whites of their eyes, that's what my coach used to say." Mr. Higle hands me a plate and gestures to an empty chair. "Glad to have you here, Josh."

"Thanks, Mr. Higle. Happy Thanksgiving."

Mrs. Higle motions for me to hold out my plate, and scoops a massive pile of goo onto it. It is by far the most disgusting-looking thing I have ever been served and between Gran and the Center, that's saying something. But it smells heavenly.

"You don't have to eat that," Matt's little sister tells me. "You can have one of my doughnuts." She points to a box of Krispy Kreme doughnuts on the counter. Not just the plain glazed ones they give out for free, but the holiday sprinkle ones. I wonder if Twig has ever had one of those.

"You don't have to eat that," Mr. Higle echoes, handing me a fork, "but I get first dibs if you don't."

By the way Matt's already halfway through his, I can tell the cinny-bun's outward disgusty-ness is deceiving. I take a small bite, not sure what to expect. It's like my mom's French toast mixed with cream cheese and filled with a river of heaven.

"You like it?" Mrs. Higle asks.

"Oh ma Gah," I manage around a second mouthful.

"Drink some milk," Matt warns. He nods toward an empty glass and scoots the milk jug toward me. "Without milk, these things reach toxic overdose levels in 3.4 bites."

After breakfast, I help clear the plates. Mrs. Higle waits until it's just me and her in the kitchen and says in a fake-casual voice, "So, you have plans for Thanksgiving, Josh?"

I nod. "Dinner at Gran's."

She puts a hand on my shoulder and turns me so I have to look at her. Her eyes are the deepest, kindest mirrors and I see myself reflected in them. Not some homeless, thrown-away kid, but her son's best friend. The one she let hold the flashlight when she read *The Berenstain Bears and the Spooky Old Tree*. The boy she taught to ride a bike and eat cherries without swallowing the pits. *My dad is gone*. The words are there, ready to come right out. If I tell her my dad is gone, maybe she can help me figure out what to do. Maybe she can let me and Twig stay here. *My dad is gone*, I try to say, knowing that she will be the one adult who gets it, who can help, but before the words come out, Mrs. Higle squeezes my shoulder and says, "I know boys and their fathers have their differences, but your dad loves you so much, Josh. Holidays are the time to work all that out. You go on home and tell your dad we said 'Happy Thanksgiving.'"

Thanksgiving with Gran sucks. Always, but this year especially. She hates turkey, and without Dad here to insist we have it, Grans announces she's making ham slices and potatoes au gratin. And by that, she means Spam and some dehydrated potatoes from a box mixed with packaged cheese powder. Mac's wife took the kids to her mother's, so he comes over about two o'clock and camps out on the couch, drinking beer. Twig and I can't even play *2K* because Mac's clogging the TV up with football. Twig is pretty much ignoring me anyway. He's on the floor, leaning against the side of the couch, reading a book with a skull and crossbones on the cover. He looked up when I came in but went right back to his book.

I wait for Mac to go into the kitchen for a beer and then squat next to Twig. "We need to talk."

"I'm good." He turns the page.

"Twig, we need to talk about what's going on with Gran."

"Gran's Gran. There, we talked about it."

I resist the urge to grab him by his ear and drag him into our bedroom. Instead I reach into my jacket and pull out the holiday-sprinkled Krispy Kreme. Some of the icing is stuck to the napkin I wrapped it in, but for the most part, it looks pretty damn good for being shoved into a pocket. "I got you something."

The battle's over as soon as he sees the doughnut. He may be a sullen preteen, but put a doughnut in front of him and he's five years old again. He follows me into the bedroom and plops down on the bed with his hand out. I give him the doughnut.

"I'm sorry that I didn't get a chance to talk to you before I left."

He shrugs and licks the chocolate icing from around the edge of the doughnut.

"I wanted to tell you . . ." I stop, unsure what I actually want to tell him. He knows Gran is a horrible person, but he has to live with her. What can I say that won't make that impossible? "Look . . . that money Dad left . . . it isn't enough for both of us to live here. So I'm staying at Matt's just for a few days."

"It's been a few days."

"I know . . ."

"You just left me here with Gran."

"I know, Twig, but—"

He stops messing with the doughnut and looks right at me. "How would you feel if I did that? If I just disappeared like that?"

The bottom drops out of my stomach. "I need you to be safe, Twig. I need to find Dad and—"

"You. *You* need. I need things too. Nobody asks what I need."

"What do you need?"

"I need you. My brother. Everything else can suck, but when you come home at night, I know we're going to be okay."

I pull him into my arms and hug him so tight, it feels like my body will just absorb him into itself and keep him safe. After a few seconds he squirms and mumbles something into my chest. I loosen my hold. "What?"

"I said, 'I can't breathe.' And you smooshed my doughnut."

He opens his hand to show me the smooshed doughnut, icing coating his fingers. Sprinkles decorate the front of both of our shirts.

"Sorry, little dude. But think of it this way"—I pull my sweatshirt up to my mouth and nibble a few of the sprinkles—"now you have a handy snack for later."

We head down to the court while we wait for dinner. Sun's out and someone shoveled the snow off, leaving a few slushy puddles we can easily avoid. Some of the kids are there and we get a nice pickup game going. TreyAnn's on her best behavior, actually passing to Twig for a change. We're tied up and I head to the net, calling for the pass. A big kid is between us, and Twig stops dribbling. He finds me and instead of sending a bounce pass, he holds the ball in both hands, bends low, and granny-tosses that ball so high, I have to shield my eyes from the sun to see it coming back down at me like a baseball knocked out to center field. I slap it to the ground.

"What the hell was that?"

"A pass," Twig says. "You were open."

"That was not a pass."

"Yes, it was."

"Oh yeah? What kind, then? A chest pass? No. A bounce pass? No. What?"

"It's an Ollie oop."

"Don't never let me see you throw the ball like that, you hear?"

"Why? It woulda worked if you just caught it."

"Boy, you play like that in school, they're gonna laugh you off the court."

"They already laugh me off the court, remember?" He holds out his arms toward TreyAnn and the rest of the crew, who are indeed laughing. They stop, though, when I give them a look.

When Gran calls us for dinner, Mac's already bellied up to the table. Apparently, Heineken goes great with Spam and rehydrated potatoes au gratin because he finishes off the six-pack and eats so much that Gran doesn't get to use her little plastic containers. She doesn't yap at him, though. Instead she pats his belly—which is now so stuffed, he could play Santa without any padding—and asks if he wants pie. The thought of pie turns my mouth into Niagara Falls. Gran never buys sweets and certainly doesn't cook pie. I'm hoping for apple, even though I know pumpkin is the tradition in most families. I hop up to get plates and something to cut the pie. When I come back over to the table, Gran's passing out little boxes. Nothing says "Happy Thanksgiving" like cold cherry turnovers from McDonald's.

Halfway through the "pie" someone bangs on the front door. Mac's face goes pale.

"It ain't her," Gran tells him, but he heads for the bathroom just in case. Gran grumbles about common decency and not disturbing families on holidays. When she opens the door, she doesn't say hello or "Happy Thanksgiving." She just says "What?" and then half turns to tell me, "Some slut's out here looking for you."

I know instantly it's Ruthie. She's the only girl who would turn up at my house on Thanksgiving. Or any day. Twig trails behind me as I race for the door, but I step outside and shut the door in his face.

"Ignore my gran. She's a total shit, even on the holidays." I start to wish Ruthie a happy Thanksgiving, but I only get as far as the first syllable when I realize she is not having a happy Thanksgiving. Her cheek is really showing the bruise from the night before. Her makeup's all smudged under eyes so puffy, she looks like she's been crying all day. I take a step toward her, not sure what to say.

She blurts out, "Chick's missing!" and flings herself into my arms with a sob. It's so cold outside, my teeth chatter while I stand there trying to calm her down so I can find out what happened.

When she comes up for air, she tells me she's looked everywhere and can't find Chick. "He wouldn't do that," she insists when I ask if maybe he went home for Thanksgiving. "He's hurt or something, I know he is."

Her teeth are chattering too, and her body is trembling from the cold. A winter wind whips her hair around her face. I keep brushing it away so I can see her. I half consider bringing her inside the trailer, but she's already upset enough without being subjected to more of Gran. I lead her over to Gran's Datsun and we climb into the back. We can still see our breath, but at least we're out of the wind. I rub her arms hard and fast, trying to warm her up.

It's hard for me to work up any worry over Chick. For one, he's an asshole; plus, he's been gone for all of what? Twelve hours? My dad's been missing at least a week and he was fricking stabbed. I don't see any of them falling over themselves helping me track him down. Still, Ruthie is freaked, so I take a deep breath and arrange my face to reflect some concern. "He was there when I left last night. Did you guys have a fight or something?"

She shakes her head. "No, we don't fight! He fights with you. With Stan. Not with me. We were sitting around at the Castle and my stomach growled, so he went out to get me an Almond Joy. He's sweet like that, taking care of me. But he was gone so long, I fell asleep. I woke up in the morning and he still wasn't there. He wouldn't just leave me alone like that."

"What time was that? When he left to get the candy bar?"

"I don't know. After you left and before the seven-thirty train. That's what woke me up—the train."

It dawns on me that Chick could have gotten arrested, trying to nick the candy bar, but Ruthie pushes aside that explanation too. "He had money! We're keeping some back just in case Stan takes off like . . ." She doesn't have to finish that sentence.

She's crying again and I hold her. I try to think about Chick and where he could be, but Ruthie's hot breath against my neck makes it hard. "Hey," I say into her hair, "we'll find Chick. Let me go grab my coat."

I go inside and tell Gran I have to leave.

She mutters, "Family don't mean nothing to kids these days."

That's funny considering she is at that moment sitting on the couch drinking beer with a married man. It's Twig I feel bad about leaving. He looks up when I say I have to go out and tells me that the fourth quarter's just starting. That's his way of reminding me there's only about another hour of putting up with Mac hogging the TV and then we could start our Thanksgiving Marathon. The Marathon's a tradition we started as soon as Twig was old enough to hold a controller. We line up all our video games on the floor and play each one. The winner picks the next game in the series. Only three rules: no repeats, no sleep until we've played them all, and anyone who has to go pee in the middle of a game forfeits. Twig's gotten so he can beat me at *Sonic* and *Smash Bros.*, but I dominate in all other areas. We always save *2K* for last and play that until Twig falls asleep with the controller in his hand, thus breaking rule number two and forfeiting the series.

I squat down next to where he's sitting. "I know it's Marathon Day. I'll be back in a little while."

"You just got here," he whines. He's got cherry pie filling at the corner of his mouth. That, and the whining, make him seem much younger than nine.

"Twig. I promise. We'll do the Marathon."

"'Kay."

"Twig." I wait until he finally looks up at me. "I'll be back as soon as I can, and we'll do it."

"Whatever."

"I gotta take some of the money," I whisper. "Is it still in the same spot?"

He nods and follows me to the back bedroom, closing the door behind us. Ozzy is perched on the top box. I shoo him off and he scoots around to Twig.

Twig scratches him behind the ears and then lifts a blue bag from beside the bed.

"Is that—" Before I can voice my suspicion, the tinkle of kibble into a metal bowl and the crunching of Ozzy's teeth confirm it. "Really, Twig? Cat food?" I walk over and snatch the bag from him. Not just any cat food. Brand name. "This stuff's expensive!"

Ozzy is still munching away, oblivious to my anger and the fact that he's eating December's rent. Twig blinks at me. "He wouldn't eat Axl's chow and you said no more tuna. You said the money was for necessities. Food is a necessity."

"For us! Not for your stupid cat! Open the window and let him hunt for chipmunks. We need that money. How much is left?"

Instead of answering, he pets Ozzy sullenly. I lift the top box. Dad's note is back, crinkled, but smoothed. Beneath it there is a small stack of bills.

"One hundred twenty-eight," Twig tells me. He reaches behind the lamp on the desk and retrieves a few coins. "Plus twenty-two cents."

"What the hell, Twig? How much was the damn cat food?"

"Not that much! But we have to read a book for school and the library didn't have the one I needed, so—"

"So you bought it. Another necessity."

Twig's shoulders slump. He grabs the book from the bedside table and holds it out to me. "Maybe we can take it back?"

"Nah, Twig. You keep it."

I make a show of putting one of the twenties back with Dad's note. "For emergencies," I tell Twig. Then I slide the rest into my pocket. My hand brushes the picture of us all smiling on the beach. A whole other life.

On the way through the kitchen, I grab the extra turnover. "That's for Mac!" Gran squawks, trailing me to the door. If she were a normal human with actual feelings, she'd probably tell me it's too cold to go out. That I should invite Ruthie in. Or at the very least I should be careful and stay warm. But my gran stands on the front porch saying nothing until Ruthie steps out of the Datsun and I call to her, "I'll be back later, Gran." Then she yells in her harsh smoker voice, "Yeah? You better be. We got a deal and if you don't keep your end of it, you can damn well bet I'll keep mine. The lord don't abide renegers."

Once we're on the bus, Ruthie asks, "What was that about? That stuff about renegers?"

I shrug and hand her the cherry pie. My mind's more on the cash in my pocket than Gran. After the bus fare, all I have is six singles. The hundred might as well be a gold bar—nowhere to break that on the street without getting rolled. Ruthie takes a few small bites and then holds the pie in her hand, forgotten, while we watch the buildings and cars go by. The bus is nearly empty; everybody's already where they're going for football and turkey and actual pie. We get off at the Center. There's a line out the door. The meal the Center does for Thanksgiving is pretty amazing. Given the option between their sausage stuffing and Gran's Spam . . . well, it's no contest.

Ruthie's mad at me and it shows in the hunch of her shoulders as we slide into line behind someone who could pass as our mom. She didn't want to waste time coming here because she knows Chick won't be here and I had to practically drag her off the bus to get her to come. It doesn't matter that I told her three times we're not here looking for Chick; we're here to talk to Dwayne. My words don't seem to be getting through to her. She keeps repeating herself and running her hand through her hair in a way that makes her bangs stand up like a startled baby bird's. She marches right past the front desk and into the cafeteria. I let her go. It won't hurt if she asks around in there, but the real person I came to see is leaning against the wall, talking into his phone. Dwayne sees me right away and as soon as he's done with his call he comes over and gives me a fist bump.

"Sorry about the other night at the hospital. Things get crazy there. Find your dad?"

I shake my head. "Actually wondering if you saw Chick come through there? You know Chick?"

"Mm-hmm. Smart-mouthed kid. Runs with Stan and that girl you came in with. Haven't seen him since ..." Dwayne rubs his chin. "I don't know, Tuesday?"

"At the hospital?"

"No. He was in here. Ran his mouth off and got his face shoved into a plate a spaghetti. Probably shoulda taken him to the hospital; his nose bled something fierce, but I don't think it was broken." Dwayne's cell phone buzzes in his hand, but he ignores it. "Chick wouldn't have let me take him anyway. He was pissed off at me for not letting him stay. Said the fight wasn't his fault." His phone buzzes again and he glances at the screen.

"Whose fault was it?" I ask.

"Oh, it was his fault, all right. Like I said, he ran his mouth off. Does that all the time, he—" The phone buzzes again. Dwayne stops talking midsentence and reads a message. Texts something back. "Sorry, sick kid at home. Anyway, Chick, he—" The phone interrupts him again, this time with an incoming call. He shrugs at me apologetically. "I gotta go outside and take this."

I find Ruthie in the main room, talking to Stan. She's crying again and he's kneeling in front of the chair where she's sitting, holding both of her hands. Stan spots me and waves me over. "Any news on Chick?" he asks me.

"Not really. I mean, he had a fight, I guess. Got his nose busted."

Ruthie looks up in alarm, but Stan pats her arm. "It wasn't busted. Just bled like a motherfucker."

"Why didn't he tell me?" Ruthie's tears stop. "Why didn't *you* tell me? We were just all together last night and—"

"Aw, now, Ruthie. You know that boy don't like to worry you. You were already keyed up enough about Jimmy Dean, didn't want to make it worse."

"It was Jimmy, then? What'd they fight about?"

Stan gets to his feet slowly and rubs at his neck. "Fucking Jimmy Dean. I told you, he wants in on our turf. Came to us after Ricky over at Wixler's ran his mouth off when we cashed out from the last job. Got pissed that me and Chick said no to him joining in and he went after Chick. Took a few guys to separate the two of them. But he was okay when he left and you saw him yourself last night. If Jimmy Dean meant to hurt him, he'd a done it right there."

"I still don't know why he didn't tell me."

"Men do strange things to protect their girls."

"Protecting me would be telling me about the fight so I could watch out for Jimmy Dean. By not telling me . . . that just leaves me walking around unprepared."

She has a point, but Stan pshaws her. "I got your back. I'll take care of you."

Ruthie gives him a look that could blaze a path right through Lakeville's zone defense.

Ruthie and I spend half the night looking for Chick. Each place we go, I ask about my dad, too (despite Ruthie's earlier reminder that this isn't about me, and Stan's warning that I could make things worse), but no one has seen either of them. We wind up back at the Castle, sitting in the soft glow of Dory's blue light. We lean against the wall, the blankets of Ruthie and Chick's bed wrapped around us, Ruthie leaning into the crook of my arm. Although I feel bad for running out on Twig and for how worried Ruthie is, and I know Chick'll kill me if he shows up and finds us here like this, this is the best Thanksgiving I can remember.

CHAPTER

12

I'M SITTING UP ON THE SIXTH FLOOR, MY LEGS DANGLING out into the swirling snow, studying the old brick Oliver factory across the way, when I hear Ruthie coming up the steps, calling my name. I don't answer. I don't have to. It's not like she won't see me as soon as she reaches the top step.

She takes two steps toward me and slips on the iced-up floor, her arms shooting out like a pop-up umbrella.

"Careful. It's slick."

"No shit."

She half wobbles, half skates across the floor to me, skidding to a stop against my back and I brace so we don't go over the edge. She folds herself around me and the press of her cheek against my shoulder blade, her body against my back, is like coming in for that first sip of hot chocolate after a daylong snowball fight—warm and soft and home. I wish the temperature would plummet and freeze us here like this forever.

"You thinking of jumping?" she asks. Her voice is quiet, serious.

Without even thinking, I tell her the truth. "Stan said I should quit looking for my dad. That he pissed off Jimmy

Dean, so he stole your money and is hiding somewhere to keep Jimmy Dean away from us. Stan said if I keep looking for my dad, I'll lead Jimmy Dean right to him."

"Yeah? You don't believe that?"

I shrug.

Her chest rises and falls against me. Rises and falls again. She's waiting for me to go on, but the words are too jagged. They jam up in my throat. Ruthie breathes in again, giving me the slightest squeeze. She lets out her breath, her grip relaxing, and the wreckage in my mouth twists. Words tumble out. "Maybe he left because he got sick of being responsible for us. Maybe he's hiding from me."

Ruthie lays her head on my back, and we sit quietly for a few minutes. Then she asks, "Why you wanna find him so bad?"

I keep looking at the Oliver plant, watching the way the snow clings to the brick of the old smokestack, covering the first and last letters so it says *LIVE*. "I guess . . . I dunno. He's my dad. He's supposed to be here. Twig needs him. I just don't know how he can walk out on a nine-year-old kid."

"Maybe it's not about Twig."

"How could it not be about Twig?"

Ruthie shrugs. "Sometimes people just think about their own shit. What if he's just thinking about what he needs and doesn't even know how what he's doing is affecting you guys? You can't make him an adult. He might be a father, but you can't make him be a dad."

I look down at the ground, study the way the wind agitates the snow. She's not telling me anything I don't know. As long as I can remember, my dad has drifted. Lighting here, lighting there. But after Mom died, he got a real job at a construction company. Seemed to have settled a bit, found a spot to stick to. Even after he lost that job, he still was mostly with us. Guess he fooled me. "How long did you know him? My dad?"

"Maybe a year? Stan pulled him into a few jobs in Michigan with us, but he never stayed long. He was funny. Always telling these cheesy jokes. Then Stan tells us we're all coming here to help Tye with a gig. That there would be plenty of cash for all of us. Never works that way, though. Somebody got a job . . . they might need more hands, but they don't really want to share the cash. Tye was different. He welcomed us right in. Brought us to the Castle. Showed us the ropes."

Hearing that he would take them under his wing like that while leaving me and Twig to fend for ourselves makes my mouth go dry. "More than he did for me."

Ruthie tugs me gently, guiding me so my back's against the wall. Then she shifts around and her cheek is against my chest and she's on my lap, hugging me for real. After a few seconds, she leans back so she can see my face. "He always talked about you going to college. Didn't want you to mess up and lose your shot like he did."

"Yeah. But how am I supposed to do that when he left me to deal with everything? Kinda hard to get a scholarship when you gotta pay all the bills and watch your little brother."

Ruthie nods against me. "I can imagine. Maybe him leaving is about you, but in a good way. Maybe Stan's right and he's trying to keep you safe. Jimmy Dean has been all over us lately."

I rub my head and don't say anything, so she presses on. "Or maybe the money got to his head and he ran off. Thousand bucks can do that, right? Could be he's living it up right now in a penthouse in Vegas. Bought himself some new clothes, looking fly. Girl on each arm, tossin' hundos in the air like he just don't care." She holds my gaze until I crack a smile at the image. My dad, trading in his camo jacket and faded jeans for a pimped-out suit and some smoking-hot babes. "Maybe he's hiding from life in general. You said it yourself. Some guys do that. He's done this before. Disappeared, right?"

I nod. "But he didn't take that much, right? Just a couple hundred?"

She gives me that head tilt of hers. "Almost a grand. We were gonna use it to get a place somewhere. Me, Chick, Stan, him, and you guys."

I barely hear anything after the word *grand.* Dad definitely did not leave a grand under that pillow. Maybe he really did split. Except . . . if he had a thousand dollars, why did he leave us such a random amount? Not enough for December rent. Not an even three hundred or two-fifty. Why $227? The odd amount, the crumpled bills, the scrawled note . . . all of that points to a man in a hurry to get away—*from*, not *to* something.

All of it makes my head swim, so I toss out the first thing that I can think of to change the subject. "How'd you meet Chick?"

What the fuck? Why would I ask her that? I want to smack myself upside the head. But it's too late. It's like the shutters roll down and the closed sign goes up. She shifts her body off my lap and stares out toward the smokestack.

"He's a good guy. Smart. Funny as hell."

I nod, knowing some part of that must be true or he couldn't get a girl like Ruthie.

"We met at the old folks home. You know, the one over by the river? I was working there, passing out trays, and he was sitting by the fake Christmas tree, next to this little old lady, his nonna. He had brought her some chocolates for

Christmas and she didn't have anything to give him back, so she took off this old scarf she always wore over her hair and gave it to him. He acted like she'd given him a car! She laughed when he put it over his head, but when he tied it around his neck like a freakin' ascot, she looked so happy."

She gets up and reaches for my hand, pulling me from the floor. I follow her down the stairs and over to a pile of clothes by the night-lights. She rummages until she pulls out a pair of Chick's pants. "He got me something for Christmas already. I found it looking for clues on where he could be. He hasn't even wrapped it yet."

She digs into the pocket and pulls out a small object. Unwraps the wad of tissue around it and holds it up for me to see. It's tarnished and whatever stone that once sat next to the diamond is missing, but the way it makes Ruthie's eyes sparkle, it might as well be fresh off the jeweler's table at Tiffany's.

Her eyes fill with tears. "He wouldn't have left me, Josh. Something happened to him."

"Then we better find him," I tell her.

Stan comes in, stomping his feet and rubbing his hands together to get warm.

Ruthie stuffs the ring back into Chick's pants and non-chalantly drops them in the pile. She dashes over and plants a quick kiss on Stan's cheek. "You look half frozen," she says, brushing away the snow that's caked in the frill of hair over-hanging his collar.

Her actions are weird, sugary, like a feint to draw Stan's attention from the pile of laundry. And Stan's eating it up.

"Colder than a bitch's brass bra, I'll tell you what."

"Yeah? But you seem like you're in a good mood," Ruthie says. She's all upbeat, like she didn't just show me an engage-ment ring from someone who's MIA. But then I realize that she's doing the same thing I do around Twig, Matt, the rest of the guys. Put on a smile, play a game. Anything to keep people from seeing how messed up I really feel.

"Ayuh. I gotta little surprise for my best gal. Cashed in the copper." He pulls out his wallet and dips into it. Hands Ruthie a thick stack of bills. "You too, Joshie. Now you got a couple bucks to get you some grub."

He holds out some money and I take it, fanning it to get a count. Thirty-five bucks. He reads the look on my face. "Rest is going toward what your dad took."

"Yeah, about that . . . A grand? My dad took a grand? You can't really expect me to pay all that back. How am I supposed to do that? I got an agreement with Gran. If I don't—"

Stan chuckles. "Get a load of this guy, sounds like a deadbeat dad, don't he? 'I gotta kid to support!' Copper don't rake in the big dough. You want more, you gotta get in on the bigger jobs. But first, we gonna find our boy, Chick, right, Ruthie?"

I wonder if he knows about the ring. My guess is no, or he'd be less likely to believe Chick would just walk away.

"Yes! Josh and I were just about to head out." Ruthie grabs my coat and coaxes me into it. Zips it up for me. I recognize the play, but let her guide me toward the stairs.

The three of us spend half the day retracing the same steps, talking to the same people, looking in the same places that we've already searched. Ruthie gets quieter and quieter with each *No, I ain't seen him* and *He hasn't been by in a few* until she is down to one-word responses to anything me or Stan say. We wind up at the Center at dinnertime, so at least there's that. Stan sees someone he knows and goes over to shoot the shit with them. Ruthie and I get in line. I try to distract her by telling her about Nick's unfortunate piercing. I'm to the best part, where the piercing gun goes off and Nick screams like someone kicked him in the nuts, but Ruthie's not laughing. She's not even looking at me. I glance over my shoulder to follow her gaze just in time to see a girl about our age stroll not so casually into the bathroom.

"Who is that?" I ask, but Ruthie just takes off, beelining it for the bathroom.

I follow her, pulling up short at the "Women Only" sign over the cavernous entrance. Going into the women's bathroom is a surefire way to get bounced from the Center. Maybe even banned. I lean against the cool concrete wall, unable to shake the feeling that something's going down in there and Ruthie might need my help. I decide to give it a ten count before I—

Ruthie comes out and marches right past me toward the food line, which has died down now. Her face is flushed, blotchy. I fall in line with her, asking what's wrong.

She starts to say something, but Stan appears just behind her, asking, "What do you mean, what's wrong? Something happen?"

Ruthie's mouth snaps shut. Her eyes flit to mine, telegraphing *Shut up*. Her whole face changes, like she put on a mask or something, shifting from distraught to delighted in a heartbeat.

"Oh my God, Stan!" she gushes like she's twelve or something. "You won't believe who I ran into!"

Stan glances around, but Ruthie doesn't wait for him to guess. "My old friend Thalia from Kzoo!" Ruthie leads us through the food line, nodding as the servers offer options and chatting a million miles an hour about Thalia and how

great it was to see her after all these years and how we definitely need to catch up to her again so Ruthie can introduce
her to me and Stan but not today because Thalia had to run.
I am 100 percent sure that girl in the bathroom was not
some long-lost friend, but the way Ruthie lasered my mouth
shut with her eyeballs tells me not to call her on this.

We find an empty spot at a table and set our trays down,
Ruthie droning on and on about all the ways she and Thalia
used to get into trouble back in Kalamazoo. Stan loses interest quickly and starts scanning the other tables, one leg
bouncing under the table like it's running a marathon. I
listen carefully, wondering how much is true. Did Ruthie
really have a friend named Thalia? Did they terrorize the
school librarian like she's describing?

As close as I want to be to Ruthie, I've only known her a
week. Honestly, who do I know? Who can I trust? As close as I
was to Stan, that was more than five years ago and I was only
a kid. And my dad? Stealing money, leaving me to figure out
his shit. Gran? She'd rather dump Twig off to strangers than
help me take care of him. Suddenly something she said to
Mac the night I opened Mom's boxes floats back up to my con-
scious brain: *You won't have to put up with it much longer.*
I can't get past the feeling that they're planning something,
that she means he won't have to put up with *us* much longer.
Maybe Gran's plan is to dump Twig off at the Department
of Child Services and skip town with Mac. Maybe the deal
she made with me isn't for the rent. Maybe it's just to get
some cash to make their escape easier. I picture the red
Volkswagen pulling up to Gran's trailer. Some social worker
dragging Twig out of the only home he's ever really known.

Twig needs a way to get in touch with me if something
happens. The money in my pocket isn't much, but it could
probably buy a couple of cheap phones. Except if I spend that

money, I'll have no emergency cash if I have to run away with Twig. Who am I kidding? This money isn't gonna solve anything.

Ruthie pauses her story long enough to shovel a forkful of potatoes into her mouth and I jump in before she can swallow. "You mentioned bigger jobs," I say to Stan. "Is there something I can get in on?"

Stan's leg stops bouncing and he stands to clap me on the shoulder. "See? That's what I was just saying, Ruthie. We gotta keep moving forward. Keep busy till Chick comes back. Ayuh, I'll let you in on a little something, but not tonight. Tonight we gotta keep moving on those manholes. Get everything out before Jimmy Dean figures it out."

I want to argue—why waste time on the little things?—but Stan's already up and making his way toward the door. If I push Stan too hard, he might get pissed and shut me out, and some cash is definitely better than no cash.

Ruthie gives me a hard look, but she follows us back to the Castle to get the tools and then up onto the tracks. Stan's leading the way, excited to be back at it. He carries the front of the tarp, with Ruthie and me at the rear. She's quiet and shrugs when I ask if she's okay.

"Who was that girl at the Center?" I whisper. "I mean, really?"

"Thalia."

"Oh okay," I say, not even trying to hide the fact that I don't believe her.

Ruthie frowns at me but doesn't offer any more details. Instead she yells to Stan, "Hey, where you going? We left off here last time."

Stan keeps walking like he didn't hear her.

"Stan!" Ruthie stops and jerks the tarp to get his attention. "It's this one."

"No, it ain't," Stan tells her. "Two more up. While you two been back there making goo-goo eyes at each other, I been counting. We got two more to go."

Ruthie drops her side of the tarp. "What the fuck do you mean by that?"

Stan sighs. "Nothing, Ruthie. I'm just tired, is all. It's getting late. Can we just get this done?"

She stands there glaring at him for another few seconds and then lifts her corner of the tarp again without a word.

Stan leads us farther up the tracks, then says, "Ayuh, this one here."

Ruthie mutters under her breath that if he wants to skip two holes, it's fine with her. Stan turns to me and holds out his arms, palms up. "What do you think, Josh? You want to start here or humor Ruthie and go back to open up the ones we already done?"

Taking sides between these two would be like getting in the middle of a fight between a grizzly and a wolf. A rabid wolf. Either way, I'd end up missing more than a chunk of flesh. I shrug. "I don't know where we stopped. We're here now, so let's get to it."

Ruthie doesn't speak to either of us while we work. It takes much longer without a fourth man, and I can see why they were so keen on getting me to help when Dad left. Stan's jaw is set like he's red-hot pissed about something. We hit two holes and haul the copper and tools back to the Castle. As we're stashing them behind the bushes, Stan's hand slips and the tarp drops with a loud clatter that could wake the dead.

Ruthie and I freeze, but Stan kicks the bush, making even more noise.

"Stan." Ruthie's voice is sharp.

"What!" he yells back. "I'm out here doing the work of two people because your dad and your boyfriend"—he jabs his finger at each of us in turn—"decided to take a hike. Forgive me if I'm fucking tired, okay?"

"Which is it, Stan? Did Jimmy Dean go after them or did they take a hike?"

Stan stills, glaring at Ruthie through slitted eyes. "Fuck is this? We got a problem now? You blaming me for your man walking off?"

Ruthie crosses the space between them in two big steps, gets right in his face. "Yeah, Stan. I'm blaming you. You and Chick haven't exactly been getting along lately. Matter of fact, Tye—"

"Whoa! Okay." I reach for Ruthie's arm, but she yanks it away. "I think what Ruthie means is—"

"What I mean is, I am sick and fucking tired of Stan insinuating that Chick left because of me." Her voice cracks, but she keeps going. "He would not do that."

She's still up on Stan, yelling right in his face. He likes Ruthie, I know that, but Stan doesn't let anyone talk to him like this. I have to stop it before Stan gets so pissed that he kicks her off the crew, throws her out of the Castle. I edge closer to them, not wanting to be the spark that ignites either one of them. "We know that, Ruthie, don't we, Stan? That Chick wouldn't've walked away from her? That's not what you're saying, right?"

Stan turns his face to the side, his jaw working. He shakes his head as if to clear it, then steps back from Ruthie. "Naw, honey. Man would have to be batshit crazy to walk away from a girl like you. I'm just tired, I already told you."

On a scale of one to Stan, that's as close as she's ever gonna get to an apology and I think she knows it. She swipes the sleeve of her coat over her eyes and storms off toward the Castle door. Stan and I finish putting the tarp away in silence. He walks right past the Castle door. I hesitate, wondering if I should give Ruthie some time to cool off. I could go to Matt's. His mom would probably let me crash there again. But I'm worried that Ruthie might interpret my absence as taking Stan's side. Plus, I don't want her to think I took off like everyone else.

She's sitting on the pallet, picking at one of her fingernails, when I lift the curtain. "You want company?"

She closes her eyes and holds out her hand to me, pulls me down next to her. She doesn't speak, just curls up against my chest. After a bit, she starts talking. Not about Chick or Dad or scrapping, but just like we're two kids hanging out. Telling me about this book she found on a park bench—it was all dog-eared and missing its cover. She informs me that she sat right down on that bench and read the whole thing. "It was so weird and funny and, oh my God, I couldn't put it down."

I'm getting good at recognizing her plays. This one is straight out of Mr. Crouch's psych class—sublimation. Of course, Mr. Crouch would be just as likely to tell me I'm projecting my own defense mechanism onto Ruthie now and he'd be right. It's how I get through school. Talk about the team whose ass we're gonna kick next, the crap ton of homework for APUSH, the new kid on the bus. Just talk. Talk about anything to drown out the rumbling of my stomach and keep my mind off my fucked-up life. I squeeze Ruthie's hand and grant her the grace of letting her sublimate. "What was it called?"

"How would I know? The cover was missing. It was about this guy whose house is about to be destroyed and he is rescued by an alien and a depressed robot and they find out—"

"Forty-two."

"What?" Ruthie sits up and slugs my arm. "How did you know that?"

"It's the answer to Life, the Universe, and Everything."

"You read the book?"

I nod and tell her my dad used to bring home books all the time. Sometimes the books were moldy or missing pages, but usually they were worth reading. It's good to see this Ruthie again, the smiling, chatting Ruthie. Most of the girls who hang around the team at school either don't want to talk about books or treat me like I'm a dumb jock for not having read the books they read. But Ruthie is different. She leans in when I tell her there's a whole series of Hitchhiker books.

The more she says, the more I know I don't know about her. She is a contradiction. The opposite of expectation. She has read a million books, but can't remember the names of any of them. She's been to Disneyland, but not the beach. She stopped going to school halfway through eighth grade, but has a bigger vocabulary than most of my teachers.

I've talked to my share of girls, but when you have no car, no cash, it's hard to take someone on a date. Plus, girls notice things that guys don't; they ask questions. The last thing I need is some girl finding out I live in Oak Creek or that Gran is a pothead or I'm practically homeless, except now even the "practically" is gone. And what if a girl did find out and blabbed to the guys? I've seen how they look at the kids who ride the bus in from Ashland Grove, south of town. Like they're less than. Guys like Mason would use that against me in a heartbeat.

But with Ruthie, it's different. She doesn't judge, doesn't ask questions. She's seen Gran's trailer and it's not like she lives anywhere better.

"I really had a friend named Thalia," she tells me.

"Yeah? But not the girl at the Center."

"Yeah." She leans back, her hands folded on her stomach. "Can I ask you something? You and Stan got some history, huh?"

It's like she opened the floodgates and I tell her a lot: what it was like growing up at the junkyard, Stan teaching me basketball. Mom, Dad, and Stan cooking breakfast on the weekends. Stan's dream of starting a restaurant with my parents. The stories just flow out until I've told her more about me than any of the guys know. Even Matt. Not everything, though. Not about soccer tryouts. Not about the day of the fire.

Ruthie drifts off, but I lie awake for a long time. All those memories swirling in my head. We didn't have everything that Matt and the other guys have, no big houses with beautiful lawns, no minivans; we lived in a junkyard, rode the bus. But we had laughter and love and each other. Then Mom died and we moved in with Gran and we haven't had much laughter. But there's still love. I think about what Ruthie said, that Dad was working toward getting a place for us, Ruthie and Chick, too. How Stan's been talking about that same thing. And I wonder if that's possible. Building a family out of the loose scraps we've become.

CHAPTER

13

STAN SHAKES ME AWAKE SOMETIME BEFORE DAWN. "C'mon. We gotta see a man about a horse."

"What?"

Stan jerks his head toward the stairs. I rub my eyes and try to roll out of my bed, but I'm not in my bed. I'm twisted in the blankets on the floor of the Castle, wedged between Ruthie and the wall. It takes me a few seconds to untangle myself and ease out without waking her.

I pull on my shoes and coat and find Stan waiting for me on the stairs. "What's up?"

"You wanted in on a bigger job."

I push, but he won't elaborate.

Watchman stirs as we pass. Warns us that the cops have been rousting buildings near the tracks.

"Any word if they're headed this way?"

"They're mostly concentrating on the south side of the tracks. Cleared out a few buildings. Them guys are out under the bridge now."

Stan grumbles that the cops will use any excuse to mess with people just trying to get by.

A heavy snow coats the ground when we reach the street and fat, fluffy flakes are falling. I jerk the collar of my coat up around my neck and fish my sweatshirt hood out from beneath it. It won't keep me dry long. The streets are just waking up; cars roll slowly through intersections that look more like ski runs than roads because of the piles pushed up by the plows. My shoes are soaked, and my feet are already so cold, they're on fire.

I follow Stan past the Center, down several alleys, and into the parking lot behind Biggly's Drugstore. He walks up to the back door, which is bolted shut with a huge padlock. Yellow tape warns that this area is a CRIME SCENE and that we should NOT CROSS. Stan glances around and then pulls a crowbar out from under his jacket.

I grab his arm. "Stan, what the hell? We can't break in there."

He shrugs me off and wedges the crowbar between the lock and its hasp. It doesn't budge, just leaves scrapes in the flaky white paint. Stan walks around to the side of the building and down a narrow alley. Steps lead down to a basement door. No padlock on that one, but the crowbar isn't much help there, either.

Biggly's might be shut down, but the stores around it aren't. People could arrive any minute to open up for the day. "Stan, c'mon. We gotta get out of here."

"Quit being such a fucking baby," Stan growls. He steps back, looking for a way in, and lets out a deep "Ha!"

He points to the left side of the door. "See this? They left us an invitation. Dumbass installed the door hinges out."

It only takes a few seconds for Stan to pop the pins out of the hinges. The door comes loose. He motions for me to enter. "Ladies first."

I hesitate and Stan gives me a not so friendly shove between the shoulders. The basement is dark, but Stan came prepared and flicks on a flashlight. I follow the beam between two rows of mostly empty shelving. Stan doesn't stop to explore the basement, just heads straight for the stairs and takes them two at a time. There's a locked door at the top, but this one is easily jimmied.

Early morning sunlight filters through the store's windows, split into squares by thick metal security bars, casting jailhouse shadows. Stan tucks his flashlight into his pocket and heads for the back of the store. I intend to follow him, but the row of books in the school supply aisle catches my attention. There's that second book in that dragon series Twig wanted. I glance around out of habit, but it's just me and Stan in the store. Stan's already rummaging around out of sight. I slip a copy of the book into the waistband of my jeans.

Glass shatters somewhere at the back of the store and Stan calls, "Josh!" Then he says quieter, "Hol-eey cow. We hit the everlasting jackpot." Then loud again: "Get your ass back here and help me load up this shit."

The shit turns out to be cold medicine. Cases of it stored under the counter in the pharmacy. I know what that stuff is used for and it isn't congestion.

"Stan. This is different from taking some old copper nobody's using."

"Here, stuff these under your jacket." He's loaded boxes of the medicine into trash bags and presses a bag against my chest.

"Stan—"

"Goddamn it, Joshie, we ain't got all day. Somebody's gonna notice that busted door. You don't wanna get caught, just do what I say and get a move on."

"Man, I ain't no drug de—"

"Look!" Stan shoves the bag so hard against my chest that I stumble back into a countertop. He presses the bag forward, bending me back into the sharp edge of the counter. "Why you think I'm here? For me? For Ruthie? We were doing just fine until you showed up; now you tell me you gotta get some money to take care of Twig. You don't want to do this? Fine." He lets the bag drop to the ground at our feet.

I picture that red car pulling away from Gran's with Twig in the back. Him living in some group home or getting shipped off to some family. Never seeing him again. No way can I let that happen. But this? Stealing meth ingredients from pharmacies?

"Oh, I know what you're thinking." He laughs. "That you just need to keep things afloat until your dad comes riding in on a white horse to save you boys. But how's that working out for you so far? And that dream you got? Dribbling that basketball right outta this life? You really gonna do that? Go off to shoot hoops at some college while Twig gets sent off to some orphanage?" Stan stabs his finger in my chest. "You gotta wake up sometime, Joshie. Look in the fucking mirror. You're Tye Roberts's kid, not Michael fucking Jordan. Born in a junkyard and that makes you just another dog like the rest of us. Now you pick up that bag and do what needs to be done."

He stands there, his hands on his hips, just waiting. I drop my eyes to the bag.

"Right?" he says. "Ain't got no fucking choice."

He is right. I pick up the bag and stuff it under my jacket. Next to Twig's book.

Maybe he isn't the only one who's right. Gran always said I was nothing but garbage.

It takes half the morning for Stan to arrange to meet with someone who might take the meds off our hands. We ride the bus to Walmart and Stan actually pays the fare, making a big show of it, like he's ordered up a limo or something. Once we're at Walmart, Stan surveys the parking lot, looking just as conspicuous as every drug dealer I've ever seen on TV. Eventually he spots who he's looking for, a dude with hair so greasy, it looks like he shampoos with Crisco. Crisco Guy jerks his head toward the left side of the building. Stan flips me a ten-dollar bill and tells me to go grab some sandwiches from the deli. The pills must be worth big money to turn Stan McScrooge into Mr. Moneybags. While I wait in line for our footlongs, I picture the two of them out there, huddled behind the building in a corner under a broken surveillance camera, exchanging cold pills for cash. That's America for you.

I find Stan leaning against the shopping cart return, both hands stuffed deep into his pockets. It's like he's got a couple car batteries in there, charging him up so he's almost vibrating with energy.

"Good news?"

"Ayuh." He pulls a wad of cash partly out of his pocket, discreetly flashing it at me. "I'm setting aside a quarter of that toward your share of getting us a place. We keep working hard, we'll buy back Sal's. You and me, Twig and Ruthie. We'll—"

"My dad, too, right?"

"Huh?" Stan snatches his sandwich from me, unwrapping one corner and taking a huge bite. "Yeah, of course Tye, too," he says around a mouthful of salami. "Hell maybe even old Chick'll turn back up and join us. One big happy family."

I don't realize how hungry I am until I see that sandwich. I break it in half, devour one portion, rewrap the rest for Twig. That'll give him a break from Gran's boxed dinners and the crackers in the bedroom closet. He needs normal.

He needs a home with a family that will watch over him and keep him safe. Me and him and Dad. But Stan and Ruthie? Chick? All of us living together? I think about that on the way back to the Castle.

Ruthie wakes up midafternoon and comes over to where I'm working on my physics homework, by Dory and Elmo's dim light. "You been up awhile?" she asks.

"Yeah. Helped Stan with some stuff."

Her stomach growls. I subconsciously glance at Twig's sandwich, sitting atop my jacket. She motions at the papers on the floor in front of me. "Why do you care about that?"

"My homework?"

She squats down to look at the diagram I'd been sketching. "Yeah. Didn't you get the memo? Homeless kids don't go to school."

"They do if they want a basketball scholarship."

"You're going to college?" I can't read the look on her face.

I shrug. "Was."

"Not anymore?"

I don't know how to answer that. All my life that's been the plan. Get good grades. Play good ball. Go to a good school and have a good life. What does that even mean? Truth is, I never thought much beyond getting out of here. I drop my pencil and lean against the wall, the book I pinched for Twig jabbing me in the back. I pull it out. The cover's cool. Dragons in a midair battle. Two kids huddled together behind a tree. If I get that scholarship, where does that leave Twig? Hungry. So broke he can't even buy a book. Ignored by Gran. Out here on the streets with Stan? No fucking way I'm gonna let that happen. I slide the book across the floor toward my pile of stuff.

Ruthie picks up my diagram. "What is this?"

"It's a Rubens tube. Shoots flames out to the beat of music."

"How's it work?"

I explain the physics of it, how the sound waves control the flow of gas, making it look like the flames are dancing to the music.

"What song you gonna use?"

"'Sail.' Or 'Radioactive.' Probably 'Sail.'"

Ruthie nods appreciatively. "That's some cool shit, but I still don't see how that's gonna help you in life. None of the stuff they teach you in school does."

I know what she means. There's more times than not when I sit in class and think why the hell do I need to know the square root of 108 or that it was Copernicus and Galileo who figured out the Earth revolves around the sun, instead of the other way around. But then I'll watch the way everyone at school's attached to their phones like mindless zombies and no one stands up for anything anymore and I think that's just like what happened in *Fahrenheit 451*. Or how that book we read last semester in Davis's class—*The Hate U Give*—got the whole class talking about the metal detectors in our school and the off-duty cops in the hall. It was like half the kids hadn't even noticed them.

I try explaining some of that to Ruthie, but my words trail off when I notice her staring down at her fingers, which are picking at a frayed tear in her jeans. She doesn't even notice that I stopped mid-sentence. "Hey," I say softly.

She looks up, startled.

"What's up?"

She shrugs and tosses her head dismissively, but the crease doesn't leave her forehead. Her stomach growls like it's going to digest itself. "God, I'm famished."

"Wanna grab lunch?"

Ruthie smiles wanly. "You gonna take me to brunch at Tippecanoe?"

My hand wraps around the cash in my pocket. I could take her to Tippecanoe. I could take her to any restaurant in town.

She jumps to her feet and crosses over to a pile of stuff in the far corner. "Truth is, I wouldn't be caught dead in that place with their fancy omelets. I'll take a good old blueberry muffin over that crap any day." She comes back and plops down next to me. "Ta-da!" She holds out something wrapped in plastic.

I unwrap it to find what was, probably, at some point, a blueberry muffin. In its current state, it looks like maybe the Hulk tried to help wrap it. But it smells wonderful and so I break off a smooshed chunk and hand the rest back to Ruthie. She nibbles around the edges, taking tiny bites like a mouse. Her mind seems a million miles away. I reach over and touch her hand. It's gotta be so hard on her not knowing where Chick is or if he's coming back. But she doesn't look sad, just really deep in thought. Like she's puzzling something out. "You wanna talk about it?"

She takes another few bites, chewing slowly.

"If you don't want to tell me, that's fine."

Her hand with what's left of the muffin falls to her lap and she looks at me like she did that first day—sizing me up. "I . . . Have you . . . ?"

Whatever she was gonna say is drowned out by Stan clomping up the steps, calling my name, shouting that he's got another job, but we gotta go right now.

I ignore him and squeeze Ruthie's hand. "What?"

Ruthie's mouth is a thin tense line and it's like she's about to tell me what's bothering her, but Stan sweeps through the curtain yelling, "Josh! You coming or what?" and Ruthie yanks her hand away from me, ducking her head as she digs in the blankets like she's looking for something.

"You good?" I ask, even though it's pretty clear she's not.

"Yep," she says, not even looking at me. I follow Stan out into the night, but I can't stop thinking about the way Ruthie's face snapped shut when Stan popped through the curtain. Like it was him she was closing off against.

CHAPTER

14

RUTHIE SHAKES ME AWAKE. I TRY TO PULL HER BACK INTO the blankets, but she shoves me off. "Come on. Get up."

I prop myself up on one elbow, my mind sifting through the jumble that time's become, trying to figure out what day it is. Pretty sure it's Sunday. There's not even a glimmer of light seeping through the edges of the boarded-up window, so it must be pretty early. Ruthie kicks my shoes toward me and tells me again to get up. "We gotta go."

"What? Where?"

"Remember those holes we skipped? Need to check 'em."

"For what?"

"You gonna lay there asking me questions all day or get up and help me?"

She sounds just like Stan, but I know better than to tell her that. I sit up and fumble around in the semidarkness to wedge my feet into my shoes. "Sure, yeah, we can do that. I just gotta make sure I get to Twig in time for the Hot Light."

Ruthie shoves my jacket at me and tugs me toward the stairs.

Watchman's snoring so loud, he doesn't hear us as we pass. Outside, Ruthie trudges right around the back of the building and ducks behind the bushes to get the tools. I scamper after her, but as soon as I touch the tarp, I wish I'd brought gloves. The tarp is supposed to protect the tools from the elements, but there's nothing to protect the tarp and it's slick and slimy with either bird crap or mold. I sure hope it's just mold. Still, I can't help making a disgusted sound.

"Quit being such a girl," Ruthie says. She bends past me and grabs hold of one corner, yanking hard.

The tarp is heavy and harder for just the two of us to get out from behind the bushes. I asked Stan once why we had to hide the tools. It didn't seem like anybody ever went back behind the Castle. Stan said, "Keeps them safe from inquiring minds, like Jimmy Dean. Can't live among beggars and thieves and expect not to get your pocket picked."

Once we're clear of the bushes, I can see the sticky stuff all over the tarp is dark, not white like bird crap would be. Ruthie's already pulling at the tarp, unfurling it so the tools clatter onto the ground. She wipes her hands on her pants.

"What is that shit?" I ask her.

Ruthie jerks her head away. "Gonna help me or what?"

She bends down, grabs the shovel, crowbar, wire clippers. I scoop up the rest, thinking it'd be nice to have Stan's help. "Why don't we leave them in the tarp like usual?" I suggest.

"We can't walk around with that in the middle of the day. Somebody sees that, they'll think we're lugging around dead bodies."

Sure as I am that Chick hit the road, my mind puts together the sticky stuff with an image of him rolled up dead in the tarp and I drop the crowbar on my foot. "Is that blood?" I point to the stain on the tarp.

Ruthie gives me a look I can't read. "Could be. Not like you didn't punch the shit outta me on top of this thing."

"Wait, what? No, Chick punched you! He was trying to hit me and—"

Ruthie's expression changes to something I *can* read and my mouth clicks shut.

We tuck the mostly empty tarp back into the bushes.

The gash in the fence isn't obvious at first and we bicker for a second, Ruthie saying I passed it up, me snapping back that maybe she'd like to lead. After a few more steps I see why we didn't spot the hole. Zip ties stretch the fence together, as ineffective as stitches in a shotgun blast. Ruthie says that's typical, people are always trying to keep us out or in or wherever they ain't. Only question is, who is it this time? Cops? Guy who owns the lot? Somebody from the railroad? Doesn't matter to the bolt cutters.

As Ruthie's clipping the ties, I see a small scrap of fabric caught on one of the jagged edges of the fence. Ruthie's so focused on working the jaw of the cutter into the zip tie that she doesn't notice it waving in the slight breeze up near her shoulder. When she bends to snip the lowest tie, I snatch the scrap, secret it into my pocket, and when Ruthie stands back up and flashes me a triumphant grin, I grin back. *No problem*, I make my face say. But my fingers worry the cloth, turn it this way and that. Fold it, unfold it, twist it into a tiny ball.

It's not just a snippet from some railroad official's coat. It's purple with a frayed edge that I'd know anywhere, and Ruthie would too.

I tell myself it doesn't mean anything except that Chick's been through here. And he has—when we went out to scrap, we came this way. There's no telling how many other times he came through here with Stan and Ruthie before I joined the crew. Except Ruthie'll read more into it, like it being here has something to do with the fence being sealed off.

Like maybe the police caught Chick back here, arrested him or ran him off. Beat him, maybe. I can't help thinking about the tarp and its stain. But it can't mean any of that, so I leave the piece of fabric in my pocket and duck after Ruthie through the newly opened hole.

It's uphill to the tracks. Our feet slip on the loose gravel and I wish for a free hand to steady myself. I lean forward and let the heft of the tools pull me up the incline. Once we're on the tracks, we fall into an easy gait, me on point, Ruthie's breath coming in short puffs behind me.

I measure distance in two-hundred-foot increments, the distance between one manhole cover and the next. Most people could walk along here and never spot one of them. But after watching how Stan paced them out, I can spot them pretty easily. We go about half a mile from the Castle, passing by nine holes the crew did before I joined and the ones we've done since. As soon as we pass number fifteen, I start counting steps until I hit two hundred, then lay my tools down, as quietly as possible. We're up over Lafayette right near the bridge and no telling who's sheltering down there. Cops drive through there every so often and the last thing I want is for one of them to hear the clatter of metal and come up here to check it out.

Ruthie brushes away all the gravel, exposing the lid, flat and black as a burnt-out star.

"Give me that crow."

I hand her the crowbar, watch her jam it under one side and lean hard on it. I add my weight to hers and the cover slowly lifts. Now's when Stan and Chick would get their hands under it, help pull it up, roll it away. But it's just us. Ruthie gives a three count then throws her weight on the bar so I can get the head of the shovel under the lid. The crowbar clatters to the ground as Ruthie releases it to help me lift the lid the rest of the way off. It weighs about as much as the two of us put together. We get the cover on its side and Ruthie leaves it to me to roll the thing out of the way. I don't let it go too far, knowing that we gotta put that sucker back on.

Ruthie shines a light down the hole and I feel around for the ladder's top step with my foot, the metal like ice beneath my belly as I slide in. At the bottom, I call up for the wire strippers, but Ruthie says, "Leave it."

I blink up, trying to see her face, but all I can see is the dark smudge of her head haloed by sunlight. "What?"

"I said c'mon."

She moves away from the hole and I climb back out. By the time I surface, she's already scraping gravel away from the next hole.

"Ruthie? I think there's copper in there. Isn't that what we're looking for?"

She ignores me and wedges the crowbar under the next cover.

"Hey. You want to just cover this one up, then? Ruthie?" We can't just leave the holes wide open like this. The sun's coming up. If a train comes along, the conductor is sure to see that somebody's been messing with the equipment, and they'll report it. "Ruthie?"

I can hear her huffing and puffing trying to pry the next cover off, but there's no way she's gonna budge it without my help. I trot over, but she turns her back to me and continues to work the crowbar. "I just don't understand what we're doing out here if we're not gonna strip the copper." I circle around her, trying to get her to look at me, but she keeps her head ducked so her hair hangs over her face as she works the crow. "Ruthie? Come on, this isn't getting us anywhere."

"Then go home! I don't need you!" she snaps at me, and then she's on the ground, curled around herself, sobbing.

I kneel in front of her, pry her hands off her knees and hold them. She still won't look at me. "Hey, I'm sorry. I'm not going anywhere. Come on, let me help."

She takes one of her hands and swipes at her tears, then looks up at me.

Man, how could Chick have walked away from those eyes? Maybe life on the street got too hard for him. At the Center they call kids like that Justins—rich kids who run away from home because they don't like the rules in Mommy and Daddy's McMansion. They hang around on the street until it gets too cold or they get too hungry and then they go crying home. Chick is older, maybe twenty-two, but rich people don't kick their kids out when they hit eighteen; they just move them down to the basement and give them a car or something. Maybe he went home, someplace warm, like Florida or Cali. Or even right here, in one of the high-rise apartments looking down on us. Maybe he'll toss aside his fur-lined blanket, set down his mocha latte, and saunter over to the window. Look down and see me and Ruthie out here in the cold, and—what? Feel bad? I would have said, *Hell, yeah, he'd feel bad.* Maybe even invite us in to get warm, have a drink by the fire. Give me a few bucks from his trust fund so I can buy Christmas for my little brother.

Except guys who'll ditch you when the going gets tough probably forget you just as easy.

And he ditched Ruthie, too.

Her mouth twists like she wants to tell me what we're doing here, why I had to get up at the crack of dawn. "What?" I coax gently. "Please just tell me."

"That girl at the Center? She told me some shit about Stan." She pauses, studying my face. I don't know what's so hard for her to tell me, so I just nod, wishing she would spit it out already. "Stan and Wade had a fight the night Wade went missing."

"Well, yeah. Wade joined up with Jimmy Dean. . . ."

Ruthie scoffs. "That's what Stan wants us to believe. But Kelli was there. Stan told Wade the only way anybody leaves his crew is in a casket."

Now it's my turn to scoff. "Yeah, but that's all just bluster, right? Stan being Stan."

"That's what I thought too, but think about it. Stan fights with Wade, Wade disappears. Stan fights with your dad. *Poof!* Gone. Chick blows up at Stan and now he's gone, too?"

"But my dad left a note. He told me he was going—"

"Then Stan skips these holes. Stan, who has fucking OCD or whatever the fuck, *skips these holes.* I'm not trying to convince you, Josh. You asked why we're out here and I'm telling you."

"This is crazy! I've known Stan all my life."

"Yeah, I know." Ruthie shakes her head. "Look, just help me check this other hole, all right?"

She's wrong. But I can't say no to her, so I squeeze her hands and pull her up. We work the cover free with the crowbar. It comes off easier than the last. Maybe because Ruthie had already been working it, but whatever the reason, I'm thankful. My muscles already ache from just the last one and my hands are so cold, they have lost not just feeling, but the memory of feeling. I roll the cover to the side. When I turn back, Ruthie is crouched completely motionless at the hole's opening, staring down into it. My pulse shoots up and I scamper toward her.

"Ruthie? What? What is it?"

I reach out to touch her just as a train rounds the bend. "Ruthie? We gotta move."

She just keeps staring down that hole, muttering something. I shake her hard, she doesn't turn, but her words get louder and I can hear her now, saying the same thing over and over—"Oh jeez. Oh man. Oh jeez"—and now I'm really scared because whatever's down that hole knocked all the cuss words right out of her.

The train's getting closer and I know if we don't move, the engineer's gonna see us. But even though I don't want to, I have to see what's in the hole. I scoot closer and follow the beam of her flashlight over the gaping lip of the hole. There's something down there, something *wrong*, but the light is trembling in Ruthie's hand and my brain can't make sense of it. I grab at the light, knowing that the thing in the hole can't possibly be what it looks like, but then the train horn blares and Ruthie's arm stiffens. The light stills and so does my heart.

A foot.

There's a foot tangled in the wiring.

CHAPTER

15

RUTHIE DOES NOT WANT TO GO BACK TO THE CASTLE and I get it, I do. But there is nowhere else to go, at least not together. She finally gives in. Luckily, Stan's not around when we get there. We lie together most of the day, staring at the blacked-out window with its fake stars. Ruthie doesn't cry, but she doesn't talk, either. Neither do I. We just lie there, bundled in the blankets Chick left behind.

At some point, Ruthie sleeps. I know because she slips down under the blankets and turns into me, her warm breath even against my neck, her thin arms snaking around my bicep. I know it's not me she's holding, but I hold her back, pull her closer.

The scrap of purple is a fierce ember in my pocket.

Stan ducks under the sheet just as I finally nod off. "Josh?" he calls.

I don't respond. He comes over and pulls the blankets down to see Ruthie's face against my chest. He sucks his teeth. "Joshua?"

"Don't wake her."

"You the one dreaming. She don't love you."

I know that, of course I do, but still my throat clenches. He frowns at me. "What you playing at?"

Ruthie stirs against me and I want to put my hand across Stan's mouth, push his words back down his throat. I try to speak, but it's as if I'm talking around a mouthful of marbles. Stan looks at me like I'm an idiot. I swallow hard and try again. "We found him. He's dead."

Stan's face scrunches up, like he's trying to hear someone talking to him through a crowd.

I fumble in my pocket for the bit of scarf. "Chick," I say, holding the small purple scrap up to Stan.

Ruthie stirs again at the sound of Chick's name. A slight smile plays around the corners of her mouth. She must be dreaming about a time when he was still here, when they were together. Maybe laughing as they rolled down that snowy hill the first time we all scrapped together. Maybe some tender moment I wouldn't know about. I gently pull away from Ruthie and bundle her in the blankets like a cocoon. Even though she knows because she was there, I don't want what I'm about to say to filter into Ruthie's subconscious and stain her dreams while she sleeps.

Stan's just staring at me. He lets me lead him to the other side of the curtain. I hold out the scrap again and he takes it, rubbing it between his fingertips. I tell him again that we found Chick and then the whole thing is spilling out—how me and Ruthie went scrapping without Stan and found a hole with the lid partway off and the foot dangling in the cables and Chick's body hanging upside down, things I only half remember—like Ruthie and me climbing into that hole and working to get Chick down, me leaning him against the wall, her kissing his swollen face and taking off her coat to drape it over him like a blanket, like he might get cold without it to keep him warm, then Ruthie curling into

Chick's lap like a little kid, like she might stay there with Chick's body until the cold and the dark and time itself took her to wherever the rest of Chick had gone. I tell Stan how I pried her from Chick's lap, dragged her out of the manhole, carried her down the track to the Castle as she pummeled my back, relief flooding over me as she went limp with exhaustion. Stan listens without interrupting. When I finally run out of words, his chin dips to his chest. "Wish it could have been different," he says, thumbing the scrap.

There's nothing to say to that, so I do the only thing I can. I crawl back onto the pallet and pull Ruthie close to my chest. I'm exhausted body and soul and I really want to just close my eyes and forget all of this, but . . . my thoughts keep circling around Ruthie's words. Stan is a hard man, I know, but he has to be hard to survive on the streets. He can't let people walk all over him. Maybe he did threaten Wade. Maybe he and Chick fought. Maybe they were out there scrapping and Chick fell. Maybe Stan knew and didn't tell us. But murder? I can see Stan at our kitchen table, laughing with my mom and dad; Stan lifting Twig out of his high chair and dancing with him to "The Purple People Eater" on the radio; Stan's hands over mine on the ball, showing me how to line up the shot. No. No way Stan did this.

Ruthie dozes off and on all that day. I sit on the pallet near her, my mind churning it all together, now and before, Chick and Ruthie, the fire, losing Mom, Dad holed up and bleeding somewhere, Gran. Twig waiting all day for me to take him to the Hot Light, going to bed not knowing if I just disappeared like Dad. I feel so fucking powerless. And angry. What the hell was Dad thinking, just disappearing on us like this? My whole life, he told me to keep my eye on the prize, get myself a scholarship. And I was doing it too. I was supposed to be headed out of this shithole and he just plunged me deeper into it.

I think about taking the money I have, going down to Greyhound, putting it all toward whatever ticket will get me the farthest from here. I picture different versions of that. Colorado or Connecticut. Alone or with Ruthie, maybe Twig, too. But by the time my watch beeps its school-day alarm, I know the only thing I can do is keep on keeping on. Get up, go to school, earn that scholarship so I can get a real job and come back for Twig. Meanwhile, I gotta scrape together whatever money I can to keep Twig living with Gran.

I ease out of the blankets without Ruthie even stirring. Stan's snoring away, propped in the corner. I touch his shoulder and he leaps up like he's spring-loaded, a knife in one hand.

"Holy fuck, Stan!" I cry, dodging out of reach reflexively.

Stan shakes his head to clear it and lowers the knife. "Ain't nobody taught you not to creep up on a man? What you want?"

"Can you stay with Ruthie today?"

Stan looks at me like I just asked him to staple his foot to the floor. "She doesn't need a babysitter. I got places to be."

"I know. I just think we shouldn't leave her alone for a while, is all."

"Where you going?"

"I need to get to school. I've got a test and a big game. If I miss, Coach is gonna—"

Stan thumps the toe of his boot on the floor. "Co-aaa-ch," he says, drawing out the syllables like a kid teasing his older sister about a crush. "Why you care what he thinks?"

"It's not really him or what he thinks." I pause, trying to figure out how to explain it better to Stan than I did to Ruthie. "I just want better for Twig than what I had. I want to get us a house. A home." I can see it in my head. A kitchen like Matt's, with one of those breakfast nooks that the whole family can sit at. I'd buy a nice frame for that picture of us all at the beach, Twig holding Mom's ponytail and laughing at my silly face, and I'd hang that on the wall behind the table.

"I told you, I got a plan for us all. You don't need school for that. You and Ruthie stick with me, you'll have a real home soon enough."

"Yeah?" I try to keep the skepticism from my voice. As far as I know, Stan's never had a real home, except when he stayed in the old farmhouse with us. He's never had a job except helping my dad scavenge for the junkyard and now scrapping. And until I can get Ruthie to see she's wrong about Stan, I doubt she's gonna want to keep working with him.

He bats me in the chest with the back of his hand and nods. "Yeah. I got a plan. Remember Sal's?"

"The saloon?"

"The *restaurant*," he corrects. "Soon as I get enough money to buy her from the bank, we're gonna open her back up. You on register. Ruthie can wait on tables. Twig can bus. Hell, maybe even old Tye'll show back up to help me on the grill. We'll live above it. Cozy little family."

It's a nice dream, but I've seen that place. It'd take a ton of work to get it looking like anyplace people would pay to eat. And as far as buying it, not even that is gonna happen unless the price of copper scrap and cold pills surpasses the price of diamonds. No sense arguing with him though.

"Can you stay here today?" I ask again. "For Ruthie?"

"Ayuh. She's our good girl."

I scrounge around in my backpack for a sheet of loose-leaf and write Ruthie a quick note, letting her know I'm headed to school and I'll be back ASAP. I prop the note against the half sandwich I was saving for Twig so it's the first thing she'll see. I finger the little blue fish in my pocket and consider leaving it with the note. It might cheer her up, give her a bright little spot to focus on. But a plastic key chain is a crap way to say *I'm sorry your boyfriend is dead*.

CHAPTER 16

THE BUS SLOWS, THEN ROLLS RIGHT PAST ME AT THE stop. Traffic is backed up and I sprint the two blocks, hoping to catch it at the intersection of Byrkit and Lincolnway. The snow is thick and wet and my shoes and socks get totally soaked. Luckily, some old woman is moving up the steps at the speed of molasses, so I make it in time. I'm opening my mouth to ask the driver why he didn't stop for me, when I see it's the same guy who threatened to run me over last time I saw him. I pay my fare and take a seat. The bell for first period already rang and I can't stand the thought of having everyone in the class stare at my wet jeans as I squish my way to my seat, so I hide out in the bathroom until passing period.

I know I should be going through my binder, trying to get a handle on where I'm behind in classes, but I just can't bring myself to pull everything out of my backpack while I'm sitting in a fucking toilet stall. Plus, my eyes will barely stay open. Each time I blink, my eyelids grate across them like they're made of sandpaper.

I'm at my locker, grabbing my book and calculator for physics, when Nick finds me. "Dude! If I didn't know you better, I'd be seriously panicking." He's smiling, but the look in his eyes is the same one he gets when we're down by ten and I foul out.

I rack my brain for what could have Nick's panties all in a bunch. As if he can read my mind, Nick says, "No, no, no, no. Please tell me you didn't forget about Psycho Mop!"

"Oh man, that's what you're tripping about? APUSH? No, man. We got this."

I keep rummaging in my locker so I won't have to look at him. Mr. Mopkinovic doesn't give normal tests. Maybe if he did, it wouldn't matter that I forgot to study. But Mr. Mopkinovic, affectionately crowned Psycho Mop because of the perverse pleasure he gets out of mopping the floor with the unprepared students in his APUSH classes, makes all his tests debates. He puts us in these circles facing each other, gives us each a role to play, and we have to debate whatever topic he throws out as if we were those historical figures. But Nick and I figured out how to line up so we're always facing off against each other. I prep him for the debates and we don't bring up anything off-script. That way we both get decent grades.

When I can't stall any longer without risking my fourth tardy in physics, I shut my locker and turn to face Nick. "We'll go over the plan at lunch," I tell him, then drift into the river of freshmen flowing toward the science hall, hoping he won't be able to track me.

As soon as the bell rings, Miss Wismer tells us to get out our calculators and put everything else on the floor and I'm reminded of what else I forgot to study for.

Wet pants, wet shoes, failed physics test, no time to study for APUSH.

By the time lunch rolls around, I'm seriously considering bailing, but Nick spots me in the hall and practically drags me to our table in the cafeteria.

"You got notes for me?"

Matt laughs. "Dude. Let the man get his food first, he's not looking so good. Seriously, you been eating?"

"I'm fine, Mom," I shoot back, and all the guys at the table laugh, but boy, am I grateful for the chance to hop in the food line. It's tater tot day and while I know they're gonna be undercooked and mooshy, they smell like manna from heaven. I'm tempted to ask for an extra serving. It's not like that fifty cents would make a difference when I'm miles from being able to pay Gran. But I keep moving through the line and let the lady scan my ID without adding in any extras.

Between bites, Nick and I come up with a strategy for Mop's debate. It won't get us an A, but it'll pass. We're on our way to APUSH when I overhear a couple of guys talking about dogs in the building doing a drug sweep. That happens a couple times a year at Woodson, so I would have kept walking, but the words "break-in" and "cold meds" float through the throng of voices. There's nothing to worry about, I know. The cold medicine was in boxes, in trash bags. There is no way my jacket's got any residue on it. Still, by the time we get to APUSH, I'm so worked up, I've forgotten most of our plan. Mop tells us to circle up for the test. Nick lines up across from me. We get assigned Trist and Polk, which I know we just went over, but my brain keeps thinking about dogs sniffing at my locker, cops taking me in. I just can't focus. Nick carries us enough that we might actually pass.

The bell rings and Mop calls out, "Mostly good things today, gang." Everyone starts packing up and he adds, "Josh, stick around, will you?"

I wait by his desk until the room clears, knowing he's going to call me out for being unprepared. He doesn't, though. Instead he tells me if I ever need an extra pair of pants or a clean shirt, I can stop by his room. He keeps a change of clothes in case a kid pukes on him or something.

My face flushes and I clench my arms to my sides. I had planned to shower and scrub out the pits of a few shirts at Gran's, but since I never made it there, I'd grabbed the least dirty shirt I could find.

But Mop shakes his head. "No, it's not that," he says. "Your pants. Looks like you spilled your lunch." He points down to my pant leg. I have to twist the fabric around to see it, but at the bottom of the left leg, there's a nasty-looking stain that apparently passes for spaghetti sauce from a distance. My stomach drops at the thought of the police dogs catching a whiff of that.

I mumble something by way of thanks and jog toward the gym. It's too late to stop at my locker if I want to make the bus for the Elkhart game. And I want to make that bus. Otherwise, I'll have to spend double what I got in my pocket on an Uber because the Transpo buses don't run there. Not to mention Coach hates when guys don't ride the bus—says away games are about traveling together, team bonding, not just showing up someplace. The team's already cleared out of the locker room. I snatch my gym bag and race out to the parking lot. The bus is loaded up and idling. I sprint down the sidewalk and bound onto the bus, expecting Coach to hand my ass to me on a platter for keeping the team waiting, but he's not on the bus. I slide into the seat in front of Matt with a sigh of relief.

"Where's Coach?" Matt asks.

"What? How should I know?"

"Coach was on the phone while we were loading up. Got a call and said your name."

"Jeez, man," Nick cuts in, "we thought the cops busted your ass." It's clear from his tone that he's joking around, but his words still cause my pulse to race. While I'm trying to think of something clever to say, the guys get to talking about the cops being at Woodson. They shoot around a few theories, but nobody knows much. Just that they think someone might have been trying to sell some of the pills to area high school kids.

Coach clomps up the steps onto the bus and barks my name. I swear, he's the only one who can make "Roberts" sound like a synonym for "shithead." Coach holds out his cell phone. "Call for you."

I'm pretty sure I'm about to get punked. I'll get on the phone and one of Coach's pals will introduce himself as the coach from San Bernardino and offer me a full ride. Then all the guys will gather around and laugh at me for being such an idiot. But we're supposed to be on the court in Elkhart soon and the irritation on Coach's face is about to start spewing out of his mouth.

I stand up, but Coach tells me to grab my gear. That can't be good. I hoist my gym bag and follow him off the bus. Before he hands me the phone, he covers the mouthpiece and tells me, "My wife works over at the middle school and called when they couldn't reach your grandma."

I take the phone and turn away, cupping my hand over the mouthpiece to filter out the thrum of the bus motor. "This is Josh?"

"Joshua Roberts?" a woman's voice repeats on the other end of the phone.

"Yeah. Um, can I help you?"

"This is Mrs. Nelson. I'm the secretary at Pokagon Middle School. We've been trying to reach a family member about an incident involving Woodrow."

It's after three—Twig shouldn't still be at school. Did he miss the bus? If he had, wouldn't she have just said, *Hey, your brother missed the bus*? Did the bus crash? As if she anticipated the panic rising in my throat, the woman rushes on to say that Twig is fine, but that it is imperative a parent or guardian be reached immediately.

"Did you try our grandma?"

"Yes. She . . . uh . . . isn't available."

"Well, sometimes she doesn't get to the phone right away, but if you try—"

The woman clears her throat softly. "It wasn't that she didn't answer the phone. She informed our social worker that she isn't available. They want to go out to the house. I know Craig has you on his team, so I told them to hold off until I could get you on the phone."

"But—"

"We need someone to come to the school immediately."

"My dad . . ."

"We were so sorry to hear about his death. Your grandmother must be so distraught to send you boys to school so soon after a parent's death. But we just can't have Woodrow here if he's going to behave like that. Frankly, we don't know what to do to impress upon him—"

I'm holding the phone so tight, my fingers ache. Mrs. Nelson has finished whatever she was saying. She's waiting for me to respond, but all I can do is stand there clenching the phone against the side of my head while her words flow in one ear and out the other like wisps of smoke.

"Josh?" my dad says from behind me. Only, when I turn around, it's not my dad but Coach. His hand closes over the phone and eases it from my grasp. He says, "Hey, Janie. We're on our way."

Coach leans into the bus and says something to the driver, then comes back and scoops up my gym bag. He takes ahold of my elbow and walks me across the parking lot to his big red Chevy truck. He tells me to buckle up, like I'm some little kid who doesn't know how to ride in a car, then leans across me and pulls a pack of Twizzlers from the glove box. Coach doesn't say a word the whole drive and that's just fine with me.

My thoughts rebound back and forth between believing Mrs. Nelson and knowing it's bullshit. There's no way my dad is dead. Every time my dad disappears, I know he's coming back. I can feel him out there in the world, even now. He's gone, but it's different from how my mom is gone. Some people say that after their loved one passes, they can feel them, up in heaven or wherever, watching over them. It's never been like that with my mom. Sure, I get whiffs of her perfume or some woman in the mall will smile at me a certain way and my mom will be in there, but that's all just neuropsycho bullshit. Memories floating up.

But with my dad . . . it's like we're connected by those little dashes Coach draws on the playboard. No matter where Dad goes, there're these dashes stretching out between us. I might not know his next move, but I know I gotta be ready for the pass.

Coach pulls up in front of Twig's school. He puts the truck in park and I reach for the door handle. "Josh," he says. The word sounds strange on his tongue, so different from the usual "Roberts." I turn back and his face is different too. Not sci-fi different, but different enough that I know this man in the truck isn't the same one on the court with me and the guys. He stares past me out the window long enough that I start to reach for the handle again, but he stops me with a hand on my arm. "I'm sorry about your dad. You know we were friends back in the day—"

"He ain't dead," I tell him. His mouth is still gnawing on a bit of licorice and it's tempting to watch the motion of his jaw, but I force my gaze up. Meet his eyes dead-on. There's pity in his expression, but I don't let it land on me. I keep my mouth tight, my eyes hard, and say it again real slow like he's the kid now. "My dad is not dead."

Nobody talks to Coach Nelson like that. His jaw goes still and I wait for him to lay into me, but instead he nods slowly and says, "Let's go see about that brother of yours."

Coach points to a chair in the school office and I sit. He chats with Mrs. Nelson, who turns out to be a pretty brunette with purple-framed glasses. She leads him down the short hall toward the principal's office. Before I know it, he's walking back out with Twig, who is watching his feet so carefully, it's like he thinks the tile might evaporate under him.

"Seems your dad isn't the only one who's dead," Coach says to me. "Woodrow here killed off Santa, too."

Coach drops us off at the entrance to the trailer park. Twig stuffs his hands into his coat pockets and trudges off toward Gran's. I let him get around the first bend before I trot to catch up. "Hey, we gotta talk about this."

The only sign that he hears me is that his pace picks up.

"Twig, why'd you say those things, dude?" I grab his arm and spin him to face me. I'm expecting the sad face of my little brother, but it's like Twig aged ten years since I last saw him and all that time anger has been boiling up inside him.

His shoulders square off against me. "What do you care?"

I ignore the question and repeat my own. "Why'd you say Dad is dead? You know he's not, right?" I want to tell him that Dad is fine. Except I don't really know that. And Dad being fine means that Dad is fine abandoning us. That can't be any better to tell Twig.

"Whatever. Leave me alone."

Twig starts walking again and again I swing him back around. He shrugs off his backpack and slams it to the ground. "Why don't you just leave me alone?" he screams.

His words push me back a step and I trip over the curb, landing on my ass. Twig towers over me, arms stiff at his sides, punctuated by balled fists. "I told my class Santa's dead because he is dead. Mom's dead. Dad's dead. If I ever believed in God, I'd say he's dead too because that's what people do. They die."

"Twig, I—" I start to get to my feet, but he shoves me back down hard.

"You? You, Josh? You're dead too. Just a ghost pretending to give a shit about me." He picks up his backpack and takes off running through the side yard of a trailer.

I'm so pissed, I nearly yank the trailer door off its hinges. "Gran?" I yell, storming through the kitchen to the living room.

She's sitting on the couch, watching TV in her robe. "What? What are you yelling for?"

"We had a deal. I paid the rent; you were supposed to take care of Twig."

She picks up her "I Heart Puppies" mug and sips calmly, then she sets it down and looks at me. "What happened?"

"The school called you. They needed someone to come get Twig and you said you weren't available, so they called my coach. Coach had to get off the game bus and go to Twig's school and get him."

"What did he do?"

"He told his whole class that Santa is dead."

Gran laughs.

"He said Dad is dead." She keeps laughing. I want to knock the smug look off her face. "Where did he get that idea? Did you tell him our dad is dead?"

"Said he *may as well be* dead for all the good he is. Him and Santa are just as likely to walk through that door."

"Twig's nine! You don't say shit like that to a kid."

"He's gotta grow up sometime. What good does it do for him to go around thinking strangers are gonna give him presents? It's about time he knows the truth. Santa isn't gonna bring him anything for Christmas and his daddy ain't never coming back. Now, if you don't mind, I was watching my soaps." She reaches for her mug, but I grab it first and hurl it at the TV. It shatters against the crucifix on the wall.

"I paid you to take care of Twig!" I yell at her. "If you're not gonna do that, what the hell am I giving you money for?"

Gran does not get up. She doesn't yell or turn red in the face. She doesn't even look at me. Instead she picks up the remote and presses the volume button. The TV gets louder and louder until the TV doctor's voice echoes throughout the trailer, drowning out any sane thought I might have. I have to get out of there before I do more than knock Jesus off the wall.

I'm halfway across the kitchen when Gran mutes the TV. "Rent's due the first. That's Friday," she says.

I stop, one hand on the door handle. "I'm working on it."

"Yeah? Well, 'working on it' ain't the same as getting it done, is it? Pay up or find someone else to take care of the little shit. In fact, you might want to start getting right with the idea of him going someplace else."

The TV volume comes back on. It's like she tossed a cup of lighter fluid on the flames already licking at the edges of my hatred. I storm back into the living room. "What does that mean?"

She ignores me.

My foot wants to kick that fucking TV, but I force the sole of my foot down, down against the inside of my sneaker, down against the crusty carpet of that ratty trailer. My hands ache with the desire to punch something. To punch *her*. I stuff them into my pockets and my fingers find Dory and the slick surface of the family portrait. If I ever want to give Twig a real family, a real place to live, I need time to figure this out. Time I won't have if I lose my shit on Gran. Even if she deserves it.

"I'll have the money, okay? Just don't do anything without talking to me." I march out of there without waiting for a response and ignore the "No promises!" she shouts after me.

CHAPTER
17

TWIG IS OUT IN FRONT OF THE TRAILER, BOUNCING A basketball against a tree trunk. Each time it rebounds to him, he hurls it with all the force he can muster. I should get back to the Castle. Make sure Ruthie is all right. I can only imagine what she's gonna do when she wakes up and finds Stan sitting there. But at least Stan can keep her safe. Twig only has me.

"Come on, little dude. Let's go get some dinner," I tell him.

He catches the ball and tucks it under his arm. Eyes me suspiciously, obviously still pissed. "You probably have somewhere important you gotta be. Game or something. I'll just eat some crackers from the closet."

"Nothing more important than my little bro. Let's get some food."

"For real?"

"Yeah, for real. Missed the Hot Light yesterday, didn't we?"

He rolls the ball just under the edge of the porch so no one will take off with it.

We're quiet on the bus, which is fine by me. I can tell he's still upset, but sometimes it's best to give the little dude his space. My brain ricochets between wanting to ask if Gran's said anything to him about staying somewhere else and not wanting to scare him. Wanting to tell Twig about finding Stan and knowing he was so little when Stan left that he wouldn't know who I'm talking about. And then there's Stan's plan to get a place for all of us. There's a glimmer of hope in that and I want to share it with Twig, but I don't want to get his hopes up only to have them dashed if that doesn't work out. Or if Stan turns out to be the homicidal maniac Ruthie thinks he is.

The after-school Hot Light is still on when we get off the bus, but just as Twig reaches for the door handle at Krispy Kreme, it flicks off. The guy behind the counter's a douche and won't give us the free doughnut even though the whole conveyor belt's full of them.

"It's okay," I tell Twig, reaching for my wallet. "Just pick whatever you want." I know even a few bucks will put a substantial dent in the little cash we have, but damn it, is it too much to ask for a fricking doughnut once a week?

While Twig drools over all of the options in the display case, the guy goes to check someone out at the drive-through window. The other worker, a girl so short that I almost can't see her over the counter, tosses two hot doughnuts into a bag and holds it out to Twig. She waves off my offer to pay.

"Thanks, but we don't want to get you in trouble," I tell her.

She reaches behind her and snags a bottle of milk and gives that to Twig as well. "My dad owns this store," she says with a wink. "Now get outta here."

I can't remember the last time I've had milk, actual milk. Gran buys that powdered shit that you have to mix with water before you pour it over cereal and the milk at school tastes like the cardboard carton it's served in. This milk is creamy and rich, even if it is slightly not-cold. I have to stop myself from offering to trade Twig my doughnut for his half of the milk. He needs the calcium and vitamin-whatever more than he needs empty sugar.

The doughnut cheered Twig up a bit and now he's acknowledging my existence. He's so wrapped up in telling me about the snake that his teacher brought in last week that he follows me halfway across the Walmart parking lot before asking where we're going.

"Gotta get something," I tell him. He goes back to his story, stretching his arm out to show me how long the snake was and using both hands to simulate the way its mouth unhinged to swallow a mouse. Sometimes I wonder if I was ever that innocent.

We walk past the coats and I wish I had a credit card. Twig really needs a new coat. Pants too. Kid looks like a scarecrow, his bony wrists and knobby ankles showing.

He lingers as we pass the book section, running his fingers over the raised title of *The Return of the Dragon Keepers*. The same book I snatched at the pharmacy. "It's the sequel to my favorite book and the library doesn't have it. Who does that—gets kids hooked on a book and doesn't order the sequel?"

"Gotta leave something for ... Christmas," I tell him, and drag him away from the books.

We find what I am looking for in the electronics section.

"No way! A cell phone?" Twig's drooling over the new iPhone, which is strategically displayed right next to a compatible VR system. "Oh my God! Can I get this one? Evan has one just like it and there's a basketball game where you are actually in the game, like looking through Jordan's eyes and ..." His words trail off as his eyes meet mine.

I walk down the display to the Tracfones. The cheapest one is $29.99. Not as bad as I thought, but for two that's sixty bucks. The lowest minute card is another twenty and by the time we walk out of the store, I've barely got twenty in my wallet with ten times that due to Gran in four days. It'd help if I had some clue how to get Stan to actually give me the money from the cold medicine. Plus, there're the manholes we haven't hit yet. My stomach clenches at the image of Chick hanging upside down by his foot. Not sure I can get myself to climb down in another one after that. No way am I asking Ruthie to.

I tell Twig we can grab dinner at the mall.

His face lights up. "Real food? Like, buy it?"

"No, dude. But samples are still real enough, right?"

"Yeah," he says, but we both know that's not true.

For once I'm glad I don't have a car. The mall parking lot is jam-packed. Like everyone realized there are only twenty-eight days left until Christmas and they must buy everything tonight. The food court is just as crowded, but we luck out and a group is clearing out of our usual booth just as we walk in. As soon as we sit down, I take the phones out of their packaging and activate them. "You know how to use this?"

Twig rolls his eyes.

"We only have sixty talk minutes," I tell him. "And sixty texts. If I text you and you respond, that's two texts. We gotta make this last so we have it in an emergency. Try not to use the phone, okay?"

"How much data did you get us?"

"No data." I hold Twig's phone out to him, but he ignores it, so I set it on the table.

"What's the point? We can't use them, so why waste the money?"

"In case you need me. I want you to be able to call me if you need me."

"I wouldn't have to call you if you would come home."

I take a deep breath and remind myself that Twig is only nine. "We just talked about all this, remember? Gran won't let me stay there. I gotta stay with Matt just until I find Dad. I'll come by as much as I can."

"You said every Sunday, but you don't even show up. And we missed Thanksgiving Marathon. Why can't you just come home? Or take me with you. I could stay with Matt too."

"Twig, I'm doing the best I can. Please take the phone in case something happens."

Twig stuffs the phone into his pocket and scoots out of the booth, headed to the arcade. My backpack's still in my locker at school, so I can't work on homework. Not sure I could focus on it anyway. My head hurts and I let myself lean back in the booth and close my eyes for a few minutes.

Next thing I know, someone's shaking me awake. I think it's Twig, but I open my eyes to see our mall's version of Paul Blart towering over me.

I sit up fast, my heart thumping in my chest, sure he's about to arrest me for the pharmacy break-in. But he's not pulling out his cuffs or calling for backup. He's looking at me like my very presence is contaminating the food court.

"You can't camp out here, sir," he tells me.

I start to get to my feet. "Oh yeah, no. I'm not—"

He cuts me off. "There's a shelter over on Michigan Street. I got their card if you need it. You can't sleep here. Respectable people are trying to enjoy their food."

I glance around at the other booths, all those respectable people watching our exchange with an equal mix of disgust and curiosity. I search their faces for someone from school who can tell this cop I belong here; I'm not some homeless guy. But their faces tell me to rethink that. Unshowered, dirty clothes, sleeping in a booth. I grab my gym bag and hold it so it at least partially covers the stain on my pants. It's actually a good thing no one from school is here. I'm halfway to the door before I realize I left Twig in the arcade. I walk back through the food court, my skin itching from everyone's eyes crawling over me. Twig is playing *BurgerTime* with a girl his age. He squawks indignantly when I grab his arm and drag him out of the arcade.

Twig doesn't speak to me the whole way to the bus or on the ride back to the trailer park. When we get off, I walk over to the bus stop and sit down. Twig's face is closed-off, angry, and I can see that he wants to just walk away. He doesn't, though. He stands a few feet away from me, arms crossed, studying something up the road.

"Sorry," I say.

Twig jerks his shoulders dismissively. His face stays hard.

"Twig, man, I'm sorry. I know you never get to play. I just had to get out of there."

"Why?"

Now it's my turn to shrug. What am I supposed to say? Some mall cop hurt my pride? But Twig is looking at me. Waiting for a real answer. "Sorry," I say again. "I just . . . freaked out a little."

Twig slips his hand into mine. "S'kay. I don't like *BurgerTime* anyway."

"I know. But still."

"Yeah."

We start walking toward the crappy busted-up asphalt that serves as the park's basketball court. Twig's still holding my hand. He's too old to do that and not get crap from the kids at the court and I'm ready to pull my hand away when he says something so quiet, I almost don't hear him. I ask him, "What?" But he shakes his head and keeps walking.

I pull him to a stop. "What'd you say?"

"It's not *BurgerTime*."

I replay the tape in my head of him standing at the arcade console. Big letters over his head, BURGERTIME, creepy hot dogs and pickles dancing across the screen. "What do you mean?"

"I'm not mad about *BurgerTime*. I just wish we wouldn't have missed dinner."

"Yeah." I nod. "Sorry, little dude. Least we had a doughnut."

He squinches up his nose and starts walking again. I agree: my stomach's already burned through that doughnut.

TreyAnn's crew is at the court. They call for us to join.

"Not today," I tell them. It's getting dark and I just want . . . what? To get back to Gran's trailer? Said no one ever. To get back to the Castle? I know Ruthie needs me, but right now I just want to feel halfway normal. "You know what? Okay."

Not two minutes in Twig does his granny pass again. Only this time he yells it: "Ollieeee—oop!" The ball sails into the air. Way into the air. It descends straight at my head. That throw is me getting thrown out of the mall, Chick dead in a hole, Ruthie crying in her sleep, Dad walking away,

Gran treating me worse than a fucking renter. I reach up and smack it to the ground. "God bless it, Twig!"

"Josh!" Twig shouts indignantly. "That was right to you!"

I don't really hear him though, because my own voice echoes in my head. *God bless it.* The phrase reverberates and changes. *God bless it, Joshua.*

I kick the fucking basketball as hard as I can. It flies right into the side of a trailer, denting the cheap-ass aluminum. Everyone scatters, leaving me and Twig to face the angry owner, but he must not be home.

"I'm sorry," Twig says in a tiny voice. "No more Ollie oops, okay, Joshie?"

I should tell him it wasn't his fault, that I don't give a damn about the Ollie oop, but my throat is so tight, it's all I can do to suck in a thin stream of oxygen. Just enough to breathe. Talking might tear my throat open and so I don't.

At the trailer Twig says he's sorry again. I don't want to leave with him thinking me kicking the ball was about the Ollie oop. I mean, it was, but not just about that. I swallow hard and tell him I had a bad day. "I shouldn't have gotten so mad about the game. It's just a game."

"You like to win," Twig says matter-of-factly, and that's true, but it's not the truth.

"I like my team to win. It frustrates me that you won't pass the ball the way I showed you. I think it would make you a better player." I don't say "good player" because both of us know Twig will never be good at basketball. But he could be better. "I just don't know what you're thinking when you throw it like that."

"I'm thinking we are a team. Me and you. I can't throw the ball the way you want with my noodle arms." He dangles his arms for effect. "But I can Ollie oop the heck out of that ball. It might work if you caught it."

CHAPTER
18

BEFORE I EVEN STEP FOOT IN THE STAIRWELL, I CAN HEAR Ruthie and Stan arguing. Their voices funnel down the shaft, reverberate off every surface. Watchman shakes his head when I pass, telling me to shut them two up before they bring every Tom, Dick, and Jimmy Dean crashing down on our quiet little Castle.

Ruthie catches sight of me on the stairs.

"He won't let me call the police," she says.

"I told her, calling the cops on Jimmy Dean is like trying to douse a fire with kerosene."

Relief washes over me. If they're bickering about calling the police on Jimmy Dean, that means Ruthie's let go of the idea that Stan is going around killing everyone.

"Calling the police means catching whoever killed Chick, whether it was Jimmy Dean or someone else." The way her eyes cut to Stan on the *someone else* part of that sentence makes my pulse race.

Stan tilts his head. "Someone else? Who else but Jimmy Dean is gonna do something like that?"

"Could have been an accident," I cut in before she can answer.

"An accident?" Ruthie shrieks, and I think of Watchman's warning to lower the noise level.

Even Stan's shaking his head. "I don't know what Chick was doing out there, but he wouldn't've gone scrapping alone. Maybe he hooked up with Wade and Jimmy Dean, planned to cash in without us—"

The whole time Stan's talking, Ruthie is shaking her head *no, no, no* until she finally just yells right over him. "We're supposed to believe that you just let Wade trot off to join Jimmy Dean? 'Nobody leaves my crew unless it's in a casket'—isn't that your motto? Wade isn't working with Jimmy Dean and you fucking know that. So where is he?"

Jesus, Ruthie. My hands fly up to my head, like they can keep everything from exploding out of my brain. Stan's nostrils flare and a vein bulges in the center of his forehead. "What kind of shit is this? Josh? You hearing this?"

"Yeah, uh, no. Look, she's distraught, okay? She heard some shit from this girl she knows and—" I turn to Ruthie, reaching out to try to calm her, but she steps back, leaving my hand just hanging there.

"I'm *distraught*? Hell yeah, I'm motherfucking distraught. The shit I heard is the truth, which is quite a change after all your fucking lies, Stan. And you know what I think? I think you warned Wade not to leave and when he didn't listen, you killed him. Chick too. You couldn't stand the thought of someone walking away—"

Stan holds up his hand to Ruthie, whose whole face is red with anger. "Crews change all the time, Ruthie. Wade and Chick are no different than a hundred other guys I worked with. They want to go, go! You gotta ask yourself why would I do anything like that? It would jeopardize everything we been working toward. I've been busting my balls trying to keep you kids safe. Safe. From shitheels like Jimmy Dean.

Why you gonna listen to some tweaker lot lizard over me? Why not just come ask me straight up?"

Ruthie is still shaking her head, but at least she doesn't look like she's about to go for his throat anymore. Stan runs his hands over his face. "Look, we all know Chick was smart. He wouldn't have been messing around out there alone. Either he was working with someone or they lured him out there. Things went bad and they shoved him into the hole. Ain't nothing we can do to take that back. So we gotta worry about us now. Got to be smart." He taps his temple. "Gotta make sure if they come for us, we're ready."

"So we should just keep trusting you, Stan? You brought us here! Told us you had this great plan, that we were all gonna live together. I believed you! Chick—" Her voice hitches, but she swallows and keeps going. "Chick believed you! And look where that got him. He's . . . he's . . ." She dissolves into tears.

I step between the two of them and wrap my arms around her. She sobs into my neck and all I can do is whisper "I know, I know" over and over. Eventually the sobbing slows and she lets me guide her to the blankets. I tell her about the shit with Gran. Just trying to get her mind off of Chick. It doesn't work. She listens for a while, then shifts the conversation back to him, telling me more about their life together.

I must have dozed off talking to her, because when Stan shakes me awake, Ruthie's sound asleep, her head in my lap.

"We gotta talk about Jimmy Dean," Stan says.

I ease Ruthie onto a bundle of blankets and follow Stan up to the sixth floor. His pacing makes me nervous, partly because he's so agitated, but mostly because the floor up here is so slick. Last thing we need is for him to slip over the edge. He ignores my suggestion that maybe he should come closer to the wall, and starts raving about going after Jimmy Dean.

"I know what you said, but is there any chance it could have been an accident? Maybe he hit his head or something."

"Yeah? Then where's the copper from that hole? Was it there, Josh? Oh, and I suppose that after Chick hit his head and got stuck hanging upside down in the wiring, he reached back up and pulled the cover on? Just for shits and giggles? Jimmy Dean wants in on the action. He done this."

My brain seizes on the image of our scrapping tools lying scattered on the ground around that hole. I hadn't been able to take care of them and Ruthie too. "Oh shit."

"Shit's right. If Jimmy's after the copper—"

I cut him off. "It's not Jimmy Dean I'm worried about. I left the tools. Ruthie freaked out and I had to carry her, and we just left everything."

Stan runs both hands through his hair. "We gotta get that taken care of now. Like, right now. Jimmy Dean'll see that stuff sitting out there and he'll be on it like shit on a shingle. He'll pull a crew together and they'll strip all the copper from here to Elkhart before we can—"

"Stan."

"—even get some guys to join our crew. Not to mention—"

"Stan!"

He stops and looks at me.

"A train passed us while we were working. If the engineer saw us . . ."

"Shit!"

"What I'm saying is, maybe the cops are already there. Wouldn't be all bad—they'd take care of Chick. Go after Jimmy Dean—"

Stan smacks me upside the head. Hard. He leans into my face. "And whose fingerprints are all over that place? Police show up down there, that's what they're gonna find. Our tools—guaranteed your prints are all over that shit. Tools, manhole cover. Ladder. You moved the body? Guess what, dumbass. Prints on that, too. Police gonna look one place and one place only. Right at you. Then they come looking for me. You fucked us both."

"I'll just . . ." My voice trails off as I remember the stain on my pant leg.

"Just what? Tell them you were doing a little illegal scrapping?"

"You said no one would care about us taking the copper. That it was obsolete!"

"Fact that no one needs it don't mean they want us making money off it. They'd rather let it rot down there than have someone like us be able to use it. Don't matter that we're not getting rich off it, just feeding ourselves. We can starve to death for all they care. We can die and they won't even notice. They won't give a shit about Chick—just finding out who's been messing with their shit. And what if Ruthie's right and Wade's dead too? If they can pin that and Chick's murder on you . . . Well, don't think they'll hesitate any more than they would scraping shit off the bottom of their shoe. That's what we are. Shit on the bottom of their shoe."

Chick is dead down in a hole. No matter how much I didn't like him, he doesn't deserve that. But Stan is right—our prints are all over everything. The blood on my pant leg is Chick's. My stomach lurches. I swallow hard to keep from puking. For once Stan's the calm one—no pacing, no hand-rolling, no tugging at his hair—and I'm a mess.

Stan puts his hand on my shoulder. "We can fix this."

"How?"

"We just gotta go clean things up. Get the tools, wipe down the rest."

"What about Ruthie? We just gonna leave her here?"

"This is for her. You don't wanna see that sweet girl in jail, do you? She's sleeping. She'll be fine."

I tell Stan I need a minute to grab something. That's true, but I really just need a fucking minute. This day has been like three weeks long.

I could only fit so many clothes in my backpack when I left Gran's, not that I had a lot to begin with, and I can't remember if I brought a change of pants. I rummage through my small pile of clothes, but there're only a few rather fragrant shirts mixed in with dirty socks and under-wear. I eye Ruthie and Chick's larger pile, but Chick was one scrawny-ass dude. The only thing that held his pants up were his hip bones. I search the pile and find a pair of sweatpants, but there's no way I'd be able to squeeze into them. I settle for the pair of shorts in my gym bag. I know I'm gonna freeze, but at least if we get caught moving the tools, I won't be wearing more evidence than what we went to clean up. I fish my wallet, the picture, and Dory out of my jeans, planning to stuff them in my gym bag, but instead they wind up in the pocket of my shorts. I grab one of Chick's old hoodies and yank it over my head, thankful for an extra layer between me and the cold.

It's so late that we don't have to worry about anybody seeing us as we slip out the back of the Castle and across the field. As we get close to the tracks, Stan waves me back. He jogs, hunched over, up the hill and peers down the tracks toward the Lafayette Bridge. I follow his gaze, but from my vantage point, I wouldn't know if a whole army was up there. It's so cold, my teeth are clacking louder than any train. Stan stands up straight, looking up and down the track before giving me what I assume is an all-clear sig-nal. The moonlight glints off jagged panes of glass in the buildings above us and I wonder for the first time if there are other guys holed up in those buildings. The Castle can't be the only abandoned building people have broken into and turned into a haven from the streets. But I don't see any signs of life as we pass below. Not that anyone would be moving around much this time of night.

The first hole is just as we left it—cover off, wide open. Stan doesn't even slow as we near it. He just walks right past it to the next one. The one where Chick is. Nothing has changed there, either. If the engineer spotted me and Ruthie, he either didn't care enough to call it in or whoever answered the call didn't care enough to do anything about it. The tools are splayed all over the place. Because I don't want to think about Chick down there in that hole, I start gathering them for something to do. I stack them up while Stan stares down the hole, rubbing his chin. Eventually he says, "Maybe we just leave him down there. No place else to bury him with the ground this hard."

I don't know what I thought we would do—roll him up in the tarp and carry him to a cemetery? Conveniently find an open grave and bury him without anyone noticing? But leaving Chick here never once entered my mind.

Stan snaps at me, clicking his fingers close enough to my face that I can feel them brush the skin of my cheek. "You gonna stand there or help me?" he asks. Without waiting for an answer, he disappears down the ladder. When I don't follow, he yells up at me to get my head outta my ass and get in gear.

Despite the circle of light above us, it's dark in the hole. Neither of us thought to bring a flashlight. I can make out Chick leaning in the corner where we put him, Ruthie's coat tucked up around his shoulders. Stan shoves a rag in my hand, tells me to wipe everything down, get all our prints off any surface. I turn away from Chick and wipe the cables and pipes and walls, even though I'm pretty sure we didn't touch any of them. When I turn back around, Stan's just standing there watching me, his hands on his hips.

It reminds me of the way Coach looks when I'm slow at a new drill, or the way Gran looks at me when . . . well, when I breathe. "What?"

Stan just shakes his head and looks at me like I'm a frickin' idiot. I feel a rush in my chest that makes me want to knock that look off his face. Instead I swallow hard and ask again. "What? Why are you looking at me like that?"

"Because smart as you are, you're a fucking idiot."

My hands are on him before I can help it, flying out to shove him hard in the chest. He stumbles backward but doesn't fall. Everything in his face changes, hardens, and I have just enough time to think I probably shouldn't have pissed him off before he comes for me. Two steps and he's got a fistful of my shirt, lifts me off my feet and slams me back against the concrete wall so hard, black spots dance at the edges of my vision. His teeth are bared inches from me. Spittle flecks my face as he growls. Literally growls. Like a dog. Or a wolf.

Stan taught me a few defensive maneuvers back when I was a kid, but that crazy-train look in his eye right now tells me there is no way I'm getting out of here unless he lets me. I force my eyes down and—this is the hard part given the pounding in my head—I laugh. Like we're just playing around. "Man, you got me good," I tell him. "You still got it, old man." I shake my head and laugh again, trying to keep panic from pushing my laughter into hysterics.

Stan tilts his head, looks me hard in the eye. Then, like someone flipped a switch, his face relaxes and he laughs too. He releases me and claps me on the shoulder. "You're a dumbass, but Old Stan'll take care of you." He gestures toward Chick. "Didn't occur to either of you two that leaving Ruthie's coat would lead the cops right to you?"

"Wasn't thinking." Getting Ruthie back to the Castle had been the only thing on my mind.

"That's for sure." Stan bends down and snatches the coat off Chick. Tosses it at me. He nods at the ladder. "You head up, I'll wipe the ladder as I follow you out."

"We really gonna leave him here?"

"Got any better ideas?"

I think again about calling the police, but as good as we wiped this place, there's still a chance the police would find my prints or Ruthie's.

CHAPTER
19

I GET TO SCHOOL EARLY THE NEXT DAY, HEAD STRAIGHT for the locker room before Mr. Jansen can show up to prep for his gym classes. Most of the lockers are empty or locked, but there are a few lockers with clothes in them. Sweats, T-shirts, a jockstrap so yellow and old, I nearly puke. Finally find a pair of jeans that's only one size too big for me under a bench in the back. I go back to one of the unlocked lockers and grab a towel and some bodywash. My own pants are stained and so long without a wash that they practically walk by themselves, so I step into the shower fully clothed and lather up. The stain doesn't want to come out at first, but I strip and squirt some bodywash right on it, then scrub it against the showerhead until it's mostly gone.

I'd forgotten how good a hot shower could feel. Bathing isn't exactly a top priority with Stan and Ruthie and even if it were, the only running water at the Castle is the constant stream of melting ice through a hole in the ceiling that's the size of a Buick. I stay in the shower and let the hot water scald off layers of me. I can almost see the versions of myself swirling around the drain. Josh, the kid who climbs down manholes scrounging for scrap metal. Josh, who's secretly glad Chick won't be coming back because Chick's girlfriend smells like strawberries and maybe, just maybe, might be the real answer to life, the universe, and everything. Josh, the guy who funds his grandma's pot addiction by paying rent. Josh, whose mom died in a house fire because he faked being sick to get out of soccer tryouts and whose dad hates him for that and a million other reasons Josh will never know. Those Joshes drip down onto the tile and seep through the tiny holes in the drain, down deep into the septic system that flows beneath a school where everyone thinks Josh is a straight-A student and shooting guard who dates cheerleaders and is headed to college on a basketball scholarship. I stay under the water until I almost feel like I could be that Josh.

I wring the water from my old clothes, roll them up in a towel, and stuff them in my gym bag, planning to hang-dry them at the Castle. I scrounge a clean pair of undies and a T-shirt from my gym bag and slip on the found pair of jeans. I can't help sighing like one of those people in a fabric softener commercial. These pants are not only clean, they're a million times more comfortable than any jeans I've ever worn. Soft and flexible. A definite upgrade from Wranglers. The pockets are not as deep, though. My wallet doesn't fit in the front pocket, so I tuck it in the back. The picture and Dory, though, they're still riding up front.

The pleasure of the shower and a new pair of pants is quickly wiped away by the look on Miss Wismer's face as she hands back my test in first period, a big *SEE ME TO DISCUSS* scrawled across the top in her perfect purple penmanship. The last thing I want to do this morning is discuss—the physics test or anything—so I skate out the door at the end of class without meeting her eye.

Somehow I make it to lunch without falling asleep in class. I grab a tray and slide it along, nodding as the cafeteria workers hold out ladles of noodles, meat sauce, green beans. The guys are at our regular table, but Matt spots me approaching and coughs loudly, killing the conversation.

Two ways I could play this. Plop my tray down, start eating like nothing's wrong, or ask them what the fuck they were just saying that they can't say to my face. Too tired to play nice, I pick the latter.

Nick's hands are steepled, pointer fingers pressed to his forehead. His foot taps against the table leg in a quickstep that makes the trays vibrate. Matt scooches over to make room for me, but I don't sit. Instead I repeat the question.

"We're just worried about you," Matt says. "You let Nick down on the test. You missed the game, made Coach miss the game—"

"Jansen had to sub in as coach," Mason interjects. "That lasted about five minutes before he went all Bobby Knight. Ejected. We forfeited the game. Against *Elkhart*. So that means—"

I don't need Mason to tell me what a forfeit against Elkhart means. I want to tell them—well, Matt and Nick, anyway—about what happened with Twig, that Coach stepped up for me in a way my own grandma, my own dad won't. But telling them that would lead to questions about my family that I don't want to answer, especially in front of Mason. I'm also too tired to blow up, so I don't even raise my voice when I tell them, "It's not my fault Jansen can't keep his temper. Not my fault that we're gonna have to show up hard in the prelims to get to state. Not my fault that I've been carrying Nick on every fucking test since freshman year. But yeah, if it's easier to blame me than to step the fuck up as a team, that's fine. Enjoy your lunch."

Matt calls after me, but he's just another voice in the chorus of people who can go fuck themselves.

I can't stand the thought of going to APUSH and hearing Mop's recap of everyone's debate-slash-exam, which will probably conclude with his disappointment in a few specific people he would not name but would definitely give hard eye contact to. And practice? No way do I want to give the guys another opportunity to rub my face in how I keep letting the team down. So I grab my backpack and walk out the side door between the gym and the library. One nice thing about not having a cell phone—a real one—is that no one can blow it up when you take off.

Ruthie is still curled up in the blankets when I get back. I know better than to try to cheer her up. You can't just cheer up someone who has lost someone they love. I learned that from all the teachers and school counselors who tried to help me after Mom died. And the way we found Chick was just plain messed up. Since I can't get the image of him out of my head, I can only imagine how it's impacting Ruthie. But just letting her give in to despair also seems wrong. The whole way back to the Castle, I'd been thinking about ways to lure her out of bed, to get her up and moving, with something else to focus on.

After I lay my wet clothes out to dry, I sit down next to her and pat her arm gently. She stirs and makes a soft sound. "Hey," I say.

"Hey."

I tell her about what happened with Twig. Him telling everyone that Santa's dead, the school calling me. I start slow and quiet, stretching it out like a story, building it until she gradually sits up, hanging on the details. "That poor little guy," she says when I get to the part about shoving me in the snow. "His poor heart."

"Yeah," I agree. "The worst part is he thinks Santa doesn't exist."

Ruthie gives me the side-eye. "Really? That's the worst part? Not that he thought your dad was dead?"

The worst part was actually when Twig said I might as well be dead, but I don't tell her that. "I don't think he thought Dad was really dead. I just . . ." My voice catches and Ruthie takes my hand. "It just makes me so sad that he's given up on all the magic in the world already. I want to give some of it back to him, but I need some help. We used to live in a junkyard. It's still there. Maybe we could find my old bike and fix it up for Twig for Christmas. Show him the whole world doesn't completely suck."

"Okay, Josh," Ruthie says. "We can do that."

Ruthie moves slowly, like she's aged a million years, but she gets her shoes on. I reach for her coat, but hesitate. The last time Ruthie saw her coat she was tucking it around Chick's body. Even if it doesn't have blood on it like my pants, I don't want to trigger her. But Ruthie reaches past me and picks up the coat. She holds it to her face, eyes closed, breathing in whatever of Chick lingers in the fabric. My stomach clenches, thinking about potential dead people odor, but it must be good smells, like his cologne or something. She gives a little nod and then opens her eyes and puts on the coat. Luckily, there's no blood anywhere I can see.

We get off the bus in front of the junkyard and even though it was my idea to come here and the whole way over I've been chatting up happy memories about growing up in a junk-yard, the sight of the green corrugated metal hits me like an elbow to the gut. The woods have all but claimed the junk-yard; vines and weeds cling to the fence, camouflaging the gate, obscuring the Pick a'Part sign with its welcome and hours and ENTER AT YOUR OWN RISK.

"Josh?" Ruthie tugs my hand, but my knees and hips and feet have seized up like the hinges on a rusted-shut door. The only muscle that I can get to move is the one in my neck and it's shaking my head in a small repeated no. Ruthie touches the side of my face with her hand and stills my head, draws my gaze away from that green fence and into the depths of her eyes. "Josh? You okay?"

I feel my head switch directions, bobbing up and down instead of side to side, but I'm not okay. Ruthie doesn't ask any more questions, and for that I am grateful. It's not like I've really thought this through. In fact, I'm just about to tell her maybe this isn't such a great idea, maybe we should just turn around, when Ruthie drops my hand and goes to the gate. She brushes aside some vines that look like they could be poison ivy if they weren't so big, to expose a lami-nated sign from the city: PROPERTY CONDEMNED. KEEP OUT. A chain with links thick as Polish sausages secures the gate. She lifts the lock and gives it a hard yank, but the only thing that comes free are the flakes of rust that now coat her palm. She brushes them off on her pants, leaving a burnt-sienna smudge that looks more like an autumn leaf than a handprint. I watch her walk the fence, apparently hoping for a gap like the one in the fence behind the Castle. There are no gaps in this fence. The chain link ends where a stone wall begins—the metal of the fence cemented into stone. Ruthie looks up, like she's considering climbing over, but an old tattered shirt smeared with red paint waves like a warning flag in the razor wire at the top and makes it clear that won't be happening. I remember Dad and Stan putting that shirt up there, laughing about how it'd keep out them damn Howe boys from up the way. Mom hated it, though, saying it made our place look like something out of a Stephen King movie.

I think about letting Ruthie come to the realization that there is no way in without a key, but next thing I know, she's climbed three rungs up the fence and is feeling around the top of the stone wall where gnarly vines hang brown and dead from a stone pot. That pot had been Mom's rebuttal to the bloody shirt. She'd planted red geraniums and purple petunias and tended them each afternoon after she got back from the diner. Now Ruthie rummages under the dried-out vines and drops down from the fence triumphantly, holding the key I'd hoped she wouldn't find. Maybe putting keys under flowerpots isn't the best security system.

She leaves the lock askew on the chain as she pushes the gate open. "You coming?" she asks.

I want to say no. But I know if I say that, Ruthie will ask harder questions, ones I don't have words to answer. So I say, "Hold on a sec." It's silly and superstitious, but leaving a lock hanging there seems to beg for some kid to come along and lock that gate behind us. I pull the lock out of the chain and toss it with the key still in it into the weeds just inside the fence.

Ruthie flings her arm out, gesturing for me to lead the way. It's been years since the fire and I've never been back, but a map of this place is burned into my heart the same way we all remember where we grew up. I'm used to the way the piles of junk loom over us like walls and the way the paths cross and recross. I take first one turn then another, headed toward Dad's old workshop. I don't realize Ruthie has stopped until I hear her let out a slow whistle. I turn back to see her standing in the T-junction of the path to the old house and the one to the sandpit Twig used to love.

"Man, this place is like a labyrinth."

"Maze," I say under my breath. "Stay close." I start down the path again. Used to drive Dad crazy when Mom would tease him and Stan about their labyrinth. "Jeezus, Rosie, anyone can build a labyrinth!" he'd grumble, and then rant about how labyrinths are easy because you just gotta plan one path through and the rest is all dead ends. "The real skill is making multiple valid pathways hidden among all those dead ends."

"Huh?"

I turn back to see Ruthie still standing in the same spot.

"You gotta stay right with me. It actually is a maze."

"Whoa, no way!" Ruthie laughs. "A fucking maze! Got a minotaur in there?"

"Just a few harmless monitors," I tell her, and when she looks puzzled, I point halfway up the wall behind her where several computers stare back through their busted-out screens.

We're far enough into the yard that a faint hint of burnt rubber drifts on the winter breeze. I instinctively veer off to the left, away from its source. Ruthie skips to catch up and slips her hand into mine. There's very little snow on the ground but enough that I can see paw prints here and there—raccoons, squirrels, maybe a coyote or three. No footprints. Not that that means anything. It's far enough out of town that maybe no one has thought to come here for scrap metal, but it's weird that Stan hasn't. Maybe the memories are just as hard for him. After all, he was here the day of the fire. It's because of him that me and Twig made it out alive and Mom . . . made it out.

We turn another corner and come to a part of the yard where the wall's caved in and the path is blocked. It's the section Stan affectionately nicknamed Millionaire Row. Ruthie lifts a tarp and silver glints in the early afternoon sun. She trails her hand over the plates and silverware cascading down from a huge pile of dinnerware.

"Whew-ee," she says quietly. "Is this stuff real?"

"Nope. Anything worth anything is long gone."

She picks up a platter as long as her arm and fingers its intricate patterning of grape leaves. "Sure coulda fooled me."

"Me too, but not Stan. He could separate cash from trash with a glance. 'All that glitters ain't,' he used to say."

"Still says," Ruthie corrects.

"Still says," I agree. It's funny how being in the junkyard has changed everything in my head to past tense, like after we left here, time just stopped and all the memories and the people in them clung stagnant and stale like leftover smoke on charred curtains.

"Might not be real, but this shit's still worth something. We should come back here with a wagon."

"And do what? Have a garage sale? I can see us now, out in front of the Castle having ourselves a big ole garage sale." I say it with a country twang that earns a grin from Ruthie.

Ruthie tosses the platter back onto the heap. The clatter is immediately answered by a deep rumbling growl from the other side of the pile. Ruthie's eyes grow wide and she mouths the word *Wolf?*

I shake my head. Last time I checked, wolves were not a thing in northern Indiana. Coyotes, however . . . I reach for her hand and lead her back the way we came. Just as we get back to the intersection that leads off to Dad's workshop, a huge black dog steps into our path, legs wide apart, hackles raised. A glob of foamy drool drips from bared teeth.

"Axl?"

The sight of him is so unexpected and overlays so perfectly with the past that for a second I'm not even sure I actually see a dog. The dog growls again and despite its threatening stance, it is definitely Axl. Which means what? Dad is here? Ruthie's hand flutters against my arm and she whispers a faint "Run" under her breath. I whisper back, "Don't."

"Hey, Axl. Hey, boy." I bend to one knee and whistle, my arms out wide. The dog tilts its head to one side, all *You talking to me?* and I have just enough time to second-guess the dog's identity and the wisdom of putting my face in the path of all those teeth before the dog is on me. Ruthie is screaming and I know I should let her know it's okay, but Axl has me pinned, swiping my face and neck with his thick paintbrush of a tongue.

A sharp two-toned whistle cuts the air. Axl's tongue gives me one last swipe and then he's off and loping toward a figure at the junction of the paths. Ruthie kneels beside me, running her hands over my face and neck like she can't believe I have a face and neck, but I can't take my eyes off the man resting his hand on Axl's head, same as he did every day the bus dropped me off at the junkyard gate.

I stumble to my feet.

Dad says, "Go on home."

"But—"

"You need to get on home." He turns away and walks up the path toward his workshop. Axl hesitates, then turns to follow him.

I take half a step, stop, take another step, stop again. Questions dart through my mind, wasps with razor-sharp stingers.

Ruthie puts her hand on my arm. "You just gonna let him go?"

Dad's about to the bend in the path when Axl glances back at me and I manage to breathe out a harsh "Wait!" It's not loud enough for anyone but Ruthie to hear. I clear my throat and force the word out louder. This time Dad stops, but he doesn't turn around. Axl gives a small whine.

"Dad . . ." I walk toward him. "I just . . . we need to talk, okay?"

He shrugs but doesn't tell me no. When he starts walking again, I look at Ruthie.

"Don't worry about me," she says. "I'll make myself at home. Maybe do a little shopping."

I worry about Ruthie getting lost in the junkyard, but if anyone can find their way around, she probably can. I jog to catch up to Dad. Axl drops back to my side and my hand drifts down to rest on the solid muscle of his back. The door of Dad's workshop is so overgrown with weeds and ivy, it looks like Sleeping Beauty's castle after the hundred years of sleep. Dad ducks through it all. The inside of his workshop hasn't changed. An old-timey pinup calendar over the workbench, tools neat on their pegs, chains sleek and oiled hang from the ceiling. Clearly, he's been coming here often.

Axl trots over to the workbench and flops down on a tattered old pillow. Dad picks up a wrench and cranks on a motorbike he's got up on a stand. I watch, hands in my pockets, not sure how to start the conversation I'd been waiting to have or even what I'd hoped to get out of it. As I watch him loosen and remove the handlebars, I shuffle questions in my head, rewording, reordering, rejecting. Finally I say, "Dwayne said you were in the ER. That you got stabbed."

Dad sucks his teeth. "Dwayne needs to mind his own business."

"Are you okay? What happened?"

He pats his torso up and down with open palms. "You see me. I look hurt? Got into a pissing match with some asshole. He cut me, but I'm fine."

"Jimmy Dean?"

Dad turns to me, his forehead wrinkled. "How do you know about Jimmy Dean?"

"Stan said—"

"Stan?" Dad tosses the wrench into a drawer, where it clatters against a bunch of other tools, startling Axl. "I told him to stay away from you kids."

"What? Why? What's going on, Dad?"

He reaches for a can of WD-40. "Josh, you gotta go on home and let me handle this."

"What home? Gran's? She hates us. We need you to come home so—"

"Damn it, Josh. Your gran is a hard woman, but she's not evil. She just wants money. I left you that cash so you could take care of everything. Give her the money and she'll quit—"

"You didn't even leave me enough for a month! Gran kicked me out! She called DCS. Someone came to the house, Dad! What if she sends Twig away?"

"She ain't gonna do that. You just gotta have Twig stop eating so much. I restocked the snacks in the closet before I left. Make him eat that. Get yourself a job."

"Get a job? How am I supposed to do that when Stan's making me work off the money you stole?"

"What the—I didn't steal any fucking money."

"Stan said you did. Thousand bucks."

Dad sets the can down on the counter and walks over to the shed's little window. He braces his hands on the top of the window frame and leans his forehead to the glass. Axl whines and goes over to him. After a minute, Dad pats Axl on the head. He comes back over to the bench and pulls out a stool, motions for me to sit on the other one.

"I didn't tell you none of this because I want you to steer clear of it. That was my one condition. I do this, you boys ain't nowhere near it." I start to ask him what he agreed to do, but he holds up a hand and keeps talking. "I'm gonna tell you some things and I want you to listen carefully. One, Jimmy Dean stabbed me over nothing. I'm fine, but he's dangerous. You stay away from him. Two, I don't know what money Stan is talking about, but if he's telling people I took it, it's for a good reason. Bit of subterfuge to throw people off the scent or something. But you're my boy and you deserve to know I did not steal anything. That money I left you, I earned it free and clear. It's all I got to my name. Three, I owe this to Stan. He tried to help me with something a long time ago and when it went sideways, he took the heat. Didn't get nothing for it. Now he's asking for a favor and needs my help."

"What's the favor? Let me help."

"Are you not hearing me? This job is . . . I can't do this thing if it puts you boys at risk. I need to know you're safe. If this job goes bad, there's gonna be fallout and I cannot have it raining down on you."

"Then you gotta walk away from that job, Dad. If it's that dangerous, you should just tell Stan no."

Dad squeezes his mouth with his hand, shaking his head. "I don't have a choice. I do this or he's gonna do it without me."

"So let him!"

"You don't understand! Last time I tried to back out of a job with Stan, someone died!"

"Wait—Stan killed someone?"

"No! No, not Stan. I—"

"You? You killed someone?"

"No! Jesus, Josh, just shut up and listen, will you, for once in your goddamn life? Nobody was supposed to get hurt, but they did because I didn't show up to do what I was supposed to do. That death is on me. Stan made it so I walked away clean. Now Stan wants what he's owed. I do this thing or . . ."

"Or what?"

Dad grinds the heels of his palms into his eyes. "There ain't no 'or.' I gotta follow this through. You boys won't be with Gran much longer. Just stay put for now. We'll get you out of there when the time is right."

CHAPTER
20

I READ SOMEWHERE THAT WHEN WE DON'T KNOW WHERE
to go, we go home. That's sappy as hell, but it's really the
only explanation for how my feet lead me back through the
maze and down the other path, where I wind up standing
under that sycamore tree. My old tire swing leans against
the trunk, its rope frayed and forgotten. Axl gives it a sniff
and then trots past it toward the cement steps. I call him
back. He comes, giving me a woeful look.

"I know," I tell him. "I just need a minute."

But it is going to take more than a minute for me to wrap
my head around all this shit with Dad and Stan. Instead I try
to shove it aside, looking at what's left of the life we had with
Mom before the fire. Axl's old doghouse is still there, weath-
ered and worn. There's no sign of his big old bowl. Maybe
Dad took it over to the shop. Just behind the doghouse, a bit
of metal glints from a bramble of winter-dried bushes. Axl
follows me over to it, trampling down the weeds. The metal
is the kickstand of my old bike. God, how I had loved that
bike. It had come in one day on a pile of junk in the back of a
pickup. Dad and Stan had tossed it into the heap with everything else, but I dragged it out, wiped off the dirt and grime.

It didn't matter that the bike was pink—nothing a little silver spray paint wouldn't fix. "Some junk really is junk," Dad warned me. He caved in, though, helping me replace the bent and broken spokes and mount a seat we salvaged from another bike. Dad told me how he used to put baseball cards on the fork and I'd thought that was cool, so I borrowed some of Twig's Pokémon cards and did the same. Twig had been too little for me to ride him double, but oh, how he'd loved to spin the wheel and listen to the *ticka-ticka-tick* of the spokes hitting the cards. I wonder if he remembers that. I pull the bike from the weeds. The cold metal stings my fingers. The rain and snow has done a number on the bike, too—the front tire is so flat, the tube bleeds out. Chunks are missing from the foam under the seat and what's left is stiff and reeks of cat pee or something worse. Charizard and Mewtwo are gone; the only evidence of their existence is a bit of moldy cardboard clinging to tattered tape. I pull at the tape, ball it up, and flick it into the weeds. I lean the bike against the sycamore and turn to face the house.

The smell has been there, tickling my memories. I'd ignored it while I fiddled with the bike; now the tang of twisted metal and blackened wood assaults me.

I swallow hard and walk over to the cement steps. I chip off the caked-on layer of dead leaves and dirt-crusted snow from the bottom step with the toe of my shoe, exposing four handprints. I lay my hand over each one—baby Twig's, smaller than my finger; nine-year-old mine, barely filling my palm. Phantom heat warms my hand as I place it over Mom's print. Lastly I fill the indent of Dad's handprint with my own.

Axl stands next to me on the step, looking up at the house and whining. It's stupid, but the longer I avoid looking at the house, the longer I can pretend that the horrible burned smell is coming from the dump. The light is stretching long across the yard now though, and Ruthie, even if she is in shopper's paradise, will be half frozen. My hand moves from the cold concrete to the thick matted fur at Axl's neck and I turn to look up at the remnants of my childhood home.

The door is closed, its green paint chipped and peeling, the three descending windows, which had always reminded me of the arched windows in a castle's keep, nothing more than jagged shards. The doorknob turns easily in my hand and the door swings open. So weird the way the fire devoured some things and left others—this door, old, but untouched by fire on one side, blackened and charred on the other, the wall around it scrawled black by flame. I'm not sure why I bothered to open the door, to enter through it. The huge picture window that Mom loved so much would have made an easy entryway as well. All the glass is gone, the lacy red curtains, the dangly spider plants in their macramé hangers, the paper snowflakes Twig and I draped across the glass, all gone. Mom loved the way the late-afternoon sun streamed through that window—she used to catch her breath and make us study how the flowers in the sofa cover blossomed from blues to purples, the yellow yarn in the carpet melted like golden threads, the spider plants grew long legs and danced on shadows across the floor as midday faded to twilight. The sun streams in now, shifting light gray to dark, gray to black, black to blackest black. Axl leaves paw prints in the ash, sniffing the gray hulk that used to be Mom's chair and the hall where Twig and I raced Hot Wheels. I wonder if Axl remembers the smells of our family in this place or if the fire has decimated even that.

I almost smell gingerbread and greasy egg sandwiches, fallen pine needles tracked across the floor as we dragged in a tree Dad cut from out near the fence, Mom's bitter coffee and Stan's syrupy egg scrambles on Saturday mornings.

Twig, talcum-coated, fresh from his bath, oil and cigarette smoke clinging to Dad's overalls the way flour and cinnamon clung to Mom. The acidic rust of melted metal floods my nostrils, drowning out those memories.

I cough and sputter, reach out to the wall to stabilize myself, but the room tilts and all I can see is black smoke rolling across my bedroom ceiling, filling my room like thunderclouds. Strips of paint peel from the walls and slide to the floor. The shelf near the door splits with a crack and my River City Raiders trophy tumbles to the floor and shatters, the tiny orange basketball dribbling under the bed. Through the blackness I hear Axl barking and Twig's hysterical wails. I roll off my bed, but the thick smoke presses its fingers into my nostrils and claws at my eyes. I stumble toward the door and shriek as its handle singes the flesh on my palm. The door shatters in front of me and I fall back only to be grasped by hands I cannot see in the thick smoke. And then I'm blinking against the brilliance of the sun and a blue, blue sky. I'm drowning again, strangling on fresh air, like my body has forgotten how to breathe, but the air is forcing itself into me. Stan's face blots out the sun. "Twig!" I scream, but the insides of my throat are scraped raw. The word lurches out, a jagged shard that is instantly snatched away by the blare of an approaching siren. Axl is barking and barking and Stan shakes my arm, tugging at me and—

"Josh? What the fuck?" Ruthie squeezes my arm, hard. "I've been looking all over for you." Her grip on my arm softens and the crease between her eyebrows disappears. "Oh man. Your lips are blue as fuck."

She puts her mouth on mine. I want my lips to feel hers, warm and wet. I want to kiss her back, put my hands in the tangle of her black hair, pull her to me. But instead a sob wells up in my throat and Ruthie stops kissing me and wraps her arms around the shaking, weeping mess of me. My knees buckle and we collapse onto the porch, but she doesn't let go. She pulls me tighter and I roll into a ball, my head in her lap, and she strokes my hair, whispering "Shhhhhh" while my tears soak into her jeans.

When I finally come up for air, Ruthie does not ask any of the usual questions, like "What's wrong?" or "Are you okay?" She doesn't pat my back awkwardly or avoid eye contact. Instead she jumps to her feet and announces that if I'm done bawling, she's freezing her fucking tits off, which makes me laugh so hard, I snort, and then she's laughing too and just like that we're back to normal.

She heads up the drive toward the gate.

"Hey, hold up a sec," I call. I jog over to the sycamore and grab the bike. It's the reason we came out here in the first place. Ruthie's mouth twists at the tangled mess of rubber and steel, but she doesn't say anything as I lift it and put the crossbar on my shoulder. She takes my hand and Axl trots along behind us, not toward the gate but back toward Dad's workshop.

Dad is still working on the motorbike, prying at the pedals. He doesn't look up when we walk in. I lean my old bike against the wall under the window. "Don't touch this," I tell him. "It's mine and I'm coming back for it."

Axl trots with us to the gate. I'm tempted to take him with us. But Transpo doesn't allow dogs and it's a hell of a walk to Gran's. Plus, he seems happy here, a guard dog again with a real purpose, not shut up in the pen behind the trailer.

I bend down and take his big head in my hands, pressing my forehead against his. "You gotta stay here," I tell him. "You got a job to do, okay? Keep Dad safe."

He sits and watches as I dig the lock out of the weeds and secure the gate. Ruthie puts the key back under the flowerpot. We stand by the road, waiting for the bus to come by. It's so freaking cold, we bounce up and down to stay warm. I can't remember the schedule and never would have caught it this late when I lived here as a kid anyway. Just when I'm about to suggest we start walking, the bus rounds the curve at the end of the lane. It lurches to a halt in front of us. I look for Axl, but he's already gone back to Dad.

CHAPTER

21

O N THE WAY BACK TO THE CASTLE, I TELL RUTHIE EVERY-thing Dad said. She clicks her tongue and rolls her eyes.

"What? You don't believe him?"

"About someone dying? Oh, absolutely. About it being an accident? Him not taking the money?" She shrugs. "What's he gonna say?"

"But he's living in a workshop in the junkyard, so if he did take it, where is it? And murder? No way. My dad's a good guy."

"A good guy who took off on you and your little brother."

"Yeah. And that makes him a shit dad, but murder is a whole other thing. There is no way my dad and Stan killed someone."

Ruthie bites her bottom lip and stares out the window.

"Say it."

She drops her head, picks at a bit of dirt under her fingernail.

"Come on, it's obvious you don't agree."

"He's your dad, Josh. Maybe you don't see him clearly, you know?"

"So you worked with him on some things, right? He ever do anything to hurt anybody?"

She shakes her head. "No, but he never once said no to anything Stan told us to do. And Stan had us doing some pretty shady shit."

When I press her, she tells me how they ripped catalytic converters out of cars in broad daylight, broke into houses and gradually gutted them while the owners were on vacation. "Don't get me wrong," she says, "I'm not a saint. I was right there with them. But Stan's different lately. He's out of control. And your dad? I think he'd follow that man to hell and back."

It's too much to think about, so I close my eyes and lean against the cool glass of the bus window. Ruthie shakes my arm when it's time to get off, tells me she needs to make a stop. I trail along, my thoughts swirling so much that I don't really care where we're going. We're walking through tent city under the bridge on Michigan Street—the one place where the cops and the homeless seem to have called a truce—when Ruthie abruptly starts climbing up the embankment. I know right away where she's headed: the tracks are up there and so is Chick. I scramble after her, calling her name quietly so that no one gets curious enough to stick their head out of one of the tents. She doesn't stop until she's up on the tracks.

I tell her it's not safe for us to be out here like this, but she says all she wants is to make sure Chick is okay. That no one has messed with the manhole. I can't exactly say no to that, so we walk up the tracks to Chick's spot. There's no sign that anyone's been up here since me and Stan, but that's not good enough for Ruthie. "We gotta check on him," she says. She starts scraping the snow away from the edges of the manhole with her bare hands.

"Ruthie, we can't open that. We don't have the tools with us."

It's like she can't hear me, or doesn't want to. She just keeps digging at the snow and flagstones, turning the snow red as they scrape her skin raw. I kneel in front of her, but she shoves me away and keeps at it until I catch her frozen hands and pull them to my chest. She struggles hard, trying to twist away, but I hold on, begging, "Ruthie, stop. Please, just stop," until she relaxes into me, crying. I wrap my arms around her, holding her tight.

"Why aren't we helping him?" she asks. "We can't just leave him here."

"I know. We'll get him out, okay? Just not tonight."

"You promise? You won't let Stan just leave him here?"

"Promise. We'll get him out. But we have to have a place to take him. Okay? And we'll need the tools."

She pulls back to study my face. "I promise," I tell her again. She swipes at her tears with a coat sleeve and lets me lead her away from Chick.

Stan's approaching the Castle from the opposite direction as we walk up. He claps his hands and calls out, "There's my crew!"

Ruthie eyes him suspiciously. "Well, aren't you in a great mood. What's up?"

"Nothing, nothing. I just thought maybe we should get some pizza tonight. Been a hard few days. Need something to take our minds off Chick and Jimmy Dean and—"

Something shifts in the darkness at the corner of the building. "Yeah? I been on your mind a lot lately?"

Stan whips around. A match strikes, partially illumin-ating a man's face. A thin silver scar arcs from his brow to his chin, bracketing the left side of his face like an unfinished parenthesis.

"You trash-talking me to the kiddos now? Blaming me for your shit?" the man says calmly, quietly. He brings the match to the tip of a cigarette clenched in his teeth and sucks in.

There's a click and a glint of steel in Ruthie's hand and she's hurling herself toward Jimmy Dean, yelling, "You motherfucking murderer!" Stan and I scramble to catch her, but a hand reaches out of the darkness as she nears Jimmy Dean, knocking the knife to the ground and spinning Ruthie around, wrenching her arm up behind her back.

"Feisty little woman you got here," the second man says. He's short with arms as thick as pythons.

"Let her go," I say.

My whole body is rigid, ready to rip his face off, but Stan, in a voice smooth as silk, says, "Hey there, Jimmy Dean." As if we are just a couple guys meeting for a game of pickup.

"Stan, Stan, Stan," Jimmy Dean says. "You've accused me of a lot of things over the years, but murder?" He holds his hand to his chest. "Me? That's a low blow and pretty funny considering your track record for mysteriously misplacing your people. Who is it this time? Let me guess . . . Chick?"

"Stan." I want to tell him we can take these punks, but Stan's hand is on my arm.

"Boys," he says, nodding at the darkness around us. Now I can see why Stan didn't beat the shit out of Jimmy Dean right away. We're surrounded.

Stan's hands hang limp at his sides. I've seen him do this before, trying to take the tension down several notches. Sometimes it works. He keeps his shoulders bunched up around his ears like a boxer who just stepped into the ring with Ali, in case it doesn't. He can't quite keep himself from rocking, just a little on the balls of his feet. He turns back to Jimmy Dean. "Call your dog off her."

Jimmy Dean ignores the command, his eyes shifting to me, sizing me up. "So this is Tye's boy, huh?"

"Nobody you need to know." Stan's hands flutter against his pant legs and then still. I'm glad I'm not counting on him in a poker match. "You can just clear on out now. Ain't nothing for you here."

Jimmy's teeth flash. He flicks the cigarette onto the ground at Stan's feet. "Yeah? All that scrap you been cashing in . . . must come from somewhere. Maybe you need some help seeing as how all your crew keeps disappearing?"

Ruthie struggles against the dude holding her, but Stan goes still. The hairs on my neck tingle.

"What? You think nobody knows about those little errands you boys been running? Bright lights, big city. Somebody always watching. Whatcha say, Stan? You need an extra hand?"

"You giving out free jerkoffs, Jimmy Dean?"

Slowly, Jimmy Dean walks right up to Stan. I'm sure he's going to kill him and probably me and Ruthie, too, but he shakes his head and laughs. "Those balls of steel gonna get you hurt one day."

"But not today," Stan says.

"Not today," Jimmy Dean agrees. He jerks his head at the guy holding Ruthie and the guy releases her with a shove that sends her staggering toward me. I go to catch her, but she gets her feet under her quick and turns back, ready for a fight.

Jimmy Dean pats Stan on the shoulder and saunters off down the sidewalk, his posse following.

Stan storms up the stairs past Watchman without the usual greeting. Ruthie and I race after him.

He yanks a box over to the blankets and sits on it. "Circle up," he tells us, pointing at another box. I drag it over and sit, but Ruthie sits on the pallet, twisting the blankets in her lap.

"What the fuck was that, Stan?" Ruthie asks. "How did he find us?"

Stan's rocking on that box, elbows on knees, hands rolling. "Just give me a second to think this through."

"But he was in our building! He knows where we live! What if—"

"Give me a goddamn minute to think!"

She looks like she wants to tell him what he can do with that minute, but her mouth snaps shut.

Stan smacks his hands on his legs and smooths them up and down. "Okay. I been telling you guys Jimmy's not someone to mess with. You believe me now?"

I nod. We both look at Ruthie. She hesitates then nods.

"All right, then. All right. Old Stan's got this. We just need to stick to the plan and keep ourselves to ourselves, okay? Can you guys do that? Stop poking around asking questions?"

He's treating us like little kids. Only telling us half the story. "We wouldn't ask so many questions if you'd stop hiding shit from us. Why'd you lie about my dad?"

Stan raises an eyebrow. "What do you mean?"

"We went to the junkyard, Stan. My dad is there. Been there all this time, but you said he wasn't."

Ruthie leans forward, nodding. Stan runs his hand down his face. "Yeah, yeah, okay. I know Tye's there. Known all along. This job we're doing, if it goes wrong, we don't want him getting blamed for it. Got a guy over in Omaha punching a time card every day says 'Tye Roberts' on it. Rock-solid alibi. But your dad didn't want you to know none of that. Wanted to keep you clear of what he's doing." He eyes me carefully, legs bouncing. "Your dad say anything else?"

"Yeah. He said he didn't take that money."

"Ayuh. Felt bad lying on him like that, but we were down a man. Needed you to feel accountable for your dad so you'd help us and I was right, wasn't I? Old Stan was right."

I'm not having it. "So where's the money? If my dad didn't take it, where is it?"

"Fair question." Stan nods. "Still got every red cent. Saving it up, just like always."

"What?" I am getting sick and tired of Stan's roundabout answers. "I've been telling you I need money for Gran's rent and you keep stringing me along when you coulda just handed me the money?"

"You're not listening. I'm holding the money. It's safe. You said rent's due the first. That's two days. I got you. But we got to keep working so we replace that money. Pile up as much cash as we can so when this job comes through, we're golden. We'll buy that old saloon, fix her up real good. Okay?"

The fight is draining out of me and Ruthie has gone quiet. Stan keeps talking. "I know I haven't been on the up-and-up with you, but Old Stan takes care of his own. We just keep working this plan, before you know it we'll be sitting pretty in our own restaurant."

Ruthie huffs. "But you're not taking care of us. Chick is dead. Probably Wade, too."

"Ayuh. But the three of us? We're gonna be just fine. Twig and Tye, too."

Stan holds out his fist for a bump, but the same doubt that's swirling in my head, I see on Ruthie's face. Stan has a response for everything but no real answers. After a few seconds Stan pulls his fist back, bouncing it on his knee with a quick nod.

CHAPTER

22

I WAKE UP TO STAN TAPPING MY ARM WITH A RUBBER-banded stack of bills. "There ya go. Two hundred. Keep her happy a little longer, then we get Twig here with us where he belongs."

I stare at the cash in my hand, not quite believing Stan came through this easy. "Yeah, yeah," I tell him. "Hey, thanks, man."

"Don't thank me, that's a group effort. We should hit more of the holes tonight, recoup some of that."

"Absolutely," I tell him, but I'm already planning the day. For a hot minute I think about how great it would feel to show up at school and take the whole team out for pizza. But after the way they rode my ass for missing a few days . . . Hell to the no on that. I'll just wait for Twig to get out of school, then head over to Gran's so I can check on him. Make sure he's not getting into any more trouble with his teachers. Soon as Stan heads out, I shake Ruthie awake. She's as shocked as I am that Stan forked over money. I tell her that I want to spend the day working on Twig's bike.

"What about your dad?"

I shrug. "Haven't figured that out yet. I just know I'm not gonna let him stand in the way of Twig getting a Christmas present."

Axl greets us at the turn in the path, grateful that Ruthie happens to have a bit of beef jerky in her pocket.

"You just carry that around in case you meet a random dog?"

"Happens more than you'd think," she tells me, then adds quietly, "Chick likes it."

There's a padlock on Dad's workshop door, a smaller version of the one on the front gate. I hadn't realized how tense I was until my shoulders relax, knowing that padlock means Dad isn't here. Part of me was hoping he'd be here. That maybe he had time to think about what I'd said and change his mind.

The key is under a rock next to the door. Axl shoulders the door open and pads right over to his pillow. The bike is where I left it, leaning against the wall under the window. Spiderwebs condo their way from seat to derailleur and across both handlebars. First things first, that seat has got to go. Whatever nastiness was frozen into the foam has defrosted and reeks so bad, my eyes water. I use a piece of pipe to relocate two spiders. The gaps in the foam make it easy to see the bolts connecting the seat to the rod. Although it's rusted all to crap, it comes off easily. I toss it out the door into a pile of old parts. There are a few seats in the pile, and Ruthie sorts through them. None look any better than the one I just trashed. Ruthie lets the last one drop with a dejected *thump*.

"There's one more place to look."

Ruthie and Axl follow me out into the junkyard. I lead them around several turns to a place I used to spend hours as a kid. Dad and Stan called it the Shoppe, which they pronounced "Shop-pay," as if it were some fancy store. It was their version of the odds and ends that line the checkout lines of grocery stores—things that might attract the attention of the people who came here looking for a side mirror to replace the one that got busted off their car or an old post to fix up a gap in their fence. Like smart businessmen, they routed all their customers through there.

As we come around the corner, Ruthie draws in her breath. "Is that a coffin?"

I can't believe how stupid I am. Who does this? Brings someone who just lost their boyfriend to a coffin. "Ruthie, I—"

"This place is amazing," Ruthie says. She's staring at the treasures piled all around—bins of dull flatware, old vinyl albums, ornaments and costume jewelry hanging from fake Christmas trees. The dirt is littered with white flecks and right in the middle of it all, the casket rests like a boat on a beach of broken shells. "What's in there?" Her feet crunch on the shards of broken glass glimmering in muddy, melted snow.

"Open it and find out."

When I was a kid, I was terrified of that casket with its cracked lid. The first time Dad brought me here and told me to pick out a Mother's Day present, I thought some dead lady was gonna spring out and eat our brains. Now I think this is one of the prettiest places in the junkyard. I tell Axl to stay so he doesn't cut his paws. He gives a low woof and a look that says *You're not the boss of me*, but he listens.

Ruthie pauses with both hands on the lid of the casket and looks back at me, as if to ask if it's really okay. I give her an encouraging smile. As the lid opens, she lets out a gasp. "My grandmother collected these!"

Ruthie picks through the pile of mostly busted-up plates and cups and bowls, stacking the cracked cups, setting aside the broken. "My grandma would have loved this one," she says. There's sadness in her voice, but joy, too, and I realize that maybe bringing her here wasn't the dumbest thing I could do. A bit of pale green catches my eye. I gingerly lift an ivory cup out by the handle, sliding it out from under the rubble. The pale green is one of three shamrocks, green stemmed, flaked with gold.

"Oh. That's just beautiful," Ruthie says.

I hold the cup out to her. She wraps both hands around it and presses it against her mouth, inhaling, like she's breathing in something delicious.

"I wish it were full of hot cocoa."

"Coffee with Irish cream," she corrects. "My grandma was Irish."

"Mine too," I say.

"She is?" Ruthie half laughs. I can imagine what she's thinking after seeing Gran standing at the trailer door in her Thanksgiving attire—ratty gray robe over baggy sweatpants and Cubs T-shirt.

I shrug. "My mom always said we had some Irish, but I actually don't know how far back."

I don't tell her the rest of that story, that I'd come home from first grade with a family heritage project. When I'd asked where our family came from, Mom said, "Ye old Emerald Isle of Ireland." Gran had snorted and told her not to fill my head with shit. "He needs to know where he's really from," Gran said. Mom had gotten upset and gone outside for a smoke, so Gran helped me write *Trailer Park, Indiana*, on my paper. She let me take it to school that way.

Ruthie reaches to set the cup back in the casket, but I tell her she should keep it. She throws her arms around me like I just handed her a whole set of fancy-ass china and a mansion to keep it in.

"If you really want to show me how thankful you are," I tell her, "help me find a seat for the bike."

We sift through several piles before she announces that she's found the perfect seat. Perfect seems far-fetched since we're searching in an abandoned junkyard, but when she holds it up triumphantly, I whistle. I trace my finger over the Bulls insignia.

"Oh man. Twig is gonna love this."

We take the seat back to Dad's workshop and I clean it up while Ruthie pries off the gnawed handlebar grips and unravels the tape from the handlebars. "We need something to get the tape residue off."

One of Dad's old shirts is looped through the handle of the kerosene can. I douse it and hand it to her. She hums under her breath as she scrubs. I tell her about the bike—how much I loved it as a kid, how I hope it will help Twig see that the whole world doesn't suck. It's not that I think it'll restore his faith in Santa Claus, just maybe give him a few minutes where, his feet on the pedals and the wind in his hair, he might feel like he's soaring above the trailer park, Gran, Dad, the crappy kids, everything. When we've done all we can for the day, I ask Ruthie if she wants to grab some food.

Ruthie's stomach gurgles and we laugh. She hangs the rag over the edge of the workbench to dry.

"Come on, buddy," I call, but Axl's so cozy and warm on his pillow, he doesn't want to follow us back into the cold. "Can't leave you locked inside. No telling when—or if—Dad will come let you out." I lean down to scratch him behind the ears, but sunlight glints against something metallic on the far side of Dad's workbench. I reach across the counter to run my fingers over the smooth foil wrap of a Pokémon card pack. Unlike everything else in the shed, there's not a single speck of dust on it.

Axl lumbers to his feet and stares up into my face.

"I know what you're thinking," I tell him. "But this doesn't mean anything."

Still, I slide the pack down the workbench over toward Twig's bike.

CHAPTER

23

RUTHIE DOESN'T WANT TO COME WITH ME TO GRAN'S TO pick up Twig. I don't want to leave her alone, but she insists she's fine. "I got some shit to do," she says.

I can't blame her for not wanting to see Gran again. And she does seem better. Not okay, but better. So I leave her at the Castle and take the bus to Gran's. The whole way there I can't help thinking I should have made Ruthie come along and that maybe the only reason I didn't was so that I wouldn't have to feel bad if Gran treated her like crap again.

The sun has broken through the perma-cloud that hovers over most of northern Indiana and the temperature is a balmy forty-five degrees. That type of weather would send most of the world inside to warm themselves by a fire, but around here people get so grateful for anything that resembles spring, they come staggering out of their trailers like Punxsutawney Phil squinting up at the sky. The playground's full of kids—or maybe just Mac's children—and even though it's pretty early, it's game-on at the basketball court. Twig isn't on the court. He isn't waiting on the stoop when I get to the trailer.

Gran's not on the couch. I can hear pleading in her voice behind the closed door of the bedroom, but not what she's saying. I lay out ten twenties on the kitchen counter by the microwave.

Twig's in the back bedroom, reading with Ozzy curled on his lap. He doesn't look up when I come in.

"Hey," I say.

"Hey," he says back, but he doesn't put the book down. Ozzy gives me the evil eye.

"What's up with Gran?"

Twig rolls his eyes. "Mac. They've been fighting a lot lately."

I perch on the edge of the bed. "You still hate me?"

Twig lets out a sigh worthy of Gran. "I never hated you. I just—I got mad. You're never here."

"Yeah, I know."

Now it's my turn to sigh. There's so much I haven't told him. I probably should have fessed up about my deal with Gran right from the start. Then he'd know why I'm not around, why he has to be careful and stay out of trouble. But he's just a kid. And a kid shouldn't have to worry about their grandma dumping them off to strangers. Then there's the whole thing about finding Dad. It's not fair to keep that from him. To let him think Dad might be dead. Except, what's worse—a potentially dead dad or a for-sure dad who can't be bothered to come home? I settle with telling Twig about the scrapping. That me, Stan, and Ruthie are scavenging for buried treasure like pirates and his eyes light up and he's full of questions and by the time we reach the mall, we're best friends again.

On the way back to the bus stop, a horn blares. I turn, thinking it's Matt or one of the guys, only to see Coach's red truck. He pulls into the next parking lot and jumps out of the truck. Doesn't even wait for us to get to the corner before he's shouting, "Roberts! Where the hell have you been?"

I stick my hands into my coat pockets, hunch my shoulders into the wind, and keep walking, like I can't hear him, don't see him. Twig's hand slips into my pocket and folds itself in mine. Coach stands there as we walk past him, probably stunned that someone has the audacity to ignore him. We get a few more steps before he comes after us. He grabs my shoulder, spinning me away from Twig, and before I can even think, I reel at him, my fist flying, but the punch never lands because Coach steps in and throws both arms around me, patting me on the back.

"I thought we'd lost you. Can we talk?" he says, and all the fight goes out of my body.

He drives me and Twig to McDonald's.

We grab a booth near the back of the restaurant.

Coach hands Twig a couple tens. "Order us some milkshakes and fries, okay?"

That's more than okay with Twig. He takes the money and damn near skips off to get the food.

"Roberts," Coach says.

I look out the window. I already know what he's going to say. That I let the team down. That he was counting on me and I didn't show up. That if I don't get my ass in gear, he'll kick me off the team. It's like he thinks I owe him. Just because he helped me get Twig out of trouble at school. That'll be the first thing out of his mouth: *You owe me.*

But he doesn't say any of those things.

Instead he says, "Josh."

He waits for me to look at him.

"I thought we lost you," he says again.

It's a struggle to keep my eyes from rolling. I could understand him being mad that I missed the game, but this whole *I thought we lost you* routine? Give me a break. "Just cuz I missed school today?"

"They found a body down by the railroad tracks. Kid about your age. They're not releasing the identity. I just thought . . . Well, everything with your dad and then you go missing . . ."

My heart thunders in my chest. *They found a body.* I want to ask whose body, but I force myself to stay cool. "Missing? I'm not missing."

"When you weren't in school this morning, they tried to contact your grandma. She said as far as she knew you took off just like your dad. You've been reported missing."

I wonder if they still put the faces of missing kids on milk cartons. I can just see last year's school photo on the side of a pint of chocolate. A few years ago a kid at Southview died in a car accident and the whole school held a vigil in the parking lot. Decorated the kid's parking spot with sidewalk chalk and balloons and shit. Only reason anyone at Woodson would care about me missing is they might get an hour out of class to hang out in the parking lot. Except maybe a few of the guys. Matt and Nick. I think about the body they found and wonder if it's Chick. Wonder if Ruthie and Stan know. I wonder if there's gonna be a funeral. Ruthie would want to go, need to go, even if it's not here in South Bend.

Coach is looking at me expectantly, in that *I just asked you a question* way. He must know by the blank look on my face that I haven't been listening. He lets out a slow breath, then asks, "What's going on? Why haven't you been at school?"

There's a million smart-ass things I could say, but what comes out is the truth. "I was taking care of a friend."

Coach chews his lip and nods. "You're a good kid, Josh. You care about your friends and your little brother. But here's the thing—you ever been on a plane? They have these oxygen masks—"

"I know. You're supposed to put yours on first before you help someone else."

If we were on the court, Coach would have benched me for interrupting him, but here, in the red pleather booth at McDonald's, he says, "That's right. Do you know why they say that?"

"Cuz if you pass out from lack of oxygen, you'll die."

"Mm-hmm. And if that happens, the people you helped with their masks will still die. There won't be anyone there to make sure they brace for impact, to help them off the plane. Heroes need to live through the crash or the good they do won't matter. You have to come back to school, Josh. You have to graduate. That's how you're going to help your brother."

On the way back to the trailer, we stop off at the Gas n'Go so I can grab some candy for Ruthie. Twig picks out a Mega bag of M&M's. I figure what the heck, rent's paid, and give him a nod.

I'm digging in my pocket for the cash when Chick's picture on the front page of the newspaper catches my eye. Headline above it reads: "Railroad Killer Strikes Again." I tell the cashier I'll take the paper, too, and fold it under my arm before Twig can see it. He's too preoccupied trying to get that bag of candy open without wrecking the re-zip.

At Gran's I head straight for the bathroom and sit fully clothed on the toilet, reading the article. It includes few facts, but does identify Chick as Melvin Charles Bransford Jr., son of Brenda and Melvin Charles Bransford Sr. Apparently Chick disappeared a few years ago from his hometown of Kalamazoo. The police have linked it to the death of another "transient" and are looking for a suspect in both murders. A picture of the other victim shows a guy about the same age as Chick. Its caption IDs him as Wade Esposito, a South Bend native.

I know I need to get back to the Castle and let Stan and Ruthie know about all this, but right now I just need a minute. Hanging out at Gran's will give me a chance to catch my breath.

Gran is all dolled up, a football game on the TV. Sure signs that Mac'll be showing up for dinner.

"Josh is gonna be on *America's Most Wanted*," Twig tells her.

She frowns. "Yeah, what're you up to now? Selling crack?"

Figures Gran would assume the worst. "He means missing, not wanted. After you told them you didn't know where I was, the school reported me missing."

"We ain't that lucky."

Mac comes in with takeout from Ho Ping House for dinner. Twig doesn't even let him set the bags down before he's searching through them for the crab rangoon. I don't blame him; Ho Ping is a zillion times better than the food court places and Gran's idea of takeout is a big tub of greasy chicken from the grocery store. I'm halfway through my fried rice before I realize Gran hasn't said anything about me eating their food. She also hasn't really looked at Mac. He's talking, practically nonstop—going on about Notre Dame and how his brother got him tickets for his birthday and the price of concessions was *re-dick-ulous*. But Gran is absolutely silent. Usually she hangs on every word Mac says, chiming in with her own stories here and there. But tonight she stares at her fork as she shovels fried rice around her plate.

After dinner Twig challenges me to *2K*, but before we can even get the system turned on, Mac's voice booms through the aluminum can of our trailer. "No, I still have to go. Just not with you. I can't do that to Michele and the kids . . ." The start-up music for *2K* drowns out the rest of his sentence.

His work boots thunder across the floor. The door slams. After a brief silence, I hear something I've never heard before. Not when she sliced her hand open and needed seventeen stitches. Not when the cockatiel she'd raised from a chick died. Not even at Mom's funeral.

Gran goes into her bedroom and closes the door quietly. Although she's not sobbing, for all the privacy of the trailer's thin walls, she may as well be.

"Any idea what all that's about?" I ask Twig.

Twig doesn't take his eyes off the game. "Some trip. I dunno. Maybe you could spend the night, though?"

I follow him to the back room and wait for him to brush his teeth and complete the usual getting-ready-for-bed rituals.

"You're not really staying, are you?" he asks.

"I can stay for a while," I tell him. I lie back on the pillow. Twig pulls Ozzy into bed and snuggles him. He scooches so his back is pressed against my side in a way that allows him to cuddle with me without really cuddling with me.

I'm wide-awake, my body nearly vibrating with the need to move, kinda like it does when I'm holding a form on the court, waiting for the other team to fall for our screen. In those moments, every instinct tells me to make a break for the ball, drive it to the hoop, even though my brain understands offense alone can't win the game. I wonder if this is how Dad feels when he's home. Like he's supposed to be out there, doing something, and if he just stays home, he'll lose.

Pretty soon Twig's breathing levels out and he's asleep. I lie there for a few more minutes, fighting the need to go check on Ruthie. Twig's my brother. He deserves a few more minutes, to settle into a deep sleep so I don't wake him when I leave. But fear of waking him isn't really what's keeping me in that bed. He asked, *You're not really staying, are you?* Not pouty or anything, but the flat way he said it is even worse. It means he's quit expecting much from me. *I can stay for a while.* The words had come so easy, like the refrain of a song sung since childhood. As I shift away from Twig and sit up, Dad's pile of boxes catches my eye and I realize why those words seem so familiar.

The whole way to the Castle, I think about how to tell Ruthie that the police have found Chick's body. She knows he's dead, so that's not the issue. Maybe she'll be relieved that he won't be in that hole anymore, that the cops will return him to his family and he'll have a proper burial. But when I tell her that Chick's been found, she crumples to the floor. Stan shoots me a look I can't read and starts pacing.

Ruthie lets me hold her there on the floor, both of us on our knees. I stroke her hair until she calms. "I thought maybe you'd be relieved that he can be buried now," I say.

Ruthie nods. "I know I should be. All I can think, though, is this means he's being taken away from me. His parents are gonna come and get him and take him somewhere and I won't know where. I can't ever see him again."

I think about Stonybrook Cemetery. How sometimes it doesn't matter if the grave is a thousand miles away or right here in town.

It's late and Ruthie wants to go to bed. I tuck her in and tell her I need a minute to check in with Stan. She looks so small with the blanket pulled up under her chin. I can almost picture her at home, in her own bed. Her room would probably have been yellow or purple. Some bright, happy color. Actually, I bet it was blue and there were decals from *Finding Nemo* above her bed. Maybe she even had a comforter with Dory on it. What must her life have been like to make her happier here in the Castle, with water leaking down from the roof and that ratty old blanket? "Be right back," I say with a kiss on her forehead.

Stan's sitting against the back wall in the far room. I slide down beside him.

"This is so fucked up."

"Ayuh. Why'd you tell her?" Stan asks, his voice low so Ruthie won't hear.

"Why wouldn't I?"

"Now she's upset all over again."

"No, she was never not upset, Stan. Why'd we have to just leave Chick there? We should've gone back and gotten him."

"And done what? You know as well as I do, there was no place we could put him that would've given Ruthie any peace."

"Do you think the cops are gonna figure out we were there? You know, after he died?"

He flicks my question away with a swipe of his hand. "Naw. If there'd been any fingerprints or DNA or whatever, the cops woulda shown up at your gran's. Since you're here, I think we're okay for now." I'm pretty sure that's not how DNA and fingerprints work, but I don't interrupt him. "What we need to worry about, the only thing that's changed, is how we're gonna get the scrap outta the rest of those manholes. The cops found two bodies, they're gonna be all over that place."

I don't say anything. Stan is acting like everything is fine, like dead bodies in manholes are just par for the course, but I can't even wrap my mind around it. A month ago I was just a normal high school kid. He shows up and my whole world goes FUBAR.

He must sense my turmoil, because he reaches out and pats my knee. "You're a fixer just like me, Josh. Wanna get in there and take care of everybody. But sometimes you gotta ride it out. It's too bad we lost Chick, but we can't keep sitting around counting our losses. We gotta keep on."

It's like he and Coach are reading from the same play-book, but in different languages: *Put your mask on. Ride it out.* It's easy for Stan and Dad to talk about this big plan to buy the restaurant, but I just can't see any way the two of them could pull something like that off. Even if they could, how long would it last before one or both of them gets bored and wanders off? Only person I can really depend on is me. All I really want to do is bail. If there was some way I could take Twig and Ruthie and get the fuck out of here, I'd pull that rip cord in a second.

CHAPTER
24

I'M DRIVING ACROSS MONTANA OR IDAHO, SOMEPLACE with big skies, Ruthie sleeping on the seat beside me, Twig reading a book in the back when the whole car starts shaking and I'm vibrated right out of my dream. It's my cell phone vibrating in my pants pocket. Fifteen missed calls from Twig, but no voicemails. I check my texts and there's a whole string of them, all from Twig:

> 8:10 a.m. Josh? Call me ASAP
> 8:11 a.m. Josh Gran's acting weird
> 8:12 a.m. She's packing all my stuff in a garbage bag
> 8:14 a.m. Josh I think Gran called the social worker to come get me.
> 8:15 a.m. I don't know what to do
> 8:15 a.m. Where are you?
> 8:17 a.m. Josh?
> 8:17 a.m. I need you
> 8:20 a.m. CALL ME!!!!!!!!!!

The last message was sent at nine o'clock. Two hours ago.

They're here to get me Josh. I NEED YOU!

I stuff my feet into my shoes and grab my coat and am out the door and down the steps before I realize that Ruthie is calling my name, asking what's wrong, telling me she has to talk to me about something. There's no time to stop, though, not if Gran did what I think she did.

I luck out and catch the bus just pulling up at the corner, run through the trailer park. In addition to Gran's Datsun, two other cars are parked in front of Gran's trailer. A red Volkswagen Beetle and a police car. Its lights aren't on. That has to be a good sign.

I storm into the house, ready to take Gran's head off for what she is, a lying sack of shit, ask her why she took money from me if she's just gonna turn Twig over anyway. And what the fuck was with Ho Ping House last night? Some kind of last meal for Twig? But Gran's sitting at the kitchen table and from the looks of things, she's putting on a good show. The social worker is holding her hand and a female cop is sipping coffee, a notepad open on the table. I walk right past them to our bedroom, but there's no sign of Twig. I check in the closet and am on my knees checking under the bed when the cop's voice makes me jump.

"We already searched the whole trailer," she tells me.

"Where is he?"

"Your grandmother thought you might know."

I get to my feet and look her square in the eye. The crinkles around her eyes remind me of the way Mom's eyes looked when she smiled. I shrug my *No clue.*

She sighs and sits on the bed. "My name's Dana. Can we be real for a minute?"

I shrug again. "What else we gonna be?"

"Being a cop is a hard job. I see stuff that no one should ever have to see. Most of the time, no matter how hard I try, I get there after everything's already too far gone. But once in a while I get to make a difference. Lisa out there, she's from the Department of Child Services. She just wants to make sure everything is okay with your brother. Your grandmother called Lisa because she needs some help caring for him. That just starts with a conversation. But we think your brother got scared when he heard them talking and might have run away. That's where I come in. When a kid's missing . . . that can go either way. Only real factor is time. The more we dance around pretending you don't know where he is, the less likely I can make a difference here. Why don't we start with this? How did you know Woodrow was missing?"

My hand twitches, instinctively starting for my phone, but I don't want her to know about that, just in case Twig tries to reach me again, so I throw my hands up, gesturing toward the front of the trailer. "I see a police car. What am I supposed to think?"

She nods thoughtfully, then pulls Twig's cell phone from her pocket. "So all these texts didn't clue you in?"

I pinch my lips together to keep from stammering, but she doesn't wait for a response.

"Look. I'm worried about your brother. He's all alone and I need to know where to start looking for him. Even if he's safe now, he might not be for long. There are all kinds of people out there and, truth is, some of them would see a little boy on his own as a target. You have to help us out, Joshua. You're his big brother. You know him best."

"What are you going to do when you find him?"

"We will sit down and consider what's in Woodrow's best interests."

I suck in my lip and look at her. "For real? You gonna keep him safe?"

She flashes me the Girl Scout salute.

"He likes to hide in the little cubby at the top of the slide."

Her eyes light up. "Where's this slide?"

"Around the corner at the playground."

She squeezes my upper arm, tells me to stay with Gran in case Twig comes back, and takes off on foot in the direction I point her toward. As she runs, she calls it in on her walkie.

As soon as she's out of sight, I head through backyards back to the bus stop.

Krispy Kreme is a bust. I didn't really think he'd be there, but I had to check. There's only one other place Twig would go, and that's where I find him. He's playing *NBA Jam* and there's enough quarters sitting on the console to keep him in the game for at least twenty more minutes. I watch over his shoulder for few minutes before he acknowledges me.

"Don't worry, I didn't break the twenty."

"Yeah? Where'd you get all these quarters?"

"Gran's laundry jar."

"Nice!" Gotta hand it to the little dude—scrapper in the making. I slip one of his quarters into the slot and press start for player two.

He smiles, that blushy, shy grin of his that makes his eyes twinkle, and instantly I want to wash my head out with soap to get rid of the image of Twig ever needing to scrap. He deserves to put that brain of his to better use.

"Got a plan?" I ask him.

Now he glances at me, then back to the game. "I'm not going to juvie."

I laugh. "Dude! They're not trying to take you to juvie—that's for bad kids. Like jail, only for kids. They were probably gonna—"

"They're not taking me anywhere!" Twig shouts loud enough that a few adults in the booth just outside the arcade look our way, their foreheads wrinkled with concern. Twig's arms are stiff at his sides. He looks like a human exclamation point.

I jerk my head toward the adults. "If you want to make sure of that, you might want to lower your voice. You're freaking out the parental types."

Twig's lower lip trembles. "They are not taking me anywhere."

"You ain't gotta tell me that. If they take you away, who will I stay up all night playing *2K* with? Who's gonna help me dominate the Oak Creek asphalt?"

Twig goes back to playing the game and the adults turn back to their conversation.

Just in case there's any doubt, I tell Twig, "They're not taking you anywhere. I am."

After we time out of *NBA Jam*, I tell Twig to grab the rest of his quarters; we gotta get out of here before people start looking for us. I can't remember if we ever told Gran any of the places we go. It's not like she keeps tabs on us, so probably the only way she'd know is if Twig let it slip in casual conversation. And why wouldn't he? It's not like it is some big secret.

Twig reaches down beside the game console and picks up his backpack like it weighs more than he does. It's stuffed so full, the seams strain. Poor kid must have crammed everything he owns in there.

"Here, let me carry that," I offer, but he *no thanks* me and clutches the backpack against his chest like he's carrying a baby. I get it. Living with a woman who garbage-pails anything that can't move fast enough to get out of the way of her cleaning frenzies has taught us to guard our possessions. The bus is pulling up as we step outside.

When Twig asks where we're going, I just tell him we're going to see Ruthie. He likes her and so that's answer enough. I don't tell him that we're going to the Castle. That's too hard to explain. You don't use the word "castle" with a kid like Twig without invoking images of Hogwarts and where we're going is about as far from that as it gets.

I expect Twig to be scared of the Castle, but I think he's so relieved I didn't send him back to Gran or off to juvie that he's keeping any complaints to himself. The only time he fusses at all is when we're in the corridor for the stairs and Watchman lets out that evil snarl. Then Twig practically crawls up onto my back. Can't blame him. It still raises my hackles no matter how many times I hear it. Plus, Watchman creeps it up extra this time, adding some hissing that seems to come from right underneath us. I wish I could throw my voice like that.

I show Twig how to use the metal pipe to signal that it's just us. Watchman is on the landing like usual. I introduce Twig.

"Twig, eh?" Watchman says. "'The jungle is but one twig short of impenetrable.' That's from our English friend Barrowcliffe. He was writing about an actual jungle, but damned if that don't sound profound when you hear it like that."

"Watchman? You talking to yourself again?" Ruthie's voice drifts down the stairwell. "Keep that up, we're gonna have to get you a straitjacket."

Watchman laughs.

"It's us, Ruthie. Me and Twig."

Twig takes the stairs two at a time, despite the heavy bag threatening to topple him back down.

"Well, if it isn't my favorite little man," Ruthie says. She folds Twig into a big hug.

I smile. "Yeah, Twig's gonna hang with us a few days, aren't you?"

"That's great," she says in a tone more suited to Glinda the Good Witch than my normal not-peppy, not-really girlfriend.

Stan high-fives Twig. "Joining the crew, kid? Gonna run with the big dogs?"

Twig shrugs. "I guess so."

"Well, we better give you the lay of the land, then. You probably already met the Watchman?" Twig nods. "Let's show you the roost. You can leave your pack here when we're around." Stan motions for Twig to ditch his backpack in the corner by Dory and Nemo. "Just don't leave it alone when nobody's here to watch it. Things have a way of walking off sometimes." Stan heads toward the stairs and Twig trails after him, still carrying his backpack.

"How long is he staying?" Ruthie asks the second they're out of earshot.

"Until I can figure something better out."

"*Better*? Better than sleeping on rags in an abandoned warehouse that probably has higher rates of mold than penicillin? Breathing in lungfuls of asbestos from all these busted ceiling tiles? Better than wondering if Jimmy Dean—" Her voice breaks here, but comes back in full rant. "It's bad enough we're staying in this shithole, living this shit life, but you really fucked up dragging him into it, Josh. He's just a kid."

"Don't you think I know that?" The words come out harsher than I intended. Ruthie's eyes go wide then blink quick—*blink, blink, blink*—but I keep going, afraid if I stop now, I won't get the words out and, goddamn it, I need to get this out. "We already live a shit life, Ruthie. You're not the only one with baggage. We lost our mom, our dad would rather live in a junkyard than take care of us, and that *bitch* who is supposed to be our grandmother"—and now *my* voice cracks—"just tried to turn him over to the state. Yeah, he's just a kid. And so am I. We're doing the best we can, so either help us out or keep your opinion to yourself cuz I have enough people riding my ass lately."

I expect her to yell back, tell me to shut up, step up, man up. I expect maybe she'll hit me, a hard shove to the chest, to emphasize my fucked-up-ed-ness.

But really I expect her to walk away. Maybe part of me wants her to. God knows everyone else in my life has, so maybe it's better to just get it over with.

What I do not expect her to do—and what she actually does—is nod. She crosses her arms and leans back, sizing me up. "All right, okay. That's what it's gonna have to be. That right there is what *you* are gonna have to be. You want to keep Twig out here, you can't let people walk all over you."

"Ayuh."

I turn to see Stan and Twig back from an extremely short tour. I'm not sure how much they heard, but enough for Stan to come at me, holding out his hand. I go to give him five, but he clasps my hand and pulls me in for a bro-hug, slapping me on the back with his other hand. "There's our Joshie. Got your big dog teeth now," he says, and there's something in his voice I've never heard before. Not from Dad or Coach or Gran. Something in the way he steps back to size me up. It might just be pride.

Stan says dinner's on him on account of our new bunkmate. Says not to ruin our appetite chewing on cardboard or anything while he's out tracking down some grub. Ruthie pulls out the deck of cards and asks if Twig knows how to play Kings in the Corner. He doesn't, so she deals us each a demo hand. Twig sits between us, his backpack tucked under his arm like a security blanket. We get through three hands before Stan is back, with a rotisserie chicken and a box of biscotti.

"Weird combo," Ruthie tells him.

Stan shrugs. "End-of-the-evening special. Caught 'em just before they got tossed in the dumpster."

He pops the plastic cover off the rotisserie chicken and the smell is like Christmas, so powerful that we all lean in, like the smell itself is an appetizer. We don't have any forks or plates, but Ruthie pulls off a drumstick with her bare hands and holds it out to Twig. He starts to reach for it, but his backpack lurches forward. Twig scrambles to grab the backpack, but I snatch it up before he can. Something inside the bag is frantically wanting that chicken.

"Twig! Did you seriously—" But I don't need to finish the question because I can see by the ugly, yowling face squirming out of the top of the pack that yes, he seriously.

"Oh my God. Has he been in there the whole time? Poor kitty." Ruthie leans over, reaching for the bag. I try to warn her that Ozzy is not of the cuddly persuasion, but she lifts the damn cat out of the bag and holds him close to her chest, cooing at him like he's a baby. Apparently, Ozzy only hates me.

"His name's Ozzy," Twig tells her. He offers Ozzy a tidbit of chicken, which the cat wolfs down in one swallow. Much as I hate that cat, I feel sorry for Ozzy being stuck in Twig's backpack. I'm gonna have to talk with Twig about taking better care of that cat.

"Your dad name him that? Ozzy?" Stan laughs, leaning over to scratch Ozzy under the chin. "Course he did."

"How'd you know that?" Twig asks.

"Your grandpa hated, I mean all out *hated*, heavy metal. Your dad used to rename all the pets after rockers just to piss him off. Ozzy, well, that's an easy one. Black Sabbath. But then there was Hendrix, Slash, Bono. Remember that old dog you guys had at the junkyard? Axl?"

I always thought Axl was named after a car part. We lived in a junkyard, after all. Now's not the time to bring up the junkyard, though. Or to mention that Dad took Axl when he left us at Gran's. Twig's eyes are twinkling from Stan's version of Dad, and I don't want to bring up the bad parts right now.

"Bone-o is a good name for a dog," Twig says.

"Not bone-o, *Bon*-o," Stan corrects. "You never heard of U2?"

"Yeah, I heard of YouTube. I'm not an idiot."

Ruthie ducks her face behind Ozzy's to hide her grin. "Apparently your big brother dropped the ball on properly expanding your musical palate."

Ruthie and Stan start throwing out band names to quiz him on who he's heard. Twig cracks up at Toad the Wet Sprocket and then we all start making up weird band names and I have a new favorite song. It is the golden chorus of Twig's laughter, mingling with the rainbow tinkle of Ruthie's giggle, underscored by Stan's deep baritone. Looking at the three of them—well, four if you count Ozzy—laughing as they take turns feeding Ozzy bits of chicken, their joy lit up in the indigo glow of Dory's faint light . . . I think maybe this is what family is. Not offering your grandma cash to take care of your little brother. Maybe it's Stan and Ruthie, me, Dad, and Twig. Maybe Stan's crazy plan to buy the restaurant, make that a home—*our* home—isn't so far-fetched.

CHAPTER

25

EARLY THE NEXT MORNING, TWIG ROLLS OVER IN HIS sleep and smacks me right in the mouth. It's not like I was getting much sleep anyway. It's hard to sleep sandwiched between Ruthie and Twig. Not to mention, Ozzy making himself at home right on my chest.

I lie there trying to fall back asleep, but my mind won't stop racing. There's so much I need to do. We'd set up a small bed by Nemo and Dory for Twig. He was reluctant to lie there by himself, but as soon as I handed him the book I snagged from the pharmacy, he settled right down while Stan, Ruthie, and I talked over options. Stan was all for rolling him into our crew.

"He's little and could scoot right down those ladders, maybe even get some of the wiring that's out of our reach in the tunnels."

Ruthie shut that down right away. "He should be in school."

Ruthie had a point, but sending Twig to school is an absolute no. "If there's one place the police will be looking for Twig, it's at school. "

"And anyplace you are," Ruthie added.

Which meant I wouldn't be going to school either. Easy for Coach to talk about oxygen masks and bracing for impact, but if the ground below isn't any more stable than the plane you're in, you gotta find another option.

Stan tells us now that Twig's here, we might be able to move up the timeline a bit on the big job.

"What does that have to do with anything?" I ask.

Stan shrugs. "Not saying it does. Just saying, I might be able to move things up." Stan and his half answers again.

Soon as me and Ruthie lay down, Twig had come padding over and snuggled between us.

I scooch off the pallet carefully, trying not to wake anyone. I pull on my shoes.

"Where you going?" Ruthie mumbles sleepily.

"Gonna work on the bike," I whisper. "Can you keep an eye on him? Just until I get back?"

She pushes up on one elbow. "What about what Stan said? That you might lead people to your dad?"

"I'll be careful."

The whole way to the junkyard, I plan how to pimp out that bike and picture Twig's face on Christmas morning. Axl hears me at the gate and comes trotting up as I latch it back behind me. We go to the workshop together. No sign of Dad, which is cool. I spend half the morning straightening bent spokes, searching piles of old bikes for a new chain, and trying to get the sprocket to turn smoothly.

I'm about ready to call it a day when I remember the rides I used to take with Mom. She had a basket on the front of her bike and would always bring a couple books and some snacks along on our rides. We'd collect pine cones or lilacs along our route and she'd ferry them home in that basket. Twig might like that kind of basket on the front of his bike for his books. Maybe even for Ozzy to ride in. Not that Ozzy would actually be willing to do that, but just in case. I call Axl and we head toward the old house to see if Mom's basket is salvageable.

The snow has melted since I've been here, and the dank must of wet earth smothers the lingering odor of the burnt-out house—mostly. Axl trots up the concrete steps to the green door and whimpers.

"No, come on, boy. Let's look around back."

He whimpers again and noses the door open.

"Axl! Come!" I yell, but he disappears into the burned remains of the house.

I race up the steps and stare into what's left of a hallway I don't want to go down. "Axl?" I step into the living room. Now I can smell the charred wood, but there're also hints of gingerbread. *Just your imagination*, I tell myself. *Yeah, and that snoring you think you hear probably is too*, my imagination tells me right back. We're both wrong and I know it, so I keep my eyes from looking at the once-yellow wallpaper curled up into stiff black flakes on the right side of the hall. I don't look at the busted glass frames hanging empty or the blackened carpet crunching underfoot. I don't look left, either, where the door to Mom and Dad's room is nothing but a blackened slab hanging askew on its swollen frame. The morning sky is a haze of gray, but it lights the hall enough for me to see the open door for the stairwell ahead. I start in that direction, but Axl whines. The sound isn't coming from the stairs. It's coming from my parents' room.

"Axl?"

He whines again.

Dad's voice floats, soft and ghostlike. "Hush now."

For a second I'm five and he's carrying me down this hall to those stairs, telling me it was just a bad dream and I should—

"Go back to sleep, boy."

Axl barks. I give my head a shake to rattle my brain back into its seventeen-year-old cranium. "Dad?"

Something thuds in the darkness, there's a click, followed by the unmistakable sound of a tent zipper.

A flashlight bobs toward me, but there's enough sunlight filtering in through the burned-out roof that we can clearly see each other without the light.

"You're living here?" It's not a question, really, as I can see that yes, he is living here. But I can't help saying it that way. Of all the places Dad could go, I don't understand why he would pitch his tent in the same room Mom died in.

Except, I do understand.

I'm trying to figure out how to retract my question because I don't want to make Dad say it out loud or maybe I don't want to hear Dad say it out loud, but he ignores the question and asks what I want.

"I was just working on that old bike for Twig and Axl took off."

"That's it?"

"Yeah."

"I thought maybe you were going to try to drag me back again."

"Well, you made it pretty clear that what you got going with Stan is more important than coming home. So, no, I'm just here for the bike." Dad tosses his head in frustration, but I keep talking. "You should know, though, I was right. Gran called a social worker from the Department of Child Services. They came to get Twig."

There's a quick hardening of Dad's jaw and a flash in his eyes. "She wasn't supposed to do that. Did they take him?"

"No, I've got him."

Dad shoves his hands into his pockets. "We're so close, Josh. We can finally have a real life. If we just ride this out."

"Ride what out? Dad, we're living in the Castle with Stan. We don't have water or heat. Chick is dead and—" Dad is shaking his head, his lips screwed up like he's biting back something bitter. "What?"

He looks at me, his eyes sharp and hard. "It's just another week."

"Until what? What are we waiting for?"

"Just go on back to the Castle. You boys'll be okay for a few more days."

"Then come with me. Why don't you just come back and we can stay together at the Castle? We can help you with whatever you have planned, Dad. It doesn't have to be like this."

He runs his hand over his mouth, squeezing it. All the hostility he threw at me last time is gone. He just looks defeated. I reach out and put a hand on his arm. "Come on, Dad. What happened to you?"

He steps away from me, still shaking his head. "Same as you. We lost her. Can't get that back."

"I know we lost her. But that was years ago, Dad. You stepped up and took care of us. It wasn't the life we all wanted—a life with Mom—but we had you. What happened to change that? What are you doing living here?"

He looks down at the floor, and the tip of his worn boot toes the packed ash. For a second I think I reached him, that he's going to tell me what happened to change things, that we can fix them and go home to Twig together. But instead he says, "There's some blame that's too big to talk about. Some crimes too devastating to forgive. You and me, we can't have this conversation because 'hate' isn't a word I want between us, son. Walk away. Just let me be. Wait for the plan to come through."

He looks right at me and I see the blame right there in his eyes. The real reason he left. It's the same look that was on his face that day as he stood in this same yard, damp from the spray of fire hoses, holding Twig, whose shrieks of "Momma!" filled up the whole world, drowning out the shouts of the firefighters, the blare of the ambulance, and my dad sobbing that we killed her.

There's nothing I can say to tell him how sorry I am for that day. For the look on Mom's face when I said I couldn't go to school, the pain in her eyes as she lay on the ground, choking on the blackness in her lungs. No words big enough to take that all back. Anguish twists my gut. My head is pounding with a wordless fury and I know if I try to speak, a meteor will fly out of my mouth and incinerate us both. I lurch out the door. A good dad would come after me. He'd tell me he was wrong to leave us, pull me into his arms, and promise to be the father he knows he should be. He does not follow, but his voice chases me.

"Get back here!" he yells. "Get back in here right now!"

His anger is a fishhook in my cheek, jerking me around to face him. Axl gives a small whine, and for the first time I notice that he's followed me. He looks from me to Dad and back to me. Axl whines again and that's when Dad's words finally register. He's yelling, but it's not me he's calling.

"You get back here!" he yells again.

Just like that, the lure loosens, falls away, disintegrating and taking my rage with it. Leaving a big gaping hole.

I lightly touch the top of Axl's head and we head down the path away from Dad. Axl accompanies me to the gate and watches as I lock it back up. I wish I could take him with me, but I can barely feed myself.

I don't go to the bus stop. There's too much inside me to sit still for the ride back to town. My throat is so dry and tight, I can barely swallow and my chest aches like I've been punched in the gut.

I walk away from Dad. Away from the junkyard. Away from town. Down roads I don't know, past farmlands with falling-down barns I've never noticed. I walk away until my legs ache more than my chest and my thoughts are drier than my throat. I could keep on walking. Maybe then Dad would go back to Twig. The image of them happy together swirls around and around, like a ripped page tumbling across a cracked landscape, but there're other images there too. Me and Mom and Twig and Stan at the house while Dad was off searching for a big score two towns over. Mom getting us ready for school, getting herself ready for work while Dad drank coffee and talked about this big job or that one. Mom helping me with homework while he packed a duffle and said he'd be back in a week, two weeks, a month. Stan nailing a bottomless bucket to a wall, teaching me to shoot, playing with Twig, while Mom cooked dinner and crossed off days on a calendar, waiting for things that never came.

CHAPTER

26

A S SOON AS RUTHIE SEES ME, SHE STARTS RANTING about how Stan wants to go scrapping and it's too dangerous after the cops found Wade and Chick. She doesn't even ask how things went with my dad.

Stan looks up from a card game he'd been playing with Twig. "So what are we supposed to do, Ruthie? Start collecting pop cans like Watchman? Boost car stereos like Mickey Kyle? We got something good and can't let a couple idiots who got themselves—"

"Shut the *fuck* up!" Ruthie screams at him. "Chick didn't get himself killed. You got him killed by not paying attention when things got dangerous. And now you're doing it again, trying to drag me and Josh, and now Twig here—Josh, he wants to drag *Twig* out there with us—out there when you know it's not safe! Josh?"

"I can't do this right now," I say. I tell Twig to get Ozzy and come on. He asks where we're going, but I just ignore him and head down the stairs.

"I need to talk to you!" Ruthie calls after me. I know I should go back, but I can't right now. I wait outside for Twig. He comes trudging after me, carrying Ozzy.

"Hungry?"

He nods.

I hadn't really thought this whole thing through. Knowing Ruthie and Stan, they didn't think to feed him either. We head toward the Center, but I already know that's out. For all I know, there's an Amber Alert out for Twig. Or maybe they figured we're together and I'm a runaway too. Or his abductor. Which also rules out the mall. Christ on a cracker. Can't go to McDonald's or anyplace we'd have to pay. I shouldn't have wasted all that money on those stupid cell phones. Shouldn't have given Gran two hundred dollars just to have her turn around and throw away Twig. Shit. Shit, shit, shit.

"Stan thinks I can help you guys. Is it really as dangerous as Ruthie was saying? Just going down in a manhole and getting copper?"

"It's not going into the hole that's dangerous. It's . . ." I hesitate, not sure how to explain about Wade and Chick, but Twig fires another question at me.

"Is Dad dead?"

"What? No."

"Ruthie says those guys are. Dad worked with them and he's missing and—"

Shit, Ruthie. I stop walking and look him right in the eye. "Dad's not dead, Twig."

"I'm not a little kid, Josh. If Dad is dead—"

I grab him by the shoulders. "Dad is not dead. But we can't keep waiting on him to take care of us. We got to grow up and take care of ourselves, okay? So I need you to stop acting like a fucking baby!" His head jerks as I shake him with each syllable and his eyes go wide. My hands fall to my sides. "Damn it, Twig."

But it's not Twig I'm damning. It's me. It's true we can't count on Dad, but it's my fault we're standing out here in the street instead of back at Gran's playing *2K*. My knees buckle and I sit down hard on the cold cement. It's my fault we were even at Gran's. If I had just gone to school. Not made such a big deal about stupid soccer tryouts. If I had let Mom go to work that day . . .

I don't realize I'm crying and saying all that out loud until Twig's words overlap mine and drown me out. His arms are tight around my neck and he's crying too. "It's not your fault, Joshie. It's not your fault." I nod and wipe at my eyes. Nod again like I believe him, like his words are helping. "It's not your fault," he says again.

But how would he know?

We wind up eating peanut butter crackers from the Gas n'Go and washing them down with rusty water from the bathroom sink. Ozzy eats two whole crackers from Twig's pack, snarfing them down like he hasn't eaten in days, even though he got a ton of chicken just last night. I let him lick the crumbs from my pack, which he does greedily, then he thanks me with a low growl that implies he'd like my fingers for dessert. Twig and I split a box of Lemonheads. Not gourmet, but not exactly dumpster diving, either.

By the time we get back to the Castle, things have settled down. Ruthie waves us over to a spot on the floor where she has set up a board game. Life. The edge of the board looks like a Chihuahua gnawed on it, but otherwise it looks brand-new. She already has the money all dealt out.

"How do you play?" Twig asks. He drops to his knees and spins the wheelie thing.

"Pick a car," she tells him, then whispers to me over Twig's head, "I boosted it from Goodwill."

There's a note of apology in her voice and a softness in her eyes. Whatever happened after Twig and I left,

Stan and Ruthie seem chill now. The four of us sit around the board in the dim light of Nemo and Dory, and, for all the messed-up-ness of our lives, I think maybe this could work. Maybe it's time we stop waiting on Dad and make this work.

CHAPTER

27

THERE'S NO ONE TO WATCH TWIG, AND SO HE COMES with me, Ruthie, and Stan to scout out another lead. Some guys are headed out to the Landsome Hills area to help with a harvest.

Twig tugs on my arm and asks, "What kind of crop are they harvesting? It's winter."

I shush him and tell him not to ask questions.

The guys we're supposed to meet are waiting on the sidewalk outside of the Rusty Nail. Sounds like the name of a bar, but it's a scrapyard a few blocks south of the Center. The guy who runs it is rail thin and about a hundred and sixty, sporting a thick black mustache and eyebrows thick as squirrels' tails. Stan shakes hands and introduces him as Randy.

Randy points at a ragtag group, naming them in turn. "Liam"—blue Cubs hat—"Frankie"—worn leather jacket with Hells Angels scrawled graffiti-style down the front right breast—"Greg"—thin dude. The way they're all standing apart makes me think they didn't come as a matched set. Randy squints at Twig. "What's with the kid?"

"Part of the deal," Stan says.

"Yeah? This his babysitter?" He looks Ruthie up and down in a way that makes my skin crawl.

She steps forward, not one bit intimidated. "I'm the driver."

He tosses her the keys and leads us around back to a beat-up pickup that looks like it could have belonged to his grandpa. "Drive out US 12 and you'll see the field I'm talking about. Tools are in the back."

Stan had started to walk toward the truck, but he turns back to Randy. "You're not coming?"

"You get the shit. I sell the shit. That's the deal."

"Shotgun!" Twig shouts, scampering into the passenger seat. That leaves me and Stan in the back with the rest of the guys.

US 12 is smooth, and riding in the back of a truck full of guys makes me think about how I used to ride in the back of Matt's truck and picture how it would feel to leave Dad and Gran behind. I never really thought about where I'd go. Other than away games at Wakarusa or Lakeville, I've never been out this far into farm country. The old barns with their sunken roofs resemble ancient relics left to ruin. They remind me of the Castle, with trees pushing up through the foundation and water seeping from the ceilings. Once Psycho Mop told us, "Though farm and factory fail, fear not. Progress is wrought." He never really said what kind of progress comes from abandoned buildings and bankrupted families. To me it just looks like failure.

"Up ahead there on the left," Stan says.

Rising out of the dust is a stone entrance with a sign that declares we've reached Farmington Hills. No hills in sight. No functioning farms, either, but I guess selling homes in the land of make-believe is highly lucrative, because the sign also says: LOTS STARTING AS LOW AS $170,000.

There's an iron gate and a guardhouse, but the gate's open and the guardhouse stands empty and we drive right up a newly paved road black as freshly poured ink. Around the first bend there's a cluster of half-built houses. No glass in the windows yet, no locks on the doors. Just plenty of brand-new plumbing, like low-hanging fruit ripe for the picking. Ruthie pulls in there and the truck lurches to a stop. I wonder aloud where the work crews are and how Randy knew no one would be here, but Stan tells me to quit asking stupid questions.

Stan opens the door for Twig and tells him to leave his backpack in the truck and come on. The look on Twig's face suggests that he will not be leaving the pack in the truck.

I lean over and whisper, "You brought, Ozzy, didn't you?"

Twig nods. "Couldn't leave him in the Castle."

"Are you kidding? He'd have been in heaven there with all the mice to hunt." I think of Ozzy's fat, lazy face and re-consider the mice part, but lying on the blankets probably would have been more fun for him than being hauled around in that bag. "He'll be okay in the truck," I assure Twig. "The sun's bright enough to keep it warm in here without roast-ing him."

"Nope," Twig says. "Ozzy stays with me."

I make a grab for the pack, but Twig scampers around to the back of the truck, where the guys are handing tools down to Stan, who sorts them into piles on the ground.

Stan scowls at Twig's backpack. "Told you to leave that in the truck. You're not just here to supervise—put that down and load up on these tools."

Twig twists the pack around to his back and picks up an old-fashioned magnet, the red U-shaped kind with two silver tips. Ruthie grabs a crowbar and a shovel; I get the socket set, a hammer, and the voltage tester. Once the other guys have divided the tools among them, Stan leads us into the first house. The house is framed in, most of the exterior walls are up, but the freshly sawed wood smells so much like Krispy Kreme, my mouth waters. Although there is a front door, there is no doorknob. It swings open easily, no crowbar required.

Inside, Stan tells Twig, "Go test anything metal. If the magnet sticks, it's cheap. If the magnet doesn't stick, that's what we want."

Twig looks around uncertainly. No door handles, no doorknobs. Not much metal.

"C'mon," I tell him.

We head down to the basement and hit the jackpot. The drywall hasn't gone in yet. Pipes and wires crisscross like a den of snakes. I show him how to use the magnet—which seems like common sense but isn't. With this many guys, it only takes us about forty minutes per house to rip out the copper plumbing and any wire and pipe that might be worthwhile. Randy claps his hands when he sees the haul in the back of the truck. He and Stan dicker a bit over cash, but in the end, Stan comes away with a thick roll of bills. "Come back tomorrow. I might have something else for you," Randy tells us.

All the way back to the Castle, Stan talks about Randy like he's the answer to our prayers. His head is in the clouds about that saloon downtown again. About how it's got an apartment above it and we just need to keep doing what we can to bring in some cash until the timing's right on the big job and then everything will be fine. Ruthie tells him we want that too, but we got to be smart. Can't be getting caught.

Stan waves her off. "You just let Old Stan do the worrying. Everything's gonna be A-OK."

Ruthie's right, though. This stuff with Randy just seems too easy. A crew going around ripping out the guts of new subdivisions is sure to attract attention. And meanwhile, we're just sitting here, waiting for that big job with Stan. It's like I told Twig, we gotta grow the fuck up and take care of ourselves.

The snow is coming down heavy by the time we get back to the Castle. Stan is in a great mood, teasing Twig good-naturedly, telling him they should build a snowman and see if they can make it come alive. Twig might be young, but he's way too old for fairy tales. Still, the two of them go around back while Ruthie and I head inside.

I tell Ruthie what I'm thinking. That maybe we should stop waiting on Dad. Figure out some other way to get the money for the saloon and if we can't afford that, maybe an apartment.

"Maybe we could get jobs," I say, "like at McDonald's or some shit?"

Ruthie laughs then realizes I'm serious. "How you gonna do that with Twig? Can't leave him alone. Plus, soon as they run a background check on you, cops will show up asking about him."

I don't think McDonald's runs background checks, but she's right. A real job comes with too much risk.

"Hey, I been trying to talk to you about something," she says. "The funeral's in Michigan. Day after tomorrow. I'm gonna hitch there and back."

"We'll come. Me and Twig." It's not that I want to go to Chick's funeral, but I don't want Ruthie to have to go alone.

But Ruthie's shaking her head. "No. I'll only be gone a few days. I'll be back before you know it."

CHAPTER

28

IN THE MORNING SHE'S GONE. DOESN'T EVEN WAKE ME UP to say goodbye.

It's so cold in the Castle, me and Twig huddle up under the blankets, Ozzy shivering between us. Around lunchtime, Stan tells us we're gonna go get warm somewhere. We bring the blankets with us, wrapping them around our coats as an extra layer. Stan takes us to Our Lady and tells us to sit tight while he hits up the cafeteria crew at the Center for some leftovers. Twig still has some of Gran's laundry money. We pile the blankets in one of the big dryers and heat them, pressing our hands against the hot metal.

Stan's back, stomping snow off his boots onto the green tiles, just as the blankets finish their cycle. My stomach rumbles as Stan hands us each a bag of ham and potatoes. We eat it right out of the bag with our bare fingers. Mom would have scolded us for that and Gran woulda smacked us one, but Stan just laughs. "That's some good old shit, huh?"

Twig unzips his backpack so Ozzy's head pokes out, and feeds him bits of ham.

"We can't stay here all day," I tell Stan. "The manager's been giving us the evil eye since we got here."

Stan glances at a short dude glaring at us through his office window. "Receptionist at the Center said we can get us another space heater from the church. Some bigwig dropped off a load of them. I'm thinking if me and you go in separate, maybe we can each get one."

"Yeah, and the good news about fire hazards is they really heat up the place."

Stan scowls. "We ain't burned it down yet, have we?"

We bundle back up and head for the door. Twig gives a cheerful wave to the manager and tells him to have a nice day. We no sooner step outside than I hear someone yelling my name. I grab Twig's hand and keep walking, to make it look like maybe he's got the wrong guy or I don't hear him, but I can't help sneaking a side glance and that's when Matt jumps out of the car he's riding in, leaving the passenger door wide open. His mom yells after him.

"Dude!" Matt shouts. He stumbles as his foot catches the curb and for a few seconds it looks like he might face-plant, but he catches himself and sprints toward us, alternately yelling "Dude!" and "Josh!" like I might not realize I am the reason for his mad dash from a moving vehicle.

His mother gives up calling after him, maybe intimidated by the blaring of horns behind her, and steers the car around the corner down a side street. Matt's mom is cool and all, but there's no way I want her to find me standing here with my "missing" little brother whose face might be pinging an Amber Alert all over the Midwest by now. Even the coolest adult is gonna go straight to the cops for this.

I tell Stan to take Twig and I'll catch up. It's too cold for them to stand around and argue.

"Hey, Matt." My words are muffled because he's smashing me in a giant bear hug. When he lets me up for a breath, I put my arm around his shoulders and tell him it's great to see him. Even though it's only been about a week, there's something different about him. We don't have time to compliment each other's haircut or new shirt or whatever right now, though. While I'm talking, I lead him around the back of Our Lady and into a pawnshop. I'm hoping his mom doesn't follow us in.

There's a whole display of used games and I make a beeline for that. "Did you see they have a new edition of *Black Ops*?"

"That's where you been? Getting your game on while the rest of us been thinking you're dead or something?"

I laugh and hold out the game to him, but Matt grabs me by the shoulders and makes me look at him. "Did you not hear me? We thought you were *dead*. And there's a freaking Amber Alert out for Twig, man. What the fuck?"

"Well, I'm right here." It's not fair to be irritated at Matt for being worried about me. After all, two guys were found murdered and I have been AWOL.

"Yeah? But where have you been? Who was that guy?"

Suddenly the difference I'd half noticed is written all over Matt's face. Even when the team's in the hole at halftime, Matt wears a *Like, what's up, Scoob?* grin. But now he is not grinning and has more worry lines than the old guy in *Up*.

"Sorry, man. I had some stuff to take care of."

He nods, but the lines deepen. "Coach said your dad—"

"Coach talked to you guys? What the hell?"

"*I* talked to Coach. Dude. I know you have shit with your family and even though the guys were pissed that you missed the big game, I get it. Family first, right? But you blew off Nick and then didn't show up for physics and we all got zeros even though I offered to do your part of the presentation . . . Man, that project was supposed to bounce me up to a C plus! Coach benched me and Nick. I had to explain to my dad why my grade is shit . . ." Matt seems to realize that he is rambling, and blushes slightly. "I was worried, is all. Not like you to leave a brother hanging."

I glance toward the door. "Speaking of brothers, Twig's waiting for me next door."

Matt's blush deepens. "So that's it? You ditch the team, ditch me, and you don't even think I deserve an explanation?" Color is spreading down his neck now and the Shaggy chillax drawl is completely gone. "Look, I been there for you, man, haven't I? You show up, need a place to stay? No questions asked. You wanna be dropped off at the CVS instead of . . . somewhere else? I got you. But this isn't about your pride anymore, bro. You're about to fuck up everything that might get you outta here. Tell me what's going on. Let me help you."

Part of me wants to say yes. To get in the car with Matt's mom, go get Twig, and let them drive us away from this. But as nice as his family is, they are still gonna call the cops and the cops are gonna separate me and Twig. There's just no way this ends with a happily ever after. So I laugh at Matt and tell him he sounds just like his mom. "I'm fine, Mrs. Higle. Had to work some crap out, like I said. I'll be back in school tomorrow."

Matt nods slowly, side-eyeing me. "Okay, dude. Whatever."

I pick up the nearest game and pretend to study the specs on the back of the box. "Sorry about your physics grade. I'll talk to—"

The bell on the door jangles as Matt walks out.

The church won't give us more than one space heater, but Stan says one'll do. Watchman's not on the landing, but who can blame him? He probably went someplace warmer. We tie a bag of ham and potatoes to the handrail for Watchman to eat whenever he gets back.

Stan's so eager to get the new space heater plugged in, he takes the last few stairs two at a time. He reaches our floor ahead of us and his voice floats back, low and eerie. "Christ's sake, where's Elmo?"

He means Nemo. I correct him without a thought. His disdain penetrates the darkness. I can see it in my head—the look he reserves for policemen and drugged-up zombies—and he gives me the same snappy reply he usually reserves for them: "Thanks for the light bulb, Einstein."

I keep my mouth shut. Last time someone corrected him on the contributions of Einstein versus Edison, they got a sock in the face. Besides, whether it's Elmo or Nemo doesn't matter: neither of Ruthie's sappy night-lights is working.

Stan trips on something and stumbles, thudding against the wall. "Can't see a rat's ass—"

A flashlight clicks on across the room, then another and another.

I motion for Twig to go back downstairs, but he twists both hands in the back of my jacket and hangs on for dear life.

"Fuck's this?" Stan growls. He takes two giant strides toward one of the lights, but a sickening crunch under his boot stops him.

"Aw," Jimmy Dean says. He aims the light toward the orange bits of plastic on the floor near Stan's feet. "Now that's a crying shame."

Twig hurries over and kneels, brushing the mess into his hand. "Ruthie's gonna be sad," he says as he tucks Nemo's remains into his pocket like flower petals.

Jimmy Dean keeps Twig in the spotlight. "Should be more careful, Stan. Never know who could get hurt with you tromping around."

I go to Twig and yank him to his feet, tucking him behind me.

"You all need to clear on out," Stan says, his eyes traveling around to the other men. "This is our place."

"'Ours.' Such an inclusive word. But you're not exactly the sharing type, are you, Stan?"

"What do you want, Jimmy?"

"Same as I've always wanted. A share. Been asking you nicely to cut me in on a job here and there. We could've worked together. I'm done asking now though. Where's the money?"

Stan's still holding the boxed space heater he got from the church, but his other hand goes casually to his hip. His thumb tucks in the front pocket of his jeans. Where he keeps his knife. I've seen Stan move quick, but even if he could get the blade out of his pocket, Jimmy Dean looks like a cat whose tail's been tugged one too many times. And then there's Jimmy Dean's crew, outnumbering us three to one.

"You can tell us where it is, or we can tear this place apart. Maybe search your little friends here too."

"It's in the beam over the window," Stan says.

"Now, see?" Jimmy Dean smiles a wide, wide grin. "Maybe we can be friends after all."

But as soon as Jimmy Dean turns to check for the cash, there's a ravenous growl from the stairwell. I twist around to see Watchman swing a pipe through the air, taking out one of the thugs. Stan swings the space heater box, connecting solidly with the nearest thug's head. Stan yells at us to get out of there, but someone punches Watchman and he goes down hard. I bend to help him and a guy the size of an ox grabs me by the arm. "Don't you hurt my brother!" Twig screams, and kicks the guy in the balls. The ox staggers back and trips over the cord to the other space heater, which tips facedown onto the game we'd been playing. That fake money goes up in flames in a flash, right at Jimmy Dean's feet. His guys are still coming at us, but he screams at them to never mind us, put the fire out. The money has to be here someplace.

Watchman's struggling to his feet, disoriented. The curtain has caught fire by now and Jimmy Dean knocks it to the floor, stomping on it. Stan wraps an arm around Watchman, leading him toward the stairs. I swing Twig up into a piggyback and follow them.

We don't know where to go, so we head toward the Center. I think we're in luck when Dwayne's outside, but when we tell him what happened, he shakes his head in disbelief. "The police been all over here looking for you, Josh," he says. "We got to get you inside, give them a call before all this gets even more out of hand." He unlocks the back door, tells us to head in out of the cold. Watchman goes in, but Stan kicks the door shut before me and Twig can.

"You call the cops, things gonna get real bad for these boys," Stan says, but Dwayne tells him he ought to be ashamed of himself, endangering kids like that. "I'm the only one watching out for these kids," Stan shouts back.

"That right? You the hero here? Let's see what the cops say about that. Maybe they'll give you a key to the city, Stan." Dwayne reaches into his pocket for his phone. We don't wait around for the call to go through.

Stan leads us down several side streets until we wind up at Tent City. He talks with some dude in a red hat who looks like he could have been Elvis in a previous life, hands the dude some cash. We're escorted to one of the tents along the back row. It is a long, cold night, but somehow I sleep.

CHAPTER

29

THE NEXT DAY, I WAKE UP TO VOICES OUTSIDE THE TENT, talking about the fire over at the old Chemco factory. Seems Jimmy Dean's thugs got the fire out before it spread, but I don't imagine we'll be going back there anytime soon. Not with them waiting to jump us again.

Twig and I venture out of the tent, but Stan's nowhere to be found. It's a little warmer, so Twig and I head out to find some food. It's risky visiting the mall during school hours, so samples are off the table. No Hot Light at Krispy Kreme this time of day either. We pass by McDonald's and I half wish Coach would swoop in and buy us lunch again. Even if it means listening to him rant about airplanes and oxygen masks. Easy for him to say all that when he's never had to decide between school and turning his little brother over to the system. But I'd sit through his bullshit again if it meant getting us some food right now. Those shakes and fries seem like something I saw in a movie a million years ago. Twig hasn't complained once, not once. But hunger has etched itself into his face already. The baby fat has drained from his cheeks and his chin juts out like Gran's.

We pass an old guy on the corner holding a sign. The guys who beg down by the Center should take a lesson from this dude. Cars are stopping and handing him cash like it's his birthday. I take a peek at his sign.

OUT OF WORK.
WIFE SICK. 3 KIDS.
ANYTHING HELPS.

No different from most. What is different is he's on the corner by Starbucks, not down by the tracks. Begging, like real estate, is all about location.

"Maybe we should try that," Twig says.

"Great idea," I tell Twig. "We'll just get some cardboard and write, *Please send us to foster care.*"

His lip juts out and he speeds up so he's a few steps ahead of me.

I should apologize, but right now that's too much work. Everything I got is going into figuring out where we can get some food. I'm concentrating so hard, I almost walk right past the pizza boxes sitting unattended on top of a small gray car. It's the crying that catches my attention and when I look back to see where it's coming from, I see a mom wrestling a screaming red-faced toddler into a car seat. She's totally focused on the baby.

"Wait here," I tell Twig.

Without even thinking about it, I sprint toward the car. I grab the pizza boxes and turn just as the mom stands up.

I freeze.

The look of shock on her face would be comical if I wasn't pretty sure my own face matched it.

I say, "Sorry."

I expect her to yell "Wait!" or "Stop!" But she doesn't yell either of those. Instead she screams, "Sicko!"

I hesitate, wanting to tell her I'm not a sicko who goes around stealing other people's food just to be mean. I want to tell her we're just really fucking hungry. But Twig shouts my name with terror at the same time that a brown blur leaps over the baby seat and flies out of the car door at me. It's growling a million times worse than Watchman's fake-ass growls and coming so fast that there is no way I can outrun it. My stomach drops and I drop with it, my elbows hit the pavement, and the growling, barking blur that is all fur and mostly teeth sails right over me. I'm scrambling to my feet, readying for it to turn back and come for me again, but it doesn't. It goes straight for Twig.

I shout, "Run!" then instantly regret it and yell, "No!" but it doesn't matter, because the dog reaches him quicker than my words can. Twig is on the ground and the dog is on him. The mom is screaming the dog's name and trying to pull it off of Twig and I'm kicking the shit out of the dog and beating him with the pizza box and I can't tell if what I see all over Twig's face is blood or pizza sauce until the mom manages to yank the dog off and drag it toward the car. Even then, I don't stop to look at the red stuff. I scoop Twig up and run.

I dart down one alley and then another, finally stopping behind a dumpster because my lungs are on fire and I can't run anymore. Twig is bawling and holding the side of his face. I pry his hands away and feel my stomach heave at the bloody mess that used to be a cheek. There's too much blood for me to tell how bad it is, but I know it's bad enough that I've got to get him help.

I need to get Twig to the emergency room. I know what that means, that they will have to call the police and Twig will get taken away for sure, but I don't know what else to do. The bite on his face is bad. It's still bleeding. I don't think you can bleed to death from a cut on your face, but it could get infected and it will definitely scar horribly if someone doesn't stitch it up. And then there's the question of rabies. The footage of the dog flying past me plays in my mind and I look for froth around the mouth. Dogs with rabies have froth, right? I look down at Twig, still crying in my arms. He doesn't have any froth around his mouth yet, so maybe that's a good sign.

I'm walking and walking and all the time I think I'm walking to Memorial Hospital, but my feet take me instead to the Center. I head to the back alley, looking for Dwayne, but suddenly Stan is there. He doesn't wait for me to explain, just leans down to get a look at the wound, then takes Twig from my arms and starts running. He doesn't stop at corners or spin or step carefully over cracks in the sidewalk; he just clutches Twig tight to his chest and runs.

I follow behind, struggling to keep up, calling after him that Twig needs a doctor.

Stan turns into an alley a few blocks from the Center, kicks several times on a door in the side of a building. I catch up and try the handle. It's unlocked and opens easily. Stan pushes past me into a narrow corridor. "Nancy!" he shouts. "Nancy, get the kit!"

At the end of the corridor is a kitchen, its large wooden table cluttered with papers. Stan swipes everything off of it with one arm and lays Twig on the table, still shouting for Nancy.

A thin woman with long braided hair rushes in. She goes straight to Twig, smoothing his hair away from his cheek and dabbing at the wound with a wet cloth that was white but is rapidly darkening to a brownish red. "What happened?" she asks.

Twig writhes and screams at her touch.

"You're hurting him!" I shout at her, and try to push her away, but Stan catches me from behind and hugs me so tight, my arms are pinned down by my sides. I fight him and yell that Twig needs an actual doctor, but Stan tells me to knock it off and let Nancy help Twig.

"What happened to him?" she asks again.

Stan shakes me so hard, my teeth knock against each other. "Goddamn it, tell her what happened so she can help Twig!"

"A dog!" I yell at them. The cloth is totally saturated now. Each time the woman lifts it from Twig's cheek, he moans horribly. "A dog attacked him. He needs—"

"A doctor," she interrupts me. "I know. Hand me that box. On the counter there behind you."

Stan releases me, but stands close, ready to grab me again if I don't settle down. I hand Nancy the old tackle box. It's covered with stickers—Holly Hobbie, Raggedy Ann, horses and unicorns and sparkly dolphins. She tells Stan to hold the rag on Twig's face and takes the box from me. There's a glint of metal in there—a knife—and some thread. She grabs a small bottle and a new cloth. "I'm sorry," she mumbles, and douses Twig's cheek in something that makes him scream worse than the bite itself.

I hold Twig's hand and study the book spines on the shelves while Nancy meticulously cleans the wound. Stan paces. *Differential Diagnosis*, *Small Animal Theriogenology*, *Veterinary Herbal Medicine*. At least she has some medical background.

"This is gonna hurt some, okay?" she asks. Twig nods bravely.

Stan stops pacing and comes over. "Hey, did I ever tell you about the time I met Michael Jordan?" he asks.

Twig whimpers what might be a no. Stan goes into this huge story about running into Michael Jordan at a pickup game on the south side of Chicago, which has to be pure bullshit, but keeps Twig wide-eyed and occupied until Nancy puts down her needle.

"Fifty-two stitches," she tells Twig. "That's a new record 'round here."

She steps back so I can see her handiwork. "Looks worse than it is," Nancy assures me.

Twig isn't crying anymore. He's just holding my hand and watching my face. I smile at him, but it's hard. He looks like some kid's science experiment. There's an arc the size of a baseball across his forehead. A bigger cut goes from his lip right up to his eye, which is purple and swollen shut. "Are you sure it didn't damage his eye?"

"Just missed it." Nancy's tossing her tools into the kitchen sink, but turns to look at me. "I know it doesn't look like it, but he's pretty lucky. Missed his lip and nose, too."

"What about rabies?"

Nancy looks like I asked her if Twig might turn into a zombie. "Was it a stray that bit him?"

"No . . . ," I say.

The scene runs through my head, this time in slow motion. Two pizzas sitting on top of a gray four-door Fiesta. Lady in a black coat, dark jeans, bending into the car. Screaming baby, arching its back so she can't buckle it. Brown fur, white teeth, red collar. Woman screaming something at me. But not "sicko." Just like that, it clicks.

She wasn't yelling "sicko." She was yelling "Sick 'em!"

CHAPTER

30

STAN HANDS ME A TWENTY AND TELLS ME TO GO GET
Twig some pain meds. I don't want to leave Twig's side,
but Stan says he'll get him back to Tent City. When I get to
our tent, though, Twig is hysterical.

"What's wrong? Is the pain that bad?" I fumble with the
childproof cap on the bottle of Children's Tylenol.

"No, it's the damn cat," Stan tells me.

"That dog ate Ozzy!" Twig wails.

Fuck.

Twig's backpack was the last thing on my mind when
that dog went for him. We must have dropped it either in the
parking lot where we were attacked or somewhere along the
way to the Center. I try to tell Twig that he just needs some
rest, but he grabs my hand. His whole face scrunches up, all
stitches and purple blotches and tears.

"Ozzy's fine," I tell him, but Twig is crying and begging
me to go help Ozzy. "Twig, you gotta calm down. You're
gonna tear open your stitches."

I promise to go find Ozzy if he will just lie down.

Stan is pacing outside the tent and I tell him to stay with
Twig while I go find his backpack.

Stan nods and says, "Ayuh," but I can see in his eyes the same anxious need to run that I feel. I grab his arm. "Stan! You stay right the fuck here, you understand? I'll be back in a few minutes."

"I got him," Stan says. He seems to consider something, then nods and says again more firmly, "I got him."

I run all the way to Pizza King, but when I get to the edge of the parking lot, I duck behind a truck to check it out. No cops. No gray Fiesta. No red-collar-wearing Cujo. No backpack, either. Somebody probably picked it up. I can't exactly stroll into Pizza King and ask to check out the lost and found.

I'm composing stories to tell Twig—the woman noticed the backpack and gave Ozzy to her kid; someone from Pizza King saw Ozzy and took him inside to feed him cheesy breadsticks and fell in love with him—when I notice a couple crows fighting over something near the bushes. Out of curiosity, I creep around the cars to get a better look. The crows are fighting over a smashed box of pizza. It looks like it's been run over at least once and the crows have picked apart most of what's left. But just past them, a corner of white cardboard pokes out from under the bush. I shoo the crows and am rewarded with the second box of pizza from the gray car. It's basically untouched except for a dirty shoeprint near one edge where the box is crushed. I bend to pick up the box and hear a faint yowling that could only be one thing.

Ozzy is so happy to be out of that backpack that he clings to me like he's half-drowned. I cradle him against my shoulder so I can carry him and the pizza back to the tent.

Twig's asleep when I get there, his head in Stan's lap. Ozzy wriggles for me to put him down and climbs up on Twig's chest. He sniffs at the stitches that zigzag across

Twig's face, then curls up in the blankets next to Twig. Ozzy watches me and Stan eat some of the pizza, but doesn't leave Twig when I hold out a piece of pepperoni for him. We save the last three pieces for Twig.

Stan rocks while he eats. "Kind of a shit day, huh?"

I agree that it is indeed a shit day.

Stan's gone for the whole next day. Twig sleeps most of it, clutching Ozzy against his chest and whimpering in his sleep. I think about sneaking out while he's sleeping. Going to the Castle to leave Ruthie a note so when she comes back from Chick's funeral, she can find us. But every time I start to unzip the tent, Twig stirs and I know if he wakes up and I'm gone, he's gonna freak out. So I stay put and feed him bits of pizza and read to him when he's awake. I pass the rest of the time trying to figure a way out of this mess. Twig's face is all jacked up and we're gonna get pneumonia staying in this fucking tent. I gotta fix this. But how? Anything I can come up with ends with Twig in the system.

Midway through the next day, Stan ducks into the tent. He's wearing a brown trench coat that makes him look fat. He hugs his arms under a bulgy belly.

"Hungry?" he asks. "Boom! Uncle Stanley in the house!" He spreads his arms and the coat falls open, raining individual bags of chips and brightly wrapped candy bars down on me and Twig.

Twig smiles then grimaces in pain. He reaches for a bag of Skittles, but I snatch it away from him.

"Man, this isn't real food! Twig needs some protein. Something that isn't a hundred percent sugar."

Stan bends over and plucks a king-sized candy bar from the pile. He tosses it at me. "Here, Joshie, have a Snickers. You ain't yourself when you're hangry."

I fling it back at him.

"This ain't good enough for you? Why don't you go get yourself some food, then?"

"I would if I could count on you to keep Twig safe while I go get it."

"Yeah?" Stan rubs the back of his hand across his mouth. "Last time I checked, it was you who let him get chewed up by a fucking Rottweiler."

I glance at Twig, expecting him to be watching us with his weary eyes, but he's curled around Ozzy, his back to us. I bend down and touch his shoulder. "Twig?"

He doesn't turn, just says softly, "I'm sorry."

"What?" I try to roll him toward me so I can see his face, but he clenches his body and doesn't let me. "Twig? Why are you sorry? None of this is your fault."

"Yes, it is. If I didn't eat so much, you wouldn't have to pay Gran to feed me. If I weren't here, you could go make money to feed yourself. You would be better off without me."

"That's not true." I yank on him and almost get him to turn over, but he flails his arm, smacking me in the mouth. "Fuck it. I'm going to get us some food." I point a finger at Stan. "Don't you leave him."

I go to the Center and hang by the back door until Dwayne comes out for a smoke. He jumps half out of his skin when I say hi. I manage to talk him into sneaking a bag of leftovers from lunch. He holds it out to me, but doesn't let go when I grab it.

"Can't keep this up," he says.

I let go of the bag. "Fine. I'll get something to eat somewhere else."

"Josh. I'm not talking about the food. Take this." He hands me the bag. "I'll get more for you tonight, no problem.

But you look in the mirror lately? You look anorexic. It would make your momma real sad, Josh, you and your little bro living on the streets, half starved."

"You think I don't know that? What else am I supposed to do? My dad is . . . gone and Gran ain't no kind of help."

"I know she isn't perfect, probably isn't even halfway good, but you gotta go back."

"No." I start down the alley toward the road.

Dwayne yells after me. "You can't even feed yourselves."

"Oh yeah? Watch me!"

I sound like a second grader, which only proves his point, but I storm off with a bread bag full of what smells like tuna casserole, so I'm calling that a win.

Of course, Twig hates tuna casserole. *All* little kids hate tuna casserole. And, if I'm being real, what person on earth doesn't? It's smooshy and smelly and eating it left over with your fingers out of a bread bag ups the disgusting quotient by about a thousand. Twig wants to complain. I can see it in his eyes—well, the right eye. The left one's still swollen shut. I dump a little pile of tuna casserole out for Ozzy, who gobbles it up like it's the best thing on earth, which for him it probably is, but that gives me an idea. I grab two bags of potato chips and scoop a big goop of casserole on one like chip dip. "Oh my God," I say with my mouth full. "This is A-mazing! Tastes just like pepperoni pizza!"

Stan's hunched over, sitting on the floor near the Dory light, puzzle-piecing Nemo back together with a tube of superglue. He looks up. Twig side-eyes me.

I grab another chip and scoop. "Mmmmm ... this is like ... oh yeah! Gran's Spam-alicious Thanksgiving feast—mixed with two cherry turnovers! C'mon, man, you gotta try this."

Stan grins. "They must have Big Mary on kitchen duty. When that woman cooks, it's like Willy Wonka all up in there."

Twig reluctantly takes a chip and dips the top corner in the casserole. He bites it.

"What's that one taste like?" I ask.

"Potato chips."

Stan scoots over to us and takes the half-bitten chip from Twig. "Naw, man, you need a bigger bite. Really get some of Big Mary's fixings on that chip." He gimme-wriggles his fingers. I hold out the bread bag. He loads that chip up so full, casserole hangs off the sides. He pops the whole thing into his mouth and chews with his mouth open. "Oh yeah, Mary! That's what I'm talking about! Top sirloin with crispy onions and a buttery baked potato. Some chocolate pie for dessert!"

Twig's mouth twists to suppress a grin. I hold the bag out to him. He loads his chip and shoves it into his mouth. He gags, which gets me and Stan laughing.

"Come on, boy!" Stan says. "Don't keep it in, tell us what that tastes like."

Twig chews and gags and chews some more. He swallows with a huge gulp and says, "Purple Kool-Aid."

"That's it? Mary must be slipping if all you taste is purple Kool-Aid." Stan frowns his disapproval. "Maybe we oughta call up the Center. Get that woman fired."

Twig holds up a finger. He takes another chip and dips it. "Purple Kool-Aid and"—he smacks his lips as he chews the chip and stares thoughtfully at the ceiling—"oatmeal raisin cream sandwiches, grilled cheese and tomato soup and Oreos and sliced peaches and . . . and . . . hot fudge sundaes with strawberry jelly!"

He dissolves in a fit of giggles and me and Stan can't help but crack up with him.

That night Stan says he's got to go see a man about a horse. "Clock's ticking on toward that big job," he tells us. "Couple more days and we'll be home free."

I stay behind with Twig. I read to him and Ozzy and sit there after he falls asleep, remembering the way he used to giggle when he was a baby. He laughed so easily back then, and I would do anything to earn one of his giggly baby fits. Twig deserves that—a mom and a dad in a big old farmhouse where he can laugh so hard, his belly shakes and he is happy and never has to eat frickin' tuna casserole. He may never have those things, but he deserves more than sleeping on dirty blankets in a fucking tent in the middle of winter. More than a diet of candy bars and potato chips. Man, I really fucked this up.

Twig murmurs in his sleep. I stroke his hair, brushing it away from the stitches. His head is sweaty, even though it's cold as heck in the tent, and I wonder if it's a fever. Maybe his stitches are infected. Ozzy unwinds himself from Twig's arms with a stretch and meows at me.

"I know," I tell him. "It's just hard to do that."

I'm still sitting there, with my back against the tent and Twig's head in my lap, when Stan comes back the next morning. He's all jazzed up—practically bouncing.

"Any sign of Ruthie?" I ask.

"Naw, but the plan is all coming together," he says.

Twig stirs, but doesn't wake. I shift his head off my lap and motion Stan outside the tent. "What's up?"

"Even better than we thought! At least double the money. Gonna have enough for a down payment on that restaurant by the time Ruthie's back in town."

He won't share any details. Just keeps saying we're "gonna hit the motherfucking jackpot" and laughing like a kid who downed a case of 5-Hour Energy. I want to believe that Stan's plan can solve everything, but Twig needs out of here now. Today. He can't spend one more day hungry.

"What do we do meanwhile?" I ask.

"What do you mean? We keep on keeping on."

"We need food. We need heat. I think Twig's getting sick."

"I'll bring back another blanket. Get you some more food."

"What, more candy?"

"You got a better plan?"

Dwayne, Matt, Coach, Ruthie—they all tried to tell me and I wouldn't listen. And here's Stan still clinging to his fucking plan while Twig is hurt and cold and sick. Do I have a better plan? No, but I know it's crazy to think Stan is ever gonna be able to help us build a real life. I wait until he leaves to get us more blankets and then I wake up Twig. "It's time to go," I tell him.

CHAPTER
31

I TELL TWIG TO KEEP HIS HEAD DOWN ON THE BUS. "READ your book," I tell him.

It doesn't help, though—everyone who gets on the bus stares at his stitches. Honestly, that and the swelling and the bruising are probably the only things keeping us from getting recognized. Twig is too sick to read, but he holds the book up. He follows me off the bus, only noticing where we are as he steps off and the doors shut behind him.

"What are we doing here?" Twig asks. There's fear in his voice and maybe a hint of distrust.

"Come on." I walk fast, pulling him along so he has to half jog to keep up.

"Josh? What are we doing?"

I keep walking. I don't stop to explain. I can't. My whole body is knotted, my shoulders ache, my hands are all balled up. I can barely swallow around the clump of fear in my throat. What if I'm wrong? What if Gran turns Twig over to the courts and I never see him again? I can't let Twig see any of the doubt, so I walk, stiff-legged and hunched over. Hurry us toward Gran's trailer so I can just get it over with.

At the edge of Gran's lot, Twig digs in both feet and yanks hard on my hand. His eyes plead with me. "You can't send me back here."

"Woodrow." I try for the tone Mom used when she'd made up her mind and there was no discussing it. Mom's firm but kind *I know you don't agree, but I know what's best* tone. As a kid, I hadn't liked when she talked that way, but I had known there was no use arguing. I expect Twig's shoulders to slump in defeat, but the tone I achieve isn't Mom's at all. It's Coach's. A two-syllable bark that causes Twig to recoil.

I swallow, force my shoulders to relax, my throat to open. I bend down so our eyes are at the same level and say his name again, soft. "Twig."

He stares back, defiant, angry, hurt, fearful.

"I don't know what else to do, okay? It isn't safe for you on the streets. Stan has a plan to buy his parents' old restaurant. There's an apartment above it. If we can make that happen, we'll finally have a home. But it's taking too long. You're sick. You need a warm bed. You gotta stay here while I go help Stan. I just can't keep you safe."

"If it isn't safe for me, it isn't safe for you."

"I am safe."

"Bullshit," Twig says.

I hold his gaze. I can't flinch away from the image of Chick upside down in that manhole, him and Wade on the front page of the paper. We got lucky getting away from Jimmy Dean. Those are horrible risks, but right now I have Twig's stitched-up face to think about. Twig's empty stomach. He might be right about the streets being dangerous for me, but I can't let him know that. We both need to believe what I am saying. "I need you to stay with Gran so I can work just a little more. A few more days and we'll have enough money to buy the restaurant, to have a home, Twig."

I hold out my hand.

Twig doesn't even glance down at it.

"I need you to do this for us. For me."

He hesitates long enough that I almost give in. Almost tell him I'm sorry and he's right, that this is a stupid plan and we'll find another way together. But just as I'm ready to cave in, the defiant expression slips from his face. He looks so incredibly sad. His hand presses into mine.

Gran doesn't answer when I knock, so I fumble for the extra key, disturbing a layer of crusted snow that sits like frosting on top of her potflower. A TV audience boos from the front room where Jerry Springer's voice asks if they want to hear what Debra's husband has to say. The curtain over the sink is drawn, casting an eerie darkness in the kitchen. Unopened mail litters the table. Flies buzz lazily around a half-eaten container of takeout from Panda Express, which lies on the counter, a fork sticking out of it. Dirty dishes and empty Budweiser cans float in murky sink water.

Twig looks at me with wide eyes.

"Gran?" I call.

We find her on the couch, soft snores coming from her wide-open mouth. More Budweiser cans on the floor, a half-smoked blunt balanced on the edge of the table next to a bowl of what might have once been Frosted Flakes. Twig picks up the remote and turns the TV down.

"Gran?" I shake her gently, then when that doesn't work, harder.

"Hmmm?" She pulls herself up on her elbows and looks around like she's not sure where she is.

"Gran, Twig's gonna stay here a few days, okay?"

Her head bobbles in my direction. "Joshie?" she asks, except it's so slurred, it comes out mostly vowels. "I told yer dad I'd take care of ya just as long as he don't go and shoot hisself like his daddy did. I told him I would, and I done right by you boys, ain't I?" Her eyes droop and she's asleep again.

Twig and I don't talk as we clean up the trailer and carry the trash out to the dumpster. Twig's phone is on the table where the cop must have left it. I find his charger in the back bedroom and plug it in. Jerry Springer changes to *Maury* and eventually to *Divorce Court*. Every family has their shit. I check the cupboard and fridge, but all that's there are a few cans of chicken with rice soup and some milk that's gone so far past its date that the sides of the jug swell. The stash in the back bedroom is still there—peanut butter crackers, juice boxes, and some stale but usable bread.

"I'll come back tomorrow with some real food," I tell Twig.

Twig nods. He puts his backpack on the bed and Ozzy pokes his head out.

"Turn on your ringer and keep your phone charged." I check my phone to make sure the ringer's on, then stuff it into my pocket. "You and Ozzy lock the door and take care of Gran, okay? Make sure she eats something and don't give her no more beer."

He nods again and follows me back out to the kitchen.

"We need to do this, okay, buddy? I gotta get us some money so we can take care of ourselves. You know I love you, right? You know that?"

Twig nods.

All this nodding should make it easier for me to leave, but it doesn't. I know he's not nodding because he believes any of this. He's nodding so I can believe it.

I put my arms around his shoulders and guide him toward the table where I can sit in one of the old kitchen chairs and be at eye level. "Twig. You gotta talk to me. I can't leave unless I know you're really okay with it. Just a few days."

He fidgets with something in his pocket and doesn't look at me. Gently, I pull his hand from his pocket and unwrap his fingers from the folded picture of our family. White creases divide our family: me and Dad on one side, Mom and Twig on the other. I hold it by its edges, smooth it back and forth over my pants, but there's no erasing the crease. I want to take the photo with me, but Twig needs it more than I do, so I hand it back to him.

He refolds it and sticks it back into his pocket. So quiet that I can barely hear him, he asks, "What if you don't come back?"

I wrap my hand around his and press it to my heart. "I'll come back. I promise. We'll be together in a home, Twig. A real home."

He nods.

CHAPTER
32

THE WHOLE WAY BACK TO TENT CITY I THINK ABOUT THAT promise. I promised Twig that I would come back. But what makes a spoken promise any more likely to be kept than an implied promise? Isn't deciding to have a child a promise? That you will take care of them, keep them safe, never leave them? Everyone who makes a promise believes they can keep it. Then something gets in the way and fucks it all up. What makes my promise different from my dad's? I am not going to let anything get in the way of getting back to Twig.

Stan's pacing outside the tent when I get there. "Where the fuck you been? I was gonna grab us dinner at the Center, but too late now." Stan looks around as if realizing for the first time that Twig is missing. "Where's little man?"

I'm too pissed to talk about it. "We gonna do this, let's do it."

"No, I promised your dad I'd keep you out of it."

"Well, I'm in it, Stan. Knee-deep in the same shit you're standing in. Let's just get it over with, okay?"

He doesn't say anything for a few seconds and I can almost see the gears turning in that brain of his. "Just need to stop off and grab something."

I'm relieved that we're on the move. Stan leads me to the Castle and around back to the tools. "The plan is the manholes?" I ask.

"No. Not the manholes. But we need to get something out of one of them."

We drag the tarp out and walk in silence broken only by the crunch and crackle of the frozen snow beneath our feet. The moon follows us as we duck through the hole in the fence where I found that bit of Chick's scarf, to the hill Chick and Ruthie tumbled down like little kids, and across the field where they stopped to kiss. The tracks are deserted and there's little movement on the street below as we cross the railroad bridge and pass the holes we've already scrapped. As we near the hole where we found Chick, the wind lifts strands of yellow police tape so they dance.

"Think they'll ever pin this on Jimmy Dean?"

"No, that man's as slippery as a two-dollar coat of Teflon. But things got a way of catching up to a man after time. He'll get his someday."

I don't know how much Teflon two dollars can buy, but Stan's meaning is clear enough. Truth is, we pretty much guaranteed there'd be no evidence against the real killer when we erased any signs Ruthie and I had moved the body.

Stan lets go of the tarp with one hand and salutes Chick. I follow suit. Seems like the least we can do. We salute another hole with yellow tape, presumably where Wade was found. Stan leads me to a third hole. "It's in this one," he says.

I grab the crowbar and help him ease off the lid. "I'll hold the light," he says. "You go on down and get it."

"Get what?" I ask.

"Come on, Josh," Stan shouts. "Gonna freeze my ass off. Just get down in there!"

"What's in there?" I ask again. Instead of answering me, Stan charges, his shoulder hitting me in the gut, bending me in two. I topple backward into the hole. My head ricochets off the lip of the hole and my ankle bangs the base of the ladder. I sit up, but my vision blurs.

"Why the fuck couldn't you just listen to me?" Stan says from the opening.

I look up at him, but my head hurts like a motherfucker and tears cloud my eyes. "What the fuck, Stan?"

"I told you, your dad and me got this handled. All you had to do was wait it out, everything would be fine, but you couldn't fucking listen."

"Stan!" I try to stand, but everything spins and I grab the ladder to steady myself.

"'Tell me the plan,' you said. Well, you wanna know so bad? Tonight's the night. That bitch is finally gone to Florida, and we're gonna burn her fucking trailer down. Wait a few weeks for the insurance guys to do their thing and *cha-ching*! We got the down payment for that restaurant just like I been telling you all. Just stay put, you hear me? Me and your dad, we'll settle this tonight and be back for you in the morning."

Burn the trailer? Burn Gran's trailer? No, no, no, Gran is there! *Twig* is there "Stan! Wait!"

But Stan drags the cover back on the hole and leaves me alone in the dark.

I am drowning in blackness. My throat closes and my eyes water; I recoil from the heat of flames that hide in billowing black smoke. I cough and choke and flail against the smoke.

In my panic I stumble over something and fall. My hands grope and find hair, a face. I am twelve and my home is burning and my mother is asleep in her bed choking on the smoke and I am too weak to lift her and I am choking too. I wrap my arms around my mother. We will both die here and all I can do is hold her head against my chest that heaves to draw oxygen from the smoked-filled room. I cry and tell her I am sorry that I can't save her. That I am too weak. But the smoke does not suffocate me and it takes too long for the flames to come. The air is too thin to choke me and smells of smoke, but not burning. Soon the heaving of my lungs slows and I can breathe.

I'm not twelve.

I am not trapped in my burning home with my unconscious mother.

I am seventeen. I was walking with Stan and . . . we were getting something out of a manhole and . . . he pushed me. Stan pushed me into the hole and closed the lid and left me here. In the dark. Holding someone who is not my mother. For one horrific second I think that it might be Ruthie. But the angles are all wrong and that smoke smell tickles my nose and I lean down to breathe in the scent of cigarettes and nicotine. What the fuck?

I remember the phone in my pocket and fumble with it in the dark. Its faint glow illuminates enough for me to see it's not Ruthie. It's Jimmy Dean. I feel for a pulse along the tendons in his neck, but either there is no pulse, or my frozen frightened fingers cannot find it.

CHAPTER

33

I SHOULD CALL 911.

I dial the 9 and the 1, but my finger hovers over the final numeral. What would I say? *Help, I'm trapped in a manhole? One of my worst enemies is dead and despite my finger-prints being all over the crime scene, I did not kill him?* And the police would do what? Come and rescue me and take me down to the station, where'd they'd give me hot chocolate with marshmallows and say, *Thank you, young upstanding high school dropout who kidnapped his younger brother, please inform us who committed this foul act?* And I would say, *Stan, Stan, the Trashcan Man.* That's funny, so we'd laugh together, the police and I. Except it's not just funny, it's freaking hilarious and I can't stop laughing even though the police aren't actually laughing with me because I am all alone with Jimmy Dean's body in a manhole.

It occurs to me then that I might be losing my mind.

My head throbs, my thoughts floating all separate like fruit chunks in a Jell-O brain, slowly settling into place. I'm in a manhole. Just like Chick and Wade. And Jimmy Dean. Stan threw me down here. Maybe he threw Jimmy Dean down here too. And if he did that, then holy shit . . . maybe it's been him this entire time. And now he's headed to Gran's. Where Twig is.

I have to get to Gran's.

I grab the ladder and haul myself up the metal rungs one by one, despite the fact that with each step, the world spins faster. At the top, I press my shoulder against the manhole cover and heave with all my might, but there's no moving that thing from down here. And there's no way out but up.

I hook my arm through a rung and pull out my phone again, but there's no reception. Back on the ground, I manage to get one bar. Better, but not good enough. I shuffle around the small space, scanning for better reception, until the only spot I haven't tried is on the other side of Jimmy Dean. There's no way I want to step over him, but I can't stand here wasting time while Twig and Gran are in danger. I brace my hand against the wall, and step into the small space between Jimmy Dean and the copper piping. Three bars.

I pull up my contacts, but the only number there is for the cell phone I gave Twig. I press it, but it rings and rings before going to a recording that apologizes that the person has a voicemail box that has not been activated. I text him:

Get out of the trailer NOW!

Shit, shit, shit.

I only know two numbers by heart—Matt's and Coach's and I wouldn't even know Coach's if he hadn't literally drilled it into us one day at practice.

"Day's gonna come when you need me," he'd said. "You'll be out somewhere and drink too much. Need to get home without a DUI messing up your chance at college ball. Or maybe it's good. You're at a restaurant and a scout approaches you with an offer. You don't talk to them before you call me. Got it?" We'd all responded heartily that we did in fact get it, but just to be sure, Coach had us run the stairs for thirty minutes, reciting his digits with each step, so that by the time practice was over, his phone number was burned into our muscle memory.

I dial the first three digits then freeze, my finger hovering over the keypad. Matt or Coach? They both have trucks, but Matt has parents and that could slow him down. I fumble to punch in the rest of Coach's number. Somehow I convince him to come for me and not bring the police. While I wait for him to get here, I drag Jimmy Dean over to the wall farthest from the ladder so he won't be visible to anyone looking down. I sit against the other wall, trying to get my head to stop pounding so I can think. It seems like forever before the manhole cover clangs off and Coach is shouting my name.

"Down here!"

Coach grasps my arm as I climb out of the hole. He leads me over to his truck and helps me into the passenger seat. "Where are you hurt?" he asks.

I follow his gaze to the red smear of blood on my arm. "I banged my head when I fell. But it's okay."

It's not okay, though. Stan is on his way to get my dad and they're headed to Gran's. "I need to get to Gran's," I tell Coach. I'm thinking he could drive me to Gran's, but even as I think it, I know I have a better chance of stopping Dad and Stan if it's just me.

"Hold on, there. We gotta get you checked out first." Coach reaches across me for his cell phone. His keys are still in the ignition.

"Yeah, yeah," I tell him. "My . . . friend needs help too." I point to the hole.

"Someone else is down there?" Coach rushes over to the manhole.

I pull the passenger door shut and slide across the seat to the driver's side and haul ass out of there.

CHAPTER
34

AS I ROUND THE BEND, MY HEADLIGHTS SWEEP OVER the front of Gran's trailer and Dad, leaning into the trunk of the Datsun. He looks up, startled, like he's ready to run. The truck barely comes to a stop before I slam it into park and jump out. "Dad! Stop!"

"What are you doing here?" Dad's voice is one part panic, one part relief. He shifts his body to hide what's in the trunk.

I shoot my own questions back at him. "What the hell are you doing? Where's Stan?"

Dad shushes me, looking around to see if all of the commotion has drawn any attention, but it's the middle of the night and everything's locked up tight. "You get back in that truck and get on outta here. Let us handle this."

I lean around him, peering into the trunk at a cardboard box containing several pop bottles with raggedy strips of his old shirt tucked into the tops. It takes me a second to process what they are. "You're really gonna burn down Gran's trailer? After what happened to Mom?"

"That whole thing got messed up. If I had just listened to Stan, followed the plan, everything would have been okay. But I got cold feet. This time we've got all the details worked out."

"Wait—what? The fire—that was you? You and Stan burned down our house?"

"No! I mean—yes, but it was Stan's plan. Kill two birds with one stone. That old house was falling apart. He said if we burned it down, the house would be gone and we'd get money to build a new one."

I stare at him, incredulous. "Stan tells you to burn down your house and you do it? It was our home!" My mind is reeling, trying to put together all the shit he's saying with what I remember about that day.

Mom trying to get us ready for school, me locking myself in my room, telling her to leave me alone. Mom banging on the door: *God bless it, Joshua!* Memories flood back like smoke, blurring out Dad and the Datsun, Gran's trailer, pressing into every crack and crevice, choking out what I want to remember and gagging me with what really happened. I climbed into my bed, pulled the pillow over my head so I wouldn't hear her yelling at me, so she wouldn't hear me crying. I cried like a fucking baby, screaming into my pillow, sobbing until I fell asleep from pure exhaustion. Opening my eyes to fire rippling across the ceiling. The world upside down and smoke forcing dark fingers down my throat, searing my eyes as I staggered half blinded, calling out with a voice so ravaged and raw, even I couldn't hear it over the crackling wood and shattering glass. Every breath scorched air, wanting to recoil but needing to find my mom, to find Twig and knowing, just knowing I would never make it to my mom, never be able to get to Twig. But then Stan had stepped through the fire and dragged me from the house. He'd held me against his chest and I'd clung to him, my face against his neck, my eyes pressed closed, blocking out everything except the smell of Stan, his shirt drenched in sweat and just under it all . . . the same odor clinging to Dad now, wafting from the Datsun's trunk.

Gasoline.

My stomach lurches and I stagger away from the smell, but rough hands grab me and spin me back around. I blink, trying to refocus on what's right here, right now. Dad, his mouth moving. "You're not hearing me! It was gonna be condemned and where would that have left us?"

I shake my head, try to clear it.

Dad tosses the truth like icy water in my face. "Stan's idea was a win-win—"

"Win-win? Who the fuck won, Dad? Mom died!"

He grips my arm, shaking his head. "No, you got that all wrong, Joshie. She wasn't supposed to die!"

I wrench away from him and shove him so hard, he staggers backward. "But she did die! She died and you knew he was gonna set the fire! Where the fuck were you?"

Dad's face reddens, then crumples. "I tried to call it off! It's not my fault. You were supposed to be at school! Your mom was supposed to be at work! If you would have just—"

"If I would have just what? Gone to school?" All this time I thought the fire was some random accident. That it was my fault Mom died because I made her stay home that day. But it wasn't random. It wasn't even an accident. It was him. ". . . you did this. You're the reason she's dead."

"Stan said it would make everything better! We'd get the insurance money and buy a big house and—"

He keeps talking, but I can't even look at him. All this time, it was him and Stan. He was *never* there for us. Never what I thought he was. All those years he was off trailing behind Stan from one town to the next, leaving Mom with nothing to give us but dreams of a future together and then he took that, too. Him and fucking Stan.

Stan!

I'm halfway to the trailer when Dad grabs my arm and spins me around.

"Where are you going?" he asks. He's gripping my arm tight.

"We have to stop Stan!"

"No, we have to wait here. There's a plan and if we follow it—"

I jerk away from him, thinking about Gran and Twig sound asleep in that trailer. No way has Gran recovered from her bender enough to wake up to the smell of smoke and Twig wouldn't wake up even if Woodson's marching band performed their halftime show in the bedroom. "Gran is going to die. She didn't leave, Dad. Or if she did, she came back. She's passed out drunk on her couch right now. And Twig"—my voice breaks as the reality of what's about to happen punches me in the gut—"Twig is in the trailer!"

The color drains from Dad's face and he crumples to his knees. "Oh my God. Not again, please not again."

"We can stop him!" I yank Dad's arm, trying to get him back on his feet.

I know we can stop Stan if we go now and if Dad helps me, but he's full-on crying, blubbering about how it's too late and he killed us all. I think of all the times he and Stan told me to man up when I was little. Stop crying. Grow a pair. But Dad isn't any kind of man either. Just Stan's fucking lapdog. He was never gonna be the dad we needed, because he was never gonna be able to stand up to Stan. And he's not gonna save us now. That's up to me.

I leave him crying there on the ground and soft-step closer to the trailer. Stan's smart, so I need to be smarter. I have to get close enough to see what's going on without him knowing I'm here. Before I scoot around to the porch, I glance back toward Dad, knowing he isn't going to help me, but wanting to make sure he isn't gonna warn Stan either. He's not by the Datsun anymore. I spot him at the end of the driveway running as fast as he can in the opposite direction.

Fuck him.

I turn back to the porch and force myself to stop and think. Stop and breathe.

And that's when I smell the gasoline already on the porch.

I take the stairs two at a time, but on the landing my foot hits something and sends it rebounding off the porch rail with a clang. I press myself against the side of the trailer just as a flashlight clicks on. Bright light shines through the doorway onto the porch.

"That you, Tye?" Stan calls.

I could rush him. He's expecting Dad, not me. I could knock the flashlight out of his hand and gut-punch him. I see it all in my mind, clear as day. But my mind puts something in Stan's other hand. A lighter. My mind shows Stan dropping the lighter into a pool of gas and the kitchen bursting into flames around us.

Stan waits, the flashlight's beam wavering with the tremble of his hand.

I wait, my breath jagged and shallow.

Stan waits another eternity, then the light of the beam sweeps away. His footsteps cross the linoleum and grow quiet. He must be on the carpet now. Does he see Gran? Would he care if he did? I doubt it. I doubt it very much. Maybe he'd think of Gran dying in the fire as a bonus. That there's life insurance in Dad's name or maybe mine.

I have to get Twig out of there before Stan torches the place.

I tiptoe across the linoleum and breathe a sigh of relief when I get to the carpet without alerting Stan. The smell of gasoline is stronger here, trapped in the canister of the trailer without the night air to wick it away. Gran's still on the couch. Her snores are soft and quiet like a child's. I bend to shake her awake but stop myself. In all the years we've lived here, Gran has always been hard to wake up and if you do wake her, she wakes up loud. She yells for Twig to fetch her pills, for me to quiet the hell down. If I wake her now, she'll shout at me for waking her up in the middle of the night. There would be no shushing her, no keeping Stan from hearing her. So I leave her there, asleep.

From down the hall there's loud pounding—*bam! bam!*—and the sound of wood splintering. I creep up to the edge of the hallway and peer in. Light dances from down the hall. He's in one of the bedrooms. *Don't be Twig's, don't be Twig's.* I inch forward. The light is steady now, coming from the room that is not ours, the one that no one ever goes in because Gran keeps it locked. Cabinets bang open and junk crashes to the floor.

I watch Twig's door, praying the noise doesn't wake him, doesn't pull him out into the hallway. For a second I think maybe it'd be good if Twig came out. Maybe Stan would get him out of the trailer. Then I think about Gran on her couch-island sleeping in a sea of gas fumes. How many fires has Stan set, not caring who died?

He's taking his time in Gran's room, riffling through her drawers. Looking for something.

I creep into the hall, my back to the wall, moving silently, quietly, softly. If I can just get to Twig's room . . . then what? I could lock the door behind me and hope I can get me and Twig out the window before Stan busts the door down? Hide behind the door and rush Stan when he busts in?

Before I can even get close to Twig's room, Stan steps back out into the hall and we both freeze, not four feet from one another.

"Aw, now, Joshie. I thought I told you to stay put."

I'm empty-handed, but he's not. From one hand dangles a bunch of Gran's old jewelry.

The other hand holds a pop bottle with a cloth in the top.

"I can't let you do this, Stan."

The corner of his lip twitches, then stretches into a slow grin. "That right?"

"Yeah. You had to see Gran out there on the couch. You walked right past her. You set this place on fire and she goes up too. Just like Mom."

Stan laughs. Behind him Twig's door eases open. I force myself to hold Stan's gaze as he goes on, oblivious to Twig in the hall behind him. "That old woman doesn't give two shits about you. You expect me to believe you care about her?"

"Just because she is a horrible person doesn't mean she deserves to die."

"Oh, she sure as shit deserves to die. She's the whole reason we didn't have enough money from the life insurance to buy Sal's. Guilted your dad into keeping the life support going long after Rosie was gone. Ate up all our money. Couldn't even be counted on to watch you two boys."

My blood runs cold. "You are a fucking monster."

"Who do you think I'm doing all of this for? Me? I can live anywhere. But me and your dad want a good home for you and your brother—"

"What happened to Chick, Stan? And Wade? Did they get in the way of your plan? Did you kill them, too?"

Stan's head turns away, his mouth twisting like he got a taste of something nasty. He turns back, nodding, eyes steel. He jabs me hard in the chest with his knuckles, leaves his fist full of Gran's cheap jewelry there against my chest like he's pinning me in place. "You got a lot of fucking nerve judging me. I did what I did—all of it—for you. So's you won't have to keep living with that bitch. So's you could have a life I never had. Them others, they would have got in the way, but Old Stan's been taking care of you all along. Now we'll do this thing and then you and Twig will come with me and—"

I step into him, not caring about the pressure of his knuckles on my sternum. "You are a lying sack of shit who never cared for anyone but yourself. We are not going anywhere with you."

Stan shrugs, dropping his hand to his side. "You really want to do this to your dad? He's sure gonna be upset losing you this way. Too bad you didn't listen to me. Had to come busting in here, trying to help with the plan."

"I would never fucking help you!"

"Oh, but you did, Josh. You helped me with the scrap metal and the pharmacy job. That last one'll really eat your dad up. And then setting your own grandma's trailer on fire. Cops are gonna have a field day when they find you. Won't take long for them to put two and two together, pin Chick and Jimmy Dean on you too. Cops are real good at figuring out a man who done one thing would be just as likely to do the rest. That and your fingerprints are all over both of them, ain't they?" Stan grins like he just thought of something hilarious, then leans forward to let me in on his joke. "Ayuh. Your dad's gonna be real sad, but he'll still have Twig, so he'll get over it eventually, just like he did your momma."

This fucker might have taught me every basketball move my body knows, how to dribble that ball like it's attached to my fingertips, how to hit the basket like all I gotta do is look at it, but Coach taught me to use my brain. To think. To analyze what the other player is doing and the strategy behind it. And right now I see through all of Stan's taunting for what he's really after. He wants me to see red and nothing else. That way, I'll be stupid and he can get the jump on me. But I have to play this right or Twig isn't going to make it out of here.

"Or . . . ," Stan draws the word out. "We could walk out together. Pals. You tell me how you want to do this thing."

He shifts his weight and I get a clear view of Twig, standing in his bedroom doorway with wide eyes, cradling Ozzy like a grumpy teddy bear. I have to get him out of here.

I drop my eyes, force my shoulders to fall in what I hope looks like defeat. "Yeah, you're right. Let's do this thing," I say.

Stan shakes his head, scoffing. "Can't bullshit a bullshitter, kid." He tucks Gran's necklace into his pants pocket and whips out a lighter as he brings the flame toward the cloth. I scream at Twig the only thing I can think of—"Ollie-OOP!"—and raise my hands for a pass, and Stan turns toward Twig, the cloth on fire, and Twig doesn't even hesitate, he just bends low, Ozzy's tail dragging the ground, and Ozzy flies through the air and the pop bottle smashes to the ground at Stan's feet as he shields his face from the cat coming right at him, but Ozzy sails over his head and I catch him, I catch that stupid cat while Stan dances, he dances as flames race up his pant legs and across his shirt and flames fill the space between me and Twig and Twig is shouting but I can't see him through the flames, which spill to the carpet, sending up thick smoke that chokes us, we will all die here, but there's a sharp pain in my hand and it's Ozzy biting me, the fucking cat is biting me.

I look down at Ozzy.

And through the flames at my brother.

And I run.

I run. Not out the door, not to safety, but to the flames, through the flames, and I tackle Twig, knocking him into his room. We fall to the floor, Ozzy squished between us. I kick the door shut.

Horror screams in the hall. Smoke curls its fingers under the door.

Twig has scrambled to his feet and is tugging at me, pulling at me. He's saying something, but I can't hear him over the screaming and the smoke alarms in the hallway and Ozzy's yowling because I'm still holding that fucking cat like a basketball. Twig gives up on getting me to understand and climbs up on the bed. He throws open the curtains and opens the window. He holds out his hands and I give him Ozzy. Twig drops Ozzy out the window and climbs after him. "Come on!" he shouts, and I do, I come on and we are outside, coughing and choking on the fresh air.

Flames rise from the back windows and crawl along the top of the trailer. Smoke pours from the kitchen window and the open door and there isn't much time until the fire reaches the living room.

"Gran is in there," Twig says.

Sirens wail in the distance. Too far away to help Gran.

I hear Coach's voice, it's only in my head, but it drowns out the sirens and the neighbors spilling out of their homes and Ozzy's yowling and the cheerleaders with their "Thir-TEE-two, thir-TEE-two," Matt saying "Come on, man, let it fly," Coach saying "You better nail it, Roberts," and I know I will because there's no one else to do it. And then even Coach's voice fades away and it's just me and the *whomp whomp* of my heartbeat in my ears. I stare at the trailer, flames dripping from the roof like saliva. *You still hungry?*

It opens its mouth for me and I launch myself into the blaze.

CHAPTER
35

THE PARAMEDIC SAYS IT'S JUST SOME MINOR SMOKE IN-halation, but Gran can't quit coughing. They strap her to a gurney and listen and prod. Gran squeezes our hands and tells us maybe we ain't so worthless after all. We don't leave her side until the paramedic says they're ready to go.

After the ambulance leaves with Gran, we sit on the back bumper of the fire truck, me and Twig and Ozzy, while the firefighters hose down what's left of Gran's trailer and the paramedics check us out. Aside from some singed fur and a nasty bite on the hand, we're fine—physically. Emotionally . . . looking at Twig breaks my heart. The sparkle is gone from his eyes. Not so long ago he would have been excited about the fire truck and all the equipment. Now he sits quietly and lets the paramedic look in his eyes and listen to his lungs. We saw a man on fire. Our grandma almost burned to death in her trailer. Hell, *we* almost burned to death in the trailer. How do you get over all of the shit Stan put us through? I trusted him and he took our mom, twisted our dad into something unrecognizable. Ruthie tried to warn me, but I just couldn't see it. I told Stan just because someone is horrible doesn't mean they deserve to die, but a big part of me thinks he got exactly what he deserved.

A cop approaches and asks Twig if there's anything she can get him. "Some coffee, maybe?" she asks with a wink.

"I don't drink coffee!" Twig's face twists like she offered him a mud milkshake.

"No? You prefer espresso?" She laughs.

At first Twig just looks at her.

But she keeps on laughing and the paramedic laughs too and then so does Twig and oh my God, there has never been such a beautiful sound in the world.

The cop introduces herself as Dana and tells me we met before. She sits on the bumper next to us and I think, *Here come the questions*. But she doesn't ask what we know about how the fire started or why there's an empty gas can lying by the porch. She asks if she can pet Ozzy.

"He bites sometimes," Twig tells her.

"He's been through a lot," she says. Her long fingers stroke Ozzy under the chin and Ozzy leans into it, letting her rub his neck. Ozzy stretches his front legs and steps from Twig's lap into hers. The cop says something and Twig answers and as they talk my eyes drift to our neighbors, gawking at the burnt husk of our trailer. I barely register TreyAnn waving at us from the other side of the tape with some of the other kids from the basketball court. Just over her shoulder, there's movement beside the neighbor's house. A shadow of a man stands alone, his hands in the pockets of his denim jacket.

The cop nudges me. "Zoned out there for a minute, huh? I was asking who can we call to come get you? Just until your grandmother is released from the hospital?"

Before I can answer, a hand lands on my shoulder. Even over the reek of gasoline and the thick smoke hanging in the air, the smell of Twizzlers is unmistakable.

My eyes go back to the neighbor's trailer, but Dad is gone.

"Thank God you boys are safe," Coach says. "Boy, am I glad to see you two."

For the second time in my life I feel the same way about him.

The paramedics want us to go to the hospital, just to get checked out. "I'll come with you guys," Coach says. Then he levels his eyes at me and adds, "That is, if I can get my truck keys back."

The paramedics lead Twig toward a second ambulance, Coach walking alongside them. I hang back. The cop—Dana—asks me if I'm okay.

Suddenly I am so cold. I rub my hands together and blow on them, thinking about what to say. I could say nothing, get into that ambulance and ride away. But chances are, it wouldn't be long until a cop showed up asking questions. And there is no guarantee that cop would be this cop or anyone as willing to listen to my side of things.

I lean back on the bumper and meet her eyes. "This wasn't an accident," I say. She nods but doesn't interrupt, so I keep talking. I tell her that I didn't always live in Oak Creek Court. That me and Twig used to live in a big house in the old Pick a'Part, with our mom and dad. I tell her how my dad's best friend taught me to shoot hoops and made us bacon on Saturday mornings. How I thought he was my family . . .

And then I tell her the rest.

I have to talk to over a dozen different people over the next few days. First to Dana the night of the fire, and then to the officers who come to the hospital, and then again down at the station with Dana present. Turns out she's a youth officer, which does not mean she's on my side, just that she makes sure they follow all the rules about dealing with a minor, which I still am for a few more months. Coach helps get me a court-appointed lawyer, but the police seem more interested in tracking Stan's activities than mine. Turns out he had a few different crews working in other cities and one of them was in the process of setting up a pill mill. They question me about the murders—Jimmy Dean, Chick, and Wade—but since Coach can back up my story that Stan shoved me down there, they realize pretty quickly that was all Stan.

They never ask about Ruthie, so I don't tell them about her.

Dad is more complicated.

I don't lie, but I don't give them anything either. When they tell me that Gran said he took off weeks ago, I nod. They ask if he has reached out to me since then and I tell them the truth. He left us a note and a little cash to help Gran with rent, but since he left he hasn't come looking for me or Twig.

Reporters show up at the hospital and track me to a few other places, but Coach tells me not to talk to them and I couldn't agree more. He's thinking about recruiters, but I'm thinking about Twig. He's gonna carry all of this with him; there's no avoiding that. But if I can keep our names out of the news, maybe Stan and Dad and all this horrible shit can just be something that happened to Twig, not something that defines him.

CHAPTER
36

I'VE ONLY BEEN GONE A FEW WEEKS, BUT WALKING BACK into Woodson is like walking on the surface of the moon, only without the bouncy gravity shit. I only have to make it through one day and then it's winter break. If it had been up to me, I'd have just started back in the new semester, but the school insisted I come today to get all my makeup work. The teachers have been way nicer than usual and a few even waived assignments altogether. The only thing that feels halfway normal is Ramón and Sadiq razzing me at my locker. It's weird, though, because Matt and Nick should be here with them, but neither of them come by even though they have to know I'm back. Ramón tells me the team has been placing bets on whether I ran off with a cheerleader or quit school to go pro.

"My money's on the Bulls," he says, "but no way they'll put you on the court. You gonna be their ball boy. Fetching them food and cleaning up their towels and shit."

Sadiq interrupts him. "No, man, I told you! Josh wouldn't leave school for the NBA. It's the Olympics! USA all the way, right, Josh?"

"You know it," I tell him.

Matt and Nick ignore me in class and aren't at our table in the lunchroom. The rest of the team barely acknowledges me at the lunch table, and everyone but Sadiq and Ramón laugh it up when Mason says something not quite under his breath about Coach planning to skin me alive when he sees me. I ignore him and the guys' snickers, but that's actually what I'm most worried about. Coach told me to come back, but that doesn't mean he's gonna let me suit up or even practice. I can handle sitting on the bench, but the team'll be expecting him to hand me my ass after missing a couple weeks of practice and so many games, and Coach has more than stairs in his arsenal. As soon as the bell rings after seventh period, I head straight for the lockers. I'm first on the court. I gotta show Coach that he was right when he said I belong here.

I lead the team for warm-ups, getting them started before Coach shows up from bus duty or whatever shit makes him late to practice every day. Matt and Nick don't meet my eye, but they follow me just like the rest of the team. Mason is the only one who doesn't; he goes to the other end of the court and shoots free throws. All through warm-ups I wait for Coach to show up and call me out, but it doesn't happen. When he finally comes, it's Mason's name he barks, shouting, "You're either with the team or on the bench." As we move into drills, Coach continues to ignore me, which is just fine by me. It is not, however, fine with Mason. He's muttering to the guys near him about me being Coach's pet and how he's sick of me getting away with shit. I ignore it, which only pisses him off more.

When he winds up behind me at the free throw line, he can't help himself. "Why'd you bother coming back?" he asks me. "Should just off yourself like your loser dad."

My fingers stiffen, feeling every raised pebble on the ball. But I am not gonna let that punk-ass kid with his big stupid mouth mess up my shot. Not after all the actual shit I've been through. I let my breath out slow and long, overlay the rim with the top curve of the ball, and pull the trigger.

After practice, Coach offers me a ride, but I tell him I'd rather walk. That I need the time to clear my head. He nods like he understands, but how could he? How could anyone? I take my time in the shower, hoping the locker room will clear. It's so quiet, I think everyone has left, except when I come out towel-drying my hair, Matt is sitting on the bench in front of my locker. I'm tempted to ignore him, give him back the same cold shoulder he's been giving me all day. He apologizes before I can decide what to do. Nothing big, just: "Sorry, man."

I shrug, not sure what he's apologizing for. My house burning down? Dodging me on my first day back? I step around him to get my clothes. He looks down at his phone, probably playing some game, while I pull on my jeans and a T-shirt.

"New shoes?" he asks as I put a foot up on the bench to tie my laces.

"Yep," I say, not adding that the old ones had to be thrown out because we couldn't get the reek of gasoline and smoke out of them.

"I heard you're staying with Coach. What's that like?"

"It's cool. He's a different guy off the court." Matt raises his eyebrows like he doesn't believe me. "Dude is multi-layered," I add, pulling my jacket from the locker. "Most people are."

"Guess I'll take your word on that. Need a ride?"

I start to give him the same line I gave Coach about wanting time to clear my head, but as I pick up my bag, a thought occurs to me. "Mind dropping me at the Center?"

"You mean CVS?"

I glance over to see if that's a jab, but Matt isn't the type to make a covert dig and I don't see any hostility on his face. If anything, he looks hopeful.

"Hey, I know I was a shit to you that day . . ."

"A lotta days."

"Yeah. A lotta days. Sorry, man."

Matt accepts my apology with a good-natured shrug. "Boy, was my mom pissed at me for jumping out of the car like that, though." I chuckle at the memory of the look on Mrs. Higle's face as Matt tripped over the curb. Matt laughs too.

"Maybe we can hang out over break?"

"Abso-fucking-lutely."

We ride to the Center with the music up and the windows down. Not talking, just finding a way to be normal together again. When he pulls up in front of the Center, Matt looks at me like he wants to say something that'll make it all weird between us. But all he says is, "Later, dude." One of the many reasons Matt's my friend.

Trina, Tina, Tracey comes rushing over as soon as she spots me climbing out of the truck. "Baby boy! We been worried to death about you. How are you? How is your dad? You need me to get you some food?" The barrage of questions continues as she grabs my arm and drags me through the door. I don't say a word until she's guided me past the reception desk and into the cafeteria. Then I thank her and pry myself away, telling her I need to see a man about a horse. She cocks her head at me. I don't bother explaining it to her.

Watchman is sitting with a man who's even older than he is. The man is wearing a knockoff of Bird's Sycamore jersey. Watchman scooches over when I slide onto the bench beside him and smiles when I rap my knuckles on the table in the same pattern we'd used at the Castle.

"That you, kid?" Watchman asks.

"Yeah," I say.

His face doesn't exactly fall, but the smile slips. "I thought you was Ruthie."

"Has she been here?"

"Now and again," he says.

"Like for real?" Hope flutters in my chest, but it's battling against the fear that took up residence in my heart the night of the fire: What if Ruthie never made it to Chick's funeral? What if Stan got to her first?

"Yes, sir. She been working over at that bakery on Lafayette. Brings me by some pastries. You see her, tell her I could use some of those almond crescents. You ever try one of those? Like dying and going straight to heaven. Especially with some good strong coffee."

My brain replays his words in slo-mo, like warped vinyl. At first, all I catch is *yes*. The rest bursts through in images. Ruthie smiling. In a bakery. Pulling a warm tray from an oven. Gradually the needle catches and I see the whole picture: Ruthie might be less than two blocks away from me right this moment, not starving and alone, but working an actual job. Pulling blueberry muffins fresh from the oven instead of dumpster diving for goodies past their sell-by date. I feel like I could simultaneously sleep for a week and jump so high that I could slam-dunk the moon.

"That's for damn sure," the older man says. "Matter of fact, I could use a cup right 'bout now. You want anything, Leon?"

"Bring me some with sugar. No milk, no cream, just sugar."

The old man unfolds himself from the bench and hobbles over to the vending machine.

Watchman—Leon—pats me on the leg. "You're a good man, coming to see me. I was worried how you'd turn out with Stan's hooks in you. But you got a lot of your father in you. Cream always floats to the top."

I wonder what he's heard about what happened to Stan. There was a piece in the paper and on the local station, but people at the Center don't tend to keep up with the news. "You don't like Stan?" I ask.

"A'course I liked Stan. Everybody liked Stan. But that don't mean he was good. Didn't surprise nobody he died trying to take what wasn't his."

I want to ask what Watchman meant when he said I had a lot of my dad in me and if my dad's been around the Center, but the old guy returns with two cups of coffee, sloshing a bunch of it on the table as he sets them down. "Hey, man, I gotta go," I tell Watchman, adding that maybe I'll come back by with one of those almond things soon.

I don't plan on going to the bakery, but my new shoes travel up Michigan and turn onto Lafayette. Since my feet are in them, I find myself standing in front of Muffins and Mayhem, staring at Ruthie through the huge storefront window. Her hair is tucked up in a lilac baseball cap that matches her apron and her lips are moving, like she's singing to herself as she wraps huge cookies in the empty store.

A mom with two kids passes by me. Ruthie looks up as they enter, smiling, chatting with them, patiently helping them each pick just the right cookie. When they leave, Ruthie goes back to wrapping cookies. The door hangs open on the wind, music floating out, old-style Miley from her bubblegum days. I want to step in, need to step in, but Ruthie looks so . . . peaceful. Like wrapping those cookies is giving her a chance to breathe. To not have to be so fucking fierce every single moment. If I go in there now, I'll track everything that happened in there with me. I can't be the reason she stops smiling.

The wind shifts and the door closes.

CHAPTER

37

I'M AWAKE THE NEXT MORNING BEFORE EVERYONE ELSE. I've actually been lying awake most of the night staring at the moonlight on the tree branches outside the window and listening to Twig breathing in the bunk above mine. Sleeping at Coach's is hard. Not just because my feet hang off the end of the bed or because Twig sometimes wakes up screaming from night terrors that bring Coach's wife, Janie, running. It's just too quiet. No slamming doors from neighbors coming home after finishing their third shift at work or a third pitcher at the bar. No engines idling or trains clacking. Some guys might go crazy lying there all night with nothing to do, but I have a lot to think about.

At seven I roll out of bed, careful not to jostle the mattress too much and wake Twig and Ozzy in the bunk above me. As I pull on my sweats, I study Mom's face in the framed picture that sits on the dresser. White creases divide us—me and Dad, Mom and Twig. We could probably have it refinished, but the marks tell our family story, our real story.

By the time I get back from my morning run, Twig and the twins are carrying syrupy plates over to the sink. Janie barely looks up from the bills strewn all over the counter.

Coach tells me there are chocolate chip or blueberry Eggos in the freezer if I'm hungry. That's another thing I can't get used to—so many food options. The freezer is packed full of frozen waffles; bags of fries and onion rings; packages of peas, green beans, and corn. I don't eat much, but it's good to see Twig starting to put some weight on those skinny arms of his. I pop two Eggos into the toaster—one of each—and ask Coach if it's okay if I have some orange juice.

"You don't have to ask," he reminds me for the hundredth time. "Anything in there's yours." I nod, but this is gonna take some getting used to.

"We're going to the library today after lunch," Twig tells me. I know he's excited about all those books, but it's hard to tell by looking at him. The stitches from the dog bite have only been out two days and the edge of his lip still puckers, twisting his mouth up at the corner, despite the fact that I haven't seen him smile since before the attack. "It'll take time, but gradually he'll get some of his joy back," the therapist at the hospital had assured me. The library is a good first step.

I'm out of the shower and dressed before Coach can even finish the dishes. "Got plenty of hot water," he'd told me that first night, but I don't see the point in wasting it when I can get just as clean with a quick one.

"Got plans today?" Janie asks. "I was thinking maybe you could join us at the library."

I know that she could use help wrangling three boys at the library, but I just can't picture climbing into her minivan, walking into the library like I'm part of her family. I mean . . . it's nice of them to take me and Twig in, let us stay with them and all, but it's only temporary. "Until we figure out a long-term solution," Coach had said.

The doorbell rings, letting me off the hook before I can come up with a good excuse.

Janie frowns. "Who could that be?"

Kevin and Kyle race to the door and push aside the curtain and each other to peer out the side window. "Nobody's there!" Kyle shouts.

"Ding-dong ditch!" Kevin yells.

Coach maneuvers around them to open the door. The twins trail him out onto the porch, their excited voices drifting back in. After a second, Coach calls back into the house, "Hey, Josh? Twig? Can you boys come out here?"

Leaning against the porch rail is a huge package wrapped in old newspapers. It's obvious what it is the second I see it. My eyes dart from one house to the next, one parked car to another, but the road is deserted.

Twig hesitantly runs a hand over the newspaper . . . finds his name scratched in black ink. His eyes meet mine, uncertain. I nod and he pulls off the paper, revealing handlebars, tires—a red seat with the Bulls insignia.

"It's a bike," Twig says. There's no emotion in his voice, only disbelief in his eyes. Like it might be a trick. Like believing could cost him more than he has left.

Kevin and Kyle lean around me, trying to see.

I put a hand on his shoulder. "Look," I say, pointing down at the fork where various Pokémon characters lean into the spokes. "I used to do that to my bike too. Those will make it sound like a motorcycle."

"Really?" Kyle asks. "Can we do that to my bike?"

I nod and the twins run inside. Janie follows them in, saying she thinks there might be an extra helmet in the hall closet. Twig looks like he might throw up. I glance at Coach, who takes the hint and says the boys'll need his help sorting their cards.

I wait for the door to close behind Coach before asking, "You don't know how to ride, do you?"

Twig looks down at his hand on the seat and shakes his head solemnly.

"No worries, little man. I got you."

We go inside to get our shoes and coats. Kevin and Kyle ignore us, excitedly sorting through their box of Yu-Gi-Oh! cards, picking out who gets which cards to use on their bikes. When we come back out, a helmet is hanging on Twig's handlebars.

Stan taught me everything I know about basketball, but my dad is the one who taught me to ride a bike, pushing me through the junkyard, one hand next to mine on the handlebars, one hand on the seat behind me to steady me. Twig gets on the bike and I help him adjust the helmet, trying to remember what Dad showed me first. Pedals.

"So you know how the pedals work, right?" Twig nods. "Stopping's easy; you just pedal backward. Only thing that isn't so easy is balance, but that's what I'm for." I put my hand next to Twig's on the handlebars, my other hand on the seat. Dad's calloused hands are phantoms next to mine.

The sidewalk has been shoveled, but it's still icy in spots and my feet slip once in a while as I walk, then jog, next to Twig. "Hey, man, slow down," I warn him, but he's pedaling faster and faster and before I know it, he's halfway down the block from me.

"Twig!" I yell after him. "Make sure you can stop!"

Twig slams on the brakes and skids into a snowbank, but gets right back on his bike and pedals just as fast toward me. "Beep! Beep!" he yells, coming right at me. I leap out of his way with an exaggerated cry of panic. Twig laughs maniacally, smiling so big, the scar almost disappears.

"He's a quick learner," Coach calls from the driveway.

Kevin and Kyle are donning their helmets as Twig flies by again. They pedal hard to catch up and the whole world fills with laughter and the *ticka-ticka-tick* of spokes hitting cards. Coach asks me to keep an eye on them and heads back inside.

I stand on the porch and wave back every time one of them waves at me. If you'd have told me a few weeks ago I'd be standing on a porch watching kids ride bikes in the middle of suburbia, I'd have laughed my ass off. But here I am and the pure joy on Twig's face makes it impossible to want to be anywhere else.

Just as the boys reach the end of the block and turn back, I finally spot him. He's standing several houses down, just behind a tree, watching Twig. Axl sits patiently by his side.

Our eyes meet and for a moment he's my dad. I start down the steps, feeling his hands next to mine on the cold handlebars. His breath in my ear as he runs alongside, yelling, "Look up, look up!" The pride on his face when I ride for the first time with no help. But just as quick, all of that is gone and what's left are his hands pulling gasoline-filled bottles from the Datsun's trunk. His grip on my arm holding me back. The hopeless, sad defeat on his face as he cries, "Not again, please not again."

I brace myself on the porch rail, unable to take another step. I can't even see the man who taught me to ride under the layers of Stan that have stained everything he is, everything he could have ever been. He drops his eyes, feeling what? Disappointment? What could he possibly want? After all he's done, all he *didn't* do. Did he think he could just show up here with the bike I dug out of the ruins of the life he destroyed and have us welcome him with open arms? Fuck that.

Fuck *him*.

We just stand there, separated by a road that might as well be the entire universe. Twig rides through it, oblivious to these two worlds colliding. I think about all he's lost, all he's gonna need to make it in this world. Life has been so unfair to him. The least I can do is try to give him this one thing back.

I cup my hand around my mouth and shout loud enough to be heard across the street and several houses down. "You coming?"

Dad looks down at Axl, who cocks his head at me.

I whistle and Axl takes a hesitant step in my direction, then looks back for permission. The leash pulls taut between them, then falls. Axl doesn't move at first, just looks back and forth between us.

Dad shouts, "Go on, then. Git!"

Axl hangs his head and tucks his tail, taking a few lumbering steps toward the road. I slap my thigh. His ears twitch as he lifts his head. His big brown eyes find me on the sidewalk now, waving him on. He whines and looks back one more time, then barks and launches himself across the street, tackling me with his sloppy kisses. "That's right, big guy, that's right," I tell him, stroking his great big old head.

"Josh?" Twig shouts. He jumps off his bike and it clatters to the sidewalk. "Josh!"

"I'm okay, I'm all right!" I yell back, imagining what this must look like to Twig. I scramble to my feet, grabbing Axl's leash so Twig has a second to realize that it's not the same dog that attacked him.

The twins have pulled up alongside Twig and all three of them are gawking at Axl. "That's the giantest dog I ever saw," Kevin says. Kyle asks if they can pet him.

"Yeah," I say. "He's my dog. Well, mine and Twig's. His name is—"

"Axl," Twig says. "How did you get here?"

Axl rubs against Twig's legs, careful not to knock him over. His huge tail bangs against the twins, making them giggle.

"Bigger question is where are we gonna keep him?" I turn to Kevin and Kyle. "Think your parents will let us have a dog?"

"Yes!"—"No way!" they both shout.

"Come on, boy," I tell Axl, leading him up the porch steps. "I hope you remember how to beg, because I think this is going to take some convincing."

Twig drops his helmet onto the sidewalk and runs ahead to open the front door. "Janie!" he yells. "Axl found us! Our dog found us!"

Axl steps gingerly onto the carpet in the front hall, and I realize that this is probably the first real home he remembers. He was just a puppy back at the old house and Gran never let him in the trailer. I bend down and scratch the scruff of his neck. "You're gonna like it here," I tell him. "You can sleep with me. At least until I go off to college. Then you're stuck with Ozzy and Twig."

"A dog?" Coach's voice echoes from the kitchen. The twins usher Axl toward their dad.

I go to close the front door, which we left open in all the chaos, and catch a glimpse of the bikes strewn all over the sidewalk, helmets scattered in the snow. I move them one by one onto the driveway and then, just as I'm about to step into the warm house, I don't know why, but I turn back. I peer toward the trees several houses up . . .

But no one is there.

A NOTE FROM THE AUTHOR

While Josh's story is fictional, it is inspired by conditions of poverty and homelessness facing many families in the United States.

According to the Bassuk Center on Homeless and Vulnerable Children & Youth, more families experience homelessness in the United States than in any other industrialized nation. Unaccompanied homeless youth (people under the age of 18 who have no support from their families) number nearly 2 million in the US and face high rates of depression, major trauma, and post-traumatic stress. From studies by the National Alliance to End Homelessness, 75% drop out of school.

If you or someone you know is in crisis, remember that it is not your fault. Help is available, and you are worth it.

RESOURCES:

National Safe Place, TXT 4 HELP
https://www.nationalsafeplace.org/txt-4-help

A nationwide, 24-hour text-for-support service. Youth in crisis can text "safe" and city/state/zip to 4HELP (44357).

The National Coalition for the Homeless
https:///www.nationalhomeless.org

The Trevor Project
https://www.thetrevorproject.org/resources/article/
resources-for-lgbtq-youth-experiencing-homelessness

TO LEARN MORE:

The Bassuk Center on Homeless and Vulnerable Children
& Youth
https://www.bassukcenter.org/wp-content/uploads/2015/
11/Services-Matter.pdf

National Alliance to End Homelessness
https://endhomelessness.org/homelessness-in-america/
homelessness-statistics/state-of-homelessness-2021/

Indiana State Board of Education Annual Report on
Homeless Youth Educational Outcomes
https://www.in.gov/children/files/HEA-1314-Homeless-
Annual-Youth-Report-April-2019.v4.pdf

These resources are provided for informational purposes
only.

ABOUT THE AUTHOR

KATHERINE HIGGS-COULTHARD became a writer on the limb of a Sycamore tree when she was in elementary school. Since then she's written in abandoned buildings, cemeteries, parks, and even on a tall ship, but her favorite place to write has always been the woods. Kat graduated from the University of Nebraska with a bachelor's in education and earned a master's degree from Indiana University, before completing her doctorate in education through Northeastern University. She has taught kindergarten, third, and fifth grades. Now she trains teachers at Saint Mary's College and offers writing camps and classes for children and teens through Michiana Writers' Center. She lives in Michigan and loves spending time with her family. Follow her on Twitter @michianawriter1 and on Instagram @kathiggscoulthard.

ACKNOWLEDGMENTS

I am especially grateful to Jonah Heller, my editor, for believing in this story. Thank you, Jonah. Your keen insights are often delivered with just the right amount of humor (for example, on an early draft, "LA LA LA CAN'T HEAR YOU. THIS DOG IS TOTALLY ALIVE"). Your advice lifted this story to a level far beyond what I could have done alone. Thank you to the rest of the team at Peachtree Teen for your hard work and attention to detail, especially Kaitlin Severini, for helping tweak the timeline; Amy Brittain, for proofreading with such precision; and Lisa Marie Pompilio for her stunning cover art. Special thanks also to Vimali Joseph and production team, Amnet Contentsource Private Limited (ACPL).

My writing community was essential in keeping my butt in the chair so I could write this book. Thank you to Jennifer Juszkiewicz at Saint Mary's College for organizing the weekly writing group; Cynthia Furlong Reynolds, who introduced me to the Michkids chapter of the Society of Children's Book Writers and Illustrators; my accountability partners Kristin Bartley Lenz and Patrick Flores-Scott; Kelly Barson whose advice about touchstones gave the story its heart; and Danielle DeFauw who really, truly GETS IT.

I am also grateful for my family without whose support nothing would be possible. Special thanks to my mom for realizing my ability to make stuff up meant I was creative and not hallucinating. Gratitude to my dad and my little bro for their constant support. Slam-dunk thanks to my nephew, Casey Marlin, who patiently answered all of my texts about basketball and kept me from going overboard with sports terms:

Me: *What's it called when someone throws a bad pass? Junk ball?*
Casey: *Just write "bad pass."*

To my very best readers, whose reactions informed early revisions:

- Chrysanthemum's gentle suggestion that maybe we don't need *that one scene*;
- Katie's indignation over the missing sandwich;
- Wren's tears over Axl;
- Alexander's sticky notes throughout the manuscript and his handwritten editorial letter.

With special gratitude to Erica Vitale, thank you for always being the Thelma to my Louise and the one person who has made me laugh so hard I blew milk out my nose. Thanks also to Virginia Black, whose reporting on South Bend's 2007 Manhole Murders inspired this story.

And most of all, Tom. You fill my world with music. Our days of "arting" together at the kitchen table gave me the time to write this book.